CLEAN SWEEP

CLEAN SWEEP

A NOVEL

E. B. LEE

Little Brown Dog Press

Clean Sweep A Novel

Publisher's Cataloging-in-Publication Data

Names: Lee, E. B., 1957- author.

Title: Clean sweep : a novel / E. B. Lee.

Description: First edition. | Pinehurst, NC, USA : Little Brown Dog Press, [2021]

Identifiers: ISBN: 978-1-7364560-1-9 (softcover) | 978-1-7364560-2-6 (hardcover) | 978-1-7364560-0-2 (eBook) | LCCN: 2021907825

Subjects: LCSH: Homeless persons--New York (State)--New York--Fiction. | Homelessness--New York (State)--New York--Fiction. | Mentally ill homeless persons--New York (State)--New York-- Fiction. | Social work with the homeless--Fiction. | Urban poor--Fiction. | Compassion-- Fiction. | Faith-based human services--Fiction. | Christian life--Fiction. | Art--Social aspects-- Fiction. | Vulnerability (Personality trait)--Fiction. | Communication--Social aspects--Fiction. | Social psychology--Fiction. | BISAC: FICTION / City Life. | SOCIAL SCIENCE / Poverty & Homelessness. | FICTION / Christian / Contemporary.

Classification: LCC: PS3612.E22358 C54 2021 | DDC: 813/.6--dc23

Library of Congress Control Number: 2021907825

Editing: Stephen Parolini, www.noveldoctor.com; Mary-Theresa Hussey, www.goodstorieswelltold.com; Louise Stahl, proofreading.

Cover design by Kathleen Lynch/Black Kat Design

Cover photograph © Olga Kaya/iStock; borchee/iStock

Publishing Services: Little Brown Dog Press, Pinehurst, NC, USA www.littlebrowndogpress.com

For Chick
You are my rock and my love.
Thank you for sharing a lifetime with me.

ONE

CARLI MORRIS PULLED a brown paper bag close to her chest as she walked the next city block. Ice pellets rattled to the ground, propelled by wind that rose into gusts, then settled. Carli turned sideways, hoping to shield her face, but stings of ice continued to bite, and every so often she hit a wall of wind so strong she walked in place. She spotted, in the distance, the electronic clock at First United Bank. It didn't matter that it glowed a bright red 3:01 or that she had fought the weather almost all night. The only thing that mattered was finding cardboard homes and delivering food to the bodies sleeping inside them.

When Carli came to a long cardboard box lying sideways on the Midtown Manhattan sidewalk, she called loudly, "Church Run. I have sandwiches." In truth, it wasn't one box, but several, sutured together so neatly they appeared seamless, like a plain pine casket. Sidled under the overhang of First United Bank, it cleverly escaped the icy assault. Carli waited, her shopping bag rippling in the wind, then called again, "Anyone there?" She knew the answer but needed a reply.

At last, the box jiggled. It tilted back and forth. Then it became still, and a man's voice mumbled through its corrugated walls. "Church Run?"

"Yes." Carli shifted her gaze to the end with the voice.

A bare hand shot through the seam in the side and headed toward her ankle. It stopped just short, waiting until Carli placed two packaged meals into its palm. The hand closed around them and disappeared through the slit. Seconds later, the corrugated voice came through the storm. "Thanks. Thanks a lot," it said. "Got another?"

Carli swallowed hard. "Sorry. Two apiece, but chowder and coffee are at the vans."

"Chowder?"

"Yes."

Carli slid her way to a second makeshift home; a pair of tattered blankets draped atop its cardboard frame. A shopping cart filled with scrap metal and wood stood nearby, gathering ice. Two bulging black plastic bags flanked its front wheels. Jim Hampton, her partner for the overnight mission, was already talking with the owner. "You need toiletries or anything?" he asked.

"What?"

"Toiletries."

"What?"

"You know, like a razor and soap."

"Oh!" said the voice. Something connected. "Yeah, I need a hood. You got anything with a hood? Like one of those sweatshirts?"

"Check the vans, and get some chowder."

"Sure. Okay … sure." The man sounded reluctant. Carli wasn't surprised. Surely, he heard the wind and the ice.

Carli and Jim veered across the street to two white church vans parked at the curb. They were high-mileage, late-model loaners from Samaritan Baptist Church that ran by the grace of God. God's grace was exactly what they needed. Nearly a dozen street people, men and women, were huddled alongside the vans. Carli couldn't help but wonder how everyone would make it through to spring. This was the second winter storm, and it was only November.

"Did you get around the block?" Tom asked. He and Irene had just scouted northward.

"Four across the street and three on the side," said Carli.

"We found a bunch too."

Carli saw four figures approaching. One limped. Two came as a pair. The last wore no overcoat. Shivers raced along Carli's arms, and her back arched reflexively, as though trying to invoke warmth for them both.

When Tom and Irene flung open the doors of the lead van, an older woman burst to the front of the crowd. She snatched a puffy, down-filled parka, squeezed it, tugged it, and inspected its zipper.

"Try it on," said Irene. Her teeth chattered as she spoke.

The woman pulled it closer but wanted no fitting. She left without a word, garment in hand.

"Say, any large hats there?"

The raspy voice came from a man whose body was so conspicuously arched it looked like he might fall forward. Moving in jerky steps, he used his forearms and elbows well and pushed his way in behind the departing woman. Others objected, but he pressed his point: he needed a hat. Several missing teeth and a bandage on one ear distinguished the man from the rest, but he reeked of a standard street odor – urine and sweat. Tom handed him a package of size twenty-eight briefs and a rain poncho to cover his many layers of clothes. Then Tom said, "Let's find you a hat."

Five hours earlier, the vans' shelves had been stuffed full of coats, sweaters, pants, and more, sorted from mounds of clothing donated to the church. Now they were nearly bare. Pastor Miller, clergyman of First Neighbor's Church, led the night's mission. He looked at Carli and said, "Someone will be left out tonight, I'm afraid." Carli nodded, then circled to the second van where she lugged out a fifty-gallon cooler, removed her gloves to handle the cups, and prepared to serve the last of the chowder.

A wind gust splattered the first ladleful across her bare hand. Within a minute, her fingers throbbed from the cold. To Carli's dismay, equally bare hands, or hands with tattered half-gloves, reached for her chowder. She passed the word: "Get gloves in the other van." Many nodded.

Most visitors came for food and then left silently. A few struck up brief conversations. One man looked like a burly northern lumberjack, but the burl was, no doubt, layered clothing piled around too-small briefs and an extra-lean body. Chowder soon froze to the hairs of his gray-speckled beard. He wore a calf-length trench coat over a red and black plaid jacket, a bright orange cap, and thanks be to God, thick winter gloves.

"Beautiful," he said, as Jim handed him coffee. "Beautiful."

The man's demeanor was positive, and his character surprisingly boisterous – qualities unmatched by the majority of the others. Secretly, Carli nicknamed him "Canada."

"Reminds me of my old job," the man said.

"Oh yeah?" asked Jim, straining to hear over the wind.

"Sure. Worked local trucking for eighteen years. There's nothing like hot coffee to get you on the road."

"I bet," said Jim. "Must have made a lot of deliveries."

"You bet I did." Canada sipped his coffee.

"You like it?" Jim asked.

"Yeah, 'til I got laid off."

"Oh, man ..."

"Left me no better than if I had been an independent all those years. Except, I never wanted to own my truck; it's a hassle."

"I'm sure," said Jim.

"Well, what are you gonna do?" asked Canada. "Others have it worse. And who knows, maybe we'll have a white Christmas for a change."

"Who knows?" said Jim. "Who knows? At least you're not driving in this stuff."

Canada raised his cup, as though to say, "Cheers," and moved along.

When all were served, Carli tossed the ladle and extra cups into the van. Cold chowder nearly glued her fingers together, and her pants and coat smelled like a cannery. Half her hair, wet from melted ice, clung seaweed-like to the left side of her face, and half drooped limply behind, periodically releasing ice water inside her collar. With no sleep for nearly twenty-four hours, and her back tightening like a tourniquet from leaning over the chowder vat, she yearned for the night to end. She gave the gathering one last look and caught the sound of another voice. "Hold that chowder! One more man coming." Carli wanted to ignore the request, but the man called again. "Hold that chowder." There was urgency in his voice.

"Step right up," she said. "Pull up a seat."

The new arrival laughed. The warmth of it caught Carli off guard. She stopped the ladle to look into his eyes. They were gray and surprisingly lively. Shoulder-length dark hair curled out from a baseball cap emblazoned with white letters that spelled "Police." Carli assumed it was a fake. She knew official issue read "NYPD." Canada punched the man amicably on the shoulder. Most other greetings she had seen had been secret-society-like nods, muttering, or near-wordless shouts. Carli suspected him a street fake – an imposter taking advantage of handouts to turn a quick profit. When she'd started with the mission, she hadn't expected people would take advantage of the homeless. But on this first night, the city had proven, once again, it had everything.

Carli addressed the new arrival with a quick, "How are you?" and expected an equally curt reply. He looked first at Carli's face, and then at her hands, as he answered, "Fine. Just fine. Thanks for asking. How about you?"

She stared, certain he was a scammer. Something like, "Okay, but the weather could be better," or, "Not bad," would have been typical. "Fine" was an odd answer, given the icy circumstances. Yet, that's precisely what she replied, along with, "Thank *you* for asking."

The man laughed again. She stared him down, and the strange man stared back, nearly smirking. He looked oddly familiar.

Carli quickly ladled soup. His hands reached to grasp the cup before it blew away, and, for a moment, they held it together. It was long enough for her to notice his silver and turquoise ring and gloveless hands, not cracked like the others on the street. Carli tensed. Was he staring deeply or blankly? Was he drugged? Damned soup. Finally, he lifted the chowder.

"Much obliged. Pleasure to meet you," he said. Carli said nothing, but the man said, "Hope to see you again. The name's Grant." Then he paced smoothly through the crowd, extending an occasional pat to a shoulder. Carli's hands dropped to her sides. The further he drifted, the safer she felt. With a shake of her head, she shook him from her mind. But as she snapped shut the last latch to the chowder pot, his voice rippled toward her.

"By the way ...," he began. Carli turned to see his denim jeans and rusty-brown suede jacket. "It's cold out. Get some gloves from the van." A smile began to rise on his lips. His own hands remained uncovered. Before she could respond, Grant was already walking away. He had no new clothes, no toiletries; only a steady hand on his soup.

Carli caught the eyes of Pastor Miller, who said, "Time to move on." Carli gladly slammed shut the van's back doors. Five hours of serving chowder and sandwiches to life's unfortunates had left her mind numb. There had been no time to think or sort facts. The strange man's figure faded into the darkness. She slid her eyes to the building in front of her, across the cardboard boxes embraced by its alcoves, up past the lighted windows displaying all-night business-people still at work and janitors pushing carts. She squeezed shut her eyes to the harsh spray of ice and prayed, simply, "Please, God ... help them. And give me the strength to keep helping others." Carli kept her eyes closed several more moments, realizing she hadn't prayed in earnest in decades.

Two stops later, the last of three hundred sandwiches had vanished into the paws of the night. Even a full-length dusty-rose designer down coat had found a body to cover. Thank God. The van doors clanked loudly as Pastor Miller closed them and crossed past Carli to the driver's side. "We have to check on Lucy," he said, retrieving the crumpled itinerary from the van's dashboard. "She lives in a tent by St. Mary's Church, a couple of blocks east. It says here, she worries about her dogs."

"Dogs?" asked Carli.

"That's what it says. Lila and Terrance."

All night the itinerary had directed them. What surprised Carli most was it had actual names of people and known addresses, roofless though they were. How had she missed this during her thirty years in Manhattan? Of course, she had seen them, but why the hell hadn't she thought to ask their names? Or recognized they had self-assigned street-beds? Where had she been all these years?

Carli knew the answer. She'd been tackling Madison Avenue's advertising world with a vengeance. After thirty years, she'd built her privately-owned firm, TSW Inc., into a prized agency, allowing her to sell it off for more money than she'd ever dreamed of and retire early. None of it would have happened without long hours, laser focus, and 100 percent commitment to work. What she gave up in return was life outside of work. She had friends, or at least work friends, but she felt a spiritual void, having lived for years wearing blinders. It was the polar opposite of her Catholic upbringing in her middle-class neighborhood. This first night volunteering with the Church Run was a tentative step toward reawakening a vital part of her soul. It was also a chance to scope out possible beneficiaries of her financial good fortune. The work of the Church Runs had intrigued her. Now, in the midst of one, she found the sheer need for them devastating.

Carli looked through the windshield and spotted Lucy's blue-domed tent just as it should be: snuggled in the doorway of the gray stone church. Contrasting trim highlighted its sides, making arching patterns that mimicked the church's. A lantern above the door spread a yellow glow across it, just like a manger, when there was no room at the inn. Pastor Miller eased the van toward the curb until a front tire bumped the edge. Methodically, he switched off wipers, heater, and lights and finally shut down the engine.

"There're three sandwiches under your seat," he said, looking straight at Carli. She fished them out while Jim and the rest climbed out the back.

"Lucy," said Pastor Miller as he approached the tent at St. Mary's. "Church Run here."

Lucy's door was open. She lay face down with the heels of her shoes sticking out of the tent. Two black noses poked out and quickly retreated from the splattering ice.

"Lucy? We have three sandwiches," he said. The two small dogs poked their noses toward the smell of the sandwiches. Pastor Miller leaned toward the tent's opening. "Lucy?" He squinted. "Hey, Lucy."

As Pastor Miller knelt, it sounded like Lucy made a slight sound. He called again, but another voice interrupted. Carli recognized it immediately and turned to see Grant cautiously jogging on the ice, shielding his face from the wind with one arm. He shouted again from a few yards off.

"Lucy, Lady Lucy. You trying to scare off the church folks again?" Grant strode in front of Carli and reached into Lucy's tent. His soup was gone, his hands empty. "I got it," he said. "I got the dog food." While the Church Run had made its previous stop, Grant had, apparently, gone shopping. An odd activity, Carli thought. Grant pulled a can from his pocket and crawled further into the tent. A moment later, the can rattled to the ground. "Lucy! Oh my God ... Lucy!" Grant turned to Pastor Miller. "Anyone have a phone? How long's she been like this?"

"Like what? We just got here," Pastor Miller said.

"Call 9-1-1! Tell them we have an overdose. No, a possible poisoning. Or, maybe a heart problem. Call now!" shouted Grant. "Please. I'm with Outreach. Mobile Outreach. My phone is dead."

Pastor Miller dialed.

"Dear God, Lucy," said Grant.

"Check her pulse!" Carli shouted. "Is she breathing?" Carli knelt next to Grant, and together they turned Lucy onto her back. Carli quickly removed a hat, untied a scarf, and loosened the tightly-drawn hood of Lucy's sweatshirt to reveal Lucy's neck. It was warm. She felt for a pulse. Nothing. She repositioned her fingers. Nothing.

Grant reached through layers of coats to locate Lucy's midsection. Carli tilted Lucy's head to listen and feel for air. Everyone else's breath puffed visibly into the night. The only thing coming from Lucy was an odor of bad breath.

"Well?" asked Grant.

"Nothing," said Carli.

"You sure?"

"Yes."

"You push. I'll breathe." Grant's tone was direct.

Carli looked straight at Grant. She hesitated, knowing the perils of unprotected mouth-to-mouth.

"Do it!" said Grant.

She moved two inches up from Lucy's ribcage and pushed. One thrust. Two thrusts. Three thrusts. Up to thirty. Grant administered air. Carli repeated. Grant breathed again. Carli pushed. Grant gave breaths. The duet continued. Finally, sirens screamed as a rescue vehicle neared. Lila and Terrance wailed. Lucy remained silent.

The ambulance sloshed to a stop and hurled an icy wave of slush across Carli.

"We're looking for a call … possible overdose."

"Quick!" said Pastor Miller. "Over here."

The two technicians ordered everyone aside. Grant offered details. "I saw her less than an hour ago. She looked fine. But she wanted dog food, so I left to get it."

"Then what?" asked the technician.

"They found her. Like this," said Grant.

The EMTs moved in. They checked for vitals and administered naloxone for a possible overdose. Lucy remained still. They repeatedly tried CPR and set up for shocks. "Clear!" one yelled. A shock went through Lucy. No response. "Clear!" he yelled again. Lucy still didn't respond.

"Lucy, please … Lucy," said Grant. Lucy's eyes remained open, along with her mouth. Another round of actions brought no change. The medics finally stopped their efforts. They conferred with each other for a moment, and then they began repacking their equipment. Lucy was gone. Pastor Miller gave a blessing, and Carli stepped away. She had never seen a person die. Technically, she still hadn't, but Lucy was warm, for God's sake! Carli glimpsed the tan and white dog. Both it and the little gray one looked paralyzed with fear.

"Who called in an overdose?" asked an approaching police officer.

Grant gave a slight wave, walked over, and shook hands before touching the officer's elbow. Carli listened in.

"Something you should know," said Grant. "She told me a man came by the last two nights. Told her she belonged in a graveyard. She thought her dogs scared him away. I asked her what he looked like, but she couldn't describe him. She was in her tent, and he was out here." The officer listened carefully. "We need an autopsy," said Grant, "to rule out poisoning. You know, like what happened to the other three. We both know she would have been cold by morning; would have looked like a casualty of the weather, nothing more."

The officer nodded. "I'll have the Medical Examiner check for chemicals."

Carli no longer heard the ice or wind.

"I was going to stay near tonight," said Grant. "Wish I hadn't left. Wonder if someone was watching."

The officer radioed others. "Tell Animal Control we have canines. I'm checking for tags and vaccines."

Carli watched. It seemed a longshot.

The man took ahold of the tan and white dog's collar. "Let's see, little one. Lila, eh? Yup, your tag's good." The little gray dog, too, passed the initial inspection. The officer continued with his call. "They're good. Send the truck."

Carli jumped in with a question. "Where will they go?"

"We have a place," said the man, "for all lost dogs."

"You're not going to ... I mean ... they won't ..." She couldn't say it.

"Personal effects go to the station. They get vouchered," said the officer. "Animals go with Animal Control. They get checked. Sent to the pound. Maybe adopted. They'll be all right."

One of Carli's biggest clients in her advertising life was Flippin' Dog, a "clean earth" dog clothing and supply company. Doing their campaigns, Carli had met dozens of rescue dogs turned advertising professionals. Still, the phrase "maybe adopted" unsettled her. Lucy's death had been loss enough. Carli looked at the pair of street dogs and was fairly certain no one would adopt them.

"I'll tell the people at St. Mary's about Lucy in the morning," said Grant, facing Pastor Miller. Then he slid so close to Carli their coats touched. "I see you're worried about L and T," he said. "Probably headed to the uptown pound all the way up the East Side. I'll try to confirm and send word to Lucy's church. Maybe you can check on them."

Grant stared at Lucy's body. Before Carli could ask about the pound, he took her elbow and said, "Take these. In case you decide to get them or something." He slid four cans of dog food into her hands. Then he moved away, leaving Carli propped against the stones of the church, mulling over her illogical urge to save a couple of street dogs. Surely, none of the other volunteers was giving thought to rescuing them. But she bet none of them knew the pain of having life upended when someone special was taken away. Carli had a soft spot for those who were left behind, even if they were dogs, and she didn't want Lila and Terrance to die like Lucy. Besides, Carli had her own dog once. She knew what it meant.

Moments later, the volunteers shuffled silently to the vans, now seeming more like a funeral cortege. Lucy's personal choir of angels – two street dogs – whimpered funereal tones, as Lucy was readied for departure. Then two white vans rolled along Third Avenue in single file, three lanes of empty pavement stretching before them in both directions. Stoplights on strict timers forced a solemn pace. Throughout the city, imaginary houselights silently switched off as men and women settled into cardboard-covered beds. Carli wondered how many there were.

As Pastor Miller hunched forward over the steering wheel, Carli leaned her head against the cold glass of the passenger seat window. No one said a word as the vans travelled past the numbered cross streets, from the Sixties to the silent Seventies, and on up through the One-Twenties for the bridge out of the city and trip to First Neighbor's Church. The city floated by the windows, which fogged up quickly from their warm, wet bodies. Carli took a moment to make a window within her window with a few hasty wipes of her coat sleeve on the glass. She watched the last of the city slip away. She never expected to see so many of them. Real people. Living here. And dying on the street in an ice storm.

TWO

IT HAD BEEN at least twenty years since Carli pulled an all-nighter. She navigated the icy roads from First Neighbor's Church in her SUV and arrived at her midtown-Manhattan apartment with dawn still in the offing. She felt oddly alert, thanks, no doubt, to adrenaline. Carli sank into a club chair, hot mug of tea in hand, and felt the residual sensation of ice and wind whipping against her face.

Lucy's body gave no glimpse of an excruciating end, but dying by poison sounded gruesome. She wondered who would threaten a tent person, let alone kill one, and felt unsettled by Grant's mention of three others. Carli's fingers clicked swiftly on the keyboard. Her search revealed no other poisonings. She started looking into dog pounds in the northern end of the borough. The image of two dogs being destroyed simply because Lucy had died continued to weigh heavily on her.

Carli pushed her keyboard aside as her thoughts took her back nearly forty years. She was a senior in high school when her brother Henry vanished. Instead of being a soon-to-be college graduate, Henry became a Missing Person. Together with her parents, she searched for Henry for almost a decade. They worked with police, detectives, and

special units and even re-mortgaged the house to hire private inves-
tigators.

It was never spoken aloud, but Carli knew she became the only
thing her parents had left. She felt helpless watching them grieve.
Throwing herself unfettered into work, and becoming a success,
helped steer their thoughts away from Henry, and it took her mind off
of him as well.

Retirement was still very new to her. She had seen others struggle
with it, but for Carli it was the perfect choice. She had gained the
enviable opportunity to work on her own paintings again and take on
small, yet meaningful, volunteer stints to help others. Lucy and the
fresh memories of Henry were unexpected obstacles, throwing her off
balance and suddenly making loss threatening again. No doubt, it was
the crux of her concern for Lucy's dogs.

Carli stared down at her tea and watched the dark brew swirl as
her steady breathing lifted and lowered the mug resting on her
midsection. The reflection of an overhead light gleamed back at her. It
looked like a miniature moon in a strangely off-colored sky.

Carli wondered if it was time to see a shrink, something people
from middle-class neighborhoods didn't do thirty years ago, or, if they
did, it was with the secrecy of a covert CIA operation. Back then, there
was no such thing as mental health. There was only mental illness,
and insurance didn't cover it. Who from her neighborhood could pay
for help? That's what neighbors and church were for.

At nine a.m. sharp, Carli dialed police headquarters. Saving two
strange dogs from possible death seemed crazy, but maybe a little
crazy was just what she needed. At best, it might serve as ever-so-
slight vindication for having lost Henry. At the least, she wanted to
ask questions and receive reassurances. Within minutes, Carli learned
over sixty thousand animals entered the pound a year. She couldn't
fathom it. Many went through police channels to do it and shared a
similar story: former pets of the elderly who either died at home or in
a hospital. The city used several pounds. She would start with the one
Grant had suggested.

Carli made more calls to ask about Lucy. The EMTs, the Medical

Examiner, and the police helped her piece things together. The toughest part of the calls was explaining why she was inquiring and how she knew Lucy. As best she could tell, Lucy was moved to the NYC Medical Examiner's office. An autopsy was likely planned, as Grant suggested. In the next days, she would be tagged and examined, cut and closed, and then placed on hold for two weeks in the freezer while Missing Persons searched for next-of-kin. If none were found, Lucy's body would be driven to City Island, then ferried to Hart Island for burial. The ferry would carry Rikers' inmates to dig and lower Lucy to her grave. Potter's Field on Hart had no headstones or markings. Just plots. It was strictly dust to dust in a mass gravesite. Carli pulled her hand to the center of her chest and closed her eyes. Where would Henry be buried? And had it already happened?

With eyes still shut, she reached for her phone.

"What do they look like?" asked the woman at one of the pounds.

"Small. Less than knee height. One tan and white, and the other dark gray. Both shaggy and they're tagged – Lila and Terrance."

"Would you know them if you saw them?"

Carli lied. "Sure."

Having eased her mind with the calls, Carli finally slid under covers to sleep.

Carli's dream of police sirens morphed into the ringing of her phone.

"Decompressed yet?" It was Pastor Miller's calm voice. He had already shared word of Lucy's passing with the Church Run Director and a woman at St. Mary's Church. "That man, Grant, stopped by St. Mary's earlier," he said. "Left word about Lila and Terrance. Call Sister Anna at the church. She knows their whereabouts."

Carli took the number. Then she asked, "How long have you been doing these Church Runs?"

"Twenty years. Give or take."

"Has anyone ever died before? During a Run?" she asked.

"First time for everything, as they say. Rough, wasn't it?"

"Indeed. I wonder if someone might be looking for Lucy; might never find her."

"The people at Missing Persons will do their best," said Pastor Miller. "We have to trust in them."

"It's not always that easy," she said. "I lost my brother ... he just vanished ... when I was in high school. His college roommates said he had been hanging out with cult members. They had set up on the sidewalk near his dorm. One day, the cult left, and Henry was gone. We don't know if he joined voluntarily. There's a good chance he was kidnapped."

"Oh my. I am sorry," said Pastor Miller. "How horrible."

"We searched for him," said Carli. "For over ten years. About eight years into the search, the FBI investigated that same cult. But they were zeroing in on human trafficking, not missing persons. Finally, we had to accept Henry was gone and that he might be in any country in the world. Or he might be dead. I can't help but worry that Lucy has family looking for her, and they will feel the pain and uncertainty ... of never finding her."

"I suppose that's possible," said Pastor Miller, "but maybe this will work out differently. We can hope someone is looking for her. And we can hope Missing Persons will connect with them."

"It's devastating," said Carli, "for a person to be lost. Of course, living on a sidewalk isn't great either."

"Many things are difficult to explain," said Pastor Miller. "Tough to accept, too. But please keep hope alive. And love. They are very powerful."

"Yes, I'll try."

"And, please, call or visit anytime," said Pastor Miller. "You might not be a member of the First Neighbor's congregation, but you are always welcome here. I hope you know that."

As she hung up the phone, Carli moved into the makeshift art studio in her spare bedroom. It was another perk of retirement. She knew she could walk into any drugstore or consumer retail - high end, low end, didn't matter - and be face-to-face with her branding, her professional work. Toothpaste? *Glisten* and her *Glisten Up* campaigns.

Cosmetics? *The Cool Touch of Workables* jumped off the shelves and covered the print pages of glossy publications and newsprint alike. *Living Easy?* It was hers as well. But every day she moved up the corporate ladder, she moved farther from the fine arts that had put her in the field in the first place. Her studio would become her sanctuary, her special space to refine the skills she had set aside. Moving back to where she started was her way to move forward, and she couldn't wait. But today, in the aftermath of the Church Run, with Lucy and Henry weighing heavily, she stared at a partially colored canvas and felt uninspired by the brushes at hand. Less than twenty-four hours ago, she had wanted to help the men and women on the streets. Now, she knew she had to. But how?

The next day, Lucy's church shone in the daylight, with its soft gray lines washing into the sun and its spires gliding upward with flights of pigeons. A single white rose lay on a step in Lucy's archway. Once inside, Carli noticed everything echoed – the door rattling shut, soft-soled shoes crossing the floor, and keys dropped by mistake.

"Welcome," said a woman, popping into the hall. "I've been expecting you. I'm Sister Anna." The woman's hair was pulled back and held by a simple elastic band. She handed Carli a note. "Grant's pretty sure the dogs are in the pound way up the East Side. Here's the address. He wanted to tell you in person, but he couldn't stay." The note was signed simply with the letter "G." What caught Carli's eye was it was made with soft graphite, an artist's pencil.

"I'm heading there next," said Carli, thankful the pound was the same one she had found. Then she had to ask, "Why was Lucy here, at the church?"

"Felt safe, I guess," said Sister Anna. "She started visiting a while ago, maybe five months. Lucy didn't have the dogs then, and she came for meals. We have a soup kitchen. Grant said Lucy occasionally used a drop-in center to sleep, and he tried to get her into a women's shelter.

That was before she got the dogs. Once she had Lila and Terrance, she couldn't go inside anywhere."

Carli nodded.

"It was somewhat reassuring knowing where she was," said Sister Anna. "It felt like we could keep an eye on her. Unfortunately, the police knew where to find her, too. They chased her out a few times. We're not a licensed shelter."

"Any idea why she was outside in the first place? Or where she came from?"

"No idea. Grant says they each have a story and they tell it when they're ready. You know," Sister Anna said, looking straight at Carli, "we run a pretty big soup kitchen here at St. Mary's. Six days a week. Thanksgiving is always busy, and we can use extra hands if you'd like to help."

"Me? Oh, no. I only came for Lucy's dogs," said Carli. "I don't want to see them destroyed. Do you think anyone at St. Mary's wants them?"

"Sorry, my building won't allow them. I'll ask around, though," said Sister Anna.

The smell of a hot winter's meal cooking in the kitchen followed Carli to the entryway as Sister Anna walked her to the door. Back outside, at the bottom of the steps, Carli adjusted her scarf and turned for another look at Lucy's archway. As she did, a flash of gray barely caught her eye. She turned her head around not knowing exactly where it was, but knowing it was somewhere in the thick cluster of shrubs leaning into the archway. After a careful scan, she saw it again, barely visible. Carli pulled aside several overgrown branches to slide amidst the tangled mass of shrubs. When she finally saw what it was, she froze. She had seen it before. In fact, she had fixed her eyes upon it several times in the corner of Lucy's tent when she and Grant did CPR. It seemed odd that Lucy's street-worn backpack was left behind when there was no other trace of her having ever been here. Was it left by accident? Or was its errant disposal done on purpose? Maybe, thought Carli, suddenly uncomfortable with her find, it had been left intentionally for someone else to pick up. Maybe even the person who had poisoned her. Carli stared at the pack, as though awaiting an answer. Then she lifted it by a single hand strap and brought it through the shrubs to the sidewalk. She walked swiftly away, knowing what she was doing – taking evidence – was no doubt illegal.

As Carli neared the pound, a chaotic mixture of barks rang into the streets. The odor of dogs and antiseptic filled her nostrils the moment she stepped into the cinderblock construction. Workers in yellow lab coats ferried dogs to examination rooms, playrooms, and meet-and-greet cubicles. Carli was directed to a cubicle where a young man in yellow brought Lila and Terrance back into her life. Carli hardly recognized them with their coats washed and groomed.

"These two came in early yesterday?" she asked. "From Animal Control?"

"Yes. Lila and Terrance. Funny names. Look like a full-bred Yorkie and part Scotty. The gray one, that is; Terrance." The man set them on the floor, and the dogs ventured a few steps toward Carli before a quick retreat to the corner. It was a replay of their inquisitive steps from the tent. For a split second, she thought they looked more cute than homely, a positive step toward finding a home.

"They were tagged by a local vet," said the man, "but the owner's address and phone number were made up."

Carli wasn't surprised. It was one of the few things in the last forty-eight hours that made sense. Half an hour later, she exited the pound, wondering if she was doing the right thing. She had placed the former street dogs on hold in her name. In two weeks, she could collect them, if they weren't claimed by someone else first. Worst case, she thought, she could find them a new family herself. At least they would live.

Instead of heading immediately home, Carli steered her car out of Manhattan toward the water to look across at Hart Island. It wasn't easy driving; Manhattan driving rarely was. But she had to see it. The place where all the lost bodies went. Where Lucy would go if no one claimed her. Carli drove from Manhattan to the Bronx, exited at Orchard Beach, and crossed the lone bridge to City Island. Still in her SUV, she peered through the wrought iron gate to the island's quaint cemetery, and looked past personal headstones and elaborately carved markers to view Hart Island across the inlet. All she saw there were scrub trees and crumbling buildings, but not a single headstone. The day had been strangely exhausting. A long inhale, followed by a long exhale, proved just the right medicine. She repeated the remedy fifteen times. That's how many days it would be before Lucy would ride the ferry to Hart, unless Carli could find her a way out of it. Surely, a person deserved better than to be forgotten.

THREE

THE CHURCH RUN sat on Carli like sandbags holding back a rising tide. On several occasions, she lifted paintbrushes in her studio only to sit and stare at her half-completed work. Her goal had been fourteen pieces for a one-person show. It wasn't a big thing to ask of herself; it only required some self-discipline, which was usually no challenge. Elena Lucia Rossi, a prominent curator, offered to show them in her gallery in less than a year's time. But, for the past week, Lucy kept pushing Carli back into her past, forcing her into recollections of Henry, and slowing progress.

In a neighborhood of large families, she and Henry had been an odd twosome, and he had always watched after her. When the neighborhood kids picked teams for streetball, dodgeball, kick-the-can, or bike races, he always chose her. Maybe not first, but not last either. When she couldn't keep up with the older kids, he always looked over his shoulder to check on her. It was comforting. Of course, he teased her too. Made fun of her braces all one summer, even in front of the other kids, but he always gave a light-hearted flick of his hand to her shoulder after. It was a good family and a good community. Between these and their extended family at St. Pius Church, they had all learned that there were times to look out for oneself, and there were times to care for others. With her working years behind her, Carli knew it was her turn to give back. She considered Sister Anna's offer. Helping at St. Mary's soup kitchen made much more sense than a second Church Run. Why, at her age, she wondered, was she still trying to figure things out?

The Wednesday before Thanksgiving, Carli returned to Lucy's church as a first-time volunteer in the soup kitchen. Gretchen, a four-teen-year veteran of St. Mary's volunteer serving crew, met Carli at the door. Once in the kitchen, they lined up fifty soup bowls and padded sandwiches with several pieces of bologna and cheese.

"Any questions, just ask. I've done it all," said Gretchen.

Carli kept assembling sandwiches and looked over the mustard and mayonnaise in donated deli packs. When bread ran out, Gretchen said, "Grab the croissants in the fridge. They're from Louie's Bakery. The Special Goods volunteers gather them up, along with about fifteen hundred pounds of extra food across the city, and deliver here and elsewhere. Nice having restaurants and corporations on our side. Special events sometimes have extras too."

Carli retrieved the croissants.

"It's often a hodgepodge, but it's food," said Gretchen.

Carli made sandwiches in automated fashion. Merrill poured apple juice and water into pitchers, her dangling earrings clinking in harmony with ice in the pitchers. Arnez separated cakes and pies into individual servings. Dorothy stacked plates and trays. When sandwich space was full, Carli scanned the room. She saw stainless steel coun-ters and ceiling tiles, some marked with brown water lines from the steam cast upward from boiling pots of soup. Fold-up chairs, to seat about a hundred, lined the fold-up tables decorated with plastic floral centerpieces.

At eleven fifteen, Carli stood patiently between Gretchen and Arnez. Her job was to restock as sandwiches ran low. A moth-er/daughter team was first to arrive. They knew the routine well. Knew to ask for crackers with their soup. Gretchen obliged. Sister Anna knew everyone by name. "Any word on your exams?" she asked Lanna, the older of the duo. Both heads shook a negative response.

"In a few minutes, we'll be going strong. Better fill more bowls." Sister Anna's advisory was right on target. Men and women, both young and old, came neatly dressed and not, along with scattered teens, a few with canes, and one in a wheelchair. All came for a good meal. Many looked for conversation and company. Others remained deep within themselves or mumbled to unseen companions. A communal newspaper at a crowded table caused skirmishes until the visitors established a readership queue. At a middle table, diners engaged in lively banter. Its members spewed mixed reviews of everything from million-dollar sports contracts to fashion heels. It was like a living op-ed table. Their voices quieted only to sip or slurp their soup and swallow pieces of bologna and cheese.

From time to time, a desolate soul shuffled in and put an "X" on the sign-in sheet. That's what the man with the multi-colored parka did. Ignoring a few stares, he circled several tables before choosing one in the far corner, where he deposited two large duffle bags on chairs and pounded a brown leather backpack off his shoulders to the tabletop. The combined load took up space for five.

He favored his right leg and hunched to protect it, weaving through tables to the food line. With a broad aqua-colored band across his parka's rose and mauve backside, Carli was quick to name him "Aquaman." She watched as he collected his lunch seriously, taking the maximum allowed of each item.

Half an hour to the end of lunch, Grant bounded through the door with his Police cap, rusty-brown suede jacket, and an air of confidence, or was it ownership? Rubbing his hands together for warmth, his silver ring sent light reflecting across the room. He stood in line and nodded to several at the tables. He didn't hesitate at the silverware bin. He was a regular.

"A little of this," he said, taking soup. "Gretchen, how are you today? And one of these." He added crackers. "And ... let's see ..." Grant cocked his head slightly to inspect a sandwich. "Wonderful." He placed a bologna and cheese on his plate.

After adding condiments, he looked at Carli. "I was hoping to see you here one of these days. I have a confession." A slight smile

eased up his face. Carli waited. "I don't remember your name," said
Grant.

Carli tensed, unsure how to answer. The truth is she had lied. To
everyone at the Church Run, and here at St. Mary's, she was Carli
Morris. To everyone else in her life, her name was Tessie Whitmore.
When she volunteered for the Church Run, Tessie was afraid to give
her real name. Afraid that street people might do something bad if
they knew who she was or learned where she lived. She felt vulnerable. She had even considered wearing a wig since her picture had
appeared in newspapers and magazines, thanks to the extraordinary
sale of her company. Now, she felt like a cheat, on the brink of total
exposure.

"I thought I heard you say it was Carli. That right?" asked Grant.

Carli said, "Yes." The lie grew.

"Say, did you do anything about the dogs?" he asked.

"I'm getting them next week." Her words were assertive; her inner
commitment was not.

Grant leaned toward Carli. "Here's a tip. Lila likes chicken better
than beef." Then he softly tapped Carli's arm and said, "Gotta run.
Don't want my sandwich to get cold."

Carli released a half laugh, and Grant glided into the maze of
tables. She watched him take a stand in the middle of Aquaman's
cargo chairs. Putting a hand on the man's shoulder, Grant maintained
balance while wedging his tray close to the old man's. After moving a
duffle to the floor, with no objection from its owner, Grant sat down.
For the next five minutes they dined and talked. Then, Aquaman put
the remains of his meal into his backpack, gathered his duffle bags,
checked all three bags several times each, and bumped his way past
tables and chairs and out to the street.

Immediately, Grant rose. With tray in hand, he joined three men
intent on dessert two tables over. As the three finished, Grant moved
again. His next host was the woman in her wheelchair. Several times
during this visit, Grant's laugh boomed above all else, causing Carli to
pause and look.

Mid-afternoon, Carli surveyed the remaining visitors. Their hunger was settled, and they embarked on the social aspects of group dining. It didn't matter that they were at a soup kitchen.

Following clean-up, Sister Anna walked Carli to the door. "She would be very grateful to you. Lucy, that is," said Sister Anna. "She loved them like the world, and they deserve a home."

Carli breathed in deeply. "I'm having second thoughts about keeping them. I might try to find them another home. But one way or another, they'll be in good hands."

Having a pair of city dogs seemed challenging. Letting them outside wouldn't be as easy as opening a door. She would either have to make dedicated time for it or hire a dog walker. Wasn't her life supposed to be less complicated now? Carli wasn't sure she was up for it, but she kept hearing Henry and her parents asking, "Didn't we raise you to help others? What happened to you?" They were the same questions she was quietly asking herself lately.

FOUR

A WEEK LATER, Carli finished her second day on the soup line knowing Lucy could head to Hart Island in a matter of days. She was about to leave the building, but the open door to the St. Mary's chapel beckoned her in. The room was empty. She walked two-thirds up the center aisle and sat in a pew. She rested her head on folded hands. It felt good to sit alone; lunch had been busy. The talkative op-ed table had shown again and had given rave reviews of a new show on Broadway, all edited from what they had read or heard secondhand, or simply believed out-of-hand. The mother/daughter duo had also come for lunch. Aquaman hadn't shown. Neither had Grant.

Over the years, Carli had given. Offertory after offertory. Even as a child, she had placed quarters from her hard-earned allowance into the wicker basket. Dutifully she had sung as she gave: *Dona Nobis Pacem* – Grant Us Peace. At St. Anthony's Church, in her college town, she also gave, and truly believed she was making a difference. She now sat within earshot of the St. Mary's soup kitchen and realized a billion offerings would not fill the gap of need. What gnawed at her most: they couldn't help Lucy find a way home. A reluctant prison labor force would bury her, and Lucy would be erased from humankind's memory. Carli felt helpless.

The sound of a man clearing his throat startled her. Carli turned to see Grant standing inside the doorway. "Did I scare you?" he asked.

"A bit. Why are you sneaking up on people?"

"Can't sneak up on anyone with this cold."

"Did you get some of the chicken soup?"

"Hah! The cure-all. Yes, but I couldn't taste a drop."

Carli asked, "How long have you been here?"

"Oh, not long. Just sharing a little space. Comes in handy. Space, that is. Ask an astronaut. Gives 'em a job and everything." Standing at the corner of Carli's pew, he said, "Coffee?"

"Huh?"

"Join me. There's a great little place around the corner."

Carli jumped at the chance to finally ask him questions. God knew she had many.

"Tell me about Lucy," said Carli.

"She had quite an impact on you, didn't she?"

"I've never seen a person die, and I'm wondering why she was here, in a tent."

"Why she was here is a mystery," said Grant. "Often is, until they open up a bit. Lucy was a good one. Really sweet, but paralyzed. Mentally, that is. I couldn't get her to move out of that archway. She was stuck. I worked damned hard at it. Must have stopped by her tent at least fifty times a month, but I couldn't get to her. She claimed she had no family and no place to go. Said something once about a car. My guess is she lived in one until it wouldn't run anymore or gas cost too much."

Grant opened the door to Gloria's and the welcoming scent of fresh coffee. "I almost got her to a shelter once. Sister Anna was going to keep the dogs one day, two days, a couple of weeks, undercover, of course. At the last minute, Lucy refused." Grant shrugged. "It's like that a lot. At least she got you to take her dogs. Or, maybe, we should call them her witnesses."

"I don't have them yet, but what do you mean by witnesses?" asked Carli.

"I'm convinced now that someone poisoned her. Just like the other three. No doubt in my mind. Some scum is out there, trying to send a message, and I aim to find him."

Carli bristled. "How do you know?"

"Just do. I've seen it before. They're still checking surveillance. Wish to God I had stayed with her. I can't stand watching my friends die."

After a long silence, Carli asked, "Do you think she lied? About not having family?"

"She could have," said Grant. "But what if she did? Missing Persons will have to find them."

A few sips of coffee helped Carli mull over his answer. "Tell me more about your work."

"Mobile Outreach?" asked Grant. "That's easy. Social Services runs it as a citywide program. A bunch of nonprofits hook into the funding and set up Outreach crews in different neighborhoods. I happen to work through Four Bridges, a couple of blocks from here. It has a drop-in center, a couple of social workers, and offers services that help with the first steps off the streets. About five hours a day, or night – my choice – I track down people who are out here and talk. Tell them about beds, medical help, and such. Mostly, I try to connect with them any way I can so they'll listen and try moving back inside. Sometimes it takes hundreds of contacts. They have to want it. Once inside some-where, other help follows when they're ready. I've been with Four Bridges about three years now. NYPD has another Outreach program, with nurses and everything. Of course, the city also cleans things up sometimes."

"To think, that night at the Church Run, I thought you were just getting soup," said Carli.

"Hah! I don't need to stand in an icy line for soup, but I need to check the lines for my people. I need to get any street intel I can," said Grant.

"Intel?"

"Oh, just info." Grant waved off the comment with a swoosh of his hand. "Like who might be lacing their food or bottled water with cyanide."

Carli stiffened at the thought of it. "Do you have any idea who did it?" she asked.

"None." Grant pursed his lips together and took in a deep breath with his mouth remaining closed. Then he repeated, "None."

Carli asked about the man she called Aquaman.

"Him? That's Harry. Funny name you gave him, but I suppose it fits. Between you and me, 'cause this stuff is kind of confidential, he spends nights with another man under the FDR Drive. Right around Forty-Second Street. You know the place?"

Carli nodded.

"That's their preferred home. But sometimes they move down to Thirty-Sixth Street. Have a real nice view of the Circle Line boat tours cruising around the city's edge. I guess Harry's story started when his wife died. At some point, Harry moved in with his daughter, but she kicked him out on account of his PTSD. Sometimes, he makes a bunch of noise at night. It scared his little grandchild. He's a Vet, and help's available, but he ran into complications and gave up on the government. It's been at least two years. Every so often, the police round him up, along with Grudge."

"Grudge?"

"An amputee who parks his wheelchair alongside Harry's trestle. They look after each other, one Veteran to another." Grant sipped his coffee. "Occasionally, the squad puts them in a drop-in center or on a ferry to a Staten Island center, but they always go back. Sometimes, they return on the after-midnight ferry. They want to be home, and the trestle's their home.

"I think you know the mother/daughter duo, Lanna and Kris, from the soup kitchen," said Grant. "They stay at a women's shelter. The man of the house walked out years ago. Kris, the daughter, is in her mid-thirties, though she looks like she's a teenager, and she's occasionally, well, suicidal. Lanna's taking classes to be a nurse. She can't pay rent, take care of Kris, and afford food. Government assistance is all they have. Kris needs drugs to stay well but often refuses. As an adult, she has that right, except when she's having bad thoughts. Then Lanna can step in, thank God. Hopefully, Lanna will get her degree. Then, she'll have a paycheck and benefits, but she'll need someone to watch her daughter.

"You've seen Marvin and Leo too," said Grant. Carli knew them as part of the talkative op-ed table. "They're interesting," he said. "Work the soup kitchens to the bone. Marvin usually sleeps at the drop-in room at Four Bridges with one chair per person, no bed, but a chance at breakfast and a shower. Sometimes Leo joins him, but usually Leo shacks up alongside the streets in the mid-Forties. He trusts himself more than anyone else and refuses to go on public assistance. He says it's a matter of pride. Unlike Kris, he'd be better to leave drugs alone."

Most of the ones who visited the kitchen had homes of some sort, but something else was missing. A few worked night shifts and saved on money by "going to church." What Grant made crystal clear was getting out was do-able, but it was like climbing the Empire State Building ... on the outside.

"Sorry to grill you," said Carli. "I've worked with lots of people, but none were as down on their luck as the ones in the soup kitchen. Mostly, I worked with ideas. I mean, what does advertising have to do with basic needs of food and shelter?" Carli quieted. She hadn't meant to share a word about her former work. Grant didn't seem to care. Nonetheless, Carli tried covering her tracks with an additional thought. "I retired a short while ago," she said, "and wanted to help. The Run intrigued me, but the soup kitchen seems better suited."

"Keep up the questions, and you'll have to join Outreach. You seem to have a passion for helping. We need that."

Carli laughed.

Grant looked her directly in the eyes. "Don't assume the soup line visitors didn't once have very different lives. Some of them even in the corporate world." Grant's tone had changed. "And I wasn't kidding about joining Outreach. I'm a pretty good judge of certain things, like needing to help and having the right kind of passion. Most people ... well, they turn away from all of this as fast as they can, as though living on the street is a communicable disease. Clearly, you know it's not."

Carli, with her fake name, and insecurity in her newfound world of tough lives, felt like a cad. Thank God, Grant had to leave to check a woman in the park. Carli left the diner and walked, as though drawn by a line of fishing filament, to the river along the city's eastern edge. She stared at the blue and gold glimmer on the water. This bench, she thought, taking a seat, might be someone's bed tonight. As her navy coat wicked heat from the air, she considered the strangers who had become family for lack of lunch money, and city-dwellers in donated suburban clothing. She envisioned a man in an aqua-striped coat, a woman thrusting her arms around the ragged tires of a worn-out wheelchair. She heard the rough outline of Grant's laugh. And she thought of Lucy. Why was she poisoned? Carli considered her plans to take in a pair of street dogs, ready or not, and also the fact that she was living a false identity, with no easy way to erase her lies. Despite the hardship she saw at the soup kitchen, Carli felt her life was more a mess than anyone else's now that Henry had burst back into it. A tear rolled down her coat collar to her lap. Carli wanted to return to work and leave this emotional turmoil. Writing a check would be easier than reaching out to strangers.

FIVE

CARLI PACKED Lila and Terrance into two new crates and slid them into her car for their ride to freedom. According to Grant, Lucy had already made her trip. Once home, Lila and Terrance huddled under the kitchen table. Bits of ham and chicken lured them into the open long enough for quick snatches and retreats.

Over the next days, Carli frequently sat on the floor across the room, content to watch and toss tidbits. She was going to give herself time to decide if they were staying, but, within days, Lila and Terrance's scampering antics had sufficiently captivated her to know they were hers. She took great comfort in having the extra little bodies in her life. They masked some of the apartment's quiet hum, a hum that contrasted starkly with the powerhouse energy inherent in her former day-to-day at TSW Inc. Did she miss that world? Mostly, she missed the people. On an impulse, Carli dialed Kristin McConnell, one of her creatives still at TSW Inc. and Carli's first hire.

"Sister!" Kristin shouted. Carli pictured her in her green-and-orange-print top with black slacks. It was funny how you got used to the office attire of co-workers, as though they were family.

Carli shrieked in return, excited to catch Kristin on the first try. Kristin gave the scoop on a couple of old accounts and on surprising changes in personnel. Carli shared news of her latest endeavors – the Church Run, soup kitchen, and Lucy, Lila, and Terrance.

"No!" said Kristin.

"Yes."

"No," Kristin repeated.

"I kind of did it for Henry," said Carli. "You know, my brother." Carli rarely talked about Henry anymore, but Kristin and Carli went back fifteen years. In that time, they had discussed pretty much everything.

"I get it," said Kristin. "But you, the workaholic, got a couple of dogs?"

"Like I said, after Lucy, I kind of had to."

Kristin was a dog person. Had a little French bulldog named Friedrich, a name Kristin and Carli had come up with when they recklessly tossed out names one night in Kristin's apartment. Carli had said it as a joke, after seeing the brand name on Kristin's room air conditioner. But then the name stuck. Carli felt like a godmother of sorts, having helped choose his name. Over time, Friedrich definitely grew into a Friedrich. He was unique. And it wasn't beyond Kristin or Carli to add a French accent to his name on account of his being a Frenchy. Friedrich didn't care either way.

"Are you getting the doggy line from Flippin' Dog?" asked Kristin. "You know ... jackets and bandanas? Please say yes, so they match Friedrich."

"Oh my God, yes." Carli knew the line well. For fourteen years, she had overseen Flippin' Dog's branding and advertising and had helped launch its digital. She had put them in nearly a thousand specialty boutiques and helped promote a line tailored to mass-market distribution online and brick and mortar. Carli was ready to shop. She looked at Lila and was shocked to see her reaction to Carli's excited conversation. Not only was Lila staring intently, but she was wagging her tail. "Oh, wow! You should see Lila," said Carli, followed by, "Oh my God, no!"

"What's wrong?" Kristin shouted back.

"My car must reek. I totally forgot about Lucy's backpack. It's in the back of my car. Holy crap."

"Eww. Sounds bad. Why do you have her backpack?"

"I just picked it up," said Carli.

"You took it from her?"

"No. It was left behind. I was airing it out before I opened it."

"Oh my God. Sounds like a cue to ask about your paintings."

"Yeah, right. Good idea," said Carli. "I'm making progress. And it's frightening. I don't have to sell anything, brand anything, or fit a budget. All I have to do is paint. I haven't felt this free in forever."

"Sounds heavenly," said Kristin.

"Yes, but freedom can be overwhelming. Anyway, I started a couple of waterscapes, and I might head to the Cape for a few days. Of course, now I have to figure in a couple of dogs. Want to dog-sit for me? Even better, do you want a couple of new family members for your little guy?"

"Friedrich!" shouted Kristin.

Carli heard Friedrich bark. Kristin dodged the pet-sitting subject and brought up Carli's birthday instead. "We're throwing you a party. You know that, right?"

"Of course," said Carli. "Like always. Tell me when and I'll be there."

Carli opened her SUV's door and stared at Lucy's backpack. It no longer smelled horrible, but it continued to radiate a clear message: "Danger!" Carli's midsection tightened. She never should have taken it. Her first instinct was to toss the pack in the trash, but Carli couldn't help but wonder what a homeless woman would keep. And whether, God forbid, it would hold a clue to her death. She decided to open it right in the garage.

Two dog sweaters lay on top. One blue quilted and the other red and black plaid. Seeing something familiar was a relief. Carli knew immediately, from the distinct rainbow-colored logo, that they were made by Flippin' Dog. A smiling dog, upside down and airborne, as though mid-flip, looked back at her. It was her design. She couldn't believe it. Four pairs of dog shoes sat underneath, also Flippin' Dog brand, and also welcome finds. At the bottom of Lucy's backpack, Carli saw a pair of yellow dog slickers. Flippin' Dog had decided against rainwear. Had decided to market fall and winter wear exclusively. She had never fully bought into the omission of rain gear, but that was a client decision. The rain slickers were PetWorld brand. She lifted them from the bag and inspected them. They were sturdy. The fabric was breathable. And ... there was something visible in their snap-shut pockets. Seeing it nearly caused her to drop the first slicker as though she were holding a live snake. Carli unsnapped the pockets and carefully pulled out the first of three photographs. Suddenly, Lucy had a past.

"Of course. To keep them dry," said Sister Anna. "I would have kept them in my own pocket, but Lucy ... well, she was certainly unique."

Carli spread the three photographs atop Sister Anna's desk. Together, with the spotlight of a desk lamp, and taking turns with a magnifying glass, Carli and Sister Anna inspected them.

In the oldest, a long-roped swing hung from a tree, in front of a big Victorian home. With feet out straight, and head back, a young girl rose through the air, pushed by another girl, cut off, in part, by the picture's ragged edge. An archway of roses, maybe red, but impossible to know from the black and white image, revealed a mid-summer scene.

Carli flipped it over to view smudged pencil lines bobbing through creases in the paper.

"It has an address," she said. "Looks like Maple Lane, but it's not clear. The house number on the door is Forty-Three."

"Every town in America has a Maple Lane," said Sister Anna. "Besides, we don't know if these were Lucy's or if she was just a collector."

"Yes, but look ..." Carli flipped over the other photos.

"Uh-hum." Sister Anna turned one of them back to the front side. According to the caption, she was face to face with "L and T" in nineteen forty-something. A man and woman, young, beautiful, and handsome, smiled back, surely married. She, in a dark Sunday dress with matching jacket and Sunday hat, and he, in a Sunday suit. Both had dark, well-coiffed hair, and she had high cheekbones and clip-on earrings, which painted elegance across her portrait. Sister Anna said, "L and T, huh?"

"This one is the jackpot. This couple near a lake." Carli flipped the photo.

Sister Anna read out loud the pencil print description. "Lucy and Will. Nineteen seventy-five. Elmsville Fair." She looked at Carli, with eyes alert.

Carli nodded and returned the photo image-side up. She had stayed up well past midnight the night before, searching for towns called Elmsville. There were at least sixteen on the East Coast. Aerial and street views narrowed her best bets to three. None of them looked quite right, but she was planning to visit the first one on her shortlist tomorrow.

"It does look a little like her," said Sister Anna. She gave a pensive nod and said, "But so long ago."

"I just want her off of Hart," said Carli. "If this is her home, it's where she belongs. Everyone deserves to go home." Carli had considered claiming Lucy herself and paying for the homeless woman's private burial. She stopped short when she considered someone else might try to find her. Some day.

Sister Anna nodded again. "Of course, but if you don't find her home or family right away, Missing Persons might do well to have these. Maybe her bag as well."

"I agree, but I have a feeling about this."

Carli addressed the soup line with little attention to the details of serving. Lucy occupied every thought. Convinced that Grant would want Lucy returned to her real home, she approached him as soon as he arrived.

"Don't be surprised if you don't find anything," he said. "Or if it's not a happy homecoming. People have a way of moving on and forgetting. Remember that, but good luck."

Carli watched him do his lunchtime rounds and heard his words many times over in her mind. Had he moved on as well? But, of course, her family would want her back. She certainly did.

SIX

CARLI WOUND through the countryside on forest-lined roadways and thought the landscape approaching Elmsville, Connecticut, looked promising. She turned off her audiobook fifteen minutes from her destination and replaced it with inner questions. Like how she would explain her visit. And explain she was looking for a dead woman's home. A dead woman she didn't even know, and maybe one who had enemies. Carli noticed her grip on the steering wheel tighten as she steered her car down the highway exit.

As roads narrowed and posted speed limits decreased, Carli suddenly smiled and shouted out loud, "Weirdness be damned!" It felt good to follow her instincts. She trusted herself and knew something good would come of her trip.

Carli glanced at a sketchpad and pencils she had set on the passenger seat. If this was Lucy's hometown, she wanted to capture the moment – the house and the tree ... everything. At last, she made the final turn onto the heavily shaded Maple Lane. The house numbers went down from number Two Hundred Thirty-Six. She took her foot off the accelerator and stopped at number Forty-Three. Even if it had undergone extensive renovation, the house out her window did not match the photograph. A giant evergreen stood in front, practically engulfing the house. No swing could ever fit under it; its branches were so full. In fact, the tree looked like a wonderful candidate for the Rockefeller Center tree lighting ceremony. Carli traveled Maple Lane end to end four times, scrutinizing each house. With every turn of her tires, hope melted away. It was worse than chocolate ice cream dripping from a cone onto a new white shirt. Carli didn't bother to turn on her audiobook or radio for the hour and a half drive home.

The next morning, Carli made copies of the photographs and relinquished the originals and Lucy's backpack to Missing Persons. She inquired if more had been learned of her family and, equally important, cause of death. Missing Persons was getting nowhere. Lucy hadn't matched anything in the national databases. Death by poisoning was news to them. The Medical Examiner hadn't mentioned it.

Carli hated admitting to Sister Anna and Grant that her visit to Elmsville was a disappointing dead end. Most of all, she hated admitting it to herself. The upside was the city escape had immersed her in more expansive landscapes. It proved valuable when she approached the partially complete canvas in her studio. Broad brushstrokes came more freely. Color options suddenly seemed plentiful. In an odd way, the Elmsville wild goose chase unlocked her arms and opened up her brain and her muscles to translate and express. Years at TSW Inc. had pushed her creativity to the limits but had drawn her away from her inner emotions and connections with the earth. Carli finished painting for the day, cleaned her brushes, and gravitated to her Elmsville shortlist, ready to schedule her next trip. Then she called Sister Anna to volunteer for another day at the soup kitchen. Maybe she could handle the emotional stuff, after all.

"Welcome back," said Gretchen. She made Carli feel like an old friend, exactly as her mother made visitors to her home feel ... when their family was still whole. Carli settled into the routine of food prep and set up, realizing it didn't feel so new anymore either. Mastery was reassuring. As some of the regular diners filed past, Carli studied them with new eyes, now that she knew something of their stories from Grant. She found herself jumping into a couple of conversations, even if only for a few moments. When Marvin passed with his tray, talking over his shoulder to Leo about Yankees baseball, she mentioned the pitchers had done well in the World Series, even though it was month-old news by now. Marvin and Leo looked at Carli, looked at each other, and laughed out loud. Then Marvin said, "Sounds like we've got another fan here. Just what we need." Leo agreed, and he showed it with a shout and fist pump.

Near the end of lunch, Aquaman came in with his usual bags in tow. "Take a couple more," said Carli. She put four extra rolls into a bag for him, knowing Aquaman Harry was Grudge's food delivery man. Then, she loaded him up with anything he was willing to take. He thanked her several times over with a simple thumbs up and was especially grateful for the mixed bag of cookies. It got a thumbs up *and* an appreciative nod. Carli watched him eat, pack, and leave, in his customary manner. She wondered how they faced their struggles day after day.

The next day, Carli exited the city as soon as traffic thinned. Elmsville, New York, wasn't far, but the main road leading into the town of two thousand was a two-laner with hills, curves, and an occasional gear-grinding, traffic-slowing, freight truck. Was she crazy? No, she reassured herself. It was the least she could do.

Maple Lane wound gently through a canopy of old trees, and was narrow and unpaved; a country lane in its truest sense. Carli crept along as though in a boat in smooth water, easing upon number Forty-Three. She let the engine softly idle and lowered her window. An arbor and stately white oak looked back. The tree was in the same place as in the photo but towered overhead. It had grown so much it shaded a good part of the house's front and even spread several branches above the roof. The swing was gone, but Carli saw it in her mind's eye, gliding, with a head-swung-back girl soaring happily, released from the weight of gravity. When a car rattled up behind, Carli quickly released the image.

It took several peeks through drawn shades, and a glimpse of Lucy's house photo, before Mrs. Thompson cracked opened the door to Forty-Three Maple Lane. The homeowner knew little about Lucy, except that her last name had been Birdwell until she married and became Lucy Stemple.

"Lucy Stemple," Carli repeated.

"It was on the land records," said Mrs. Thompson. "Not the person we bought it from, but a while back. The person to see is the woman in the tax office. Her name's Mia. And see if you can find Thelma, the old Tax Collector. She's the one you really ought to talk to. Retired a year or so ago. Lived five houses away as a child. Every time I used to pay a tax bill, Thelma brought up some memory or another. It seems Thelma and Lucy stayed friends even after Lucy married and moved. My living here made me someone special to her. But it's Mia who's there now. Go talk to Mia first," said Mrs. Thompson.

Carli felt fortunate to have found Mrs. Thompson. She headed into town, feeling even more fortunate that it was a small enough place that everyone talked, especially Thelma. Elmsville possessed a few small stores, a coffee shop, a town hall, and two churches. Carli looked over the whitewashed brick government building with a 1923 cornerstone marking the edge of an addition. Elmsville also possessed a long history. Carli let herself in through one of the building's well-worn double wooden doors.

The tax office took up space down a stairwell at the end of a narrow, dimly lit hall. Handwritten signs gave directions. In the quiet one-person operation, Mia invited Carli in moments before she reached the room; she proudly announced she'd heard her coming.

Carli explained the purpose of her visit and, within fifteen minutes, Mia and Carli found every home Lucy and her husband had owned, which was two. For the next thirty minutes, they chatted about Elmsville. Mia was a long-term resident. She suggested Carli see

Doctor Reynolds in town since he knew everyone, and also the woman named Thelma. "Lucky for you," said Mia, "Thelma's still in town. Give me a day to contact her and pass along your information. My guess is she'll be happy to talk."

When Carli left Elmsville she felt like she was in the middle of a brainstorming session for a new advertising campaign. It was both exciting and unsettling. There were so many ideas swirling, she knew she was making progress but hadn't a clue how it would end. Carli was used to a project team of at least ten. This time she was in it alone; it felt odd. First thing back home, Carli phoned Pastor Miller.

"I found Lucy's home," she said. "Her childhood home."

Pastor Miller sounded grateful for the news.

"Only, I haven't found Lucy's family just yet. I wonder if you'll help make the connection." Carli gave details as she knew them. Pastor Miller was delighted to help. All they had to do was await Thelma's call.

"Crossing fingers," said Pastor Miller.

"Yes," said Carli. "Crossing fingers. And ... there's something else you should know."

"Oh? What's that?"

"My name isn't Carli." Silence followed until she volunteered more. "I didn't know who we would meet on the Church Run. I was afraid to share personal details. My real name is Tessie Whitmore." She paused another moment, before adding, "I made a lot of money selling a company I built from scratch. The sale made headlines. I didn't want people we met on the street to find me. I was afraid of the possibilities."

"I see," said Pastor Miller.

"Even people who aren't desolate, often look at you differently if you have money. And assume things about you. I don't want that either," said Carli.

"So, now what?"

"I don't see a good way to change back to Tessie. I'd like to meet Thelma as my alias."

"You're okay with that?" he asked.

"Yes. For now, I'll consider it a nickname. I had a good friend named Carli in college."

After her call, Carli looked over her first paintings. It was time for an objective critique. Although not quite done, they didn't shatter the earth. They were hollow, for lack of a better term. The power they exerted came from subject matter alone—crashing waves and white-caps—and not from her technique. Nothing grabbed her emotions. Carli considered them average first attempts. Tomorrow she'd get on with another. Being this rusty was frustrating.

Thelma couldn't wait to meet Carli; Lucy was a big part of her life's fabric. But how had she taken the news of her old friend's demise? Surely, Mia had shared details.

The meeting was awkward, and then painful, even though Carli omitted the cause of death. She had been a bit vague with Mia, as well. After all, poison had not yet been confirmed. Pastor Miller filled in details of the Church Run night. His compassion was soothing. Then Carli revealed specifics of Lucy's trip to Potter's Field. Thelma leaned all the way back in her chair, as though needing support from its full surroundings.

Carli scolded herself for not handing the mess to Missing Persons and bowing out. Now it was too late; Thelma was part of her life, tears and all. Save one or two close friends, Carli had remained mighty adept at keeping her life private, and relationships emotion-free. At least Pastor Miller was with her to handle these sensitive parts.

"I'm sure the neighbors will help. Bring her home, that is," said Thelma. The woman in front of Carli was, indeed, a lifelong friend to Lucy.

Pastor Miller offered more supportive words. Carli could only nod.

"That photo of the home ... It was her childhood home," said

Thelma. "Lucy moved out when she married. Her older sister, Georgia, died in mid-life. Her mother and father – Lila and Terrance – are gone too."

Her parents, thought Carli. And her dogs. They had the same names. Yes, the two terriers were Lucy's ticket home. Lucy had carried an ID after all.

Thelma continued. "Her marriage ended when William died of cancer. They lived in the town center when they married and then moved a few blocks toward the edge of town. That's where she was until she left."

"When?" asked Carli.

"It's almost a year now."

"She and William didn't have children?" she asked.

Thelma shook her head. "She couldn't. She would have been a wonderful mother. She babysat a lot of the children here. See that sparkle in her eyes?" Thelma glanced toward the photograph of Lucy and Will. "It was always there, beautiful sparkling blue, like the lake. William went, and then she got sick. The sparkle vanished."

"Sick?" asked Pastor Miller.

"Diabetes. Heart trouble," said Thelma. "The doctor here, Doc Reynolds, once told me it could change a person's moods. Lucy got depressed; she completely changed."

Carli and Pastor Miller remained silent.

Thelma continued. "'Why would I want to stick myself with a needle every day?' Lucy would ask. Pills wouldn't work for her. Lucy told me nothing would work and said it was none of my business. That's why I talked with the doctor. It wasn't like Lucy to speak like that."

Thelma nodded and sat silently, as though remembering the moment. Then she said, "Lucy sold her house out of the blue, and said she was heading south. She said she would consider giving herself shots. It sounded fishy. But it's all she said. After that, she never wrote, never called, never said, 'Boo.' We all thought she meant Florida."

"I am sure this is overwhelming," said Pastor Miller. "Illness can, indeed, change a person's outlook on life. Losing her husband must have been difficult as well."

"There's more," said Thelma. "Lucy and William put a lot of money into his treatments. It burned right through a big line of credit. She never told me how much. Didn't want us to know how bad off she was. When she sold the house, she didn't get much, I'm sure. I think the finances scared her into moving."

Thelma closed her eyes. "I can't believe she was so close and living in a tent." A tear trickled down her face. "We all would have pitched in." When Thelma opened her eyes, she added, "That girl pushing the swing ... that's me. Could I keep it – the picture?"

"I'll make you a copy and frame it," said Carli. Even though she felt a tear welling up and a lump forming in her throat, she knew she had done the right thing for Lucy and for Thelma. The truth was still better than being lost forever.

"I found them," said Carli. Grant listened. "Lucy's home, her parents, and her friend," she said. "Pastor Miller and I visited Lucy's hometown."

"It must have been hard on her parents," he said. "How old are they?"

"Actually, they died. So did her husband. No children, either. We spoke with Thelma, a lifelong friend. She knew Lucy well."

Grant held out his hand. "Congratulations. Better than Missing Persons. It couldn't have been easy," he said. "Any idea why she came to the streets?"

Carli heard his question, but a stronger voice inside her was privately asking herself why Grant's handshake was so familiar. She knew thousands of people and had shaken many of their hands. At one point in her career, Carli started grouping people she met by their handshake: natural, bone-crushing, limp noodle, firmly elegant, and several more variations. It was an intriguing exercise, nothing more. She pulled herself away from her thoughts to answer Grant. "Thelma said she lied and left. Said she was likely fighting illness through denial. It seems Lucy had diabetes and heart problems. Thelma also said Lucy was depressed. And she was pretty certain Lucy was nearly broke from paying for medical treatment for her husband."

Grant slapped his hand against his jeans and stomped his foot on the ground. "Damn it! Damn it!"

Carli stepped back. Unlike the handshake, nothing about Grant's outburst was familiar.

"I missed it. Completely missed it." Looking to the sky, he said, "That sore on her hand, never healing, should have been a dead give-away. Along with her moods." He snorted with self-reproach. "Lucy went through a box of chocolate bars faster than anyone I know. Said she had to eat them before the dogs got to them because chocolate would make them sick. Not once did she talk of it. Bet she knew it would kill her. I should have seen it."

"Diabetes isn't something you can see."

"Sometimes there are signs, like with everything else," said Grant. Laying a hand on her shoulder, he added, "Sorry. I hate missing clues. I thought I had gained her trust. Thought she would turn to me for help."

Carli didn't know what to say.

Carli picked up Thelma at the expressway exit outside the city. With cataracts and aging reflexes, Thelma wanted to carpool through city traffic. It was 11 a.m. when they arrived at the Department of Corrections to plead for Lucy's return.

"Did the police see these?" The day's attendant shuffled through the photographs.

"We found them after she was buried," said Carli. "I gave the originals to Missing Persons."

Thelma got straight to the point. "This is no place for Lucy. I have her birth certificate, marriage license, house deed, and plenty more old photos. If you need dental records, I'm sure I can get them. We want her back home. We have a very nice cemetery. And there's a place for her next to William."

"Who's William?"

"The love of her life," said Thelma.

"Thought she didn't have family," said the attendant.

"Not alive, but she's got family, all right," said Thelma. "And it's time they spend the rest of eternity together."

The man looked up.

"I don't know what it costs," Thelma continued, "but there're plenty of us in town to raise what's needed. It's just not right leaving her here. She deserves better. She's not a Missing Person anymore. Never really was, anyway. She just left."

"I'm kind of new here," said the man. "I'll see how we handle this and get back to you."

Carli and Thelma left with hope and a prayer. "I can't thank you enough," said Thelma, "for finding us."

"I had to," said Carli. "I know how losing someone feels."

"Oh?" said Thelma.

As Carli drove, her story of Henry spilled out. By the time she dropped Thelma at her car, Carli and Thelma had formed what would become a lasting bond. For all the years Carli had kept her family's tragedy bottled inside, hidden from all—save for a few special friends like Kristin—she had just learned how good it felt to finally let it out again, especially to someone else who understood. When Carli arrived home, she walked straight into her studio. A Victorian home, with a girl on a swing, began to take shape. Carli had found her muse.

SEVEN

"FOUR WEEKS at the soup kitchen, or maybe it's five," said Grant. "Time to celebrate! Actually," he said, looking directly at Carli, "we have to talk. Join me after lunch. Down the hall." He glided to the tables, where plastic poinsettias had replaced the autumnal plastic mums. Christmas was less than a week off.

Aquaman had a new yellow hat, maybe from a Church Run, or maybe from a thrift shop. Grant gave its tassel a playful tap before chatting and then moving to catch up with Lanna. He followed with a visit to Leo, Marvin, and the others at the op-ed table. The lunchroom was more crowded than usual. The cold was bringing more people inside for a break from the weather. Carli wondered how they were holding up outside, in particular, Aquaman with his new yellow hat. After another visit, Grant disappeared, likely to meet with Sister Anna. No doubt he passed Bruce on the way. Carli always felt uneasy when Bruce came for lunch. Today was no different.

Bruce mumbled his first words as soon as he entered the soup kitchen. "Ugly garbage," he said to no one in particular. "Know what I mean?" he asked the room. "Garbage slime." Bruce paused and then said, "Real good. Real good." He walked to the sign-in table, sliding one shoe noisily across the floor, as though he couldn't lift it off the ground. Bruce asked, "What ya gonna make today? Huh? And where're ya goin'?" Bruce continued, leaving several seconds between his sentences. "Where're ya goin'? ... I don't know. Maybe there's a road outta town. Press on the gas, bud." Bruce hovered over the sign-in paper a few seconds before he grabbed the pen and loudly scratched his name across the page. He accidentally ripped the paper and dropped the pen to the floor in the same motion but didn't notice he had done either. He just stepped toward the serving line with his invisible companions.

Bruce suddenly shouted, "Fuckin' crap!" A couple of faces looked up, Carli's included, even though he did this nearly every visit. "Someone's gotta fix the water here," he said. Bruce's voice rose into a crescendo and fell again. Then he took hold of a plastic tray and looked over the food selections, with his head down and nothing more than a sweep of his eyes. "Someone's gonna fix the water out there. Did you hear me?" Bruce increased the volume again and moved closer to Carli, but he wasn't talking to her. She had answered once before, only to learn he hadn't noticed her. This time, he looked not at Carli but at the broccoli in the bowl between them. "The water needs fixing," he said again. He took another loud shuffle along the food line. "Lousy garbage slime. Looks like rain. Storm's a comin'. Huh?" He said nothing more as he eyed the soup, but Carli saw him grinding his teeth and moving his mouth as though chewing invisible food. Suddenly, he exploded. "Fuckin' shit!" Just about everyone looked up this time. Bruce didn't notice. Didn't see a single staring face. Bruce left his tray on the shelf above the sandwiches and stomped to the coffee pot. With several jerky shakes of the pot, he half-filled a mug. With a few awkward scoops, he added sugar. Then he paced. Like usual. Back and forth from the sign-in table to the start of the food line. Slowly. Pausing. Shuffling. And continuing his conversations, "Real hard time coming. Real bad. Fuckin' slime." He began waving his arms as he spoke. Coffee splashed out of his mug. "What ya got there? Huh? You goin' somewhere?" Bruce looked to the clock high up on the wall over the door and said, "Storm's a comin'." He paced toward Carli again and said, "You don't have to do that," and after a pause added, "Huh?"

Carli nodded once and let him stare at the broccoli. He would leave soon. Coffee with extra sugar was his usual meal.

Grant held Carli's chair, seated himself, and immediately made his proposal. "I need your help with Outreach."

"What?"

"Maybe once a week. Just like now, but working the streets instead of the soup line. Days only. Nights are mine."

"I don't understand," she said.

"Sister Anna agrees you'd be good for it, and it's tougher for me to find the right help than it is for her getting extra hands for the lunch line. Volunteer position to start, but might turn into a paying job. You need a job?" he asked.

"Are you crazy?"

Grant ignored her question. "Oh, that's right, you just retired. Well, it's like I told you before, I work for the nonprofit called Four Bridges. Work out of its drop-in center a few blocks from here. About thirty other people do what I do. Most work in teams. I work on my own, by choice. We regularly meet with the people who are making their homes on the streets; ask how they're doing, try to nudge them inside or to get medical treatment, if needed, and learn what's stopping them from getting off the streets for good. Some groups only send out people who have come from the street. Other nonprofits don't have any workers or volunteers with street time. Four Bridges sends out both. I need help with a couple of women. Two in particular. I doubt they'll ever trust a man, so that leaves me out, and I haven't seen anyone make any progress with them. I'm frustrated with this continued failure to connect. I mean, no one is reaching them. We need to change it up. I'd like to see if you could get through their shells."

"And you think I'm qualified? You're nuts."

"I disagree. I see the way you talk with Lanna and Kris and some of the others here at the church. Noticed you got a couple of fans in Marvin and Leo. It seems to come easily to you."

"It's not as easy for me as you think, and this sounds totally different," she said.

Grant proceeded with details. "We'll give you a cell phone. I'll do better at keeping mine charged. It's kind of a weakness of mine. I'll give you plenty of support getting started."

Carli shook her head. "Do you have any idea what my regular life is?" she asked.

"I don't care about your outside life. I mean, I care ... but it doesn't matter to Outreach."

"What exactly would I be doing? I mean, I just retired and have plenty of things to do. I wasn't looking for a job."

"You meet these two women, although I'll introduce you to some of the men who are out there too, so you can see how I handle them. But no one's been able to reach the women. You'd be like a specialist. Your task would be to visit them, talk with them. Make sure they're still alive. See if they need help. Well, we know they need help. But you see if they're ready to accept it. Everyone out there is different. It's just talking to a couple of women."

"I want to help. I really do. But in some little way. I have a pretty major commitment already, doing my painting and preparing for a show. Serving lunches is easy. Getting into people's lives isn't what I do."

"Well, here's the thing ...," said Grant. "Getting into people's lives is what I do best, and I know you have it in you, for who knows what reason. You, alone, knelt to assist in trying to save Lucy. That's after you volunteered to help on a Church Run. Doing a Church Run, in itself, puts you on my radar screen. And, it's not like you had competition for little L and T. No one told you to find Lucy's house and family either. Something is pushing you. I can tell."

Carli was frightened by Grant's words but was even more frightened by his certainty and the truth of it.

"One day a week," he said. "Actually, just part of a day, like the soup kitchen. Maybe two, if you want. Part-time. Volunteer. Think about it."

Carli shook her head again. "You must be ..."

"Think about it," he interrupted.

"Okay. Okay. Don't get your hopes up."

Grant folded his arms across his chest and smiled. "A bit tougher than I expected, but a good start." Uncoiling his body, he gently tapped his coffee spoon on the table in rhythm with his words. "Don't think long. Say yes."

Joining Outreach was a preposterous idea. Who did Grant think he was, asking her like that when he didn't even know her? Carli meant to give it no thought at all, but it poked at her every time she thought of Grant sitting in the lunchroom and connecting with people. It jumped to mind as she ran errands, unloaded groceries, and painted. In particular, it snared her two days later as she sat on a Central Park bench in winter wraps, on the edge of Columbus Circle. She had given herself a day to sketch uptown. It was now or never to exercise her artistic brain.

The Plaza Hotel sparkled, dressed in its holiday best. Shiny black limousines lined the street in front, and horses clopped past, carriages in tow. On the nearby sidewalks, peddlers sought out customers, and, midday, a wave of people splashed into the streets and then receded, their hunger satisfied by upscale meals and food cart cuisine. Late afternoon, Carli finally set down her pencils and swiveled around to look into the park itself. Two men in multiple layers of coats, hats, and hoods slept upright on a bench. One sat with his head tilted against the rail, his mouth opened wide to the cold air. The other hunched over, his chin buried against his chest in the creases of his overcoat. Three benches away, another man lay curled up in the fetal position, asleep. A month ago, she would have glanced and done nothing more. Today, thanks to Lucy and the soup kitchen, she stared and wondered who they were.

Carli walked slowly along Fifty-Ninth Street, following the edge of the park. Who else was out? A man studying his newspaper while eating looked the same as others, except for the hole in the knee of his black slacks. A twig of a man said hi to all who passed, perhaps a friendly neighbor, except he reeked of alcohol. Carli managed to say hi back at him, but nothing more.

She watched the people, nearly invisible to most, for a long while. Twenty minutes were spent on a woman in a bright blue coat. A matching hat covered her head. She glowed. Her three black plastic bags on the ground, and four more bulging on the bench, were joined by a small, rusted, four-wheel shopping cart.

The woman pulled a roll of newspaper from one of her bags and then fished out a pair of high heel shoes, blue to match the coat and hat. She carefully folded the well-worn paper around the heels and placed them on the bench. Out next came an olive-green sweater and a second pair of shoes. Other items were already wrapped. The women removed their paper and wrapped them again with new. Old paper was lightly pressed and smoothed by hand and then piled on the bench. The woman checked the deepest corners of her first bag before folding it neatly and placing it on the bench. She weighed it down with the wrapped blue heels.

Bag two came next. Three sweaters, five pairs of pants, and two more shoes were either wrapped, unwrapped, or both. Carli lost track, but the woman probably did not. Bags three and four brought more of the same. Bag five was reserved for newspapers. Bag six was different as well. Labored tugs brought forth the bedroom. One rolled-up sleeping bag, a piece of foam, three blankets, and a gray, flattened pillow, barely an inch thick, emerged. From within the blankets came a pillowcase. From it, the woman pulled pieces of paper, which she unfolded, observed, and refolded. Carli thought of Lucy's photographs as the woman also pulled from the case one small box, pill bottles, a ball of string, and three large gray and white feathers. The inventory was returned to the pillowcase and carefully settled inside the blankets. The final bag had a collection of socks and a brown leather satchel, which was left unexplored. Carli supposed it was filled with more knick-knacks, but what if it held secrets, as Lucy's dog coats had? What if it was this woman's ticket back home? Carli wanted to grab the satchel and look inside.

———

Throughout the night, the woman in blue periodically sauntered into Carli's thoughts. It was as though Grant had stationed her there for Carli to discover. Could she actually help someone like the woman who packed clothes in the park? As disconcerting as it was, Carli was considering Grant's proposal. He had sensed her deeper need, as if someone had told him her personal reason for wanting to help. It was as though he knew her. Certainly, she could spare half a day a week, but wouldn't she be better playing it safe at the soup kitchen? She knew the routine. Wasn't looking to get any more involved.

The next day, Carli tried to catch Grant at St. Mary's to ask him her questions, but he was nowhere to be found.

"He does this sometimes," assured Sister Anna. "Goes to another kitchen downtown, I think. Actually, goes all over, as far as I know. Wherever he needs to go to find them. Sometimes he disappears for weeks at a time."

"Say, what do you know about Outreach?" asked Carli.

"I know it does a lot of good work. That's what I know," said Sister Anna.

"Has Grant ever talked about any women in particular? Ones he can't connect with?"

"No one in particular," said Sister Anna. "But I do know he thinks you might make some connections. That's what it takes."

"I don't know why he would think that."

"I don't know, but he seems to get it right more times than not," said Sister Anna.

Carli checked Gloria's and ordered coffee to reconsider the offer before returning to her studio. As a blast of cold air blew her napkin from the table, she turned toward the open door and saw a man in a familiar yellow hat and aqua-striped coat juggling his duffle bags between a set of tables.

"Oh no, not today. We've got our business hours. You should know that." The waitress practically slammed Carli's coffee mug onto the table and continued talking while lifting her chin toward the wall. "Either you order, or you're out. The sign's right up there."

Carli looked in the direction of her nod. The sign was clear: bathrooms were for customers only.

As Aquaman Harry fumbled through a pocket, two men in suits tried to pass. His bags blocked their path, and the men showed their impatience through a pair of matching scowls.

"Always trying to wash up here," said the waitress.

Carli said, "I know him."

"Really? I just figured he was homeless."

"He is, but he goes to the soup kitchen. I know him from volunteering."

"Well, he comes here every week, sometimes stinking real bad. Hate to turn him away, but it bothers the paying customers."

Aquaman shuffled outside. Other places would turn him away too. With three days until Christmas, most tables bulged with gift bags, but his bags were different.

Carli slapped down several dollars and left. Harry was already half a block away, even though his pace was slow. The uneven weight of his shoulder bags caused a lopsided walk, as usual, and several people bumped him off balance as they passed. He glanced from one side to the next, as though checking a rearview mirror. By block's end, he was sidling close to the buildings, retreating from the pedestrian mainstream. Red lights caused others to fidget, but Aquaman waited patiently. He passed most stores with little fanfare, but a travel agency caused a five-second review.

After trailing him for four blocks, Carli finally caught up. She had seen enough bumping and sidling. She had felt enough anger. Anger with others, but mostly with herself. She could have shared a table or, at least, bought Harry a coffee. She did nothing. The only way around her anger was to take action.

"Hey, Harry," she said. "Don't know if you remember me. I'm Carli from St. Mary's."

Harry swung around to look her straight in the eyes. After a moment he said, "I know who you are. You're the one with the cookies." He nodded as he spoke, and his hat's yellow tassel slid along the side of his face.

"Right," said Carli. "Right. Say, how's your new hat working? It looks good."

Harry shrugged. He looked like he wanted to say something, but didn't know what to say. So, he nodded, nothing more, and his tassel swung once again.

"Well, I saw you and wanted to say hi. Hope your day goes okay." Carli pulled a few dollars from her bag. "You might not need it, but, please, take this ... in case you want something else for you or Grudge, and don't want to walk all the way to the kitchen."

Harry stuffed the bills into his coat pocket and nodded his thanks. With a slight wave, he continued on his way. Carli watched until he was nearly at the end of the next block. Maybe, she thought, joining Outreach wasn't crazy. When Harry passed through the next crosswalk, Carli muttered under her breath, "Dear God, I'm listening. I hope I'm hearing you right." Almost immediately, she found herself rubbing her hand on her coat collar, something she knew she did with her shirt collars at work when she felt anxious but equally resolute. It told her something.

EIGHT

CARLI'S PAINTING was becoming more natural again. She credited it to the heart-to-heart she had with herself early one evening, sitting in the cushy gray club chair in her bedroom studio. Across the room she saw her floral sofa, standup mirror, crowded bookshelf, boxes, and knick-knacks, including a twenty-ounce "shot glass" from a trip to Tijuana. Her mind and heart shouted in unison: get rid of it! Painting and sketching in a cozy home worked in high school. And it worked in college, in the small family-style art department of Castle College of Art. She was an office artist now. Cozy clutter fostered daydreams, not completed work. Carli needed good light, open space, freedom from distractions, white walls—like the walls of her former office—and a business-like studio.

She hired Luis, a one-person operation, to paint over the warm gray walls of her spare bedroom. Bright white, not yellow-white, not linen-colored, not pink-toned, gray-toned, green-toned, or any other kind of white, soon coated all four walls, doors, jambs, and moldings. She put the warm greige (part gray, part beige) carpet in her storage bin, had Luis sand the floors to the original wood color, and paid extra to have him coat them with heavy-duty polyurethane. She removed plants and squeezed the mirror and extra bureau into her bedroom.

Not even the patterned fabric headers remained over her windows when she was done. In their place, she installed mini blinds, which could allow a clear-ish view out, sunlight in, or total darkness and privacy. All this prompted her to spend three nights with Lila and Terrance at Kristin and Friedrich's place.

"Grant asked me to do Outreach with two street women," Carli said one night after dinner.

"What does that even mean?" asked Kristin.

"I don't know all the details. He said I'd visit them, try to connect with them, and, hopefully, encourage them to go inside somewhere for help. Do I look like the type that walks up to a street person and starts talking, asking how their day is going? Well ... except that it is exactly what I did a couple of days ago."

"Honest answer ... no," said Kristin. "It's not that you don't care about people, but usually you're more job-driven. Less interested in the touchy-feely side of things, especially with people you don't know. If you know what I mean."

"Exactly," said Carli. "So, why am I considering it? Why can't I let this go?"

Kristin pulled Friedrich closer. "In this episode of 'Let's Ask Friedrich,' we call upon the world-famous wonder-dog to ask, 'Why is Tessie considering something that makes no sense?'"

Carli laughed as Kristin gently turned the tips of Friedrich's rounded ears and said, "Wait ... he's looking for signal. ... Yes ... we have it. Friedrich says, 'I haven't a clue,' but he also says, 'She might know more than she thinks she knows. She'll figure it out.'"

"Well, thank you, Friedrich," said Carli. She leaned in to give the dog a hug. "I think I'm going to try it. If I haven't said no yet, I must be thinking yes. And Friedrich is right, there is something else."

"Oh?" said Kristin.

"I used a fake name," she said.

"And what does that mean?"

"Everyone at the soup kitchen and Church Run thinks my name is Carli. Same with the people in Elmsville. I didn't want them to know who I really am, with my money and all."

"Interesting. How are you going to get out of this one?"

"I'm not," said Carli. "At least, not yet."

The first thing Carli did when she and her dogs returned home was hammer a picture hook to the left of the door to her newly refurbished studio. On it she placed a framed graphic for Bright Start's *Morning Magic* facial wash. It was her first solo production for Madison Avenue advertising. Granted, it wasn't as magical as she once thought, but it sold product, and it would remind her every time she entered her new workspace that she not only could but would succeed. It was perfect. Carli was considering adding a couple of dog beds, but, for now, Lila and Terrance could sleep curled into tiny balls, or stretched full length on their bellies, on a pair of towels.

St. Ignatius was a small neighborhood church, tucked into a residential block roughly ten minutes' walk from Carli's apartment. The congregation included a mix of families, younger singles, and older members, both coupled and not. She connected immediately with Father Timothy's sermons, and it was Father Timothy who steered Carli toward Pastor Miller's Church Runs. At the time, doing the Runs sounded oddly enticing; a mix of excitement and mission. During her working years, Carli had been one of the "CEO churchgoers," making it, as the saying indicated, only for services for Christmas, Easter, and an occasional other. After retiring, she had yet to make regular services, but each time she attended she felt more alive. As Carli waited for Christmas service to commence, she momentarily reflected on Lucy. Thanks to Thelma, Lucy Stemple would go home soon. She wasn't the first to be disinterred from Hart, but making real headway required a route through the City's Bureau of Vital Statistics. With Lucy now in the Bureau's book, all that was needed was the ground to thaw. The McFaddin Funeral Home in Elmsville would handle the logistics, thanks again to Thelma. Plenty of town folks were chipping in to pay for a proper burial and headstone next to William's. Carli was grateful she had shown the courage to step up and answer the call, but, mostly, she gave thanks to God that hearts could now mend because their Lucy had been found. She couldn't ask for anything more. Mid-service, when the offertory came around, Carli slid a donation among the others. It wouldn't save the world, but it sure saved her soul to be able to give.

Two days after Christmas, Carli finally found Grant at St. Mary's. She gave him her decision to try Outreach for one part-day a week. "I knew I could count on you," he said. "That *they* could count on you." He scratched a few words on a napkin and said, "Go to this address and complete the paperwork. Meet me here, at Lucy's church, as you call it, next Wednesday at eleven. We'll have you making visits in no time."

Carli asked about his holidays.

"Holidays? Quiet. Always quiet, which is good."

Early the next day, Carli visited Mercy Gonzalez, a social worker and Outreach Manager at Four Bridges. A half flight of stairs, running alongside the front of the building, led from street level to the basement level door. A remnant of police tape hung limply from the metal handrail. Carli stepped past and admired the brickwork around the 1930s entry before she swung open the door and descended the final four steps. In front of her was a room filled with people, sitting one person to a chair in crooked rows.

Grant had made it sound so simple, meeting two women. Instinct told her she was making a mistake as she looked at the people around her. These were people's lives she was about to enter. Not brands. Not campaigns. Not a simple serving to someone in a lunch line. Why had she felt so invincible, let alone the least bit qualified to help? Because Grant had said she could do it? Because she had reached out to Harry on the street? What was she thinking? Carli stared across the room and caught the flash of a waving hand. She focused more closely. It was Leo from the op-ed table ... reaching out ... to her! Marvin sat one seat to his left. Carli slowly lifted her hand in return and felt surprisingly more capable. Worst case, she thought, it wouldn't hurt to ask a few more questions. Carli proceeded through the room of chairs to step into Mercy's office, but not until she gave a light tap to Leo and Marvin's shoulders, and they, in turn, did the same to her.

Mercy was a slight woman, wearing an updo with product, and a vibrant red, yellow, and black large-print blouse. Mercy's shimmering red lipstick played beautifully off the rest of her attire. Eyeglasses hanging from a gold chain around her neck were big, bright, and green. Mercy had style and clearly wasn't shy. Not about her self-image, and, as Carli had learned from life experience, likely not about life either. In contrast to this bold exterior, Mercy exuded the warmest, most gentle welcome as she stood, extended her right hand to shake, and placed her left hand on top of Carli's as she did. All Mercy said was, "Carli, so nice to meet you," but her words and handshake combined to immediately bring Mercy into Carli's confidences.

"Please, sit," said Mercy. "And tell me what's on your mind."

"You know this is new to me," said Carli. "And it hadn't crossed my mind to join Outreach. So, I need to know if the two women I'll be seeing are ever violent," said Carli. "I don't know how any of this works."

"Vera? Sarah? Not a chance," said Mercy. "No worries there. We wouldn't have you reach out to them if they were."

"Are they anything like Bruce?"

Mercy knew Bruce. "No, not at all."

Carli felt better. "Last, I need to know why someone is poisoning street people," said Carli.

"Where did you hear that?"

"It's what Grant told the police. When Lucy died, he said they should check for poison."

"I see," said Mercy. "I don't know about poisoning. Not with Lucy. Not with anyone else. I'll have to ask him."

"No one's been poisoned? Grant was mighty adamant about it."

"Not that I know of, but I'll double-check." Then, Mercy said, "I don't know how well you know Grant. I don't expect very well yet. Our other employees and volunteers go out as teams. We try to keep tabs on just under a hundred street sleepers. Grant checks on more than anyone, and he's done a whole lot of good work. Unbelievably good work. He prefers to reach out on his own, and we give him leeway because he's so successful at connecting and persuading them to come inside for help. His methods aren't typical. Sometimes they are … well, a bit baffling, to put it mildly, but I trust him. Just like I trust his judgment in asking you to help." Mercy stared straight at Carli. "Anything else?"

Carli had decided ahead of time to finally reveal the truth. Deceiving another person, especially Mercy, would put Carli over the edge. Of course, Mercy's welcome manner made it easier. If Mercy sent her away on account of it, Carli would move on without regret.

"Before we discuss any more details," Carli started, "I have something to share. It's about my name … and it's a bit embarrassing."

Mercy looked interested.

Carli explained her name change for the Church Run and the soup kitchen. Mercy listened intently and then said, "I see. Mind me asking who you really are? Confidentially, of course."

Carli hesitated. "Tessie Whitmore. I'm Tessie Whitmore."

"I see. And I understand," said Mercy. "I thought you looked familiar. It must have been from your pictures in the news."

Carli nodded; her point taken.

Mercy took in a deep breath as she looked toward the ceiling. "Anonymity isn't something unusual when it comes to donations and charity. Maybe not so common when talking about volunteers and donated time. You're not the first person to come in here under an alias, however. Not likely to be the last either. Hell, a few of our clients have three names. IDs to match." Mercy let out a staccato laugh. "But that's a different story," said Mercy, more calmly. "You're not getting paid, so we don't have to worry about the legalities of payroll. And, as I said, plenty of people give one thing or another anonymously. Why don't you give me a name, address, and contact person. Just fill out the forms as Carli. I'll know who you are. And I'll keep it confidential."

It sounded easy. Kristin's name and number went into the system as an emergency contact.

"Well, welcome aboard. If you have any troubles with anything, get in touch. Any day. Any night. This is my card."

Carli took the card and prepared to leave, thankful to have such a good ally.

"And by the way," said Mercy. "Congratulations on your company's buy-out."

Carli looked up.

"For the record," said Mercy, "and full disclosure ... When I saw it in the news, I marked you down as someone to chase down for a donation. We're always looking for funds. But, don't worry, I'll leave you alone. Just want you to know I like seeing people succeed."

NINE

CARLI WAS as ready as she would be. She gave Lila and Terrance extra treats and headed to the street for her first day of Outreach, intent on saving two women. Despite the many unknowns, she felt certain of success. From a distance, she spotted Grant's backside, along with the stern-looking faces of two New York City police officers. Before she reached Grant outside St. Mary's, the police dispersed.

"Was that about Lucy again?" she asked.

"No," said Grant. "Something different. They're looking for leads."

"What happened?"

"A homeless man was mugged. Gave him a big gash, and nearly cracked his skull, but he's conscious. A lousy New Year's gift, huh?"

Carli couldn't believe it. It had made the news, but she hadn't caught the full story. "Do they know who did it?"

Grant looked straight ahead. "No." Looking at Carli, he added, "I talked with him in the hospital. His name's Lenny. He says he doesn't know who did it. These people get victimized pretty regularly. Usually, it's kids. The police already talked to me yesterday. They stopped by looking for anything new. One thing about being out here, Carli, you learn a lot ... about everything.

"Anyway, welcome to Outreach," he said. Grant extended a cup of coffee. "Take this. It'll warm you. Our first stop today is Penn Station." Grant glanced at Carli's hat, coat, and shoes and said, "Glad you dressed sensibly."

Together they crossed the street.

"Nervous?" he asked.

"What do you think?"

"But you couldn't say no, could you?"

"No ... I couldn't." Her voice quieted.

"You have it in you. Like it or not. The passion."

Carli shook her head. Someday she might tell him about Henry.

"If it makes you feel better, I'm nervous too," he said. His words stopped her short. "Yeah, I never had a partner before." His grin erupted into a full smile. "Much as you are going to hate this notion," said Grant, "you are not going to solve the city's problems in one day. For now, and the next couple of weeks, it's introductions only. We'll meet some of the men I keep tabs on, so you get a feel for what goes on out here and learn what's available to them. After that, I'll introduce you to the two women. So, watch and follow my lead. All we're doing is meeting people. We'll both know when you're ready to take on the women. And when they're ready to consider letting you into their lives."

"Sure," said Carli. "No problem." Watching would be fine.

Carli and Grant slipped quickly down the city blocks until Grant flashed his hand to the side and said, "We have to make a detour. It looks like Wilson." They made a beeline to a pocket park where a man with a brown bag barely held himself stable on a battered picnic table. Grant slowed, to come upon him gently.

"Wilson. It's me, Grant." He let the words sink in and slowed his approach even more. "Wilson, how are you?"

Wilson looked drowsily upward, coddling his brown bag. "Oh, Grant. Why you always asking me that?"

Wilson's salt and pepper stubble looked relatively cared for compared to his coat and clothes, which had missed many trips to the laundry and were covered with food waste. His overcoat was fully buttoned. Unfortunately, its two top buttons were missing, leaving plenty of bare skin exposed. In his one hundred proof state, Wilson, a large-framed man, looked tiny.

"Wilson, this is Carli. She's volunteering with Four Bridges. You'll be seeing her with me sometimes."

Wilson opened his eyes a bit more.

"Okay?" asked Grant.

Wilson nodded.

"Did you go in yesterday?" asked Grant.

"Yeah, I've been in."

"Safe harbor or drop-in?"

"Both."

Grant huffed a deep breath out. Wilson looked away, trying to hide his lie.

"Ernesto can't keep you in his deli, and it's too cold to stay here all day," said Grant. "Get yourself to the day center. And maybe get yourself a new coat too."

Wilson gave his coat a slow once over and came up looking confused. "What do I need that for? Took me a long time to get this one. Besides, it's got good pockets, inside and all."

Grant shot Carli a quick glance, then gently grasped Wilson's lapel with his bare hands. "Looks like about an inch, maybe inch and a half." Reaching under his own coat, Grant fished out a quarter from his pants pocket and placed it against one of Wilson's remaining buttons. "Perfect fit," said Grant. "I'll see what I can find." He offered the quarter to Wilson. "Here, take this for your food collection and get inside, my friend. They'll get you a special order of heat."

Wilson was smiling like a child. The coat was still his. He slowly raised himself from the picnic table, assessing his ability to stand, and began a side-to-side rock toward the park gate. Mid-stride, Wilson suddenly changed course to head toward the back of the park. Grant lightly grabbed Carli by the arm. "You probably want to keep facing the street."

A few minutes later, Carli heard Wilson rustling toward them through uncut autumn ragweed. "It's not like I like to do that," said Wilson, "but some people's getting more particular about their toilets. Gotta keep my ticket for the big stuff."

Carli remained silent. She had smelled it, of course, on hydrants, walls, park fences, subways, and more. With over a hundred toilets, easy, in Wilson's favorite block alone, he had given her a quick lesson, using the only toilet available to him.

Unfazed, Grant responded. "There're toilets at the drop-in. Showers too. Get a hot meal and get inside. You know where to go, right?"

Wilson knew where to go.

"I'll check on him later," said Grant, resuming course with Carli. "I've been trying to get him to rehab for almost a year. The social worker you met at the drop-in center – Mercy – she's been talking with him too. He keeps refusing. He tries self-detox. Tries AA. Then he leaves. Tries again with support. Between you and me, I think he only does it for the three hots and a bed because then he leaves, time and again. They don't call it failure. No, it's relapse. But trust me, it feels like failure, until it turns to guilt. Then it feels like impossible, and finally, 'screw it' – acceptance. Denial works to a point. When I don't see him for a while, I figure he's in the hospital. Unfortunately, it's likely only a matter of time."

"What's his story?" asked Carli.

"If what he says is true, and I believe most of it, he and his wife both worked, but then she died in some horrible freak accident. Painful and abrupt. Then he lost his only son in a military accident. After that, he couldn't keep it together enough to work. The rest just followed. Sometimes he talks. Sometimes he doesn't. Our job isn't learning all the whys of his life or anyone else's. It's fine, of course, if they want to share, but a lot usually stays bottled up. Our biggest hurdle is making a strong enough connection that they trust us and see the value of shelter, medical help, and other services. Often, it happens only when they're as far down as a person can go. Desperate.

Once they're inside, and safe from the elements, they can usually get food easier, and social workers can direct them to more professionals and resources to get to the heart of how they ended up on the streets. It's always a long road. And it's different for each one out here." Grant stood for a moment. "One of the best things we can do is show them they aren't being forgotten; that they are not alone, and that there are still plenty of people who want to help."

"Compassion," said Carli.

"Exactly. Compassion. Not pity," he said. Grant resumed walking. "What I find works best with Wilson is ... well, seeing him in the early afternoon, if I find him, and then sitting with him for about fifteen minutes, just letting him know I care about him. He likes to talk about food. Oddly enough, he also brings up perfume from time to time. Unfortunately, he's in a pretty big fog a lot of the time, and that's a barrier."

"Is either of my two women like this?" asked Carli.

"Vera? Sarah? No. Neither is doing substances."

Carli nodded. "Good to know."

"Some days, Wilson jingles a cup in the Thirties and Forties to raise cash. Thirty-Third Street is his favorite. There's a deli there – Ernesto's – that doesn't mind him being outside their door. When he's really bad, we take him to our drop-in if we can. You'll see that soon enough. When I say 'we,' I mean me; or others from Four Bridges if they see him first. There are two others reaching out to him. Some nights, he goes to a safe haven shelter. They're easier to get into than a more permanent shelter. Less paperwork involved. Fewer questions asked. Substance issues are no barrier to entry. Often, he's too disruptive to stay in another shelter anyway. Maybe a couple of new buttons will help get him inside.

"Buttons?"

"Sometimes it's the smallest connection that tips the scale. Wilson's the one who has to decide to change, though. Remember that."

Grant swung open the door to Penn Station with a hefty tug. "Next stop: Cedric's place. There's no guarantee he's here, but odds are good this time of day. Transit tries not to chase him out, but the place has to be neat, and he can't go sleeping on the benches. Cedric's usually good about it."

Carli trailed Grant through the maze of a station. In between intercom announcements she got the rundown. "Cedric is my latest success story. It took about a year and a half to get him under a roof, but he finally tried it, a men's shelter not too far from here. By day he's a can man. Spends all day collecting and redeeming cans. He doesn't want to look into any of the other options yet. For that year and a half, he wouldn't go inside because he couldn't take his cans into the shelter. Sometimes he can't redeem them and has to keep them overnight. He could go up to the redemption center, but he doesn't want to. He found a place where he can leave his cans overnight if needed, but he won't tell me where it is. He's very secretive about it. I just have to find out if he's been bussed anywhere. That would definitely put him back outside. By his choice."

"Bussed?" asked Carli.

"Yeah. Sometimes the police or the station sweep up all our people they can find, and they get bussed over to Queens or Ward's. Once there, they don't track the people through the assessment centers. They can end up anywhere. It's lousy."

"Ward's Island? Near Hart's and Lucy?" asked Carli.

"Exactly."

Grant stepped off the escalator and said, "He has his vices. Booze, definitely. Pot as well. According to Cedric, he tried crack once and has no plans to try it again. He didn't say why not. Basically, Cedric pieces life together a nickel at a time. His willingness to work this hard tells me he has potential." Grant pointed out Cedric with a quick lift of his chin. "Over there on the bench." Carli saw Cedric sitting upright, bagel in hand.

"Heyyy, Grant." Cedric's smile revealed a noticeable gap between his two front teeth. With a punch on each other's shoulder, the greeting was complete. Cedric slid his bags aside to make room. Grant, still standing, introduced Carli.

Cedric scanned Carli from head to toe, nodded at Grant, and gave somewhat of a smile, somewhat of a sneer. Suddenly serious, he asked, "You leaving?"

"Hell no," said Grant. "You, my friend, know me better than that. I just need some help. Mostly with the women."

Cedric nudged his bags aside, making room for two guests rather than one. Then he said, "I'll help with the women."

Grant got down to business. "Are they treating you right at the shelter?"

"Yeah. Okay. Not great, but okay."

"What do you mean, 'Not great'?" asked Grant.

"I don't know. It's just different."

"Of course, it's different. Sometimes different can be good." Grant allowed a few seconds for his words to sink in. "Tell me about the food. Is it okay?"

"Yeah, okay. I still get some of my own when I can."

"That sounds all right. And you got a bed, right?"

"Yeah, the bed's okay. I'm trying it," said Cedric.

"That sounds good, too. Really good. You haven't been bussed, have you?"

"No."

"So, so far, no problems."

Carli learned about some of the problems walking from Wilson's to Cedric's: thefts, attacks, other bad stuff. Coat pockets like Wilson's could be too inviting to be safe. Sometimes they got slit while the owner slept. Metal detectors at centers were good, but not foolproof. She understood Cedric's resistance.

"A couple of guys got talking to themselves," said Cedric. "One was shouting on and off. How are you supposed to sleep? This other guy was hacking away. You can't smoke inside, and I'm not saying that's what he did, but he was coughing all over the place." Cedric shrugged to end his recap, then said, "I'll give it a few more days. It's warm. Okay?"

"Wise man." Turning toward Carli, Grant continued. "This man is a can collector extraordinaire. Hardest worker I know."

Cedric beamed. Carli smiled back.

"How many do you collect in a day?" Grant asked.

"Good day? Two bags easy. Ten bucks." Leaning toward Grant, he lowered his voice. "Know a couple of really good new spots. Plus, my usual route. Keeps me in business. Plus, I just found me a great new place to take them," said Cedric. "Central Market takes every single one. No limit. I don't have to even think about that redemption center."

"Cedric, my man, you're doing great," said Grant. "Tell me, though, have you checked into assistance like I suggested? Maybe asked anyone at the shelter about it?"

Cedric was silent. Grant let him off easy. "Just keep it in mind."

"Sure, sure, but I don't want to take no one else's money and have to owe 'em anything. Besides, I already have a job."

"Well, maybe a different job would work just as well." Grant leaned a bit closer to Cedric. "You hear anything about the park two nights ago?"

"Just what's in the news." Cedric reached his eyes toward Carli. "I read the paper. Every day."

"No word from the street?" asked Grant.

Cedric shook his head. "I'd tell you. You know that."

Grant nodded and stood. Cedric gave a casual two-fingered salute, to signal the visit's end.

Once outside, Carli asked, "Do you think he knows anything about Lenny?"

"Cedric's usually pretty honest with me. I believe him."

Every few blocks on their way to Four Bridges, Grant pointed out another person he knew, or stopped to share a quick conversation. He spotted most from nearly a block away; knew exactly where to look. There sure were a lot of them, including one man prospecting for coins near the street gutter, two of four men who lived near the Midtown Synagogue entrance, a man who clucked for conversation, and a woman who only ate French fries. The woman turned away when Grant approached. Heading the final blocks crosstown, Grant pointed out yet another man, who was occupied digging cigarette crumbs from an empty package. Carli and Grant passed a young man —who looked no more than eighteen years old—pointing in the air and making repeated circular movements with his hands, as though performing mime. Finally, there was a "screamer" – a woman in a green shawl, known to start screaming without notice. Grant wasn't sure if it a ploy; a means to make the woman appear crazy enough to warrant being left alone. Once again, Carli wondered how she had missed them all. Here they were, in plain sight. And there were so damned many! What hit hardest was knowing each had once been someone's protected child.

Carli and Grant arrived at the Four Bridges drop-in center just after noon.

"Hey, any of you near the park two nights ago?" Grant's voice boomed as he addressed the roomful. "Anyone?"

Forty or so people in chairs looked around expectantly, waiting for news, but no one answered. Wilson didn't bother raising his head from his chest, but Carli was grateful to see he had made it.

"If you don't know, we had someone hurt up there. If you hear anything, you tell Mercy or me, or anyone else from Outreach. And be careful. Okay?"

A few in the group nodded.

The bodies streaming in and out of the room, past the metal detector's inquiring vision, seemed endless. All they were given was a single chair, but it was better than cold stone and far better than wind and wet flurries. A few left with a nod to the guard and a show of a single cigarette. They would soon return.

Grant provided Carli with a quick survey of the room; the assortment of broken lives was numbing. She was relieved when Grant said, "I think you're getting the gist of it. Let's go find Mercy."

Carli and Grant found Mercy in her office finishing a conversation with a man, who said, "I'll try. I understand."

As soon as the man left, Grant and Mercy exchanged glances. "Pizza?" asked Grant. Theresa smiled, and Grant led the way to Sal's, at the end of the block.

At their corner table, Mercy extended Carli a hearty welcome. "I remember my first day here like it was yesterday. I met this man, Jesu, and he lied to me." She turned to Grant and said, "By the way, have you seen him lately? I don't know if he's in or out. Still lying to me."

"Haven't seen him," said Grant.

Mercy continued her story. "He said he needed a coat. This man was so convincing, and I was new. So, dang, if I didn't make a special trip in the snow to get one. I gave him the coat, thinking I was doing the best thing in the world. The next day, the very next day, no coat. You know what he says?"

Carli shook her head.

"Said he gave it to a friend. Like hell he did. That coat that I raced to get was likely worth two vials of crack." Mercy and Grant sighed in unison. "Sometimes, you just want to shake people and get some good sense into them, but it doesn't work that way."

"Amen," said Grant. "Tough love."

"But it's not that simple," said Mercy. "No ma'am. The thing is, some want something, but they're struggling and don't want it bad enough. Or they go working at cross ends with themselves. It's like they have two heads and one says yes while the other says no. Other times, you get mad at the system instead. Look at Rudy, who I was talking to inside when you two arrived. Works at a nightclub cleaning toilet bowls. That's right, toilet bowls. You tell me how he feels telling the shelter he's late for curfew because he's cleaning toilets in another borough, and sometimes the train is late. I mean, how's a person supposed to feel? How're they ever going to keep their pride? This one's trying, and he's still getting stung. Dang, it burns me to a crisp. Say, think you can stop up at the shelter and vouch for him? I'll be calling and sending messages too."

Grant nodded. "Say, has Vera been at drop-in today?"

"Pretty sure she came and went already."

"She's one of the two I want you to visit," said Grant, looking at Carli. "Not to worry. We'll meet her soon enough."

Looking at Mercy, Grant said, "You might get a new one named

Lenny. He should be coming out of the hospital. With any luck, he'll decide to go home. But he might stop here instead."

"The one who got bashed in the head? I heard about him," said Mercy.

With lunch over, Mercy headed to Four Bridges, and Carli and Grant started walking uptown. Over his shoulder, Grant called to Mercy, "We'll send you the easy ones today, if we find any."

Carli heard Mercy call out, "Ain't no such thing, and you know it."

Another block north, Grant slowed, put a hand on Carli's arm, and said, "Here's someone you might know. He barely misses a Church Run Midtown East Side, unless he's on a business trip."

It was hard to forget Canada.

"His real name's Steven. Steven Lewis. But he never liked it," said Grant. "So, I call him Madison, or Mad for short, though he's never angry. He usually beds down outside the Midtown Synagogue on Madison Avenue with a few of his buds; the ones you saw on our way here. He's the one who suggested the name, in jest, but the name stuck. I doubt he'll ever stay inside anywhere, though he, of all of them, could."

It was good to see the iced chowder was missing from the man's beard. Carli confided, "I named him Canada." Grant laughed his approval.

"For the longest time, he thought I was an undercover cop," said Grant. "He cleared out as soon as he saw me. That's because ... well, a guilty conscience does things.

"What do you mean?" asked Carli.

"Madison makes his food money dealing, or copping, and middle-manning it, actually. He takes it to the young 'white-collars' on Wall Street, the ones the big hitters don't have time for."

Carli stiffened. "He's a drug dealer?"

"Yup, makes it look like they're making a donation, helping the needy," said Grant. "The thing is, the needy one is the person Madison says 'bless you' to as he hands them the stuff." Carli knew it happened but hadn't realized the logistics.

"I don't blame them, really," Grant continued. "Most of them have zero street smarts. They're better paying the mark-up and letting our friend, Mad, travel into the shadows to get the stuff. They can certainly afford it. Madison used to deal cocaine and crack exclusively, but lately, he's moved into heroin, what with all the opioid addictions and related legal prescription scrutiny. All these years, he's never done any of the stuff himself. To him, it's just a job. A way to stay out and earn his keep."

"So, what do you do with this knowledge?" asked Carli.

"What do you think? No one's going to rehab if they get busted for going. And no one's going to trust us to help if we send them to jail. What do we do about it? Nothing." Grant shrugged. "We're here to help," he said. "We *have* to know this stuff. Shit happens. Hits happen too. One hit. Two hits. Lots of hits happen, and one of the biggest methadone clinics in the country is sitting pretty right there, right around Wall Street."

"What?"

"Sure. Those who bid Madison adieu spend their lunch hours buying meth instead." Grant tipped his capped downward slightly across his eyes. "We're not the police. We're here to help them, any way we can."

"But he's a drug dealer," said Carli, suddenly happy with her fake name.

"I know," said Grant. "A small-time drug dealer. One of the smallest. And his buyers are going to get it somewhere. I know, for a fact, they're safer buying it from Madison than in some sleazy dark alley, production house, or car transaction." Grant picked up the pace and shouted, "Hey, Madison!"

The burly man spun around, happy to hear Grant's voice, but pulled up short upon seeing Carli. "Are you out all hours too?" he asked, once Grant made the introduction.

"No," said Grant. "I get to keep all those overnight secrets to myself."

Madison became suddenly serious. "I heard someone in the park got roughed up. You know anything?"

"I do," said Grant. "They left him pretty bad off. All for a buck or two, I'm sure, or a bit of entertainment. You keep the guys together, okay?" It wasn't a question.

"You knew him?" asked Madison.

"I checked in on him at the hospital," said Grant. "He's new."

"No idea who did it?"

"Not a clue. There's always someone trying to make the news, or maybe it was Lucy's guy trying out a new game." Madison nodded, wanting more scuttle. Grant changed subjects.

"Carli, here, has a nickname for you. Fact is, you've met."

Madison looked carefully.

"She saw you at a Church Run and calls you 'Canada.'"

Madison roared. Several pedestrians looked over.

"Call me Chipmunk if you want. Whatever suits you."

"Why not," said Grant, staring at Madison. "Names can't hurt, right? See you tonight."

"He's a good man," said Grant, "but I doubt he'll go inside anytime soon. Being in wasn't too good to him in the end."

"What do you mean?" asked Carli.

"The poor guy had a high school sweetheart and would have done anything for her. They got married young. No kids, just the two of them. Madison had a steady job, and he got laid off. Over time she lost interest. She must not have liked his oaf-like ways, and she broke his heart when she sent him out. He doesn't want to deal with alimony or any ties that'll keep breaking his heart, so he just split and left it all to her. Madison figures this is his best way out. So, I give him space and check on him. I give him credit for his spirit. Seems like he could turn it around easier than most if he'd just get past that broken heart."

"Sad," said Carli. "Hard losing someone you love."

Grant nodded. "Now, what would you know about that?"

Carli didn't answer. Instead, she said, "So, what should I call him? He doesn't like Steven, and the name Madison seems reserved for you."

"Why not stick with Canada? He seemed to like it, and he said you could call him anything you want."

"Canada it is," she said. "But I'm not too keen on working with a drug dealer." Another half block along, Carli asked something else. "The man who got hit in the park ... What will happen to him?"

"Lenny? He'll be fine. Bruised, stitched up, but recovering, which tells me it was probably just one person, not any punk kids this time."

Carli caught his eyes.

"Kids might have pummeled him dead," said Grant. "It happens more than you think. Sometimes they even set a person on fire, either out of spite or for sick fun." Grant took in a deep breath as though thinking. "No, this was one person. Probably settling a grudge."

"Someone he knew?" she asked.

"Turf war sort of thing. Just a hunch."

"Another person from the streets?"

Grant pursed his lips.

"Does Lenny know?"

"Nope." Grant directed his eyes toward Carli's. "As to where he'll go ... wherever he wants."

"They'll just let him out? To the streets?"

Grant nodded. "Unless they have a reason to keep him, but that costs. My guess is he gave them a fake address. With any luck, he'll give more thought to the shelter system or going back to wherever he came from. That's why I went to see him – to give him Mercy's contact, and to find something out ... about it all." Grant gazed right through her as he said, "You can take a breath now. Your first day's over."

Carli said, "Thank God. I'm breathing."

"Wasn't that bad, was it?"

"Bad? No. Eye-opening? Yes."

"Good. It should be. Same time next week?" he asked.

"Sure."

When warmth returned to her body, Carli flipped through her recent sketches of the city and closed her eyes. The vibrancy she tried to capture over the past weeks only served to perpetuate the myth.

The myth that all was well. She reached toward a neatly arranged row of pencils and selected a medium soft 4B. She began placing the people of the streets onto a row of empty benches lining Central Park. She struggled to create the proper angles, wanting to show a man hunching forward just enough that his chin folded into his chest but the rest of his body didn't slouch. It took three tries to lay down a man on a bench with just the right bend of the knees and extension of the legs to allow his feet and knees to hang over the edge and his head to rest on the armrest. Adding a blurred likeness of a tattered, light-colored coat was easier. Next bench over, she inserted another man's form in the likeness of Wilson. In a finished piece, with color, she would keep the lines soft and would differentiate only slightly between flesh and swatches of clothing. She wanted them to appear somewhat obscured. In life, so many remained nearly invisible.

On another blank sheet, she started a study of Canada from memory. She couldn't believe she was sketching a drug dealer. What the hell? The thing about him that stood out – and the thing she had to get right – was the expression in his eyes. While everyone's eyes gave a clear message the instant you made contact, Canada's eyes were complex, with multiple layers and meanings appearing over time. His overall aura was upbeat, but his eyes did not match. No, Canada's gaze included a hint of concern, worry, hardship, or, perhaps, it was a fight for survival. Maybe even had a slight element of defeat. Of course, they still held onto the loss of his first love. This sentiment came through clearly. How to capture it, she wondered? She made several attempts, but each time the result fell short. Art was as much about looking and seeing as it was transferring paint to canvas or graphite to paper. What was she failing to see? Carli stared at her work, and then followed her thoughts on a tangent. What would a study of all of their eyes look like? She closed her own eyes to see those she had seen throughout the city with Grant, and suddenly real-ized how strongly their eyes contrasted with the liveliness of the eyes she had seen day after day at TSW Inc. One set of eyes reflected bodies filled with hardship, drugs, struggle, and fear. The other gave news of bodies high on life, pressing to achieve, and soaring in the excitement of challenges and ideas. It was survival as success versus success well beyond. Carli faced a troubling thought: maybe some at TSW Inc. were falling, too. Hiding addictions. Feeling failure, but covering as best they could. Maybe some had more trouble at home than she had stopped to consider. Not that she had ever stopped to consider it. She thought of herself. Without Henry. Yes, it was possible. It could be any one of them, even with gleaming eyes.

TEN

"I KNEW you'd see this sometime," said Grant. It was supposed to be "Ladies Day": Carli's second day with Outreach, and the day she would meet Sarah and Vera. Instead, Carli and Grant found Wilson face down on a snow-covered table in his pocket park. They raised him unceremoniously. Carli felt pity. She couldn't help it.

"We're taking you in," Grant said. "To drop-in." They waited for Wilson to take a trip to the back wall, the same as Carli had seen before. Then Wilson and Grant moved with arms slung around each other and the look of a three-legged race team about to topple. It was only five blocks but felt much longer, particularly since Carli was transporting Wilson's bag of booze. Mercy simply nodded when they deposited him in a chair.

"Talk to her, Wilson," said Grant. "She can help."

Wilson seemed insulted. Grant pulled a chair closer, took a seat, and asked, "Do you think you can stay still? I have a gift."

Wilson looked at a packet of shiny black buttons in Grant's hand. In the middle of the drop-in center, Grant threaded a needle and began weaving it through button and fabric. Glancing at Carli, he asked, "Can you thread another? We'll get out of here faster."

Wilson's head bobbed up. "I'll do it," he said.

"Not today, man." Grant grabbed the card of needles from Wilson's hand. "You just hold tight."

Wilson's pout was clear but short-lived.

"Thought you'd never ask," said Carli. She took a seat and loosely measured some thread.

Two needles pricking and pulling at once were awkward but definitely faster. Grant was in a rush to get back outside.

"Looking good, Wilson," said Carli, once the job was done. Wilson beamed like a toothless baby as he looked over the result of their work.

Of the thousands of people street sleepers encountered each day, Carli guessed Grant and other Outreach workers were nearly the only ones who called them by name. It made sense that they welcomed Grant's visits, even if brief, which today they were. Carli wondered why the rush.

For the second time in two weeks, they found Spaceman Irving passed out on the sidewalk between First and Second Avenues as they searched for Vera and Sarah. Irving wore a bike helmet twenty-four seven and carried a hand-made jet pack of a knapsack. Three single sheets of *The New York Times* newspaper were his mattress.

"I'll check him when he's awake. Tonight," said Grant, racing past. Carli was curious as to what made this concrete spot so sacred.

A man named Bert was also out, with his flea market of sorts spread across the sidewalk in the Thirties. He displayed upscale clothing catalogs and computer magazines, with a variety of address labels, along with a tattered lampshade, assorted hardware parts, and unopened mailers with coupons. Bert sold nothing but kept an arm thrust out in front of him practically all day, waiting for loose change. Grant gave a quick shout, nothing more.

Trying to slow Grant down, Carli asked, "How did you get into this?"

"Outreach?" he said. "Just did. Business suits aren't my style."

Carli waited for more. Grant picked up the pace. Something was clearly driving Grant forward. Finally, he gave a clue.

"Lenny's out," said Grant. "I saw him very early this morning at drop-in. He said he would go, and he did. I'm wondering why he wasn't there just now, but, for his sake, I hope he stays. Or, better yet, goes home. His life's a mess. Maybe that head blow will save his life. I'm still mad at him, though."

"Mad?" asked Carli.

"Angry as hell. If it weren't for him, the street cleaners wouldn't be out, not yet, not so strong."

Carli had never seen Grant this driven. "What does Lenny have to do with street cleaners?" she asked.

"It's an expression. It means the officials are trying to get the street people off the sidewalks. The same ones we're working on."

"What do you mean?"

"It's an odd situation," he said. "The mayor's office does help, but it also moves the street people away so they don't bother the tourists or the neighbors. They're usually the biggest complainers. Lenny made the news, so the city had to respond. Sure, it helps sometimes, but it often louses things up. Forces our people to move, go places I can't find. If they wanted to be in shelters, they'd be there. Most people are too scared."

Carli jogged to keep pace.

"Thanks to Lenny's incident, we're looking at 'The Sweep,' and all my people will have to scramble," he said.

It seemed odd for Grant to blame the extra work on Lenny, but what did Carli know? Grant, on the other hand, had plenty of experience. And he spoke with conviction. Today, especially.

Arriving at the lower reaches of Central Park, Grant's eyes zeroed in on a woman in a bright blue coat, fortressed by seven plastic bags and an old rusty cart. "Are you ready?" he asked.

"Well ..." Carli's intermittent confidence had vanished.

"Don't worry. You can do it," said Grant, interrupting. "Her name's Sarah. It took three months for her to raise her eyes to me. She's not harmful, but not happy or healthy either. I think you're ready to meet. Maybe she is too."

"Sarah ... I never knew her name," Carli said softly. She didn't know if Grant had heard her, but his stare showed he had.

"I saw her once," she said. "Watched her after I sketched here one day. I told you about my artwork, right?"

Grant nodded. "Yes. You're doing landscapes and things. Getting ready for a show."

"Right." Carli nodded. "I stopped by, and she—Sarah—took out everything from her bags, rearranged it, and put it away again. Bright blue heels to match her outerwear are in bag number one."

"Shameless sapphires." Grant let out a robust laugh. With more reserve, he delivered the rest of Sarah's report. "A place in the Eighties will take her, but she needs a doctor's referral first. It's a special women's shelter, and it could get her on disability, but she needs a diagnosis. So far, I've gotten nowhere with her. I need your help on this one. Who knows, maybe you have the same shoe size."

Granted started walking. Carli remained frozen in place, contemplating her slim chance of success. "So, wait ... What do I do?" she asked.

"She might never talk with you," he said, returning to Carli's side. "You'll find out. Right now, she has to see us together. I'll introduce you. Just say hi to her. Anything more will overwhelm her."

"That's it?"

"Nothing more."

"How do you know what makes people tick?" asked Carli. "Were you a psych major?"

Grant laughed and started walking. "No. But I've met a lot of people, and maybe a lot of shrinks too. Usually, I know what people want to hear. I guess I know what motivates them." At the intersection, he said, "Turn right. We'll swing down from inside the park. I always get a better reception when I come from that direction, no idea why."

A circular trail brought them six benches from Sarah. She bobbed a string, with a metal flip top attached, up and down on the sidewalk. She was fishing, and her sport fish of choice was pigeon. With jerky spurts, a gray and white bird with coral feet approached and fled time and time again, showing intermittent curiosity and bravery. Grant guided Carli closer with a silent hold of her elbow. They soon sat directly across the promenade.

"I've seen her do this a million times," he whispered. "If it were real food, she'd have every bird in the city by now."

Sarah kept the lure bobbing until a messenger on a bicycle whizzed past, sending the pigeon cooing into the sky with a clatter of flapping wings. Sarah spat out angry caws, as though to chase the messenger's tires out of the park. Then, she cast her line anew, and another pigeon stopped to taunt and be taunted, until it, too, had reason to fly. That's when Sarah looked straight ahead, and then quickly away. Surely, she noticed them. Grant signaled it was time to visit.

"Hey, Sarah. Nice day. See you had another pigeon," said Grant.

The woman looked scared. That didn't stop Grant from a quick introduction and equally quick departure.

"That was it?" asked Carli. "I thought you were kidding about my hardly speaking."

Grant nodded.

"That was a big … big … nothing."

Grant smiled. "That was not nothing. That," said Grant, opening his arms to the sky, "was huge."

Carli's mouth dropped.

"No one builds a house without a foundation," said Grant. "It'll take you one to two months easy just to set the foundation."

Carli felt like she was in a junior executive position, or worse, struggling through her first internship. How could that meager introduction possibly lead to results?

"Glad to see you're ready to help," said Grant. "I knew you would be. Still don't know why, but I'll get it out of you someday."

———

"So that was it?" asked Kristin. Carli had phoned to share news of Outreach.

"In its entirety," said Carli. "It was a big, fat nothing. I mean, it was less than a big, fat nothing. I looked at Sarah. Grant gave her my name. Sarah stared at the bench. I said, 'Hi.' That was it: 'Hi.' And we left ... I mean, what the hell?"

"Sorry, Sister," said Kristin. "Definitely a bummer. The good news, you were ready. I mean, totally ready. Psyched. Pumped. Prepped ... On the edge of blowing it out of the water ... about to nail it, and ..."

"Okay. Okay. I get it. That's nice. Thanks for the support." Carli and Kristin broke into shared laughter. "I guess I was ready, wasn't I?"

"That was my point," said Kristin. "So, what do you think her story is?"

"I haven't a clue. Last time I saw her, she had a bunch of clothes and took about a half hour to meticulously wrap them in paper and unwrap them. It was like she was folding purchases for a customer at a department store."

"Oh, I hate that. It takes forever."

"Exactly," said Carli. "No one has time for that anymore."

"Maybe she worked in one of those stores," said Kristin.

"Maybe, but why do you think she keeps all of those clothes? She couldn't possibly wear heels out there."

"Beats me. I don't know why anyone would be outside in the first place. Maybe she has dementia and doesn't know where to go," said Kristin.

"Maybe she was evicted and doesn't have money," said Carli.

"Or was disabled in some way by some kind of illness? Or maybe she fled domestic violence."

"What if someone tries to poison her?" asked Carli. "Grant's convinced it's how Lucy died. But Mercy said it never happened."

"Sounds like she wouldn't stand a chance."

"I know," said Carli. "And she already looked so helpless. Do you think Sarah would get off the street if she knew someone might poison her?"

"It sounds like a pretty scary way to make someone move. And if Lucy wasn't poisoned, you would undoubtedly come under investigation for saying it."

"Right," said Carli. "I know. But I doubt I'll ever convince her of anything. She barely looked at me, and it's not like I know what I'm doing."

"So, what's with Lila and Terrance?" asked Kristin. "You keeping them?"

"Looks that way, doesn't it?" Carli glanced at the next cushions over on her sofa to see a bundle of paws stretched over the edges. "They're pretty easy, actually, and they make for good company," she said. "As a matter of fact, they're sleeping right here."

"Mr. Friedrich's sleeping too. In his bed. No doubt dreaming of food."

"They sure wake up happy every day," said Carli. "I never knew Friedrich was a better friend than I am."

"You saying I just dropped below L and T?"

"Funny. And funny you called them 'L and T.' It's what Grant calls them."

ELEVEN

BAD NEWS HIT the following week. Carli and Grant found Cedric sitting with arms crossed and face oozing with anger. His work gloves and stick, used to root out cans, lay between him and a well-groomed hedge outside Penn Station. After a long silence, he shared his wrath.

"They got 'em all. Found my stash. Last night." Raising his eyes slightly, he added, "Gone."

"After I saw you?" asked Grant.

"Yes. I was at the shelter. I have to find out who did it and get 'em."

"I thought you had a place to take your cans."

"They went traitor on me," said Cedric. "They won't take them anymore. Either I cross the city to hawk 'em back, or I gotta store 'em. It's not like I'm stealing or nothing. I'm keeping the city clean."

"Maybe it was the garbage collectors," said Carli. "They pretty much grab everything once they hit a spot."

"She's right," said Grant. Then he suggested, as he had apparently done dozens of times before, a different kind of work, with a paycheck and safety from the streets. Cedric wasn't interested. Cans were his thing.

Grant slipped Cedric a couple of dollars to cover the loss. Then he said, "I'll check on you later. Every business has setbacks some time or another." His words, more than the money, seemed to mitigate the loss.

A short walk across town brought Carli and Grant to Vera. Carli was ready. Thankfully, Grant gave her the green light to say anything she wanted, a nice change from Sarah. But even without knowing her yet, Carli sensed trouble and became reluctant to engage

"What's wrong?" Grant asked, jumping right in.

"One of those runt cops gave me a ticket," said Vera. "I never got ticketed for nothing before, my whole entire life."

"Ticket?" asked Grant.

"He said my box was blocking the door."

"Was it?"

"Of course. How else is it supposed to fit in here? No one ever uses this door at night because it's locked. Got to go around."

Carli listened carefully to Vera's every word, spoken with a distinct New York accent. She also heard a slight rattle in her voice, a wheezing sort of rattle, likely from age or the cold weather.

"What happened?" asked Grant.

"Well, he said I had to leave or he'd ticket me. I told him I wasn't blocking anything since it was night. He said I was supposed to go to some sort of shelter. I told him they're dangerous. He seemed shocked by the news. But then he asked if I had relatives. I told him they were six feet under. He said, 'Do you have any friends?' I asked if he had friends. That's when he told me again to leave. I didn't want to, and that's what I told him. So, he gave me a ticket ... and still made me move."

"Where'd you go?" asked Grant.

"Walked around this whole big, lousy block, then came right home where I belong. Don't you know, he showed up the next night? Only, I moved before he got me, and then I came back as soon as the lousy roach left."

Carli learned Vera had debilitating arthritis, and it wasn't improving in the cold. It surely wouldn't improve with extra walking.

"I thought they were supposed to protect us folks," said Vera.

"They are," said Grant. "Maybe he was trying to tell you something."

"Hmph."

"You've been dodging them long enough to know about that cheesy Sanitation Department Regulation," said Grant. He turned to Carli with an explanation. "It's meant to keep abandoned cars and boxes a.k.a. 'vehicles and other movable property' off the street. Unfortunately, Vera's box qualifies. When the city decides to Sweep, it goes all out. Right, Vera? Goes all out?"

Vera nodded. "Wish they'd just go right out the city. Cross the bridge and leave me alone."

"Sometimes they even enforce the 'no camping without a permit' regulation and 'everyone out of the parks by one a.m.' They'll quit soon enough, though," said Grant. "They don't like enforcing it either. Just following orders."

Vera released another indignant snort.

"Do you need anything?" asked Grant.

"Just to be left alone."

Carli and Grant departed with one message: stay well and stay safe. Then they headed to lunch at St. Mary's.

"It might take you a while to reach her, but we've got to try," said Grant. "She's plenty talkative with me but won't budge when it comes to changing her lifestyle. Something's stopping her, but I can't get to it. Maybe you can. Who knows?"

"How long have you been trying?" asked Carli.

"With Vera? Must be four or five months by now. Not too long, but she looks worse than she used to. Street life is tough on her." He paused. "It's tough on everyone."

The soup kitchen felt like a congenial family restaurant, metal stack-up chairs and all. Carli felt oddly excited when she stepped inside. She was sure others felt what she felt – the goodness of seeing Gretchen and other familiar faces and the goodness of having a "family" bound by common threads. After Grant visited with several others, he took a seat next to Aquaman Harry. From her seat at the op-ed table, Carli overheard Grant ask about Lenny's attack, and saw Harry glance up from his soup and shrug, seemingly unconcerned. Grant gave an extended stare.

After lunch, Carli asked, "What's with Harry and the park? Does he go there?"

"He does sometimes. Right around midnight. And that's when it happened. It may not look it, under his hat and all, but Harry's got good ears. And he knows I know it because we've had a couple of interesting talks. I figure he might know more than he's saying."

"Do you think he did it?" she asked.

Grant shrugged, but Carli knew Grant rarely cast a line without purpose. Harry suddenly looked different.

When everyone else left Carli's birthday celebration, Carli and Kristin shared a ride to Carli's apartment for a final toast. "Sister!" said Kristin.

"Sister!" said Carli. "To another year."

"You said it. To the best one yet." Kristin put her nose in the air, as though sniffing scents wafting past.

"You look like a dog," said Carli. "What the heck ..."

"I smell oil," said Kristin, trying to hold in laughter. "How are your paintings coming? Do I get to see them yet?"

"Yes, Rover. Come on in," said Carli.

Together with Lila and Terrance, they walked into Carli's studio. "It's coming back to me," said Carli. "Finally."

Kristin immediately crossed the room to a finished waterscape resting on a tarp. Carli had propped it against the wall to dry. "Look at this! I love it!" said Kristin.

Carli smiled. "It's my favorite so far. I don't think I can sell it."

"No kidding. I get it."

The painting was one of several ocean scenes Carli planned for her show. This one painting had evolved into the most serene moment she could have imagined capturing. One single, long wave broke gently and curled forward on the low horizon, barely a quarter of the way up from the bottom of the painting. The rest of the water was calm. Meeting it from above was a fully clouded sky, mostly white, but with a smattering of light gray puffy undersides, showing no threat of rain, but, rather, a melding together of soft-looking nebulous masses. It looked like something you would want to touch or rest upon. Or simply gaze at for hours. It was the cloud-enriched sky, as much as the slightly darker gray ocean calm, that drew one's eyes to the wave curling in between on the horizon. Except, there was something else about the scene that caused a deeper review. Maybe it was simply an odd shadow of a cloud, or, much more likely, something under the water. It appeared ever so slightly darker than the surrounding water. Was it some sort of raised sandbar? A concealed outcrop? Maybe covered with blue-shelled muscles glued tightly by their home-woven threads? Soft white brushstrokes hinted at the water having very gently washed over it, whatever it was. Carli looked over her completed painting. Everything about it was calming.

"When things are hectic out on the street, I come here and get lost in its calm," she said. "With everything going on, I wonder how I even made this one happen. It's the exact opposite of my current world."

"Well, you sure did it," said Kristin. "And I need it for my office. And my apartment. Make some prints, please! Or let me make them."

"You definitely know how," said Carli.

"Yes, I do. But something's wrong," said Kristin. Carli looked at the painting and said, "Wrong?"

"I don't know. You tell me." Kristin turned her eyes toward Carli and said, "Birthday or not, I'm going to be nosy. I know something's bothering you. What's up?"

"You know me like a sister, don't you," said Carli. She took in a deep breath and looked toward the ceiling for a moment. "You're going to think I'm crazy."

Kristin's look demanded information.

"Grant reminds me of Henry," said Carli.

"Your brother?" asked Kristin. "That Henry?"

"Yes, my brother," said Carli.

"Is that a good thing?" asked Kristin. "Or is it a downer?"

"I don't mean he reminds me of him," said Carli. "I actually wonder if he *is* him."

"What? Tessie, come on. Look-alikes are pretty common. I mean, think of all of the Elvis look-alike contests. They not only make themselves look like Elvis, but they act like him. And sing like him too."

"That's just it. Grant doesn't look like Henry, but he acts like him. Well, not exactly acts like him, but there are certain things that seem ... familiar."

"But he would know you," said Kristin. "He knows your name. And he would recognize you."

"Name change, remember?"

"Oh, right. But why would Henry change *his* name? Is it some family genetic thing, changing names? That's a joke, by the way, but I mean, really. This doesn't make sense."

"I'm telling you, Grant seemed familiar the first time I met him at the Church Run," said Carli.

"Right. And you said it was dark, and he seemed spooky. Is that how you think of your brother? Come on, Tessie."

"What if he changed his name? Came to New York after leaving college and living with a cult?" asked Carli.

"That would be weird. Not to mention totally unlikely."

"I know. I know, but ..."

"Too weird. And he would still know you," said Kristin. "And you would know him. But if you really want to find out, ask if he has a sister."

It was a simple enough solution, but Carli wasn't ready to ask.

"One more time and the shelter's history," said Cedric. Barely a week had passed, and someone had swiped his stash again. Just as Cedric had finally accepted the offer of sleeping inside, his life was upended. Grant's words were useless. Carli guessed Cedric might never move inside for good and make a different life for himself on account of his stolen cans. They left him to brood alone. Tomorrow Grant would visit again.

Wilson was nowhere in sight. According to Grant, he had become invisible for the past six days, leaving Grant to question if Wilson were finally in a hospital. Carli knew that would mean bad things but was thankful they didn't find him frozen to a tabletop.

After another quick brush past Sarah in the park, which practically followed the first disappointing Sarah meeting to a tee, Carli and Grant found Vera. She had just disembarked from an M103 city bus.

"Very interesting," said Grant. "Doesn't usually come this far up. I call her the Matron of the Fire Standpipe at Thirty-Seventh Street because that's where she likes to hang out during the day. Usually, she rides the Third Avenue and Lexington Avenue buses back and forth for heat, then stations herself at the standpipe on Third."

Vera ambled southward far more slowly than others on the sidewalk.

"She must have been riding a while," said Grant.

"How do you know?"

"In the right seat of the bus, the heater can burn the flesh right off your calves, right through the pants."

Carli didn't see any pants. All she saw was a four-inch gap between Vera's navy anklets and the bottom of her long skirt, exposing bare skin to sub-freezing temperatures.

"Usually, it's about midway back, but old bus, new bus, makes a difference where the heater is," said Grant. "Yessiree, she must be warmed to a toast, given how slow she's moving. She's savoring it. I know how she feels."

Carli couldn't take her eyes off Vera's ankles.

"Vera spends a good part of her days hugging buildings, pretending to wait for a bus. Every so often, she gets on one for the heat. Or in the summer, for the cool air."

Grant jumped the curb the second the light switched and cut an angle to Vera. The woman's legs were ashen gray from winter, but, thanks to the M103, they were likely warm.

"What do you want today?" Vera asked, barely interested in meeting Carli again.

"You need a sandwich?" asked Grant.

"No. What I need is some heat out here."

"I thought you knew where to get some of that," said Grant. "You know where Four Bridges is, right?"

"Yeah, I know where it is all right. The heat is good. But I get tired of just sitting in there. I like to see people. You know, see 'em all scurrying around. Going places. Talking to each other. Sometimes I hear them making plans to meet people on their phone calls. I wonder what the person looks like that they're talking to. That's a whole lot more interesting than watching people sit in a chair at drop-in. Too much going on out here to miss it all," said Vera.

"Oh, Vera," said Grant. "You're quite the socialite, aren't you? Either that or just plain nosy. And I go with the first one."

"You just do that," said Vera.

With Carli and Grant beside her, Vera slowly made her way to her standpipe. Once there, she seemed ready to stand awhile and watch her usual buses.

"Maybe Carli, here, can catch up with you over a cup of coffee sometime," said Grant. "She might want to hear some of your thoughts on all these people."

Vera half shrugged and half tilted her head, her meaning clear: thanks, but get lost.

After Outreach, Carli descended into Grand Central Terminal's underground café and noticed a familiar figure following her every move. Canada waved a hand slightly, and she dared to approach, thinking how odd it was to know him.

"Catching a train?" he asked.

"No, just getting coffee. With all the people and trains running, there's nothing like it," she said. "High energy, and I love it."

"Most people this time of day either need coffee or a stiff drink," he said. "Have you been out with Grant lately?'

"Just finished."

"Is it going all right?"

Carli wondered how much Grant and Canada spoke of her. She eyed his backpack and said, "Sure, but I'm not doing much yet."

"Give it time," said Canada.

"Say, you've known Grant awhile?"

"Sure. A bunch of years. Like a brother to me."

"Why do you say that?"

"Just 'cause. We look after each other. It's good to have someone watching your back."

"Maybe that's why he says he might get you inside one of these days."

Canada laughed it off. "What good would that be?"

"So, he calls you 'Madison,' even though that's not your real name. Is 'Grant' some sort of nickname too?" she asked.

"As far as I know, Grant is just Grant. Always has been. Not everyone has a nickname."

"I see," said Carli. She was sure her body sagged.

Canada gave two thumbs up.

By the time Carli settled in with her coffee, she assumed Canada was back on the streets. She looked around. Had anyone else noticed Canada was here? Were any of them, God forbid, his customers? Or worse, undercover cops ... who had just seen her with him? With her first sip of coffee warming her insides, she wondered who she was fooling. Vera and Sarah were way out of her league. She rose quickly and started home, eager to find a pair of dogs and her studio.

Sure enough, as Carli unlocked the door to her apartment, she heard Lila and Terrance scamper across the wood floor. It was their daily race to set their paws onto her knees, in a futile attempt to reach their noses to her face. As usual, they licked her hands as she reached to pat them, and their tiny bodies wiggled as though powered by their tails, which were now wagging like a pair of windshield wipers at top speed. Within a minute, she found herself nestled on the floor, with one hand rubbing each of their warm bellies. The stress of the day eased away. Then she confronted a troubling thought: Canada knew Grant as Grant, which meant he couldn't be Henry. But Grant's laugh still seemed familiar. She had heard it before. Not quite as she was hearing it these days, but something about it continued to haunt and remind her of Henry. And he was so very kind to them all, which also seemed oddly familiar. Was it possible? Or were these crazy thoughts simply rising to the top, now that she lacked her shield of nonstop work? Carli phoned Kristin to ask a favor.

"There's something I need you to do," she said.

"Your tone of voice is scaring me," said Kristin. "Am I going to regret doing it?"

"No, this time it's easy," said Carli. "I'm texting over a couple of pictures of Henry in college. I need you to accidentally—quote-unquote—run into Grant and me on the street and see if you see any resemblance."

"Tessie ... or Carli ..."

"Please. It's important."

"Sure," said Kristin. "Easy enough, but keep your hopes low. It's about as likely as Friedrich having kittens. What day are you going out?"

"Wednesday. I'll call when I know our timing."

"I can't believe you can't tell if he's your brother," said Kristin.

"I get it. But you know what college reunions are like these days, right? Men change in thirty years. My last reunion, there were a lot of them I wouldn't recognize in a million years. I was reading name tags all night. People change. I mean, Woody, who was barely the height of a parking meter, grew about two feet, added fifty pounds, and had a beard. Josh was bald, post-middle age, and looked like any other guy you see in the ad world. Carlos used to play football and was totally buff in college. At the reunion, he was skinny, hobbled around, and barely had half a head of gray hair, which was receding, no less. And glasses? Half of them wear glasses now. Their voices change. They mellow out. It's not easy to recognize them at all."

"Come on, Tessie. I'll quote-unquote run into you, but I don't expect to say, 'Eureka, you found him.' I still say Grant would recognize you, even if you aren't certain."

"Thank you. Fair enough," said Carli.

TWELVE

IT WAS several months before Lucy would be going home, as the late January ground had yet to thaw, but Elmsville was already preparing for her return. So was Carli.

"Golly, I love seeing those two," said Sister Anna, smiling at Lila and Terrance. "Make sure to get them something from the kitchen. Here's my paperwork to show the Reverend Mr. Scott. Please, thank him again for letting me join him in doing the service."

"I will," said Carli, patting Terrance. "I'm considering asking Thelma if she'd like to take the dogs."

"You're giving them up?" asked Sister Anna.

"Thelma's life seems a bit empty, now that she's retired, and it feels like they belong with Lucy."

"It's a nice idea," said Sister Anna.

"Besides," said Carli, "they might like more space to run."

"I thought you were taking them to the park. Are you sure you can part with them?"

"I'm not sure. Actually, I'm not sure of a number of things, and they definitely feel like family now," said Carli. "Still, I want what's best for them."

To Carli's surprise, Thelma's home was packed with people. Mrs. Thompson, the Reverend Mr. Scott, and several ladies of the church guild filled club chairs and sofas, as well as a series of fold-up chairs brought out for the occasion. They were gearing up for Lucy's return with the energy of a homecoming. Thelma had been right; Lucy belonged in Elmsville, even if Lucy had tried to leave without a trace.

Pastor Scott, in casual street clothes, chuckled as he leafed through Sister Anna's pages. "It says here, 'She was as stubborn as a pug, as hearty as a bulldog, but had the heart of a golden retriever.'"

Loving chuckles and nods of reminiscence circled the room.

"It says, 'She often talked of gardens and life's beauty, even in the city.'"

The surrounding faces turned more reflective.

"'She often kept to herself,'" he continued, "'but you always wanted to see her.'"

It was *their* Lucy, all right. They might not have found her in time, but they weren't about to forget her. All were still stunned she was in New York City, and not further south.

The church ladies detailed arrangements from flowers to dessert. For the simple reason that Carli had found Lucy's home, she was unceremoniously inducted into their guild and confidences.

Following the conversation, Thelma suggested a walk with Carli and Mrs. Thompson. Lila and Terrance joined. Their walk led them straight to Lucy's childhood home. Even from a distance, the house looked inviting. With a few steps past the massive old oak tree, Carli saw a beautiful new swing floating down from an outstretched branch. She all but danced to it and held out her arm to offer Thelma a seat. To her surprise, Thelma accepted. With Mrs. Thompson clasping her hands together in delight, Carli gave a gentle push to send Thelma skyward, giddy as a child.

"You know," said Carli, following Thelma home, "I've been thinking about Lila and Terrance. I'm wondering if they might want more room to run. Maybe in your yard?" She touched Thelma on the arm.

Thelma understood. "For an old body like mine, those little spark plugs might be just the boost I need. Or they might wear me into the ground. One or the other."

"Seeing as they were Lucy's," said Carli, "it might be nice if they came back here with her."

Thelma looked straight into Carli's eyes. "Lucy might have rescued them once," she said, "but you rescued them a second time. Had to go out of your way to do it, too." Then Thelma asked, "Do you truly want to give them up? You all seem so attached. Like you belong. I wouldn't want to change that."

Carli was torn between two opposing answers. Thankfully, Thelma needed time to think the offer over.

Leading Carli into her study, Thelma said, "I have photos of Lucy. We all put them together. I'll be making a display for the service and then putting them in a scrapbook." Looking through nearly a half shoebox of photographs, Carli was introduced to a very full life before Lucy landed on the streets.

"That's Lucy, with the fish, isn't it?" she asked.

"Yes," said Thelma. "Along with three of the boys. And that's me, on the other end. Used to fish all the time as kids."

"Wow, stunning," said Carli, looking at another.

"Yes. Prom. And that's her William." Thelma pulled out another photograph. "Here she is again. Playing bridge with William later in life. It's a good picture of him. Of her, too."

Carli also saw that Lucy bowled and gardened. No photo hinted of her future. Nearly all showed that sparkling glimmer of which Thelma had spoken.

"A person must embrace life," said Thelma as she leaned into an oversized armchair, another photograph in hand. "It's the little things that count." She took another look at the photo before returning it to the box and said, "Tell me about Outreach. How many homeless are on the streets? Like Lucy was."

"Thousands," said Carli. "Four thousand perhaps. It used to be more. The city has a good selection of soup kitchens and programs, like Outreach. Grant keeps track of a dozen or so. I'm only helping part-time with two women. Four Bridges, our Outreach center, sends out teams to keep track of about a hundred in total. Other organizations do the same."

"I see," said Thelma.

"Any time one comes in, there seems to be another on the street," said Carli. "A young man recently showed up at Lucy's spot. The police have been scouting around more, still trying to learn about how she died."

"Learn more about a heart attack?"

Carli abruptly stopped talking.

"I have her death certificate," Thelma said. "Followed up with a few people as well. I guess some camera footage verified it. She up and died. I'm glad it was so quick. I'm also glad you found her so fast, so nothing more happened to her."

"Heart attack ..." Carli's voice trailed off. "Yes, it was fortunate."

As Carli slid through the city to meet Grant, she spotted Wilson shuffling behind a crowd of men and women in business attire several blocks from his park. He seemed to recognize her and nodded. Carli waved but kept walking. Two days earlier, Canada had also recognized Carli as she ran an errand; had even raised his hand slightly, as her eyes met his, from across the street. Over the course of several weeks, Spaceman Irving had slept through several of her walks past his street-bed, but she knew where to check for him. For a brief moment, she took comfort in finding Bert, the "consignment store owner," and others in their self-assigned spaces and in seeing a semblance of order in their lives. Immediately after, she was furious for having accepted it and for accepting that nothing had changed on the street in a month's time. Suddenly, she was impatient.

"In this business, time isn't measured by alarm clocks, watches, or calendars," Grant said softly. "It's not measured by days. All it does is pass."

Carli glared, knowing it was true, but angry to hear it so clearly spelled out.

"Yep," he continued philosophically, "time passes. In fact, you have all the time in the world because that's what they have. Well, unless they die, of course."

"What kind of comment is that?" she snapped. "Cedric and Wilson aren't budging. Vera's hopping buses for heaters. Harry's living under a highway. The same faces show up at drop-in. Nothing's changing." Carli's passionate outburst took her by surprise.

"Not by your standards, but they're surviving. That's getting done. It beats the alternative. Vera, by the way, says, 'Hi.' Says she likes you."

Carli cocked her head.

"Much goes on in a person's mind that never makes it to their eyes or face," said Grant. "Trust me, nothing would happen if we weren't out here."

"But Wilson doesn't want to go in. Neither does Canada. Nor Sarah, for that matter."

"Often, it takes a hundred to two hundred contacts to get through to them. I already told you that once. You'll see."

"I don't want another Lucy," said Carli.

Grant steered his eyes to hers.

"I heard she wasn't poisoned, after all," she said. "Heard she had a heart attack."

"Who told you that? It was arsenic."

"Arsenic? Thelma had the death certificate. She said video footage showed her going down. And I thought you said before, it was cyanide."

"Sometimes they try to cover this stuff up," said Grant.

"Who does?"

"Anyone who doesn't want people knowing."

"What do you mean?" she asked.

"You'll see," he said. "You'll see. Trust me."

"No, seriously, what do you mean?"

"Can't tell you yet. But when I can, I will."

Carli recalled Mercy's invitation to talk if Grant's routine became confusing. She mentally penciled in a call. In the meantime, she said nothing for the seven long blocks to Penn Station. Once there, a different sort of confusion ensued. Cedric was oddly slumped near a hedge, looking more like a heap of fifty-pound rice bags tossed from the curb than the usually upright can man. Instinct told both Carli and Grant something was wrong. They jogged the last few steps.

"Holy Christ! What happened?" asked Grant.

Cedric managed a feeble response. "He took 'em before I even got them stashed." Cedric moaned out some of his pain before adding, "I tried to stop him, but he got me ... Ho, man, it hurts."

Carli was shocked to see Cedric's face bloodied and bruised and wondered if it was Lenny's man.

Grant probed slightly and Cedric winced. Then he said, "It's a beaut," and gently helped Cedric into a standing position. "There's a clinic three blocks from here. You probably just need cleaning and stitches," said Grant. "But we should see if anything's broken."

Nearly every seat of the Sixth Avenue Clinic was occupied. Several patients looked watery-eyed and feverish with the flu. Others sat with canes and crutches, and a baby screamed in the middle of the room. Grant helped lower Cedric into a chair. "Stay here with Carli. I'll sign you in and look for ice."

Cedric slumped. "I should've seen it coming," he said. "Actually, I did, and I tried kicking him but missed. That's how he got me; caught me off balance. But I landed him one before that. Right in the gut." He was almost smiling.

"You're lucky to be alive," said Carli, surprised with the extent of her concern; after all, she barely knew him. "Save yourself and give him the cans," she added, and she meant it.

"That's not how I work." Cedric turned his battered face a few inches in Carli's direction. "Maybe you and Grant can get me some blankets?"

Carli had seen plenty at drop-in. Reluctantly, she said, "Sure."

"Put these on your face," said Grant. "It's all I can find. They're too backed up to get ice right now." Grant handed two cold cans of soda to Cedric. "They'll see you as soon as they can."

"It don't matter much either way," said Cedric.

"He wants blankets for the street," said Carli.

"Thought you were getting used to the heat, man."

"The heat was good, but that cougher was bad," said Cedric. "Besides, my business needs tending. I told you before, three strikes, and I'm out."

"I hate to see it, just hate to see it," said Grant. After a few moments of silence, he added, "You see who did this?"

"Of course, I saw him, and I better not see him again."

"Who?" asked Grant and Carli, nearly in unison.

Cedric barely shook his head and pressed his lips into an airtight seal.

"I was wondering if it was Lenny's man," said Grant.

Cedric continued looking at the ground. He would be settling it on his own.

While the doctor examined Cedric, Grant chaperoned, and Carli managed a call to Kristin. "Sorry, we got delayed. It's Cedric. He's hurt, but thank god, he should be okay. Can you still do it?" she asked.

Kristin said, "Sure, no problem. I'm coming down Fifth Avenue, right?"

"Yes."

"Starting now."

With a cleaning and fourteen stitches, Cedric was free to leave. He had orders to apply ice and take a painkiller as needed. The only thing still broken was his pride.

Carli and Grant walked Cedric to the Four Bridges drop-in. Before they left, Cedric said sheepishly, "Glad you found me." Carli guessed it was his way of saying his trust was still intact, even if other things were not. Grant promised to catch the Church Run's first stop to cop a couple of extra blankets, then he and Carli trudged the half flight of steps to street level, feeling robbed. Yes, releasing Cedric to the street hurt. She could see it in Grant's stride as well.

"I'll swing by tonight to make sure he has plenty of covers," said Grant, "and that he's safe."

Barely three blocks from Cedric, Carli stopped in her tracks. "Do they always leave these here?"

Grant spotted the neatly stacked pile of cardboard boxes, flat and bundled, lying next to a church, and chuckled. "No, but I'll bet you Cedric finds them. That guy is lucky."

After another deep sigh, Grant said, "We'll get him. It's just the cans are the top dog right now." He clucked his tongue and said, "Let's go find Sarah for you, if we can."

"What do you mean, if we can?"

"The Sweep. It's pushing a lot of them into hiding. She might have disappeared for a bit too."

"Hiding?" asked Carli.

"Sure," said Grant. He was nearly into a slow jog. "I haven't seen Harry and Grudge for a couple of days. It's always my biggest clue. You'd think they'd be left alone 'cause they're not in one of the pricey tourist areas. That's where The Sweep is always strongest. But they get gathered during their Midtown forays. Sometimes they go into hiding when they know The Sweep is taking place. Easier for Harry to move Grudge voluntarily than have to gather everything on a moment's notice, all to end up where they don't want to be."

"That explains it," said Carli.

"Explains what?"

"A couple of days ago, I saw Canada moving north at a pretty good clip. And on my way to meet you today, I saw Wilson moving as well. I don't think I've ever seen him out of his park, except when you carried him to Four Bridges."

"That's The Sweep, all right. Sometimes gets pretty bad."

Another block north, Carli heard a familiar voice. "Sister!" It was Kristin. No surprise; Carli was expecting her. Carli introduced her to Grant as a former colleague and best friend.

"Is this you doing your Outreach?" asked Kristin. She addressed the question to Carli but looked straight into Grant's eyes.

"Sure is. The new me," said Carli. "Where're you headed?"

"Late lunch, errand, and then a long afternoon and evening ahead."

"Ah, it never ends," said Carli. "And that's a good thing."

"Hey," said Kristin. "Let me get a pic of my girl in her new life. You too, Grant. Get in the photo." Kristin took a couple and then circled to Grant's side to take a group selfie. Mission complete. Kristin headed to lunch.

"What will happen to Cedric if they Sweep?" asked Carli.

"He'll have to hide, like the others. But I know his favorite spots. Pretty sure I'll find him."

As Carli and Grant swung into Central Park, benches looked eerily empty. Sure enough, Sarah was missing.

"She'll be back," said Grant. "Not to worry."

Carli did worry. Even without knowing Sarah beyond a one-sided introduction, she felt oddly responsible for the woman in blue. Carli didn't fail people. Not her work people. And not her friends; the few that she had. While Carli wasn't sure what Sarah was to her yet, she knew she was someone ... important.

Carli called Mercy as soon as Grant took leave from the empty park. Carli needed answers. Without them, every attempted brushstroke would be preoccupied with Grant's poisoning conspiracy.

Mercy shone like the sun, with her big green glasses dangling against a nearly glaring yellow pantsuit. Carli knew no one else could have worn it like Mercy. Her lip gloss was fuchsia pink. A fresh euca-lyptus-lemongrass-like fragrance completed her outfit. It was good to see her.

"Missing Persons and the Medical Examiner looked at me like I was crazy, asking about poisoned street people," said Carli. "Grant looked at me the same way when I told him Thelma had video footage of a heart attack."

"Strange," said Mercy. "On all accounts. After your last visit, I asked Grant about people being poisoned. When I pressed him on details, he dropped the thought."

"Exactly what happened to me this morning. Said he'd tell me when he could. One way or another, someone is wrong. It makes more sense the city would cover something up. Don't you think?"

"Sadly, it does," said Mercy. "It also makes sense that Grant would have reliable inside information, being on the street and all, and keeping tabs with so many of them out there. Except ..."

"Except what?" asked Carli.

"Well, sometimes Grant sees things a little bit different from others. It's like I told you the day you came to do the paperwork; sometimes his methods are a bit ... well, unconventional. And they can be confusing. For all I know, it could be he's starting a rumor to dig up some other information about what really happened. Or maybe he's trying to get the police to look into something else, in a round-about way. Grant's got a unique kind of insight in that way. I've seen it before."

"So, what do I tell Vera and Sarah?" asked Carli. "That they need to be on the lookout for some sick person? That, in itself, should push them inside somewhere, instead of staying on the streets at night."

"No, no ...," said Mercy. "I wouldn't go scaring them like that. I'd just tell them to be careful, as usual. I'll ask Grant about this again."

"So, you're saying Lucy might have had a heart attack?" asked Carli.

"I'm saying I'll do some more digging. We don't need word getting out on a bigger stage through a rumor mill or making Page One of the newspapers. The first priority is safety, and having everyone on the streets mobbed by a bunch of reporters out for a story isn't safe either."

"Got it," said Carli. "But I'd like to know myself what happened. This is bizarre."

"I'm with you."

The moment Carli unlocked the deadbolt on her apartment door, a pair of dogs came skidding across the bare floor and erased the troubles of the day. Almost.

"You coming over?" she asked Kristin over the phone.

"In five."

Carli moved piles of mail off her dining table and heated a pot of tea. Then she waited. For Kristin and Friedrich.

"Thanks again," said Carli. Kristin barely had her coat off when Carli asked, "What do you think? Is he my brother?"

"You tell me. I sent you the photos."

Carli and Kristin inspected their phones, scrolling, zooming in, and comparing what they saw on the screens to the four photographs of Henry in college.

"I don't see it," said Kristin. "Really don't."

"I don't either," said Carli. "Except for how he's got his hand resting against his leg. It looks almost identical to how he's standing in this one in college."

"I see what you mean. But the eyes don't look quite right. They're a different shape. And the chin is different."

"The hair is hard to tell because of his cap. I guess you're right," said Carli. "He's not Henry, is he?"

"I don't want to be a downer, or anything," said Kristin, "but can you even get out of a cult? Or do people ever want to leave? I always thought it was impossible."

"I always hoped it could happen," said Carli, "but I think you're right. It's not the norm. And this one ... well, it got rid of some of its members for profit. I think I told you that already."

Kristin put her hand on Carli. "Sorry, Sister. I really am."

When Kristin and Friedrich left, Carli moved into her living room and pulled aside the draperies. From her sixteenth-floor window seat alcove, she stared out across the city. Lights were beginning to glimmer as residents returned home and settled in. She loved the city nightscape. Looking down to street level, she saw some people scurrying and others casually walking, as they made their ways home, or elsewhere, on the asphalt grids. It truly did look like a maze of racing rats. She could just make out interesting details, like what people were carrying, including newspapers and flowers.

In a minute, she saw Kristin and Friedrich step out of her building to begin their walk home. Kristin knew Carli well. She turned to wave. Carli smiled, and she continued to smile as she watched Friedrich's paws moving double-time to keep pace with Kristin. Then she saw him catch a worthwhile scent and pull Kristin to a screaming halt. When they disappeared around a corner, what caught Carli's eye was the atrium entryway of the Piskar Building on Forty-Seventh Street, three blocks from her apartment. It was two stories of open glass, with warmth within, and plenty of green plants. She saw bodies moving around inside, and more people entering and exiting through the revolving gateway in the glass expanse. She found herself idly staring at the glass for many minutes. In her lifetime at work, Carli had broken a glass ceiling. Why was it that others could not break a glass wall? Or any wall? Why were Vera and Sarah outside? Why wasn't life fair?

THIRTEEN

"THEY'RE THIS CLOSE," said Carli, squeezing her thumb and fore-finger so close together they almost touched. "This close," she repeated as Grant watched. "The only thing separating so many of them from heat is an inch of glass. That's it. The lobbies and atriums in these buildings practically beg for them to come in. How does this happen? How does a person choose to stay out in weather that's eighty degrees lower than body temperature? Why do they ignore police orders to find emergency shelter? Why do we have worlds of atriums and worlds on the street?"

"Talk about a lot of questions," said Grant. "Hard to know what to say." He thought a moment and began walking. "It's tangled, to be sure. Housing stock has a lot to do with it. As does all the stuff that can happen to a person when life gets complicated. Where are these questions coming from, anyway?"

"It's just so wrong," said Carli. She looked straight into Grant's eyes and felt again the sharp sting of losing her brother, and the equal sting of losing her faith.

"Come, let's check on Wilson. Then we'll look for Vera and Sarah. Clearly, you are chomping at the bit to do more."

"You said it. Let's get something done."

It soon became evident that Grant was looking for more than people. Every plant-filled atrium seemed to catch his attention. "Making fun of me?" Carli finally asked.

"Not at all. Vera lives near a good one, only a block away," he said with a smirk. "Aquaman Harry doesn't live near an atrium. But maybe he'll relocate if it's planted right." Grant continued his evaluation. "Wilson might not behave well enough, don't know. Cedric would have to stash his cans, and Sarah probably won't want to check her bags anywhere. So ...," said Grant, looking at Carli, "Canada and his sleeping buds are the option I like best."

"Great," said Carli. "Just great. Thanks."

Aside from atrium talk, visits were quiet. By Grant's account, The Sweep was moving them too damned well, and he was pretty certain they weren't going in. A double-check at drop-in proved him right.

"No Wilson," said Carli, looking across the room.

"No Cedric," said Grant.

"And no Vera." Both of them saw Lenny sitting in a chair along a wall. Grant approached.

"When I saw you at the men's shelter, you said you were thinking about heading home," said Grant.

"What for?" asked Lenny.

"You tell me."

"I don't need anybody telling me what to do," said Lenny. "Not you, my mother, my aunt, no one. Just leave me alone. I'm taking care of myself. Nobody else can do this. Just me."

Grant nodded and left him sitting. Carli had learned early that Grant chose carefully his moments to hold and moments to fold. For now, the streets had another.

The city's Sweeps meant wandering souls and messed up communiqués. The next week, Outreach was noticeably more somber as a result. Raw morning air, overcast skies, and the feel of an approaching storm didn't help. To avoid being placed inside, one had to be clever, and the ones Carli knew were. Wilson abandoned his park again, Cedric dipped into a colder alcove, and Sarah vanished, pigeon hook and all. Grant dismissed himself quickly to search for Harry and Grudge. He said his intel told him they had moved from their backup location and were temporarily housed in some hellhole of a vacant building, inhabited by birds, and with no steam grate nearby. Yes, Lenny had started a mess.

Carli found herself veering from her direct route home. On a hunch, she climbed the steps to the main branch of the library. With rows of arching windows rising high above the books, the main reading room had often seemed an idyllic place to set up an easel and paint. The light was enticing. Even with tables full of people, the room was wide-open and spacious. Carli and Kristin had discovered the room years ago, when they were caught in a sudden downpour. Soaking wet, they had splashed inside and stayed for hours.

Today, Carli walked on one large floor tile to the next, the entire length of the reading room and back. All the while, she inhaled the scent of scholarly paper that still oozed from the walls, despite the influx of keypads. Of course, she looked to the ceiling of painted sky and clouds, and was momentarily swept away by inner thoughts. Then she descended to the sanctuary set aside for periodicals. It was a masterpiece. Murals covered the room's walls in tribute to New York publishing houses: Charles Scribner's Sons, Harper & Brothers, McGraw Hill, and many others. They were all here, the buildings where it all occurred. Carli sat and slowly moved her gaze from one painting to the next, one building to another, one story to the next. How lucky she was to live in New York. She caught sight of the man dozing in a tall yellow armchair, reading light shining beside him. Canada had found soft upholstery to curl heat around his back. Even better, it was in a public building with free access to running water, toilet, drinking fountain, and enough pipe-clanking heat to open his pores to the warmth of civilization, if not civility. As Canada slept, his newspaper slid to the edge of his lap. Without warning, pity crept in. His wife had stopped loving him; look where he ended up. How could Carli feel anything different? Canada awakened with a start and looked at her through glassy eyes. She gave him a minute to scatter the cobwebs.

"How are you doing?" she asked softly.

"Good. Good," he said. It was exactly what Carli expected him to answer.

"But I've got to move on. Grant here?"

"No, he went looking for Harry and Grudge. He's been looking for you, too."

Canada nodded and then squinted for a better look at a table clock. "Oh boy, ... way past time." He started to pull himself together and added, "They need me." With a squirrely wink, he touched his hand to his pack and said, "They don't call me D. Jones for nothing."

Carli raised her brow.

"D's short for Dow."

Carli said, "Of course."

"Yup. I've got my family down there," said Canada. "They're so slick, but they come out looking for it. I can see the need in their eyes. I help them, they help me. They leave and I watch how fast they walk, and just imagine how they try to make that elevator climb faster than gravity allows so they can slip into that stall and get what they need." Carli said nothing. "If I didn't help them, someone else would. That would be a dirty shame; a loss of business and goodwill."

Carli contemplated Canada's employment and family wrapped in one. Surely, he slept with pockets full of cash, just the ticket for a shelter robbery or worse. Traces of drugs also closed options to a steady shelter or steady job.

"Say, how are you holding up with The Sweep?" she asked.

Canada clunked his bag onto the chair, a resigned look emerging on his face. It was back ... the complexity in his eyes. In a flash of a second, Carli saw pain, surrender, and a hint of lost hope. Then she detected something else. Something she had missed before. Denial. "I took a couple of subways. Spending some hours here. I'm okay."

"Sure," she said, staring at his eyes. "Sure." With a pat on her arm, Canada rambled off. She smelled the scent of banana in his bag and wondered if it was food or drug cover.

Carli turned full circle for another look at the room. Her eyes stopped on the painting of *The New York Herald's* office, late 1800s, near Herald Square. Money had certainly been spent on its construction, as it had been for many city buildings of that era. Artistic details and fine craftmanship had not been spared. Within the walls of this glamorous building, news had been captured and stories put into words for an entire city to read. Carli felt infused with its magnificence and power, until she suddenly realized that certain people had likely always been on the streets, perhaps even in front of the very building that caught her gaze. Just as they were right outside her magnificent library. Rough times were nothing new. Someone would always be out.

As soon as Carli arrived home, she phoned the one and only Elena Rossi at the fabulous Galleria Elena Lucia Rossi. Elena was one of those very soft-spoken people you literally had to strain your ears to hear, but she had very quietly become a prominent gallery head, mostly by putting together a plethora of highly-regarded and intriguing shows. She had a certain knack, owing mostly to an insatiable curiosity, a very open mind, and a willingness to take risks. Carli was ecstatic Elena had made room for "The First Showing of Tessie Whitmore's Landscapes and Waterscapes." What had intrigued Elena most about Tessie's proposed exhibit was it would be the first time that Tessie Whitmore, of TSW Inc. fame, was mounting a show of her own creative works. Elena was certain it would garner interest from all those who knew TSW for its advertising prominence. Elena, herself, couldn't wait to see it. Carli was grateful for her confidence and support.

"Hello, my darling," said Elena. "My mind has been absolutely spinning with ideas for you, but you first. What's new?"

Carli gave a hint of her first completed waterscape, the calmest of calm ocean pieces. Elena said, "I don't want to ruin the surprise, but this is killing me. Please, send a photo."

Then Carli gave updates on timing and progress. Together they discussed details of the exhibition space, signage, lighting, and opening day buzz. When shop talk was complete, Elena and Carli hit upon the subject of Outreach. Elena knew a couple of people who volunteered with Outreach in her neighborhood. Elena was impressed, but not surprised, by Carli's compassion to help. Carli suddenly felt part of a bigger mission, transcending the bounds of her helping two Manhattan street women. The grip of Outreach had bigger meaning, didn't it? Yes, Elena also had a certain knack for inspiring.

Immediately after the call, Carli stepped into her studio. It had nagged at her for weeks that she still hadn't gotten it right. Today, she finally saw what she had been missing. In the midst of the library, she caught, in Canada's eyes, that tiniest flicker of denial. It had an odd sparkle to it. A false sparkle. It was the full definition of denial – a mask and a coping mechanism that was giving Canada time to adjust to his distressing situation. It was also preventing him from tackling his pain and moving on. As she put her pencils down, she knew she had finally done it. They were ever-so-slight—the changes in shape and light—but they put denial in place.

Carli reached the base of the steps at St. Mary's and shielded her face from the mid-morning sun just in time to watch Grant leap over the same five steps to meet her.

"Ready?" he asked. "Let's go!"

He moved full throttle, despite averaging three hours of sleep a night the past three days. His commitment to finding his clan astonished her.

"I'm used to it," he said, in answer to Carli's questioning look. To be sure, Carli thought, he looked none the worse for wear. "We're doing the park first. Sarah's up there somewhere. I can feel it, but I haven't spotted her." He spoke quickly and decisively. "You look for Sarah. I'll look for Harry, in case he's poking around in there too." When they entered the lower end of the park, he finished his directive. "Meet me here in twenty minutes. No need to do anything. Just tell me if you find her … and where."

The February sun felt surprisingly warm. Empty park benches did not. God only knew where Sarah was or what The Sweep was doing to her already-shattered life. It must have been the reason Grant kept moving. And the reason Carli felt a twinge of panic.

"No sight of her," Carli reported.

"Figures. I lost a bunch of the guys, too." He gave a quick glance, distracted by thoughts, and said, "Say, look, I need to pick up the pace, catch a couple of subways, run into a few fringe spots. You might not want to come. Actually, I need to go alone. Well, you could come, but … no, better not."

Grant's words tumbled out quickly. Faster than ever, in fact. Carli was happy to give him space. Seeing him this way was frightening. Then he said, "Let's check with Mercy first."

Carli said, "Let's go." It would give Mercy a first-hand account of Grant's unusually frenzied behavior, and it might give them both a chance to ask about the poison.

Half walking and half jogging, they covered twenty city blocks in less than seven minutes, far faster than usual. Mercy barely hung up the phone when Grant barged into her office and asked, "Any luck with Lenny?"

Mercy smiled. "Hello to you, too."

Grant seemed annoyed by the reply. Mercy said, "Any luck with Lenny, you ask? Are you kidding? Of course. He's one angry young man, with a lot of petty crimes behind him, but I see something that looks promising. I spoke with his aunt. I'm hoping she stops in soon, while he's still here. It might be what starts to bring him back." Looking at Carli, Mercy said, "Sometimes, seeing someone they know does that. It reaches them. Starts to bring them awake to the possibilities."

Carli said, "Makes sense. I'll keep it in mind."

"You should know I found Wilson," said Grant. "He made them take him in. Probably only wanted the heat. Instead, they slapped him with another 'public consumption.' No doubt got a detox referral as well. So, you might not see him for a while."

Carli wondered when Wilson would hit rock bottom. It was a dire thing to wish for, but something had to steer him toward help. Carli turned to Mercy. "Sarah hasn't been here, has she?"

Mercy opened her mouth to answer, but Grant interrupted. "Sarah'll never come here," he said. His voice sounded both angry and impatient. "But you two go ahead and talk it over for as long as you like. I'm going to Clinton and the West Side. Lots to check. See you next week."

Carli and Mercy watched Grant sprint out of drop-in, barely minutes after arriving. Then, Carli looked at Mercy with raised eyebrows. Mercy nodded slowly.

"So, what was that?" asked Carli.

"Not sure. I've seen him like this a few times. I'll keep an eye on him," said Mercy. Carli would be keeping an eye on him as well.

Heading home, Carli took a detour, hoping to find Cedric, to ask how he was doing. Nothing big, but she was curious. When she found no one home, it was oddly disappointing. Turning a corner, she happened upon Vera. It was time to show some courage.

"Vera!" Carli shouted. Vera spun around. "How are you doing?"

Vera looked uninterested in talking, but, surprisingly, said, "I just saw me a movie." Carli was happy to hear it. And happy to see Vera wearing pants under her long brown skirt. It was a definite upgrade from navy-blue anklets.

"What did you see?" she asked.

"One of those kiddy films," said Vera. "It was nice and peaceful. I like to see all the little ones and their families who go to watch it, too. Just don't like the scary parts. It's too much for the real little ones."

Carli knew a movie was a great excuse to find heat but let the subject slide, asking, "Where are you headed?"

"Home," said Vera.

"Home?" Carli exploded with hope.

"You know, my spot."

"Is that really your home?" asked Carli.

Vera straightened up, puckered her lips, and glared. Carli had pushed too hard, without a proper foundation. Vera gave her a few more moments to feel the guilt before giving the lecture.

"I had my good life," said Vera. "Fifty years with the same man."
She nodded and said, "That's gone now. All I have now is checks and
vouchers and a landlord who made it tough. Medical costs go up, and I
don't feel like going to some strange place with a bunch of weepy old
ladies."

"What about your arthritis? And your eyes? Don't you want help?"
asked Carli. "You know, we even have doctors. They can come right to
you."

"No," said Vera. "That's exactly what I don't want. Doctors don't
know a thing. If they did, my husband would still be with me."

"What do you mean?" asked Carli.

"It's a long story. Too long for today."

As Carli listened, she recalled Mercy's words from day one. Yes,
Carli wanted to whack Vera over the head and knock a different kind
of sense into her. Instead, Carli ended the conversation, saying,
"Movies, huh? That sounds like a good idea." For now, she would let
her concerns go, to build a bit of trust.

When Carli entered her workspace, she felt as though the studio
was magically opening unseen arms to give her a hug and sanctuary
from the troubled world of Outreach. She couldn't wait to step up to
her easel and squeeze masses of oily pigments from their tubes.

She started with a mix of blues and greens, a dab of white, and a
smaller dab of midnight black. She lifted a thick, short-bristled brush
and started mixing. It was her third seascape. The waves were
erupting exactly as she wanted. They were powerful, fierce, seemingly
defiant; nothing could contain them. Murky green brushstrokes
created hints of sand dragged up from the seafloor to tumble ahead
part and parcel with the racing water. Sea spray shot upward. She
glared at the watery scene. In her mind, Carli heard the explosive
clash of the three waves slamming together, breaking apart, and
releasing their energy in a forward, reckless rush. She forced this
energy onto her canvas. She felt a fine salty mist filling pockets of air
and smelled remnants of seaweed, shells, and disintegrating sea life
infused in its mist. She sent the feel of this nearly sheer maritime haze
floating above her waves. Finally, she fought to combine mystery,

danger, and allure into a single tangled brushstroke of intermingled colors, to draw a person's inquisitive eyes, like a magnet drew metal, smack into the heart of the watery clamor, where a person instinctively knew he should never go. Finally, she was painting again! It was exhilarating. When Carli set down her brushes for the last time, she collapsed on her bed, with a dog on either side of her. Whatever happened with Outreach, she felt secure again with her painting.

On a sun-filled afternoon, which felt marvelously spring-like, Carli took a needed break from her painting and followed her whims from one street to the next, enjoying the stream of displays in window-glass storefronts. It was like viewing a world of make-believe. Molded mannequins waved at her and struck a myriad of poses, all in the latest fashions—seductive dresses, dinner jackets, and fashionably-torn jeans. Modernistic, straight-lined mannequins, crafted from colored Lucite, posed as though hailing taxis, but their real purpose was to share flashes of glimmering accessories – jewelry, handbags, and scarves. In instant after instant, these, and others, mentally whisked her off the streets into their made-up lives.

Displays, she thought, silently laughing, were one part each of advertising, marketing, and dream machine. When she turned away from a garish display of houndstooth, with the characteristically-patterned fabric fashioned into jackets, boots, pants, shorts, coats, and leggings, she found herself smack in the middle of Vera's neighborhood. Carli was drawn to a sidewalk cart by the very distinct scent of fresh hot pretzels. It was somewhat sweet, somewhat smoky; almost popcorn-scented, but it hinted of dough, and burned dough at that.

She was about to make a purchase when a big blue city bus rattled past. She saw Vera sitting near the window. With golden yellow turn signals flashing, the bus slowed, pulled to the curb, and pneumatically lowered so its steps better met the sidewalk. Vera hobbled off, with two others disembarking behind. It had happened before. Vera, and several others Carli now knew from Outreach, occasionally crossed into her days and her world when Carli ventured into their Midtown neighborhoods. Carli ordered a second pretzel for Vera, and while she awaited her order, she remained near the pretzel cart to observe. The familiar dance began. Vera claimed her standpipe next to Mel's Deli and waited. Two buses passed while Vera stayed put. Having just seen her arrive, Carli knew Vera wasn't leaving. As Carli received her pretzels, she noticed a police officer approaching from the other end of the block. Carli had never seen it, but inside her, Carli could feel it: The Sweep was coming for a visit. The man in blue would soon ask Vera to move along. He would ask her to stand some other place, walk herself to a shelter, or maybe move to the drop-in room at Four Bridges. No matter the intentions or understanding manner, Vera's intentions and The Sweep's were about to clash. Carli had to move fast.

She jogged toward Vera and winged it. "She's with me ... waiting for me," said Carli. As she pushed the pretzels into Vera's hands, she said, "Here, hold these." Fearing Vera would expose her lie, Carli quickly added, "I'll get us coffee," and darted into Mel's before Vera could say a word. Through the window, Carli peered at the officer waiting barely two feet from Vera. At first, he looked to have all the time in the world, but, as the seconds ticked, he seemed to be losing patience. Carli, with two coffees in hand, nodded through the window, stole four sugars, and watched the officer walk away. Carli set about delivering the steaming brew.

With hands pressed inside her pockets, Vera refused Carli's gift. With her eyes glued to a single spot on the ground, she refused to engage at all.

"Try it. It'll warm you," said Carli. She wondered if she should have let The Sweep move Vera into a warm surround, but guessed Vera would never have gone inside. At least, not for long.

Vera remained still.

"Come on, Vera. Try it."

"No. No, thank you," she finally said. "But thanks for getting that lousy cop off my back. I'm mighty tired of seeing his face. I'd think he would be tired of seeing mine too and bothering me all the time. I'd think he would get the message. I don't feel like moving. Not to mention, I don't move too fast these days."

"Like Grant said, they just have to do what they're told. The Sweep won't go on forever."

Vera said, "I sure hope not."

"I'll leave this here for you," said Carli. "Take it if you want. And I hope he leaves you alone." Carli balanced Vera's coffee on top of her standpipe, and was surprised to receive one of the pretzels back in return. It was the best she could do, given Vera did not want to move to a shelter. Thank God the mannequins had sent her Vera's way. No need for Vera to waste energy with a fruitless confrontation.

FOURTEEN

"THEY TURN THEIR BACKS," said Carli. "So many of them, just like I did – the people walking past on the street, the people in offices ... the officials in office. I mean, I've lived here practically forever, and I didn't have a clue what it was really like."

Grant's nod was one of agreement. Then he said calmly, "Yes and no. Who do you think sponsors the programs? And ... me?"

"Sure," said Carli. "But they don't know how much more there is to do. They give the same way I used to. Every week at church. Religiously! And are people really giving? Or are they buying peace of mind and taking a tax credit?" she asked.

"Hah! Not everyone jumps with two feet, but they help, trust me. The city's doing a good job," said Grant.

"Really? It seems to take so long," said Carli. "And the city is sweeping our people off the streets like cattle. I saw it happen to Vera the other day. Or almost happen."

"I heard," he said. "Good work."

"You heard? Wow ... that was fast."

"Carli, it *does* help. Besides, I've got good news."

"Lenny? Lucy's man?" she asked.

"Neither," said Grant. "I have an atrium."

"Oh, thanks. Looking forward to more sarcasm."

"I do," said Grant.

Carli checked his eyes. Grant nodded. "It's near Vera. East Side, mid-Thirties. Huge plantings and granite ponds."

"What are we doing with it?"

Grant's eyes dazzled. "We're moving them in!"

"What?"

Carli could hardly keep up as Grant rushed to show off the enormous glass enclosure.

"We're moving them in here? An actual atrium?" she asked.

"Absolutely. You had a great idea. So, I made a few calls. Worked the network. Three or four of them will fit to start." Grant smiled a broad smile. "You didn't know I was an attorney, did you?"

"Right."

Grant stopped, his face deadpan. "I was. I might not be licensed to practice in New York anymore, but I wasn't disbarred. At least, not that I know of. My old law firm did work here."

Carli remained silent.

"Past tense," he said, flicking his wrist to dismiss the topic.

"You talked with the partners?" she asked.

"Not exactly, but I have my connections. Like everyone."

Grant's open-hearted laugh echoed, only this time, Carli didn't find it funny.

The atrium was warm and extraordinarily green with clusters of tropical plants rising to a patterned glass ceiling. Granite planters made natural partitions, and water flowed smoothly across artificial rocks into inviting circular pools. The sound trickled into Carli's insides with the calm of a spa. It was the exact opposite of how the prospect of moving a few of them inside here made her feel.

"Vera is closest, just one block, and several others aren't far," said Grant. "We need our best shots. We don't want to blow it." Carli was rooting for Vera but knew she was stubbornly attached to her standpipe and alcove. "Right now, Canada and his buddies can't find a good grate anywhere without being nabbed by The Sweep," he said. "Gives us a fifty-fifty chance. Oh, Carli, it's going to be great. I'm going to like this lousy Sweep yet." Grant's laugh roared again. "My guess is Harry and Grudge won't go for it, but it's worth asking. Let's see if we can track down Vera." Grant was midway through a revolving door before Carli could say a word.

Vera was curious and willing to make a block's journey to see the mystery atrium from the inside. Her swollen joints forced a casual stroll, and Grant nearly exploded with impatience on account of it, but Vera couldn't help it. Carli remained alongside her as Grant darted ahead.

"Whoooee!" said Vera. She cupped her hands close to her face and pressed her nose practically against the outside of the glass. "Get a look at those planters. And them plants. What are they called? I know ... Philliedendrims," she said. They shuttled inside. Vera sounded ready to check-in.

"Yes, indeed," said Vera. "Mother used to have them all around the windowsills. Said they breathed life into a place."

Carli glanced at Grant and received a wink in return. Vera breathed in deeply, filling her insides with moist, warm, earthen air. It was the kind of air that revealed the plants were recently watered. Vera closed her eyes as she exhaled, then quickly opened them and turned around smiling. The smile folded back into her face as she said, "Ain't doing it. Might lose my spot. Then where'd I be?" After a short pause, she added, "I don't belong in here, but you sure know how to pick an atrium."

Vera moved to the revolving door. "You tell these atrium people to bring their plants on down aways. Tell 'em they can build a heated plant center around me anytime they want. Think I'll write the mayor a letter, maybe even tonight."

"Vera, for God's sake ...," started Grant. She raised her eyebrows, and he quickly switched course. "Ok, you win, but think about it. It's not getting warm anytime soon."

"This isn't about winning or losing," said Vera. "It's about good common sense and me keeping my real estate."

"If you change your mind, let us know," said Grant.

Leaving empty-handed was disappointing. Grant would try Harry and Grudge when he found them. The atrium seemed like a dream. How had he done it?

At night, Carli settled into her own bed, and tears slowly soaked into her pillow. Seeing Vera in the atrium, talking of her mother's philodendrons—or phillidendrims, as she called them—grabbed another memory from Carli's emotional lockbox. Carli's family used to feel so secure. Grant still seemed oddly familiar, but not familiar at all. Why couldn't he be Henry? Why couldn't she have him back? Carli's musings turned into a pity party of one. Thankfully, she was asleep within minutes.

"Madison, or Canada, as you call him, agreed to try it with his buddies," said Grant. "We toured the atrium, went over the ground rules, and they said they'd do it. Harry's sticking to the highway and, thanks to The Sweep, one of their backup locations. The atrium is too bright, and Grudge is content." Then he said, "I haven't given up on Wilson. Let's go."

Wilson was stationed in his park. "Do you need anything?" asked Grant.

"I'd take a bottle of something."

"Try some heat instead. It's better for your health."

Wilson responded with an empty gaze and, no, he wasn't interested in the atrium.

"I'll ask him again later," said Grant. "This wasn't the best time to ask, but it was worth a try. Hoping he'll change his mind."

At Lucy's church, Grant moved quickly from one seat to the next. Marvin and Leo talked of an upcoming concert, and Lanna and Kris bragged of another exam passed. Harry didn't show. Grant wanted to know why and left quickly to find out. But not until he said to Carli, "I think you and Vera are both ready for an official one-on-one visit. Why don't you look her up? Should be at her usual address."

It felt like Grant had just told her to hit in the older kids' stickball game with all the marbles on the line. Carli slowly gathered her belongings, wondering why he thought she was ready. Truth be known, she did feel ready.

From inside Mel's Deli, Carli sipped coffee and eyed the vacant standpipe. For twenty minutes, she soaked in the mixed odors of cooking oil, grilled burgers, falafel, and pickles. Finally, Vera settled herself along the deli's outside wall. Carli ordered a second cup of coffee to go.

"Vera! Hi. I brought you coffee."

Vera turned quickly, likely surprised to hear her name.

"For you. If you want it."

Vera glanced at the coffee and then settled her gaze on Carli.

"Sometimes, it helps to have something warm inside you, as well as a good coat on the outside." Carli held the cup forward a slight bit more.

Vera almost smiled. "Coffee's great, but then I'll need a bathroom."

Carli hadn't thought this part through. Hadn't known to. She balanced the coffee on the sprinkler head and placed the sugar and cream on the window ledge of Mel's. "In case you change your mind," she said. "Maybe have half a cup." Then she said, "It's good to see you. How are you doing?"

Vera thought a few seconds before answering. "I'm doing all right. Yeah, okay, I guess. I wanted to thank you for getting rid of that Sweeper."

"I knew you didn't want to move."

"Of course not. This is my space, and I intend to keep it."

Carli considered Vera's words. "What makes it so special?"

"Prime real estate," said Vera without a second's hesitation. "Plus, it's mine, and it's special. Just is. Ain't no one can take it from me."

Carli didn't understand. She stuck to her original plan, formulated inside Mel's Deli: a bit of small talk to start, and then a few seeds of more serious nature if the opportunity arose. First, she had to wait with Vera for a bus. In the distance, she saw one rumbling toward them. It wasn't long before the blue double tandem, completely full, rolled to a stop practically at the standpipe. That's when Carli asked, "How come you think the buses are all blue?"

Vera gave Carli a funny look. "Beats me."

"Could be any color at all," said Carli.

"Sure, they could. Green. Purple. Red. Any color."

"It's my favorite color. Blue, that is," said Carli. "Not necessarily bus blue, but blue."

"Blue? Nah. Mine's green," said Vera. "Always has been. But blue's okay. I think that's my second favorite."

"Well, what do you know? Green is my next favorite, after blue."

"What do you know? Almost like twins or something."

"Exactly. Something in common," said Carli. "Wonder why we even have favorite colors."

"Now, that's a good one; beats me," said Vera. "Likely some scientific reason 'cause seems like there's one of those for everything these days."

"I know what you mean."

"There's a lot of things we don't know," said Vera. "Like why those cops keep coming here to bother me."

Carli worked up her nerve. "It's like Grant says, they're trying to help. They want you to be safe, Vera. That's all."

"They just need to leave me right where I am, and I'll be fine."

"You know, when I was younger," Carli said, as casually as she could, "I lost someone special."

Vera's eyes darted to Carli's face, and she carefully listened, likely as interested in why Carli was sharing this news as in the details of the story.

"What do you mean you lost someone?" asked Vera. "Kind of hard to lose a person."

"He vanished. Into thin air."

"Thin air? That's impossible," said Vera. "Sounds like some kind of fairy tale or something."

"No. Not at all. It was someone in my family." Knowing Vera and Grant shared news, Carli hesitated to say who it was. "I looked for years but never found him. It was painful."

Vera pursed her lips as she thought over the situation.

"I'm wondering," said Carli. "Not that it's my business, but do you think anyone is looking for you?"

Vera nodded once and began to smile. "I knew this was going to come around to me somehow. And I was right." Vera said. "Well, some things just can't be helped."

"I was just wondering," said Carli. "That's all. Those cops working The Sweep are just trying to help. Keeping everyone out here safe."

Vera's next words came out as a grumble, nothing Carli could decipher, but she understood their meaning, nonetheless.

"Do you need anything, Vera? You know about the drop-in and the atrium. Just keep them in mind, right?"

"Sure, I know about them. And I've got what I need right here."

"Okay, Vera. I get it. I'll be back again. I will."

Carli left, wondering if it meant anything to Vera that Carli was watching out for her, because it was beginning to mean something to Carli.

Several days later, Carli ventured up Sarah's way, knowing full well she wasn't yet ready to wade solo into Sarah's life. Vera had been challenging enough, and she seemed one of the easier ones. No, Carli was hoping to learn whatever she could, simply from watching the woman in blue. As she followed the path into the park, who she saw wasn't Sarah. Grant smiled back from Sarah's usual bench.

"What are you doing here?" she asked.

"Resting. I've been running all day."

If it was anything like his running during the atrium visits, Carli was certain the rest was needed. "Where's Sarah?" she asked.

"Haven't seen hide nor hair, and I've been here nearly an hour. The pigeons are distraught. Bored out of their minds."

"You haven't seen her at all?" asked Carli.

"Haven't seen her for the last few days, actually."

"Days?" Carli was suddenly on edge and must have shown it.

"Don't worry," said Grant. "She'll resurface."

Carli took in a deep breath. It helped diffuse the fear. Then she asked, "When do they move to the atrium?"

"Friday," said Grant. "Atrium party for the weekend, as they say. I'm picking up Canada's group at the synagogue at eight. And good news, Wilson said he'd try it. Meeting us at Midtown Synagogue. Want to help them move?"

As a matter of fact, it was exactly what she wanted.

Come Friday night, a few minutes before eight, Carli caught Grant a block from the Midtown Synagogue. Darkness was just beginning to settle down for the night, and the restaurants were starting to fill. Before she even said hi, she asked, "Are you sure this is okay?"

"What do you mean?"

"What if someone doesn't want them in the atrium?"

"Not to worry. Rocky will handle it."

"Rocky?"

"The night man – security," said Grant. "Got to know him doing late hours."

Carli wondered why he hadn't mentioned him before.

"It's my bet Rocky will welcome the company," he said. "Nice change from the late-night TV shows. What's the difference between TV and reality, anyway? We need to get in as many as we can."

Wilson stood waiting with Canada's two street buds at the Midtown Synagogue, as planned, but Canada was conspicuously absent.

"Don't tell me Mad's off buying," said Grant. Together the men nodded. Grant sighed deeply. Then, for a full five minutes, he paced, checking the sidewalks in all directions. Finally, he gave up on Canada and started the caravan moving. As they walked at a surprisingly comfortable pace, Grant revisited the rules, with the men alternately listening and volunteering their interpretations of the "do's" and "don'ts." Everything sounded on track.

"This distinguished gentleman is Rocky," said Grant, when they stepped into the tropical paradise. "Some of you know him. He's high security. Used to live on the streets but got himself inside and got himself a job, as you can see. You three need to make it easy for him; if it weren't for Rocky, you wouldn't be here. Like I showed you before, bathrooms are around the corner. Everything else is off-limits. What Rocky says, goes."

As predicted, Rocky welcomed the company and set aside his newspaper. Instead of shaking hands, the group simply nodded. Wilson openly gawked at the height of the plants and expanse of the atrium before touching a single plant leaf, and then another, with both gentleness and apprehension. Next, he ran his hand along a tall, straight stem. One of the other men looked at the ceiling of glass before sliding his eyes to ground level and taking a rapid scan of the lobby. His examination complete, he walked to a spot between two large granite pools and set down his single plastic bag. The other member of Canada's street group followed and began settling in. Wilson joined to bring out a bedroll and pile his lone bag neatly against the granite. He started to unfold a long cardboard box. Grant curtailed the operation. "Wilson, remember, we said inside means no box."

Resigned to the different reality, Wilson refolded the box and placed it in the lineup. Settling in had taken less than three minutes.

As the men reveled in their newfound riches, Carli could only think how unusual it looked. With a ring of an elevator bell, a young man blasted into the lobby, tie loosened, coat open, and with a look that said he was ready for a weekend. He eyed the men but continued his surge toward the exit without a word. Grant and Rocky exchanged looks. The men finished settling in, and Carli decided that maybe it was okay after all – how oddly marvelous. The law firm's partners were certainly progressive.

"I know it's new, but try to settle in. I'll be back in four or five hours." Grant added firmly, "Remember, we're guests." Then Carli and Grant left the group sitting in their bedrolls, with one of Canada's men dealing cards. Apprehension crept through Carli when she and Grant stepped outside, and she saw them through the glass-front divide. Something about the atrium housing two vastly different worlds still didn't feel right, despite the indifference of the young man heading home and the partners' blessing. The thought was pushed aside when Grant asked, "Want to see if Harry and Grudge are home?"

Carli liked that Harry looked after Grudge, but concerns lingered. What was Harry really like if he was, in fact, Lenny's assailant? There was one way to find out.

Grant's swift gait took them to Harry's highway in no time at all. Carli was glad to have Grant by her side. It wasn't a place to be alone at night. Maybe not even during the day.

Grant called to Harry from a distance to let him know who was approaching. "Your turn at the barrel, I see," he said, once near the trestle.

A single steel drum, with a well-contained flame, kept the two men warm. Harry stood alongside it, while Grudge was presumably entrenched in a cardboard box on the ground. A wheelchair rested alongside, tethered to a pole by a short rope.

"What're you burning tonight?" Grant asked.

"The day's news. The only news worth a dime is we were left alone today."

Grudge chimed in, "Amen," and then emerged from the box, with a pair of crutches used adeptly to settle himself into the wheelchair.

Grant delivered two hoagies he purchased on the way over. With Grudge claiming to be famished, Carli better understood Harry's generous "take out" portions from Lucy's church buffets.

"Say, pass me one of those pine sticks," said Harry. "We can get this thing going strong, seeing as we have guests."

Grant handed Harry wood from a small pile. It had been splintered away from a pallet. At first, it smoldered. Then it shot up an impressive flame, illuminating Grudge. Harry stepped close to settle a fire-warmed blanket across his lap.

Carli had expected the air over the river to be gusty and unforgiving, which it was, but the aqua alcove had been picked with care. It was clear Harry and Grudge knew how to fuel the flame enough for comfort but how to dowse it when patrols passed by. Fire code didn't permit open burning, of course, sort of like barbecues on fire escapes. Plenty of cars drove overhead, weaving together a song of tires, but down at their level it was quiet. Anything could happen below, and no one would ever know. Carli thought about Lenny. She knew retaliation could be brutal. She feared for their lives, even if they had each other.

"You ever seen a better heater?" Grant asked. Carli knew he wasn't expecting her to answer.

"It works," said Harry.

"Nothing like real heat," said Grant.

"We'll be fine."

"I just don't want you two getting hurt."

Harry shrugged.

"Why haven't I seen you at lunch?" asked Grant.

"Didn't feel like it, with The Sweep and all. Miss the cookies, though." Harry smiled at Carli and then gazed off for a moment. "My wife used to make the nicest sugar cookies," he said. "Added lots of vanilla. I can still taste them."

"Lunch or not, remember, it's five bucks if you go to the talk next week," said Grant.

"The talk," Carli had learned, was a meeting at Four Bridges, meant to give leads, plant seeds, and maybe get someone off the street. Five dollars were given to each attendee, but she didn't see Harry adding it to his schedule.

Snaking their way from the river, Carli and Grant found a Church Run making stops. Carli recognized some of the visitors, including the woman who yelled and Spaceman Irving. She had never seen Irving awake, let alone upright. Grant looked directly at him, but their eyes did not connect. Then Grant stared down a couple of young moochers and followed with stern warnings when they tried moving in. One thing Grant hated as much as street cleaning was a moocher ripping off someone in need.

Shelves in the vans were still half full. Either the group had gotten a late start, or The Sweep was keeping too many of them away. Grant didn't recognize the driver; maybe that had something to do with it. With a few firmly planted hands on shoulders, Grant was done with the vans and ready to check on Vera. Carli was more than ready to make sure her new friend Vera was safe and sleeping soundly.

Vera didn't answer when Grant whispered a greeting, but he wasn't worried; they had found her and had found a sock tucked under the box, with just its toe visible. It was Vera's nightly signal to Grant that all was good. That was a win. "Needs her rest," he said. "I imagine you do too."

Walking to her apartment, Carli and Grant came upon a pile of boxes in front of Hannah's Bakery. They were neatly folded and bundled, just like the boxes they found after Cedric's clinic trip.

When Grant left Carli at her building, she waited in the lobby until Grant walked out of sight. Then she slipped outside to shuffle through the boxes at Hannah's. She felt fortunate to find two that were clean. Back inside her apartment, Carli manipulated the cumbersome pieces of cardboard into their original box forms and slipped one box partly inside the other. Her new construction wobbled as she slid it on the floor of her studio and closed the flaps at one end. Carli maneuvered herself through the opening at the other end of the box and, once inside, pulled shut the remaining end flaps. She wanted to know how it felt.

Carli heard Lila and Terrance sniffing and felt the box rock when their noses bumped against it. Their sounds were slightly more muted than usual. Carli felt invisible in the box's dark interior. There was practically no space to move, but she found the coziness comforting and the box protective, even though it was somewhat thinner than a piece of toast. The problem, of course, was it didn't have a heater. Was there a science to cardboard, she wondered? Were some types more insulated than others? Some stronger? What if this were her world? "Good Lord above," she whispered, closing her eyes, "please, get Vera into that atrium."

In the aftermath of the night's cold street air, Carli's face felt burning hot and continued to burn as she rested in her cardboard box. The smell of corrugated fibers filtered into her sinuses, eclipsing the smell of oil paints that coated the studio. Carli wondered how Grant could leave them night after night and wondered how they could stay.

He had never told her where he lived, though she assumed it was near so he could keep close tabs on them. Carli decided to sleep in her box. She didn't know why. She opened the flaps so her dogs could see her, but she didn't bother to turn off the lights. Crawling out would take too much effort.

A dark-gray paw poked Carli's eye and roused her early the next morning. She was surprised to see a wall of cardboard inches from her face. She was also surprised at how stiff she felt and how difficult it was to crawl out. She pushed painting aside to make a trip to the atrium. According to Rocky, everyone had vacated, with no complaints, by six a.m. Grant had looked in during the early morning. She suspected it was right after he left her.

At eight o'clock that evening, Carli again met Grant to chaperon the group for its second night inside. Once again, Canada was missing. Grant was agitated by his absence and in a noticeable rush to find him. "I'm taking the subway. Come with me," he said, his voice oddly commanding. "Madison's in Brooklyn, I'm sure. There's a place out there where he sometimes stays. And he might be getting more of his stuff tonight. First, though, I need some food."

Gloria's was lively. So was Grant. For thirty minutes, Grant ate and talked of fashions and hairstyles. His voice was loud and laced with excitement. Carli listened, unsure what to make of it. Finally, she asked, "Are we looking for Mad?"

Grant shot her a condescending look and abruptly dropped his fork to his plate. "You want to go?" he asked. He stood immediately and was halfway to the door when Carli reminded him they had yet to pay. A few yards from the subway stop for the train to Brooklyn, Grant veered into an alley, surprising both Carli and a group of teens passing out drugs. Carli didn't know if she should follow. After Wilson's lessons, she wondered if he was using it for personal business. Trash barrels, upright and not, lined buildings alongside the alley. Carli had passed it many times.

"Sometimes, Cedric uses this skanky little place," Grant called to her over his shoulder. He glared at the teens, then banged on one of the barrels. It sent a rat scuttling past and the teens running with a hail of shouts.

"Damned rats," he said. "Can pick a home anywhere, fit into anything, and there's no Sweep to move them. People? No. They have to move, piss around the city to find a place they won't be bothered. Fucking rats. I hate 'em."

Carli stared at Grant, but he took no notice.

"Cedric, you here?" he called. No one answered.

Carli and Grant rode to Brooklyn and back with no sighting of Canada, leaving Grant even more agitated than before. As soon as they pushed through the atrium door, they found their man, sitting on the edge of a granite pool. Canada spoke first. "Where have you been all night? We were ready to deal in Wilson or Rocky."

Carli saw Wilson asleep near a planter. Rocky was minding the monitors while his television broadcast a game show.

"Finally," said Grant. "Deal me in. But, first, tell me where you've been." The cards started to fly, and Grant said, "Seriously, man, where have you been?"

"You know me," said Canada. "Here and there. Subways. Outer borough. Sorry I missed it here last night."

When Grant's turn to deal came around, he shuffled swiftly and fixed his eyes on the cards as they flitted from his hand, nearly too fast to follow. With equal speed, he stacked the remaining cards in a pile on the floor.

"Card or draw?" he asked Canada with an expressionless face. "Card or draw?" he continued around the circle. Grant studied selections, discards, and faces with a continued lack of emotion. He played his cards with no hint of what was in hand, but as though he could read the others spread before him. Carli wondered if he was stealing reflections off the glass or if Rocky was giving secret nods. Both seemed impossible given the seating plan.

"Beginner's luck," said Grant, taking the fifth game, and third in a row.

"Yeah, like always," said Canada. "Things never change."

Grant casually tossed his cards into the pile, and his intensity slid quickly away, as though someone had flipped a switch. Carli couldn't wait to get home to capture the essence of the night with charcoal and paper.

FIFTEEN

THE FOLLOWING WEEK, Grant hooked his arm into Carli's as they walked, taking her by surprise.

"Um, what are you doing?" she asked.

"You were right about the atrium," he said. "Wilson loves the place, and I think he'll meet with Mercy again. There's hope, Carli! There's hope." He sounded like he had touched the moon. Within minutes, his errant conversation sounded like an uncomfortable extension of Gloria's gleeful fashion talk. "While we're here," he said, "let's see if he's in his park yet." Grant jogged off and didn't bother stopping at three out of four red lights, deciding, instead, to dodge his way through streams of moving cars. Twice he turned to check for Carli. She didn't understand the hurry, and several close calls made her scream. When they hit upon the corner park, they found Wilson minding his table, looking to be out cold. Instead of his usual gentle approach, Grant skipped forward, hopped onto the bench and up to the tabletop. "Wilson," he sang out. "What's the word?" He actually sang, and Wilson bolted upright.

"What's the secret of life?" Grant asked, holding the last note for quite a long time and spreading his arms to the sky. He could have been on Broadway.

Wilson smiled oddly and glanced at Carli. It didn't make sense.

Grant reached toward the sky again and yelled in a sing-songy voice, which morphed into a more organized tune, casual dance motions included. "Can anyone tell me the secret of life? Is it love, is it lust, is it lavender, is it lace, is it leaves or legalese? Or is it simply lies and law school, lobsters and traps, licorice and lollipops, legs and laps?" He followed with a billowing laugh.

Carli froze. She recognized the tune. The words were new to her, but the jingle was a childhood favorite. She and Henry used to sing it together in a raucous duet. Carli's legs nearly buckled as she stared at Grant. Wilson tilted his head to see Grant towering overhead. With a sharp slap on the shoulder, Grant descended and marched to the park gate, ready to move on. "Feel good today, okay?" he yelled over his shoulder to Wilson.

Carli and Wilson exchanged glances again. She was slow to catch up. When she stood beside Grant, she demanded to know, "What was that? You nearly scared him to death."

"What was what?"

"The singing and shouting. And, that song. Where did you learn that song?"

"That song? An oldy but goody," said Grant. "And Wilson ought to be out enjoying life." Grant walked on, displaying a huge smile. Then he added quickly, in a loud whisper, "I'm going to Harry's to do a bit of spying. You move in on Sarah and check on The Vera. Then, make sure everyone else is out of the atrium. I might not get there in time. Meet me at St. Mary's first thing tomorrow."

"Spying?" Carli asked. Was Grant still checking into Lenny? And since when did Vera become "The Vera"?

"Just do it," he said. "It's important."

"Wait," said Carli.

"Can't," said Grant. "Gotta go." He gave an unexpected hug and jumped into the street, jogging to cross before the next wave of cars.

"Wait!" she shouted. Grant didn't stop. Cars roared past, and Carli remained in place until a woman rushing to make the light bumped her shoulder and knocked Carli off balance. Carli wobbled three steps out of the pedestrian mainstream to a large display window and steadied herself against the glass. She saw a petrified reflection in the window; her arms were shaking. What was going on?

Carli remained glued to the glass, catching her breath and reconsidering the possibility that Grant might be her brother Henry, something she had dismissed for weeks. She watched dozens of groups of people crossing in front of her and saw Wilson exit the far side of the park before she felt able to walk. Finally, she pushed forward in search of Sarah. Carli felt oddly numb, as though disconnected and simply watching herself go through the motions. It was as though she were bouncing uptown in some weird, see-through bubble. People passed, lights changed, and cars moved and honked, but they all seemed distant, even though they were barely feet away.

She spotted Sarah clucking at pigeons and ignoring the rest of the world around her. Carli sat on a nearby bench and watched for almost an hour. In that time, Sarah looked at Carli exactly once. After, Carli paid a visit to Rocky's atrium. It would be hours before Canada and the others returned, but she half hoped to see them enjoying the inner luxury. Some luxury, heat. She did find Rocky, earning overtime, and not the least bit upset the other guard had called out sick. Carli swung through the door.

"Is everyone doing okay here?" she asked.

"Sure," he said. "They play cards for a bit and sleep. Last night, they read the newspaper to each other. Occasionally they ask me about the TV shows I'm watching. I think they're just looking for company. Reminds me ..." Rocky's voice quieted.

"Reminds you?" asked Carli.

"Yeah ... of back then."

"When you were on the streets?" she asked.

"Exactly," said Rocky.

"Do you mind me asking how long you were out?"

"Too long," said Rocky. "I lost a bunch of years, and plenty before that. I don't plan on wasting another second, thanks to the Lord." Rocky nodded as he sifted through memories. "Grant knew I could do it before I did. Helped get me to meetings, even though I wasn't very sure about them for the longest time. I kept fighting it. Finally, I started to get ahold of myself. Got one temp job, and then another, until I finally got this one. My first permanent job in years, almost ever."

Rocky was grateful.

"Wasn't too sure about this atrium thing," said Rocky. "But like I said, everything's been cool, and when Grant asked, how could I say no?'"

Carli jerked up her head. "When Grant asked?"

"When he asked to use the atrium," said Rocky. "What did you think we were talking about?"

"Grant asked *you?*"

"Uh-huh."

"Anyone else?" asked Carli.

Rocky shrugged.

"He talked to *you?*" Carli repeated. "I thought he talked to the law firm."

"Don't know anything about that," said Rocky. "But don't worry whether he did or didn't; my boss ain't gonna wake up at three a.m. to see how I'm doing my job. Grant, yes. Boss, no. As long as they're out by six, they're fine."

"What about the cameras?" asked Carli.

"These things?" Rocky gave a nod toward his monitor. "No one ever checks them unless there's a problem."

Clearly, Carli was headed for another day away from her studio. Normally she shared everything with Kristin in near real-time, but Carli first needed to absorb today's news alone. She sat in her window seat, back propped against the sidewall, considering, once again, Grant might be Henry. It seemed impossible, except his laugh, his handshake, and the silly childhood song all pointed in that direction. But why was Grant, or Henry, acting so strangely? She had never known the person she saw earlier. And why was Rocky the atrium "in"? For that matter, why did Henry change his name? Maybe there was never a cult, and Henry simply wanted to leave the family. Why would he do that?

Early in the evening, Carli finally called Kristin.

"What are you going to do?" asked Kristin.

"I have to ask him," said Carli. "But I don't know how. For starters, I would have to tell him I'm Tessie, not Carli."

"Do the nickname thing we talked about. Just tell him I started calling you Carli way back and you got used to it," said Kristin. "I'll cover for you. You know I will."

"I could tell him he looks like someone I used to know and see what he says," said Carli, "Except it will sound like the oldest pickup line ever."

"It's definitely one of the top five," said Kristin. "Pickup lines, that is."

"I just can't make sense of it," said Carli. "Maybe I'll punt."

"Do nothing?" asked Kristin.

"Exactly."

"Right," said Kristin. "Except, you'll worry yourself to death in the meantime."

"I don't do 'nothing' very well, do I?"

"Depends. Look what you did for Lila and Terrance ... and Lucy. Do you call that nothing?"

"He's acting so strange," said Carli.

"Maybe he figured it out too. Maybe he knows who you are," said Kristin.

"How could he? I wasn't the one singing our song."

"Who knows. But are you certain?"

"Not at all. One minute I am, and the next I think I'm going nuts," said Carli.

"Like I said before, maybe you want him to be Henry so badly that you aren't seeing it objectively anymore."

"It's possible."

"I think you have to out and out call him Henry and see what he does," said Kristin. "Tell him who you are, while you're at it."

"I tried," she said. "Then, I didn't have the guts to do it when he ran off and seemed like a complete stranger." Carli thought of the moment she learned Henry was missing. She had been drawing a self-portrait when her mother and father quietly entered her bedroom together. It was going to be an addition to her portfolio for college applications. After they delivered the news, the portrait was ruined by tears. She looked at it a week later and realized its tear-weathered look was as accurate a self-portrait as she could have created. For weeks, Carli had felt numbed by the news. She wondered why she felt even more numb now.

Carli hung up with Kristin and immediately phoned Pastor Miller. Her first words, "Thank you for taking the call," were met with a jovial laugh.

"When someone phones after dinner," said Pastor Miller, "I know they need to reach me. What's on your mind?"

"Divine Intervention."

"Oh, my. Is that all?" Pastor Miller laughed again, but the tone was decidedly different.

"How long have you known Grant?" she asked.

"Known Grant? Let's see ... must be a few years by now. I don't see much of him, of course. Just doing the Runs. He checks in just about every time I do one."

"Any idea where he came from?" she asked.

"What do you mean?"

"I keep seeing little things about him that remind me of my brother. I'm doing some Outreach visits now. Two women. I don't think I told you that."

"Wonderful. No, you didn't. But you said your brother joined a cult."

"Yes. At least ... we think he did. But Grant's laugh is somewhat familiar. He keeps reminding me of Henry. I was wondering what you knew about him."

"Carli, it sounds mighty unlikely."

"I agree it doesn't add up, but I can't stop thinking we have, some-how, been brought together."

"Uh-hum. Divine intervention?"

"Yes."

"Well, as you likely already know, things do work in mysterious ways we can't always understand ... or explain," said Pastor Miller. "I suppose it's possible. But at times, too, we are asked to accept things we don't want to accept. Unfortunate things ... or events ... like losses. Times like those are the biggest tests of our faith. Our strength, as well."

"When we lost Henry, I lost my faith. I guess it was a bigger test than I could accept. Lately, I have been trying to strengthen it, but seeing the men and women on the streets is cutting some of the fragile strings again."

"Happens to most everyone somewhere along the way. To one extent or another."

"I'm sure."

"You know, you could always compare your DNA. I believe it's pretty accurate. Usually, though, it is helpful to meet life head on ... and trust the outcome." After a moment, Pastor Miller said, "Talk with him. See what he says."

"You make it sound so simple," said Carli.

"Good. Maybe it is," he said. "On another note, I hear Lucy is going home soon. The weather is finally with us, even though they won't be holding her memorial until spring's end."

"Yes, we did it. We actually did it."

"I spoke with Thelma. She cried at the thought of it. Or, maybe, it was for having let Lucy slip away in the first place. Wasn't her fault, of course."

"No, of course not," said Carli. "Thank you again for reaching out to her with me. I couldn't have done it on my own."

"My pleasure. Always helps to ask for help. Speaking of which, I'm glad you phoned. Feel free, anytime."

Carli hung up, still considering the need for an appointment with a psychiatrist, and wondering if, as Kristin had said, she wanted Henry back so much she was seeing things that didn't exist. Carli closed her eyes. She realized the likelihood of Grant and Henry being one and the same was near zero. Then she thought of Canada's eyes. And she contemplated denial.

The next morning, with no appointment or forewarning of her visit, Carli sat as soon as Mercy invited her into her office. Mercy rose to close the door. Before she returned to her seat she said, "I'm hoping you are not going to waste a single minute of my time, or yours, with small talk, and you are going to tell me straight away what's wrong. Because to my eyes, something looks mighty wrong." Mercy knew how to make a person feel at ease.

"It's Grant," said Carli. "I think he's my lost brother, but it doesn't make sense that his name is Grant. Or that he would be here. What do you know about him?" she asked.

"You know, you could be asking him all these questions yourself," said Mercy. "You would likely get better answers than asking me about him secondhand."

Carli understood but wanted a different answer. She decided to open her second can of worms. Mercy listened with raised eyes. No, the atrium visits were not sanctioned by Four Bridges. When Carli brought up Grant's recent euphoria, Mercy, again, listened intently. Yes, she had seen it.

"Any idea where Grant is right now?" asked Carli.

"Best way to reach him is to call," said Mercy.

"We both know he doesn't answer his phone."

"True," said Mercy. "But, eventually, he gets back to you."

Mercy placed her hands on Carli's forearms. "I hope you found him … for both of your sakes. But, hey, keep an objective eye on it."

Carli nodded.

"And, as to the atrium, let me know what he says, if you see him, please," said Mercy. "Or, better, have him come talk to me. You and I both know no atrium has city approvals for sleeping space."

For days, Carli was forced to wait. Grant wasn't picking up her calls and hadn't cleared room for new messages. Carli found herself anxiously touching her shirt collar. She wasn't surprised, and she knew what it meant: her resolve to act was growing by the minute, but the more she had to wait, the edgier she felt. Fortunately, Sister Anna got in touch when Grant was at St. Mary's, just as Carli had requested. Carli didn't bother cleaning her paintbrushes; she just ran to catch him before he left.

"Like I said, you have your contacts, and I have mine." Grant had the gall to smile. "Rocky's a good friend and has a great atrium. Wilson, by the way, visited Mercy to ask about help. I think the atrium made him do it."

"Wilson saw Mercy?" asked Carli. "When?"

"Couple of days ago."

"I spoke with Mercy a few days ago, myself," said Carli. "Told her how it was going at the atrium." Carli's next words were slow and deliberate. "Mercy hadn't seen Wilson in over a week. Didn't know about an atrium either."

Grant looked surprised. He didn't say a word.

"Where have you been, anyway?" she asked.

"Me? Shopping. Cruise wear's out."

"Shopping?"

Grant smiled.

"What about Outreach? Cedric? Wilson?" she asked.

"They're doing great. They think the atrium's the bomb."

"The bomb? Grant, what's going on?" she asked.

"What's going on?" he said. "I told you already. The atrium is great, and cruise wear is out."

Grant's words prompted a change of plan. Instead of asking about his childhood, Carli probed for more details of the atrium. Grant dodged them well. She left to ferret out the truth.

"Like I told you," said Rocky, "one of the local cops poked his nose in last night. I told him it's cool, that it's a type of special experiment, and he left, but I know he'll be checking in again, even though he might want to help them. You and I both know you don't see this kind of thing – street sleepers allowed in these fancy places."

"Did he talk with any of them?" asked Carli.

"No. They were sleeping. Or pretending. You get pretty good at faking it sometimes."

"Does Grant know?" she asked.

"He came by but was in such a rush, he couldn't stay still. Told me to do whatever I wanted. And he had on this odd summer hat. Looked mighty funny."

Cruise wear, thought Carli.

"I figure I'll put up a couple of portable barriers so they won't be so noticeable, and ask Grant again, next time I see him."

Carli slowly nodded. "Last time I saw Grant, he was acting weird, like you said. Have you ever seen him like this?"

"Wearing funny clothes, you mean? Oh, sure. Every so often. I think he does it to start people talking. Break the ice. But, come to think of it, he hasn't done it for a while."

"Does he usually rush around so much? Lately, I can't keep up," said Carli.

"Oh, sure. Sometimes he stays forever, practically the whole night, like there's no rush at all. Sometimes checks in like usual, chats a bit, and goes. And, sometimes, like now, it seems like he's popping wheelies and roaring in and out of here." Rocky added, "I don't know if this is normal or not. But I know it's normal for Grant."

A few days later, Carli caught Grant rushing down Lucy's steps, following another call from Sister Anna. The police visit to the atrium was old news to him. A night stop at Rocky's had delivered the update.

"We had a couple of complaints," said Grant. "Had a couple more visitors too. Even Vera went into the atrium," he added. "She told me it was worth a try and liked how peaceful the water sounded. Then Rocky let Clyde in ... I don't think you know Clyde yet. A couple more pulled up inside, too. So, we got some complaints ... because it was pretty noticeable. One of them – I think Rocky said it was Clyde – couldn't get himself out on time. So, Rocky can't do it anymore. He's afraid he might lose his job. Say, how come you didn't call me about the police?" asked Grant.

Carli was too stunned to respond. A moment later, Grant added. "Lucky thing I stopped by."

Barely whispering, Carli asked, "Where have you been the past few days? I've been trying to leave messages, but you have too many on your phone. Don't you ever check them?"

"Where have I been? I've been everywhere," said Grant.

Unfortunately, Carli believed him. Then she asked, "How'd they take the news?"

Grant gave a peculiar look. "What news? Cronkite retired."

"The news they can't stay," she said slowly.

"Right," said Grant. "We need to tell them. Doubt it will bother them in the least."

Carli knew they would have to tell Madison and Wilson before they settled in again. She stared at Grant for another few moments as though to somehow siphon clues to explain his behavior. He didn't seem at all like her brother, let alone anyone she wanted to know.

As Grant turned to leave St. Mary's, Carli put a hand on his shoulder and said, "Wait."

Grant looked annoyed. He was ready to go.

"Sit," she said. "Here. On the steps."

Grant sat, and Carli asked, "What is wrong with you?"

"Wrong with me? Nothing. Anything wrong with you?"

"No," said Carli. "I'm fine, but something is wrong. You seem like you're in a huge rush and are preoccupied or something ... like ... I don't know what. Just ... different."

"Different?" asked Grant. "That's the best you got? I prefer, 'unique,'" he said. Grant stood and said, "Coming? Or am I telling them myself?"

Carli stared, silently. Then she followed to see what more she might learn.

———————

Wilson sat in his park. He accepted the atrium news without question, exactly as Grant predicted. To Carli, it seemed a setback. To Grant and Wilson, it was another fact of street life. Grant immediately left to find Canada and the others to pass along the atrium news by himself. Carli walked home. Passing Vera across the street, Carli was in no mood to reach out, not caring that a few days earlier Vera had almost accepted her first cup of coffee and had tried the atrium, or so Grant had said. Vera didn't seem to mind that Carli waved but didn't stop. Near Grand Central Station, Carli crossed paths with Harry, heading to his highway home, and displaying his familiar lopsided gait. Carli would have ignored him had he not been so close. "Heading back to Grudge?" she asked.

"Yup. Settling down early. Tonight's going to have a lot of wind in it." Harry's words rattled with disgust. Carli wanted to talk, but she couldn't make herself do it. The confusion tied to Grant and the atrium was like a full-body restraint preventing any Outreach beyond a most basic greeting. Most distressing was that Grant was in charge of the restraining straps. Carli needed to break free.

———————

Late morning, several days later, Carli walked to Four Bridges, once again. The tires and exhaust of city traffic had turned March's overnight snow shower into an unappealing mix of dark-gray slush and rivulets of dirty laundry water. Together, they made passing through crosswalks with dry shoes impossible.

"What brings you here?" asked Mercy.

Looking at Mercy's astounding blue blouse with a double-row

necklace of faux pearls, Carli wanted to say, "You," and that's exactly what she said.

Mercy got a real thrill out of it. "That's just what I needed. Today's been a hard one."

"Oh?" asked Carli.

"A couple of tough cases. I thought they were doing one thing, but it turns out they were doing something else. Weather is mighty dreary, too."

"The snow?" asked Carli. "It was beautiful ... until the city started painting over it with road oil and all. That mix of fluorescent colors—purples and pinks—always looks pretty cool skimming on top, though I hate to think where it goes."

"Ah, know what you mean," said Mercy.

"Has Grant talked with you about the atrium yet?" asked Carli.

"He's been in. He didn't want to do much talking about it. He doesn't understand why it wasn't a great idea. He still thinks they should be in there. He was mighty annoyed with the city. And with me for pressing. Have you had any trouble with him? Being angry, I mean?"

"Annoyed, yes. And impatient. But not angry. And I won't tolerate it if he goes there," said Carli. "Actually, I'm worried about him," she added.

"I'm still keeping my eye on him," said Mercy.

Carli motioned to the drop-in room. Nearly all of its chairs were occupied. "Do they ever go in? Really go inside?" she asked. "Not in an atrium, but back home?"

"Why do you think I'm here all day?" asked Mercy. "Of course, they do. Lenny? We'll get him. He and his aunt have continued to talk, and that's a great way to begin his trip back home. Rocky? He's doing great. You see him. I know you do."

"I like Rocky. You're right. He's doing great."

"Several others too. Even some you'd never know had it rough once, got themselves in and better together. Don't give up on them," said Mercy. "Can't ever do that, just ask Grant. He never gives up."

Carli was in no mood to ask Grant anything. Instead, she steered her questions to Mercy, "What about Canada? And Wilson? Cedric and ... and Vera?"

"Forgotten any?" asked Mercy.

"Well, Harry and Sarah." Carli's voice dulled.

"Don't ever say never," said Mercy.

With Mercy's shot of optimism, Carli returned to the streets to see a shimmering sword of sunlight slicing through the remaining gray cloak of clouds. In the distance, she saw a single opening to blue heaven above. All the snow was gone. She took it as a sign of good things to come.

Grant finally answered his phone, but Carli wasn't sure he was paying attention once he switched their conversation to the speaker mode. She decided to share her decision with him anyway. "I am going to visit Sarah on my own," she said. "I am as ready as I will ever be, and I don't think Sarah cares if I wait or not."

"Whatever," said Grant. "Sounds okay."

"Just okay?" She heard him yawn.

"Sounds okay," he repeated. "No one's gotten through to Vera or Sarah. Go for it."

The line was silent for a while until Grant said, "I'm thinking of quitting."

"What?" asked Carli. "Why?"

"I don't know. It's Mercy. She gave me flack for the atrium," said Grant. "You told her about it, didn't you?"

"You know I spoke with her about it. I already told you," she said.

"You did? Don't remember." It sounded like he yawned again.

"She told me you would never give up on any of them," said Carli. "Why would you quit? You're more resilient than that."

"Oh, I don't know. Forget about it. I need to go do something here."

"Grant, are you all right?"

"Yeah, I'm fine. Like you said, I'm resilient. Probably just tired."

"Well, get some sleep. Sounds like you need it." When Carli said, "And I'm going to visit Sarah," she wondered if she wouldn't be better saying, "And I'm thinking of quitting too."

———

Like Cedric's cans, Sarah's bags had cost her a chance at housing. Grant had presented the details. It was nearly a year ago, he had said, when he and Sarah made it to a shelter Uptown, prepared to bring her inside. Carli remembered his description vividly.

"She wouldn't take a shower," Grant had said.

"A shower?"

"Everyone going into the shelter gets deloused."

Carli remembered gasping.

"They spread fast," he had said. "Never knew if it was the shower or the storage situation that kept her out. Doesn't much matter," he had added.

So, the shower had been out, and so was Sarah.

Carli stared down the benches in the park. The trick would be sitting as close as possible to Sarah's self-imposed boundary without causing Sarah to draw the invisible door shut. Carli sat three benches away. Sarah stood, but neither looked at Carli nor neared. Instead, she organized her bags on her cart, and, with Carli's eyes trailing behind, Sarah rumbled along the path and out of the park. Carli had come too late. Carli returned home and cuddled next to Lila and Terrance, wondering if she would ever help anything more than a couple of dogs.

SIXTEEN

"VERA. DEAR-A, VERA," said Carli with a light-hearted voice. "How are you doing today?"

Vera turned, with a smile on her face, and said, "Oh, it's only you again."

Carli smiled. Vera was happy to see her. Carli looked at Vera hunched against the standpipe and asked, "Are any Sweepers out?"

"Yeah, they're out. But I've kept away from them pretty good."

"What else is new?" asked Carli.

"New? Nothing that I know of, except that snow came and went fast. That's a good kind of new."

"You said it. Spring's coming." Carli leaned against the deli window so Vera didn't have to look into the sun. Then she asked again, "What else is new?" It was now her standard greeting. Seemed to get Vera talking, or, at least, bringing a slight glimmer to her eyes.

"Just the usual," said Vera. "No SROs left anymore. Swallowing them up fast."

Carli had heard this gripe once before, but let her continue.

"Them developers is developing and redeveloping everything they can get their hands on," said Vera. "They keep pushing us residents out for tourists. Pricey hotel rooms they made out of 'em all."

Carli knew the city had prohibited Single Room Occupancy over fifty years before, and the majority of its rent-stabilized units and SROs had since been lost. It wasn't new news. Vera was stuck.

"They're making efficiencies now, Vera. Nice ones," said Carli. "More and more of them. Mercy at Four Bridges can tell you about them. She'll even help with the paperwork and application."

"What do I need that for?" asked Vera.

"Did you ever live in an SRO?" asked Carli.

"Ahh," said Vera. "Now we're talking."

"We are?"

"Yes, indeed. Met my husband there. In Minnix House. He lived next floor up."

"Minnix House," said Carl. "Haven't heard of it. Is it still here?"

"Oh sure. The building's here, but nothing like it used to be. Can't afford even a quarter of a closet in it now," said Vera. "Make that a closet shelf. Not even one lousy shelf."

"They redid it?"

"Oh, yeah. Only millionaires can afford my old room. That's all it was. One room. It's all I needed. My husband, too, but he wasn't my husband then. No ..." Vera paused to reflect. "We met there. He started courting me there. Used to walk me up the stairs to my room, and then continue on up to his. I used to listen to his footsteps going all the way up the stairs and then down his hall until I couldn't hear them anymore."

"Sounds romantic," said Carli.

"Romantic? Sure, it was. We had next to nothing, but it was plenty. We had a roof over our heads. Can't do that anymore. Can't afford nothing. And then they went and tored the place apart on us. Couldn't afford it. Couldn't afford much else either. We got married. We were in love, yes, we were in love. And we were also practical." Vera paused, in thought.

Carli took another chance. "Where was it?" she asked, hoping to finally be given the key to Vera's home.

"Where? You're practically looking at it," said Vera.

"What do you mean?"

"Over there," said Vera. "That one with the gold dome. He proposed right over there. Third floor. Happiest day of my life up to that point. I can still see him there."

Carli looked over Vera's shoulder and saw the gold dome catching the early afternoon sun. She knew the building. Vera was right. It was a four-star hotel with high-end clients.

"So, it's like being with him again. You standing here, I mean," said Carli.

Vera took in a deep breath and said, "I think I've gone and done enough talking for today. I need to catch me a bus."

It was another broken heart, bearing down. In a different sort of way. All Vera wanted was to be with her husband. Either back at Minnix House, or on the other side of life. No wonder she didn't want a doctor's visit or medical care. She was simply waiting it out. Vera rode off on the next 103.

———————

Carli looked out across the Atlantic Ocean while Lila and Terrance ran through froth left by waves on the shore. She was finally in Cape Cod. Lila and Terrance raced after seagulls and sniffed dead crabs and plastic containers until their little tongues hung down and they panted from happy exhaustion. Then, she settled them into her car so she could get to work. Carli had never sketched from inside a car, but it seemed a logical method for multitasking dog control and rough sketches. The water was deep-sea gray, and the rolling of the waves was longer than in New York waters. Round, water-tumbled stones covered parts of the shore, in contrast to the large granular sand to which she was accustomed. The colors of the Cape differed as well. She put it all to paper and added notes. Surprisingly, what caught her attention more than the water, were the boats. Everything from yachts, fishing rigs, oil tankers, and container ships, to two-person motorboats, sailboats with one, two, three sails, and more. Even a few kayaks passed close to shore, low to the water, looking like toys. In their unique ways, the different vessels were designed to take on the powerful Atlantic. They hit the waves at different angles, leaving behind signature trails of wake, and making a possible study in itself, she thought.

Moving to the bay side, Carli took comfort in finding marshland protected from the oceanic winds and waves. She watched flocks of birds enjoying that same comfort, along with near-shore feasts in calm waters. Carli suddenly thought of all the wildlife that routinely lived relatively unsheltered, doing naturally what people didn't do. Then she thought of Vera, with her navy-blue anklets and feisty personality, and she thought of Blazing-Blue Sarah with her pigeon hook and gentle cooing. She smiled and realized how important they had already become to her. It was wrong for them to be on the streets, unprotected. One way or another, she was going to reach them.

Several days after her trip from the city, Grant phoned. Carli welcomed the chance to talk and maybe determine his condition. Instead, she learned he was on a mission. "I haven't seen Cedric for almost a week," he said. "He's been off radar and I'm worried about him. Wonder if you can help me look. To cover more ground."

"What's the big rush?"

Her question seemed an annoyance. He wanted a yes or no answer, but Grant obliged. "He was fighting off a cough. I have a hunch it's not the flu. The way he looked a couple of days ago, he'll be toast if he runs into that can-stealing punk again."

"What do you mean, not the flu?"

"Could be pneumonia. Or worse. It's one of those instinct things."

Carli felt an odd sort of panic. She agreed to the search. Grant barked out her territory, and said, "Call me at two, whether you find him or not."

Carli immediately started walking. The only thing she found, in an hour of pounding the pavement, was a fickle wind snatching hats as it skipped through the urban canyons. Cedric remained invisible. Midday, she overlooked the financial district from the roost of steps leading to the sprawling corporate terrace of McClean Towers. A line of flags, jutting overhead from second-story flagpoles, snapped loudly as energetic gusts took hold of their cloth. Many tried to dine in the spring sun. Blasts of wind hawkishly stole their meals and whisked them away like tumbleweed. Tantalizing aromas blew past as well. From her vantage point, Carli saw spring leaves just beginning to pop on trees lining the streets below. Under their developing canopies, she spied a familiar figure. Canada, in his usual street attire, was an anomaly in a sea of men and women in dark, tailored suits, with shoes polished to a shine. Carli descended, hoping to learn something of Cedric.

Canada had leaned his backpack against the building and was using it as a seat. Carli watched him converse with a man in a suit. Then she saw him pull a silver cup from his coat. If he saw her, he didn't show it. She witnessed her first sale. It looked as much like a donation as any. In a mere five minutes, Carli saw two more donations. He was right, they needed him. She was shocked.

"No luck," said Carli, phoning Grant at the appointed hour. "I found Canada doing business; he hadn't seen him."

"An education, I'm sure. The streets are dead. No sign of Cedric anywhere here either. Call if you see him on your way up."

It was hard to imagine a homeless person missing. She called the city morgue.

"Someone else called about him this morning," said the woman.

Carli knew it was Grant, which revealed the depth of his concern. Thankfully, no one matched Cedric's description, with the familiar gap between his front teeth.

Carli started searching again for Cedric early the next morning. It didn't matter that it wasn't her day for Outreach or that he wasn't technically on her visit list. Cedric mattered, now that she knew him, or knew of him, at least. She respected his work ethic, and Cedric had a certain allure—shy but witty—that sporadically appeared, giving hint of who he might really be. Her sense of protective oversight these days applied equally to Wilson and Canada, drugs and all. How had she gotten here?

A search of Penn Station offered nothing. A couple of Cedric's known alleys were vacant. Carli was certain Grant was looking too. After scouring a five-block grid, she decided to check the station one last time. Carli barged through the Penn Station door and saw Grant walking to Cedric's bench from the opposite direction. Together, they spotted Cedric, back home.

"Thank God you're here. How're you doing?" asked Grant.

Blood spotted a rag Cedric used as a handkerchief. "Hurts a bit – my head, and down here a little." Cedric motioned to his chest, then conceded, "Just about everything hurts."

Carli touched her wrist to his forehead and conveyed her findings to Grant through raised eyebrows. A phlegm-soaked cough left another unsightly glob on his rag as if to corroborate her finding.

"You need to see a doctor," said Grant.

Cedric rose slowly, without argument.

"Three blocks," said Grant. "Walk or ride?"

"Walk," said Cedric. "Always walk."

Cedric trembled his way up the stairs.

"Where have you been?" asked Grant.

"Subways, mostly. Found a good heater. It's colder than hell out here."

Carli and Grant exchanged glances. They had left their jackets at home.

The clinic was overflowing, as always. Unfortunately for Cedric, lacerations and other wounds came first. Grant rose every ten minutes, nearly to the second, as they waited. Over the course of an hour, he paced and spoke with a receptionist three times, lost his temper once, and, with no change of queue, sat with one ankle crossed above his knee and his foot impatiently twitching.

"I'm going uptown," Grant finally announced. "Meeting a housing officer. It can't be changed. Can you stay here with him?"

Carli's art could wait. Leaving was never a thought.

When Cedric's turn finally came around, Carli helped him off with his coat and deposited him in an examining room. A few short minutes later, a doctor reported to Carli. "My guess is pneumonia, maybe tuberculosis. Has he been in a shelter?" she asked.

Thanks to Outreach, and nudges from Grant, the answer was an unfortunate yes.

"They check for it," said the doctor, "but it still runs through sometimes. We'll get samples – blood and sputum – and a skin test. Best to run an x-ray while we're at it."

Cedric had moved into the doorway to hear the prescription. "Ain't nobody gonna prick me," he said.

The doctor looked to Carli. She turned to Cedric. "It's the best way to know how to treat you."

Cedric headed toward the door. Carli gently touched his arm, but he swung his arm upward and was free. He walked surprisingly quickly, given how ill he looked. Before she knew it, Cedric crossed through the waiting room and was back on the sidewalk. When Carli stepped outside, Cedric had vanished.

"I heard," said Grant the next day. Carli had passed up another morning of painting to meet him at Four Bridges and reveal her failure. "I called the clinic. It's not your fault," he said.

"Easy for you to say. You didn't see it."

"I've got a connection," said Grant. "We'll get it done."

After Rocky, Grant's connections sounded sketchy, but she and Grant marched to Penn Station, where they found Cedric in his usual spot. "I heard you ditched her," said Grant. Cedric turned his eyes away from Carli as she settled at the far end of his bench. She thought she saw his lips curl slightly upward.

In a matter of minutes, Grant had Cedric on his feet, heading up the stairs. Reaching street level, Grant said, "It might be pneumonia, but there's a chance it's tuberculosis. You've heard of it?"

Cedric grumbled.

"It means we can't play games." Grant waved his arm in the air and smiled. "Perfect timing."

A blue and white medical van pulled alongside the curb. A moment later, a woman hopped out of the passenger side's open door. It was the first time Carli had seen mobile medical. With a mask over her nose and mouth, and blue gloves covering her hands, a woman approached. Carli was certain Cedric would bolt. Instead, he leaned slightly against Grant, who steadied Cedric with one arm only.

"Mr. Cedric, I'm Riley, your Nurse Practitioner, and I'm here to help. We need to see what's the matter with you and get you better. We'll even drive you to the hospital, if needed, to see what's going on, and start treatment. What do you say?"

"I don't like medication," said Cedric.

"It's better than staying sick like this, or worse."

Cedric folded his head further into his chest.

"Come on, man. I know you can do it." Grant gave it a try. "I'll go with you. And don't worry about your cans. I have storage all my own."

"Once you're on your own feet, it's likely just pills," said Riley. "Could be for a while, but I know you'll be feeling a whole lot better than you do now."

"Worst case," added Grant, "you meet me here every day or so, just like always, and we do your meds together."

Cedric's eyes rose for a split second to siphon input from Carli's face.

"We'll help. Just like Grant said."

"You too?" asked Cedric. He was looking at Carli.

"Sure, Cedric. When I can."

Cedric shifted his weight. After lengthy deliberation, he nodded just enough to tell Grant he would go. Grant maintained a steady hold, evidence that Cedric's trust was well-founded.

"You're on your own," Grant said to Carli, as he climbed in with Cedric. "Thanks for your help."

The next day, after four hours in her studio and a walk along the river with Lila and Terrance, Carli couldn't wait to check on Vera. "What's new?" asked Carli.

"Well, my, my ... look who's here," said Vera. She looked happy to see her, once again.

"I went away for a few days," said Carli. "But I was thinking of you."

"Oh, sure you was."

"I was. Look. I got you something. From Cape Cod." Carli handed Vera a small paper bag with tissue paper decoratively covering its contents.

"What's this?" asked Vera.

"Take out the tissue and open it."

"You got me something?"

"Yes, just for you."

Vera pulled out the paper and looked inside. "It sure is green, whatever it is."

"Here, give me the paper, so you can get to it," said Carli.

Vera handed the paper to Carli and reached into the bag.

"My favorite color. Now, how'd you know that?" asked Vera.

"Gee, I wonder."

"Socks?"

"Yes, socks," said Carli. "Two pair. One for you to wear, and one to leave out for Grant. They're long, too, so they should keep you warm."

"Oh, I don't think I'll be leaving any of these out for Grant," said Vera. "No, no. These ... these are special socks. I think I'm gonna go keeping these both inside for myself. Well, maybe one for me and my feet, and maybe I'll keep the other one next to me."

"Whatever you want," said Carli. "They're yours."

"Green," said Vera. "It was my husband's favorite color too."

Carli realized Vera was once again at Minnix House, but this time, thankfully, she seemed happy.

Vera looked straight at Carli. "It's been a long while since I got a personal gift," said Vera. "I can't believe it."

"I told you, Vera, I was thinking of you."

"Well, I guess I had better go and say thank you."

"You already did, Vera. You already did. I'll see you again soon."

SEVENTEEN

X-RAYS SHOWED the phlegm-covered fingers of TB crouching inside Cedric's lungs. It would be two weeks before Cedric felt better, and six months of medication after, but with a barrage of medication he was improving. Grant was given family privileges, allowing him to visit with a mask; TB liked to spread. In the meantime, Carli tended to Sarah.

With a cool wind shooting its final spring claws at her, Carli sketched as Sarah sat in her usual spot. Carli was merely doodling until, in an odd instant, she hit upon an idea. She reached into her coat pocket and pulled out a crumpled package of soup crackers. In a matter of seconds, a few deliberately dropped crumbs brought scores of flapping bodies to her feet. In their race to peck at the loot, they careened off one another's wings, nearly knocking heads. One flapped so near Carli's face, it set hairs on her forehead flying from the breeze. Carli hid the rest of the crackers, and the clamor stopped as soon as the final sidewalk crumbs vanished into greedy gullets. Carli saw Sarah look her way.

Exiting the park, Carli stopped directly in front of Sarah and gave her name. The woman barely nodded before shifting her weight just enough to turn her shoulder toward Carli, and her face away.

Although the message was clear, Carli said, "Let me know if you need anything. I'm here to help." Oddly, it felt like progress.

With Grant putting in extra time with Cedric, Carli finished her painting for the day and decided to check on Wilson. She found him at the picnic table in his park, resting his head on his arm, as usual. Carli came upon him slowly, as she had seen Grant do many times before, except for during their last frantic visit.

"Wilson," said Carli. "It's Carli here. How are you?"

Wilson raised his head and said dreamily, "Honey ... suckle." He closed his eyes and slowly folded his head down upon his arm. "Yup. One of my favorites," said Wilson, still resting on his arm.

"Wilson. It's me, Carli."

Wilson raised his head again and said, "I know ... who you are. I like your perfume."

Carli stared. Technically, it was body wash, but Wilson was right, it was honeysuckle.

"How do you know this?" she asked.

"I know all the perfumes," he said. He rubbed his eyes, trying to clear the fog. "Not all of the newer ones. Don't know what they're called. But I know when they go past."

"Go past?" asked Carli.

"Yeah."

"Wait," said Carli. "What are you saying?"

"What do you mean, what am I saying? Ahhh ..." Wilson closed his eyes again. "Lily of the valley lady again." He slowly turned his head toward the street and said, "Yup. That one, over there." His eyes followed a couple of pedestrians, and he said, "Blonde with the shopping bag. Must live near here. That's her, all right. Lily of the valley."

Carli looked to the sidewalk. She saw the woman. Then she inhaled deeply and caught barely a scent of perfume. It was faint. Carli couldn't distinguish it as anything specific. But Wilson could.

Carli swung her legs over the bench, directly across the picnic table from Wilson, to sit. "Talk to me," she said. "How do you know this?"

"Know what?" he asked.

"Different scents," she said.

"I don't know. Maybe I was a chemist or something."

"Chemist?"

"Maybe."

Carli waited for Wilson to give her another clue. Anything.

"It's one of the reasons I sit here," he said. "It smells nice." Wilson closed his eyes and looked to be nodding off to sleep when he said, "Honeysuckle." Carli watched his baby-faced smile rise into his cheeks. In another moment it faded, and Wilson said, "Wonder how much they spend on this stuff now." Wilson would soon be asleep to the world. Although Carli had hit a wall, she was certain a wall could have cracks.

Cedric was ready for discharge in two weeks' time. With proper pills, he'd be safe to others and to himself. Carli sat across the table from Grant at St. Mary's. Grant's request to meet had sounded urgent. "We'll have a hell of a time getting him to take his pills," said Grant. "The minute he feels better he'll balk."

"Makes sense," she said.

"There's something else." Grant's somber tone grabbed her attention. "We have to be tested."

Carli didn't understand.

"TB."

Carli's throat tightened as the words sank in.

"Can take a couple of weeks to show, and for your body to react to a skin test. We start periodic testing in a couple of weeks. Might want to take a preventative just in case." He pursed his lips, then added, "Sorry, but we got so close to him. Almost certain infection. Doesn't mean we'll feel sick. Our bodies are surely stronger than his." Grant reached across the lunch table and grazed her hand with his.

After a quick lunch, they headed to the hospital. Cedric was ready to go, dressed in a fresh set of clothes Grant had delivered the night before. Enough life had been pulsed into him that he rebuffed even the most modest hint of inside living. They began the mandatory wheelchair ride through the hospital halls in routine manner, but Grant abruptly pushed aside the attendant and began driving the wheelchair himself. Grant's driving was fast and reckless. Cedric seemed content. Grant was thrilled. The attendant protested, but Grant left her shouting far behind. Carli watched in disbelief.

At the lobby entrance, Grant sent the empty wheelchair spinning unescorted to the main desk as Cedric, Grant, and Carli stepped into a waiting car.

"What was that?" asked Carli.

"Had to get him out of there. Otherwise, they might have kept him." Then he faced Cedric and said, "Speak now, or forever hold your peace. Shelter or not?"

Cedric looked at the floor. "Not."

"Mercy could ..."

"Not."

At the drop-in center, Grant explained the routine. "I'm coming by every other day with these pills. You'll take them with me."

Cedric nodded.

"No backing out. We're pushing the limit with every other day instead of daily. Also, no alcohol."

Cedric nodded again but was fidgeting. Carli searched for clues to his movements. All she saw was a man who seemed to have lost twenty pounds since they first met, but now looked like he would live instead of die.

Cedric cleared his throat. Carli and Grant exchanged glances. Perhaps he was already balking. "Ahem," Cedric started. Carli caught Grant's eyes again, before darting to Cedric. "Miss Carli...," he began again. "I ... want ... I mean ..." Cedric continued to fidget and shift his weight from one foot to the next until finally emitting a raspy statement. "Thank you. I feel better."

His eyes flickered toward Carli's like a stun gun. "Good," she said.

"And sometime you'll have to tell me how you ditched me at the clinic." Cedric's smile revealed the gap between his front teeth. The overhead light caught his teeth just right. They sparkled like a chandelier.

Leaving Cedric, Grant asked, "Want some coffee?"

"Not today," said Carli. "I'm checking on Sarah."

"Come on. One day won't matter. She's been there for years, just like the dinosaurs in the sewer. No, a day won't matter at all."

Grant had mentioned dinosaurs a few minutes earlier, as he was leaving Cedric with Mercy. It had sounded amusing, but it had also sent both Mercy and Carli on alert. Hearing it again was equally alarming. All she said was, "Tell me what you find. I'm going to Sarah's."

It was late afternoon when Carli finally reached the park. Sarah was taking her afternoon inventory and would be leaving soon. Carli waited until all items were tallied, then followed behind. Staying close to buildings, and lagging a bit, she saw Sarah stop a few short blocks from the park, near a service entrance to a high-end apartment building. Almost immediately, a woman came out the door, left what looked like a meal, and disappeared back inside. Had Sarah been adopted? Was her real family inside? Anything seemed possible. In fact, everything seemed both possible and impossible these days.

According to Grant, Cedric proved a model patient, easily dispensing with his pills every time Grant showed. Occasionally, Carli met them together at Cedric's usual spot. Several bags of cans usually kept him company, proving he was on the mend. Carli knew, even with a newly-borrowed postal cart, that his can business was a body-buster so recently off bed rest and fettered by crippled lungs.

"I'm telling you," Grant said, gaining Cedric's full attention, "Mercy's got a job for you. If it's outside you want, you got it. Some places'll give you a bed and a job when you're ready. You wouldn't have to be lugging and storing cans. Besides, housing comes in handy."

Cedric shrugged. Nothing more.

Not long after leaving Cedric, Carli and Grant came upon Canada, with his eyes closed, face to the sky, and sunning, as he leaned against scaffolding set up aside a block-long construction site.

"Madison, my man!" Grant loved running into Canada. "Need to get you off these streets," said Grant. "My partner says she's seeing you a lot. Might make me jealous." Grant shot a smile. Carli shook her head.

"You never change," said Canada, punching Grant's shoulder. "Guess what I did?"

Grant looked curious.

"I got to another meeting."

"So?"

"Yeah. I got my five bucks."

"This must be your twenty-fifth meeting. You're only supposed to get paid the first time you do it."

"That's what they say, but some people are lucky."

"Learn anything?" asked Grant.

"Yeah. There's too much paperwork."

Grant sighed. "That's why you have Mercy. She can help with everything. Of course, if you're wanting a lawyer to read the documents, I used to know a good one. Can track him down if you want. Thing is, you have to want it."

Canada scratched his ear. Grant said, "Glad to see you're thinking it over."

Perhaps it was the relief of having Cedric back on his feet, or perhaps it was the warmth in the air, but after taking leave of Canada, Grant was upbeat and talking nonstop, with energy to spare.

"Cedric'll be off the street by summer," he predicted. "Along with your Sarah, and probably even Wilson. Never underestimate people, especially yourself. I know you're going to get to her. We might even get Lenny, and I have a good plan for Harry."

Gliding under a few spring clouds, Grant's words flowed. So did impulses. Twice he pulled Carli close to him as they walked. Twice she said something to regain distance.

"And for those who aren't in, we'll find another atrium." Grant looked to the clouds and laughed at the thought of it.

"You said last week Cedric would be out a while."

He pulled up, looking askance. "Not Cedric. We'll get him. We'll get 'em all. I know someone in the mayor's office. Election's coming up. That should help."

Before the atrium blowup, Carli had clung to Grant's positive attitude. Since then, doubt was her ally. Although his batting average with predictions was indisputably high, and the conviction of his statements hard to fight, Grant still had several hits against him, including the unresolved poison question and the atrium fiasco. Besides, she had heard these promises before.

Grant stomped through Midtown as though pressed to make a deadline. In the mid-Fifties, Carli finally asked, "You in a hurry for something?"

Grant looked perplexed. "No, but we need to go to the park."

"For Sarah?"

"No, to head to the museum. Seen some prospects. They might be going in."

"Museum?"

"The Met."

"What?" Not once had Carli seen a hint of a street sleeper at the Metropolitan Museum of Art. It was armed with guards. Real guards.

"Yeah," said Grant. "Let's go." The sound of an arriving subway train sent him into a jog down subway steps.

"Grant, I've been to this museum many times and have never seen a street sleeper." Carli yelled to override the clatter of train wheels on steel. "Well, maybe one, outside the parking garage."

Grant shouted back, "Why not?"

"There're guards jamming the exhibits."

"So? Can't evict them. Museum's free." He continued to look ahead. "It's like people going to films during the Depression and war years," he added. "They're always looking for a nice distraction. It's as nice as the atrium, and there's even more room."

Carli said nothing more, but her entire insides screamed in

turmoil. On the steps to the museum, Carli found no one with black plastic bags. She wasn't surprised. But it did seem unusual. These days, instead of noticing everyone except them, she now noticed them alone. And they were everywhere. Grant cleared a path around a tour group and headed straight for Egyptian Art. Glancing around, as though searching for someone in particular, he finally said, "This is where they could stay." He looked up at the reconstructed blocks of a centuries-old monument, with its encircling moat, and added, "They'd have a private bath and everything."

Carli was stunned into silence.

"Quick, let's check the next floor." Grant bounded up the stairs and paced the galleries, curled around corners, casually glancing in many directions before taking his steps. He looked like a spy.

"Grant, stop."

He seemed not to have heard. Then, as though pulled by strings on a marionette, he stood next to her, his face showing anger resulting from her intrusion. She nearly remained silent on account of it, but finally asked, "What's going on? There's no one here."

He blinked and resumed walking. "You're right. But they could be." He spun around. "All of them could fit."

"There's no way they could stay in here. What are you saying?" she asked.

"Forget about that for now. Let's look at the Impressionists."

"I think we ought to leave," said Carli.

"No, we really need to see this. It's special."

The last thing Carli wanted was to make a commotion in a busy museum. Especially one filled with guards. She followed as Grant started his private tour.

"He did his best work before he became famous, but most people don't know it," said Grant. They stood in front of a Monet. "Someone estimated five thousand and sixty-two brushstrokes for this one, but my bet's with six thousand at least." Grant was absorbing the fiber and fabric of the canvas. "This one he did for his mother. Used a friend as a model. Took a half year to paint," he said.

Carli stared at Grant. "How do you know this?" she asked.

"Just do," he said. "Look at these layers. All these dabs and stabs of brushstrokes. Which one do you think he did last? Which is the one stroke he put on top of all the other thousands?" Grant spun around. "Don't you just love this stuff?"

Carli wasn't sure anymore. An hour later, after rushing through three more exhibits, they parted ways, with Carli prepared to visit Mercy in the morning. In the meantime, Carli reached out to Kristin.

"I don't know what just happened," said Carli.

"Where are you?" asked Kristin.

"Home, but I came from the Met," said Carli. "Grant said we needed to search for street people in the museum."

"What? That's crazy," said Kristin.

"Exactly."

"What was he thinking?"

"That's just it," said Carli. "I don't know. He went from looking for homeless to saying we could move homeless into the exhibit space, and then he gave me a tour of some of the Impressionists. He's losing it. Something is definitely amiss."

"So, what did you do?" asked Kristin.

"I went along with it so we didn't have a blowup. I have to talk with Mercy again. This is bizarre."

"It's beyond that."

"Hope you can spare a few minutes," said Carli, speaking into her phone.

"For you? Anytime," said Mercy.

"He's running like a racehorse. Without a track."

"I assume we're talking about Grant?"

"The one and only." Carli described the latest behavior. Grant's actions worried them both. Carli and Mercy would be taking Grant under their wings, through their own sort of personalized Outreach.

"Thanks for the update," said Mercy. "When it rains, it usually pours."

"Oh?"

"Right now, Lenny's really got me steamed, jumping out of that special shelter we got him in," said Mercy. "But do you know, his mother and aunt don't even care if he's out. They're not making it easy on him, but maybe that's what he needs. Sometimes, a family just wears out trying to help. He's caused them a whole lot of pain." Carli was beginning to know how it might feel, as she contemplated her possible relationship to Grant.

———

Carli settled herself well within eyesight of Sarah, feeling relieved to have Grant handle the rest, but half wondering if he might stop by. She sketched a feathery subject in full, jerky, hesitant strut. The study turned more serious as she filled in details – five noticeably large feathers with pointed tips on the wing and more delicate plumage interspersed. Rounded, overlapping feathers along the tail. Tiny breast feathers puffing out as though ruffled by a playful April wind. Carli started down the scaly feet, and suddenly felt eyes upon her and a shadow close by. She glanced between the bird and her pad and sensed the figure move closer. She drew and shifted her eyes back and forth, each time feeling Sarah's dark blue presence creeping closer still. She stiffened.

Sarah slid within three feet. Carli selected a different pencil and glanced at Sarah. The woman's eyes were glued to the emerging bird. Sarah continued to inch over, looking between the pigeon sketch and people passing. Carli recognized the woman's odor and heard her labored breathing. Then, Sarah emitted a short squawk, that sounded like she had said, "Nice." Carli startled. She had never before heard Sarah speak a word. Carli was afraid to move but finally chanced it.

"Glad you like it." Carli took another chance, scaling out several light marks on the empty space near the pigeon's beak. She rounded and shaded. Sarah watched intently. Spongy-looking popcorn formed on the paper. "More?" asked Carli.

"Mo-re."

Two more kernels popped within reach of her pigeon. Carli drew lines higher on the page. As she did, several cooing sounds flew forth with Sarah's labored breaths. Part of an illustrated hand reached downward toward Sarah's paper pigeon, with two kernels ready to roll off its fingertips. Carli peeked at the woman. Sarah was silent. It seemed she wanted to speak, but nothing more came out. Demon silence had returned.

As Carli poked at the print again, Sarah squawked loudly. Carli looked up to see Sarah rushing back toward her bench. A young couple had slid into unguarded territory. Sarah fled to reclaim her stakes.

"See you soon," said Carli, on her way out of the park. Sarah said nothing from inside her fortress. Carli's heart soared, nonetheless.

"She spoke with me!" said Carli. She couldn't wait to relay the news, but a lot was going on at Grant's end of the line.

"Congratulations," he said.

"Sounds like you're in a construction zone," said Carli.

"One of the neighbors is moving some stuff or something. There must be a thousand people here. Let me close the door," said Grant.

It sounded as though he dropped his phone. "You always keep your door open?" Carli asked when his voice returned.

"No. Just pulled in. What did she say?"

"She said the word, 'Nice.' That's about it. But she watched me draw a pigeon."

The line was silent. Grant finally said, "Huh? What kind of poop is that?"

"Grant, she came over to me, watched, and said something!"

For another long moment the phone remained quiet. "Grant?"

"Yeah. Good. I mean, great," he finally said.

Carli hung up quickly, wondering why she had called.

EIGHTEEN

GRANT SAID he had searched the benches at Penn Station for four days running while Cedric became an invisible patient. Said he had made special night trips to no avail. On day five, Grant gave Carli the updates and, again, asked for her support. Miraculously, Cedric surfaced after their short twenty-minute search.

"How was I supposed to know?" asked Cedric. "Don't have one of those fancy watches."

"It doesn't take a watch," shouted Grant. Carli pulled back. She had never seen Grant lose his temper with a street man. Judging from Cedric's response, Cedric hadn't either. "You missed a dose," Grant added, as he pulled pills and bottled water from his coat and waited for Cedric to take the prescription. Then he asked more calmly, "How are you feeling?"

All Cedric said was, "When do I stop taking these things?"

"We've been through this," said Grant. "You know it takes time; six months. Remember how you felt?"

Cedric mumbled what sounded like an acknowledgment, but Carli wasn't certain. Grant said, "I even brought Carli away from her painting for you. Next time, be here. Okay? Day after tomorrow. We can do this."

Cedric said, "Sure. I'll be here."

Walking away from Cedric, Carli suddenly stopped. "He really *can't* tell what day it is," she said. "I mean, cans are cans on Monday or Sunday, makes no difference. Sure, weekdays and weekends look different on the streets, but not day of the week."

"Doesn't matter," said Grant. "He needs to be here when he needs to be here. Hope he gets it right." Before Grant headed off to check others, he said, "Thanks again for your help."

A few blocks from her apartment, Carli stopped at the sidewalk newsstand and bought a calendar, the first she could find. She hoped Cedric liked cats.

The next day, before painting, Carli couldn't wait to look for their patient. She found him soaking in early April's spring sun.

"What's this?" Cedric asked, as she handed him the calendar.

"To help with your pills."

"I have to take them today?"

"No. Take a look," said Carli. "Every day, you cross off the box when you get up. If the day has a star on it, wait here for Grant. He'll bring pills on the dates with the stars."

Cedric flipped through the pages. "I never liked cats."

"Why not?" she asked.

"Just creepy."

"What do you like?" Carli realized she knew next to nothing about Cedric.

"Well, ... I kind of like women," he said.

"Women?"

"Yeah. You know ..."

It didn't register. Then, it did. "Oh, no," she said. "You'll get used to the cats. They're just pictures." Cedric understood. "By the way, did you ever have a garden?" asked Carli.

"Garden? Not me. I've always been a city kid, but I like the parks. Why?"

"No reason. Take it easy, Kid."

Cedric seemed to like her calling him "Kid" and answered with the same. "Yeah, Kid. See you."

Carli heard aluminum cans crinkling gently together as Cedric settled into his easy chair. She headed to Kristin's office, hoping to give Vera another surprise.

"Sister!" said Kristin.

"Thanks again," said Carli. "I think this has potential." She hooked her arm in Kristin's for a few steps as they set off to find Vera. It didn't take long to reach the standpipe. "There she is," said Carli.

"I see her. I'm ready," said Kristin.

"Vera Dear-a," called Carli.

Vera turned. She looked surprised to see Carli with a stranger. And worried. Vera didn't say a word.

"How are you?" asked Carli. "This is my friend Kristin. Best friend, actually. We've known each other forever."

Vera nodded. "I see." Then she seemed to close down.

Carli had expected a more welcoming response. Maybe bringing Kristin was not a good idea after all. Suddenly turning to Kristin, Carli said, "It was nice running into you. I'll see you again soon, okay?" Kristin got the message. She departed quickly, and Carli filled the vacancy with an explanation.

"I'm glad you got to see Kristin. We know each other from way back, but enough of that," she said. "How are you doing today, Vera?"

Vera looked more relaxed. "I'm doing okay," she said. "I've seen The Sweepers around, bothering others, but, so far, they're leaving me alone. The sun's shining. I'd say I'm good. Mighty good."

"You look good," said Carli. "Especially good." Then she cocked her head and began to smile. "And I know why."

"What do you mean by that?" asked Vera.

"Are those green socks I see?" Carli raised her eyebrows.

"Oh, listen to you!" said Vera. "Telling me I look good because I'm wearing your socks. You ought to be ashamed of yourself telling fibs like this. Here I am thinking I'm actually looking different somehow, and it's just you doing ... whatever."

"Call it what you want," said Carli. "You look good today. And I'm going to ask my friend Kristin if she agrees."

"No need to do that," said Vera. "She wouldn't know what I look like, good or bad."

"You never know, Vera, never know. Tell me something, did you ever have a best friend?" asked Carli.

"Best friend? Of course. My husband." Vera nodded and looked into the distance. "He was the best friend a person ever could have. Not easy being here without him."

"I'm sorry you lost him." After a moment, Carli added, "I lost someone special too. I told you that already. I know how it feels." Vera raised her eyes. "It's why it's so nice to know Kristin. And some other friends. They help fill some of the void. You have some other friends? Not like your husband, but others?"

Vera shrugged. Carli had given Vera enough to consider for one day. She asked, "You need anything?"

Vera shook her head. "No, I'm good. Thanks."

"Any time," said Carli. "Stay safe. And don't forget about Four Bridges. Mercy's a good one to know."

As Carli wound her way home, she found Canada's group sitting near their cardboard bedcovers. They, too, were soaking in the warmth of the sun and violating sidewalk regulations. The Sweep was still in effect. She wondered how they were avoiding it. Good thing they hadn't taken the abrupt ending of the atrium experiment as hard as she had.

"Still here?" she asked Canada.

"Exchange is closed today. Holiday. I get a day off," he said.

"Nice day to enjoy spring," said Carli.

"That it is. Say, is Grant nearby anywhere? Haven't seen him for a week or so."

"Longer," added one of the other men. "It's been longer than a week."

Grant's absence didn't make sense, but the museum trip hadn't made sense either.

"I wondered if he had any extra bedrolls," said Canada.

"Yeah," said one of the others. "Couldn't keep them dry in the nightly rains we've been having. It's starting to smell like the sewage treatment plant around here. Like, time to toss them."

"Did you try Four Bridges?" asked Carli.

"Yup," the men said in unison. "Gone."

"Some of the ladies at church were sewing new ones," she said. "Four Bridges ought to be getting a new supply. I'd check soon. Before they're gone again. Or Church Run." It seemed like years ago that Carli had seen sewing circles of church women converting donated comforters into street-bound bedrolls. In truth, it had only been a mere couple of months.

Carli sat with the op-ed table at Lucy's Church, happy to see Leo and Marvin off the street, and many of the ones she knew enjoying each other's company. Opening Day was a good one for Yankees baseball. Off-season trades had paid off. Leo and Marvin had plenty to talk about. And they could feel it in their bones, as they said, that the season was going to be a good one.

"Any word from Grant?" Carli asked Sister Anna.

"Not today. He dashed in and dashed out a few days ago. Something seems to be troubling him. Is everything all right out there? I thought I overheard him talking to the police about poison again."

Carli beckoned Sister Anna out of the dining area. "Follow me." She took a peek over Sister Anna's shoulder and asked, "Do you have proof anyone was actually poisoned?"

"What do you mean?"

"Thelma said Lucy had a heart attack. Said it was on the death certificate, and she sounded mighty certain of it. Mercy at Four Bridges didn't know of any poisoning either, and I asked Missing Persons and the Medical Examiner's Office. I got the same answer."

"Oh? Sounds strange, but I'm sure we'll find out sooner or later. And, as to Grant's whereabouts, I'm sure he'll show," said Sister Anna.

After leaving St. Mary's, Carli swung into the park to visit Sarah. The blue coat and hat were easy to find. Carli wondered when Sarah would bag them for summer storage. Carli chose her seat carefully, as usual, settling close to Sarah, but not too close. Pigeons were plentiful, flapping wings on benches, gliding down from light poles, cooing and strutting in circles, and pecking at fallen potato chips. Quickly, Carli drew a perfect bird, perching on the back of a park bench, toenails curling around the top slat. She felt Sarah step close enough to watch her draw. In between breaths, Carli heard the word, "Where?"

"Here," she replied, tapping on the side of her forehead. "My imagination." Sarah watched a bit longer before turning to walk away. "Wait. I have the other one. Needs color. Want help." Carli had reverted to Sarah's abrupt, monosyllabic style.

Sarah turned. "Col-or." It was neither a statement nor a question.

"Yes, so I can paint this one."

Sarah turned again and shuttled away. Carli took it as another test.

Several days later, Carli settled into the park, and Sarah sauntered over for another peek at Carli's pigeons. Despite renewed requests for help, Sarah said nothing of colors or anything else. During several more visits, the scene was repeated. On a relatively quiet day, Sarah looked on more intently. Carli worked on the popcorn pigeon. Casually she said, "Gray?" and waited for Sarah to turn and leave. Instead, Sarah said, "Gray ... ey?" with a strong inflection on the second syllable and rising pitch of a squawking parrot.

"Darker gray here?" asked Carli, pointing her pencil at the wing feathers of her popcorn pigeon. Sarah nodded, with less assurance. "White patch anywhere?" Carli was going to ask as many questions as she could to keep Sarah talking.

"No ... no ... Buff ..."

"Buff?"

"Buff ... y." Sarah repeated, "Buff ... y."

Carli stopped drawing, and said, "Buff ..." She looked directly at Sarah. The woman finished her word. "... y."

Carli suddenly understood. Sarah had named her birds. How many returned on a regular enough basis to be named, she wondered? Together, they completed Buffy's color scheme.

"Next week," said Carli, "I'll show you." Sarah nodded, perhaps not knowing why, but knowing enough to nod. As she started toward her bags, Carli thought she heard her say, "Buff ... y," one more time.

When Carli next saw Grant, on the steps of St. Mary's, he reeked of alcohol and breath mints. He was barely interested in her pigeon progress and was equally cool to Vera's news and Cedric's calendar.

"Let's go find Cedric," he said, before popping another mint onto his tongue.

"It's not his day. Not mine either," said Carli. "I'm here to drop something off with Sister Anna."

"Well, let's go anyway," said Grant.

The entire way to Cedric's, Carli wondered what was wrong with Grant. She found herself repeatedly slowing to check behind her. He was dragging. Not finding Cedric, she finally asked, "What's the matter?"

All he said was, "I'd better go home," and he walked away. Carli watched him for as far as she could see, unable to find a meaningful answer to her question.

Several days later, Carli made a special trip to St. Mary's. Sure enough, she found Grant, along with the same unwanted scent of alcohol and breath mints. At lunch, he buried himself in his food but hardly ate.

"Have you been getting Cedric his pills?" she asked. His answer was a definitive yes, but Carli didn't trust him. She proposed a visit to

Cedric's, where Grant fumbled pill bottles from his pocket and clumsily handed them to Carli to administer and keep.

After a third day of the same, Carli demanded answers. "I know you're on something. What is it, and what's the matter?" she asked.

Grant looked confused. "Matter?"

"Yes."

"Mouthwash," he said coolly. "New flavor." He smiled.

Carli stared him down. "Canada and his group needed new bedrolls and said you hadn't visited them in a while. Yesterday, you looked bad. Today, too. What's the matter with you? Why are you drinking during the day?" Grant looked away, considering her words. "Did you hear me?" she asked.

Grant shook his head. "I don't know." He took in a deep breath and said, "I have to go."

"Wait." Grant didn't slow his step, didn't turn around. Carli watched his brown suede coat flap gently as he continued to walk away. She started in the opposite direction, with indecision plaguing her steps. She stepped into a deli, and indecision vanished. She set about following him home. Why was he wearing a coat, anyway?

Carli kept nearly a block between them. As conspicuous as she felt, she also felt safely hidden as pedestrians raced for buses, subways, trains, and more. His gait looked different, lethargic. After he disappeared into a corner store, Carli glided next to a woman in a red blazer and peeked in the window as she passed. Then she followed the woman in red into a bank to wait. As soon as Grant walked into view, she moved toward the door to follow.

He now carried a single brown bag, tucked securely under his arm. His hands were stuffed inside his pockets. His pace was faster. In tandem, they crossed through Hell's Kitchen, from a well-maintained neighborhood to a low-rent district, with no more doormen or brass door handles, and, finally, past several broken windows and a boarded-up building. Midway through a block, Grant dug through his pocket, presumably for keys, and disappeared from the street. She gave him a minute to settle in before walking the last block to check out his home.

"Really?" she whispered. She said it again. In front of her was the entrance to Cooper's Modern Self-Storage. It must have been where he stashed Cedric's cans, and maybe goods for others or himself. A guard sat visibly at Cooper's front desk. She turned for home, assuming Grant would do the same in due time. She vowed to never follow him again. What did it matter what he was doing, anyway?

———

Buffy emerged from Carli's canvas in magnificent color, ready for flight to its keeper in the park. Carli found Sarah watching people and pigeons with equal interest, but she only cooed to the birds.

"Sarah, I have it," said Carli. Sarah jerked up her head. Maybe it was because she had been called by name. "Buffy – your bird," said Carli. Sarah looked around, searching. She took serious notice when Carli sat on her bench.

"Buff ... y?" said Sarah.

Carli unveiled the portrait—a multitude of glimmering feathers and salmon-colored feet—on a one-foot-square acrylic board. Sarah stared, then slowly reached forward. She poked the feathers with a single finger, then gently placed another two fingers on the bird. Sarah continued to stare. For a brief moment – a mere flicker – her face seemed to light up. As Sarah's fingers slid up to the painted hand offering popcorn, the light went out. Her fingers rested, motionless.

Carli dared put her own hand on Sarah's worn coat sleeve. Sarah's eyes turned immediately to look, but Sarah remained still. *That* was progress. Carli safely balanced Buffy's portrait on Sarah's lap and left.

———

With Grant's questionable condition fresh in mind, and with word from both Sister Anna and Mercy that he hadn't shown for nearly a week, Carli added extra visits to her schedule. She wasn't about to let them down. She wondered if Grant had actually planned his absence, and was thankful to still have Cedric's pills.

Cedric, she found, had garnished his food wages for a purchase of his own. He was not the least bit timid to show Carli his new calendar. Carli flipped to May, ready to make necessary notations. Then she flipped to June, then all the way through. The calendar was a ribbon of color with stars throughout ... and naked women.

"Like yours," he said proudly.

Carli pulled a silver marker from her bag—a color unlike any of Cedric's—marked the days for medication, and handed the calendar back. Cedric seemed pleased. A visit to Wilson was next. Barely able to open his eyes, Wilson remained helplessly mum on why he knew anything about fragrances. Gaining more insight was going to wait, but one way or another, Carli was going to gently pry it out. Afterward, to her surprise, Carli found Grant rising from a table in the lunchroom of St. Mary's. His shirt was wrinkled, his shoelaces clicked on the linoleum floor as he walked, and his face was long-unshaven. The only good news was he didn't smell of alcohol or mints. Carli was certain Sister Anna, the servers, and patrons noticed. Surely, no one missed how carelessly he slid the contents of his tray into the garbage, nearly untouched. Carli caught up to him going out the door.

"Grant, what is wrong? You look ... well, ... you look bad."

"Beats me. Maybe it's the flu. I'd better go home," he said.

Carli considered Cedric's TB, but instinct told her it was something else. Carli gave him a slight head start, and then, against former vows, followed. He took the same route, and performed the same routine, including the purchase at the corner store. She followed, as before, expecting to leave before he made his final turn. This time, he didn't turn. Instead, he continued walking. Maybe he knew she was with him. Carli had a decision to make, and, for once, opted to leave before he went in somewhere. Surely, home was near. In the meantime, Carli took a taxi to Four Bridges.

Mercy invited Carli into her office and sent the door slamming shut with a single swift push. "What's going on?" Mercy asked, keen to Carli's distress.

"Grant again," said Carli. "I am sure he needs help."

"Haven't seen him much lately," said Mercy. She took in a deep breath. Clearly, she knew something. "What're you getting at there, Carli?"

"He's acting mighty strange. A couple of weeks ago, I couldn't keep up with him. More recently, I either couldn't get him going or he just didn't show. The last time I saw him, he looked ... awful. I've been covering some of his visits."

Carli detailed her latest encounters. While it wasn't her business, she had blindly waded into the middle of it. Carli felt uncomfortably like a snitch. And in her old neighborhood, snitches were unpopular.

"What do you think's going on?" asked Mercy.

"That's just it," said Carli. "I don't know. A few weeks ago, he smelled of alcohol and was popping mints like a candy dispenser. But not lately, and I don't think that explains his behavior. I figure you know him as well as any."

"He might have been using. Maybe one of those rave pills, although he's always had a lot of energy. Or we might be talking some sort of chemical imbalance, what with the different swings and all. Maybe some sort of bipolar." Several of these possibilities had crossed Carli's mind. She kept shunning them. How could Grant have problems? He was supposed to be helping others. Mercy's words made Carli's heart race.

Mercy left Grant a phone message while Carli listened in. "He's always been his own operator," said Mercy. "But when he comes in, I'll see what I can find out."

"You won't say anything, will you?" asked Carli.

"Confidential is my middle name. Has to be." Mercy winked.

Carli set off to the safety and familiarity of her studio. She had assured Mercy she would continue to help Cedric with his pills. It wouldn't take much more time and Cedric was now counting on her, even if he didn't necessarily know it. A new canvas stared back. Lila and Terrance settled into their new beds on the floor. Carli mixed a combination of deep, dark, nighttime colors. This waterscape was going to be dangerous and dark. The surrounding air was going to be dark as well. A nighttime sea, hurtling waves into a strong chop, was about to rise from a dark ocean of water, miles deep. It would be an ocean that gave chills, with but the slightest glimpse. It would have danger written all across it. Carli prepared to add a two-person dingy, severely undersized to handle the swells of this dark ocean. Anyone manning this craft was in for a tough go.

———————

Cedric sat ready and waiting with his calendar each time Carli visited with his pills. They had the routine down and made increasing time for casual conversation. It was the last thing Carli would have expected; that she would be sharing tales with a can-collecting street-man. True, Cedric was still outside, but Carli was just getting started.

Countering that success was Sarah's disappearance. Guilt grew as Carli wondered if Sarah had disappeared on account of Buffy. Carli would have given anything for Grant to appear and offer assurances that he had seen her safe and alive during one of his nighttime prowls. But Grant remained invisible. A bit of good news crossed into Carli's world early one afternoon after she said, "See you, Kid," to Cedric, and headed off to visit Wilson. She had intentionally worn a different perfume; one she had kept in her bathroom vanity for over fifteen years. At one time, it was special to her. A gift from a man she had hoped to marry. Long after the man had gone out of Carli's life, the perfume, a special musky creation, continued to keep Carli's spare bottles of shampoo company, and made sporadic appearances. She was surprised, and thankful, it retained its alluring fragrance. She removed its cap and inhaled gently. The familiar, mellow aroma made her grateful for the time she had had with him, and grateful she no longer felt heartbroken by the parting of ways.

Wilson was stationed in his park in an unusually upright position. From the sidewalk, Carli saw him turn his head even before she waved.

"You smell different," he said, when Carli sat across from him at the picnic table.

"Yes," said Carli. "It's one of my old-time favorites."

"I know that one," he said. "But I can't quite figure it out. I like it."

Then he said some magical words.

"I think ... I think I did it."

"Did it?" she asked.

"Yeah. Pretty sure." Wilson seemed deep in thought, scouring a memory bank long tinted by C_2H_6O—ethanol. It made the mental search challenging, but, finally, he said, "Might have been." Then he was silent.

"Might have been? Might have been what?"

"I don't know. Maybe one of mine."

Carli connected the fuzzy dots. "It was one of LaRusso's," she said. "LaRusso Parfumerie."

Wilson abruptly shifted his eyes toward Carli. "I know LaRusso."

Carli was certain he knew a lot about LaRusso. And not just because it had been one of the largest, most prolific perfumeries in the world, based in New York City. What she didn't know was why. She hated being so clueless.

Despite a few more questions from Carli, Wilson offered no more insight into his world of fragrances. Carli left Wilson to dig a bit deeper. It was like Grant had said over and over: they all had plenty of time.

At week's end, Carli settled into the quiet of a pew at her comforting St. Ignatius Church, hoping to find an inner calm equal to the calm of her most serene waterscape. Sitting alone, she closed her eyes and let her tangle of thoughts quietly wash away. In a brief time, she released her thoughts, released control, and was ready to accept whatever came next, in good faith. After another few minutes, however, she found herself pulled back into her present surroundings and wishing she might suddenly hear Grant clearing his throat and sounding like his old self. She silently cursed him for having let the street clan down, even beyond letting her down. Cursed him, right in the chapel, and then felt guilty for doing it. He needed support, not condemnation.

Her eyes were drawn to the cross on the wall, where Jesus hung with eyes cast downward. A thought silently crept in, and Carli tensed throughout. In the next moment, she ran from the chapel, heading straight to Cooper's Storage, with her heart pounding. The guard sat watch near the door. Carli considered her options while a man walked in off the street. The man signed in at the desk and disappeared toward the elevators. The stranger made it look easy.

Carli worked up her nerve. "I'm with Mr. Konklin," she said, after a quick glance at the sign-in sheet. She signed another alias on the line below and passed the guard without another word. With Mr. Konklin heading to room 302, Carli darted to the stairwell to make her way to the top floor, far from anyone's sight.

Cooper's was shaped like a letter H except for a more intricate grid pattern in the center. The floors were unfinished concrete; the rooms corrugated metal with pulldown metal doors. Windows at the end of the corridors offered natural light but did nothing to remove the stale concrete air. A few doors were clamped shut by heavy locks, but most remained unlatched. Clearly, the lower floors were more popular. The metal door to a room at the end squealed as Carli slid it open. She ran her hands along its thin corrugated wall until she came across a switch, which clicked loudly as she flipped on the light. Two low voltage bulbs, with wire mesh safety covers, glowed a measly yellow above. Electrical wires, stapled to ceiling crossbeams, shared space with a single fire sprinkler. The room was surprisingly spacious. Carli flipped the light switch again and moved slowly through the hall.

All was quiet until she came to a corner, where she made out sounds from a radio. Carli braced herself against the cinderblock wall and swayed her head around the corner to peer down the new hallway. She heard more clearly the radio commentary of a baseball game and saw a dim ray of light coming from a single storage room. Carli retreated around the corner, closed her eyes, and continued listening to the last inning and a half of the game. Then, someone switched off the radio, rustled in the bin, and began walking across the concrete. Carli prepared to run, but the steps grew quieter as they moved away. Carli peered around the corner once again. In the second it took to pull back into her corner, her chest had become so tight she was nearly unable to breathe. Grant was still wearing his coat. A second glance revealed toothbrush and toothpaste in hand. Carli heard his slow steps, followed by the swinging open of a door, the loud click of a light switch, and a door swinging shut.

Carli wanted to flee but would never have forgiven herself if she left without confirmation. She removed her shoes. Then she peeked up the empty hallway one more second before racing, as quietly as she could, on the balls of her feet, toward the light. Grant's room was jammed with books, paintings, and boxes. Shelves scaled upward on two of the four walls – straight ahead and to the left. They were stuffed full. A bike, stacks of shoeboxes, a lineup of black sneakers, and empty pizza boxes spilled over from another corner. A tapestry swung down across the right-hand wall, and underneath lay a mattress, with blankets and sheets flung open. The radio sat on the floor beside the pillow. Carli fled for the stairs and felt the pain in her heart spread through her chest. All that she had known of Grant had come even more unraveled. What had she gotten herself into? For all she knew, Grant was the one who had bashed Lenny. Clearly, Grant needed help.

Carli called Kristin, barely out Cooper's front door.

"Who the heck lives in a storage room? Is that even legal?" asked Kristin.

"What do you think? Of course not."

"What are you going to do?"

"I don't know. He surely needs help. No one in his right mind lives like that."

"I say you ditch Outreach and stick to painting," said Kristin.

"I can't. Grant does so much for everyone on the streets. If he goes, they go. I can't just ignore this. Besides, I still wonder if he could be my brother."

"You're still thinking about that?"

"No, not really. But I keep getting signs that he might be. What matters more is that Grant has helped more than thirty-five people move off the sidewalks, according to Mercy. That's mighty worthwhile. Somehow, I have to help him ... with whatever he has going on."

"Are you qualified?" asked Kristin.

"No. Not at all. But it takes more than doctors and specialists. It takes support. Lots of it. And many kinds of support. That's why I wanted you to meet Vera. She needs to start thinking about friends. Maybe one of them can help. I'm trying everything I can think of."

"You go, Sister," said Kristin. "You go. I get it. Really do."

Early the next day, Carli took a car out of the city with Lila and Terrance riding in the back. As Carli stood on the sandy beach, looking across the water, the two companions chased waves and seagulls alike. Soon, Carli would hand them over to Thelma, and they would rejoin their Lucy. She wished she hadn't made the offer.

Carli was surprised when Grant joined her mid-week as she left Four Bridges. He was clean-shaven and alert. Grant shook Carli's hand vigorously and said, "Sorry I had to skip out a while. Anything happen?"

"Nothing," said Carli. She looked at him from head to toe and wondered if he detected her lie.

"Let's go then," he said.

"Wait. You talked with Mercy, right?" she asked.

"What do you mean?"

"I mean, you were a mess. And we are concerned about you."

"Saw her yesterday. Sometimes I need a break from all this. Out here, I mean." He started walking. At a normal pace. Carli watched his every move. They found Cedric waiting and ready for his medications. Grant's absence seemed not to have mattered to him.

"Good thinking. The calendar, I mean," said Grant as they moved on.

"The one I got him had cats. This one's all his doing."

Grant laughed. "Sounds right." Then he asked, "Has Wilson been around?"

"Yes. No change ... except ... he knows perfume inside and out, like you said. Surely, it's a hint to his life before the street, but Wilson hasn't told me enough yet."

Grant sighed. "Yet. That's the key."

"Vera said The Sweepers are still out," said Carli. "And I know why she won't leave her real estate."

"I think The Sweep is pretty quiet," he said. "No need to check Vera, unless you want to. Saw her last night."

"You were out?"

Grant nodded. "Say, want some lunch?"

"No. I need to check for Sarah." What she most needed was space to think.

"What's new with her?" he asked.

"Beats me. I gave her the painting and she disappeared."

"Oh, Sarah's all right," said Grant. "I saw her last night too. In an odd place, actually. A clear six blocks away from her usual nighttime home, and at midnight."

"Did she seem okay?"

"As far as I could tell," said Grant. "Same as ever. You know she doesn't talk much. And not at all to me. And I said I saw her; didn't speak with her." As Carli turned to leave, Grant said, "Thanks."

She asked, "For what?"

"You know."

She stared. "What was wrong with you?"

"Don't know. Sometimes, like I said, you just need a break."

Carli didn't respond. She knew the real story was more complex.

"If you ever need alone time," said Grant, "let me know."

Carli thought for a second. "Why don't you take Cedric's pills back. I'll visit him when I can."

"Got it," he said. "And let me take you to lunch tomorrow."

"What? No way. We're good."

"Seriously," said Grant. "Meet me at St. Mary's tomorrow."

"Sure," she finally said, hoping to see for herself how Grant was doing.

NINETEEN

CARLI STEPPED through the archway of St Mary's to see Grant leaning against one of the closed doors to the chapel. "Perfect timing," he said. As he picked up a parcel with a long baguette sticking out the top, he added, "We're headed to the Meadow."

"You mean in the park?" she asked.

"Exactly. It's time to soak in this sun and watch a few softballs fly. Not to mention, celebrate."

"What do you mean?" asked Carli.

"They made it to spring. All of them. Well, except for Lucy."

Yes, she thought, they had.

Carli sat on the lawn, tilting her head to the sun. By her account, Grant was acting fine. She let her hands gently dig through the grass into the soft earth. "When I was young, I planted marigolds every summer," she said. "I loved putting my hands in the dirt."

"It's how you learn," said Grant. "By touch."

Carli turned her head. "I do. Yes. How about you?"

"I'm done learning," said Grant, pulling a few items from the bag.

"Oh, come on ..."

"No, I am. Sometimes I can't get what I see out of my head. Better to turn off the learning switch," he said.

"I doubt that's possible."

"I used to have a garden. Big back yard too," said Grant. "Did all the usual chores – weeding, mowing, watering, mulching, you name it."

"You miss it?"

"Not a bit. That was my old life."

"Sounds like what you say about the street sleepers," said Carli.

Grant gave her a funny look. "I guess it is, isn't it?"

"So ... Thelma and Mrs. Thompson are sprucing up Lucy's old gardens," said Carli.

"We can carpool to her service," he said. "Along with L and T, if Thelma's taking them."

"Yes, with L and T. Thelma finally said she would take them in."

"It'll be nice for all of them, but aren't you going to miss your two little scouts?"

"I wish they were staying," she said. "It's going to feel empty, and I definitely love them."

"Dogs are the best. Always say the right thing."

Carli laughed. "It sounds like you had a dog or two in your life."

"Me? Sure did. One," said Grant. "Kind of a weird little mutt."

"The best kind."

"Good ol' Bonaventura," said Grant.

Carli jerked her head forward and stared sharply at Grant. "Bonaventura?" she asked softly.

"Odd name, I know," said Grant.

"Bonaventura," she whispered again.

"Yup. The one and only," he said.

"The one and only," she repeated. Carli continued to stare at Grant. She felt her arms begin to shake. "Did he have a ... nickname? Something not so long?" Carli asked.

"Actually, yes. Most of the time, we called him 'Tura.' He had other names too. Like most dogs, right?"

"Tura?" she asked. Carli slowly placed her hand over her mouth, all the while staring at Grant.

"What's the matter?" asked Grant.

Carli continued to stare. She tried to speak but couldn't.

"Seriously, Carli, what's wrong?" he asked.

Carli slowly pulled her hand from her face and reached forward to touch Grant's arm. "Henry ...," she said quietly. "You *are* Henry."

"What?" asked Grant. "Who are you talking to?"

"You," said Carli. "I finally found you."

Grant turned to look behind him and asked again, "Who are you talking to?"

"You," said Carli. "Aren't you Henry?"

Grant looked pale, as though he had seen a ghost. "Of course not," he said. "Are you okay?"

"It's me," she said. "Tessie. Your sister."

"I don't have a sister," said Grant. "And why are you saying this? You said your name was Carli."

Carli pulled back her hand and straightened up. "Are you messing with me?" she asked quietly.

"Me? I'd say it's the other way around. What's going on?"

"I had a dog once. His name was Bonaventura," said Carli. She continued to look at Grant's face. "And I had a brother, too. Until he vanished from college. I thought you were my brother. He used to call me Tessie. But now my nickname is Carli."

"Quite a coincidence," said Grant. "What are the odds of another Bonaventura?"

"Exactly," said Carli. "And my dog's nickname was Tura."

Grant began gathering the extra food and wrappers.

"Where are you going?" she asked.

"Home, I guess. I thought we were done."

"Done? We barely got here. But you stay. Enjoy the day. I told Sarah I would meet her."

"Now?" he asked.

"Yes." Carli gently squeezed Grant's arm, stared at his face, and said, "Forgot all about it."

In the fifteen-block walk to her apartment, Carli was certain she didn't take a single breath.

"He's Henry. I know he is," said Carli.

"I thought you finally accepted he wasn't your brother," said Kristin.

"How many dogs are called Bonaventura?" asked Carli.

"What?"

"How many people would name their dog Bonaventura?" Carli repeated.

"Well ... probably not many," said Kristin.

"Exactly. My dog was Bonaventura. His dog was Bonaventura. And we both called him Tura for short. That's more than a coincidence," said Carli. "Composers are named Bonaventura. Artists are named Bonaventura. And a couple of musicians. I bet we had the only canine Bonaventura in the world."

"So, you found him. You finally found him," said Kristin. "I can't believe it." She gave Carli a hug and said, "You found your brother!"

"I did. And it was unbelievable. It was better than I could ever expect. Then, it was awful."

"Awful?" asked Kristin.

"He said he didn't have a sister. He looked at me like I was crazy," said Carli.

"What?"

"I don't know what the hell happened. And now, he thinks I am totally weird."

"I don't understand," said Kristin.

"Me neither. I mean, what the hell.... I didn't know what to do. I was so shocked I left."

"I guess you wait it out and see what happens. Are you certain?" Kristin asked. Then she shook her head and said, "Forget I said that. Bonaventura is a unique name. Grant has to be your brother. Why did he refuse to recognize you?"

"I don't know, but I have to find out. Oh, my God. Kristin, I found him."

Carli was grateful to find Mercy's open door. She practically collapsed into the seat on the opposite side of Mercy's desk. Today, Carli didn't notice what gem of an outfit Mercy was wearing. As soon as she sat, she said, "It's Grant. And he's a mess. So am I."

"What's going on?" asked Mercy. "Take a breath, Carli. Looks like you just had a major breakdown."

"You're telling me. The short of it is Grant's my brother. I know it. Only, he claims he doesn't have a sister. He says he doesn't know me."

"How is it you are so sure?" asked Mercy. "You had doubts. Now you seem certain."

"I am certain. We had a dog. As kids. How many dogs named Bonaventura do you know?"

Mercy nodded. "I see." She continued to nod. "And he claims he doesn't know you?"

"Right," said Carli. "He's been such a mess, on and off, that I wouldn't even know him, except for Bonaventura and the other little things that looked so familiar. Other than that, he's been drinking, and on and off looking like crap, and maybe even clinically depressed sometimes. That wasn't how he used to be. Today, he seemed fine ... until he didn't know me."

"I talked with him a couple of times," said Mercy. "I know what you're saying. This dog bit is another interesting piece. But first and foremost, what can I do for you? Not Grant, but you?"

"I have no idea," said Carli. "I feel like I'm in some surreal world. Or I'm losing my mind."

"In a way, you are. This is not your normal world. Not at all. So, this is what I want you to do. I want you to help yourself. I have a good person you can talk to, if you want. And we can also see if Grant, now, or down the line, can meet with this person, as well, and figure out what's going on with him. It definitely seems like he needs help."

Mercy called Dr. Greenberg at Avenue Partners before Carli left her office. There was too much in Carli's life, let alone Grant's, to pass over. Carli was grateful for the last-minute appointment. Before she stepped into the hall, Mercy said, "It will work out." To Carli, it sounded unlikely.

Two days later, Carli stepped up to the door of Avenue Partners, on the posh Upper West Side of the city, pressed the entry buzzer, and stepped into the softly-colored waiting room for her first appointment with a psychiatrist. She felt like a failure.

Upon meeting Doctor Greenberg, Carli knew she had come to the right place. It was high time. The first visit didn't allow nearly enough precious minutes to spill out her worries and concerns, the trauma of losing Henry, and the recent events of finding him. Maybe that was why she was given a fifteen-page questionnaire to complete at home before her second visit.

"As to your brother," said Dr. Greenberg. "He might need deprogramming. Cults can be very powerful at having their members disassociate from former connections, including family. The cult becomes the family. Depending on how long he was involved, it can take concentrated effort to bring him to his pre-cult life. The drinking and, as you describe them, mood swings, might be related to the transition away from the cult, or they could be a separate condition. I would have to meet with him to give an evaluation. In the meantime, let's you and I explore your concerns with loss." Dr. Greenberg was a beacon of hope. Finally, Carli had the help she needed. If only she had been to a doctor forty years ago.

The next day, Carli awakened, surprisingly ready to try again. Her phone calls to Grant went unanswered, so she tried to track him down at St. Mary's. No one had seen him. Three days later, Grant finally phoned. "Meet me at Lucy's church," he said. "Tomorrow." Before Carli could say a word, Grant hung up. At least, he was talking to her.

The next day, Carli sat inside St. Mary's through the entire lunchtime. Grant didn't show. She passed down the steps through the archway and started home. That's when she heard the strange rustling of branches behind her. She turned to see Grant stepping out from the tangled landscape plants near the church. He walked quickly to Carli and said, "Keep walking." Carli stopped to face him. Grant said, "Keep walking."

"What's wrong?" she asked. "Where are we going?"

"Just walk," he said. Grant pushed her lower back as they moved away from the church. "I knew you'd keep looking," he said. "And I knew you'd find me someday."

"What?" asked Carli. She stopped and turned to face him. It sounded like he was admitting he was Henry.

"You're the one, aren't you?" asked Grant.

"The one?" she asked.

"The scum who's been poisoning my friends. It's you, isn't it?" said Grant. "From Nirvu." Carli felt she might crumble to the sidewalk. She hadn't heard the cult's name in decades. Couldn't even talk about it by name. To Carli, it was still the cult, nothing more specific. Grant was as serious as she had ever seen him. He looked down on her. This, too, sent her body into full alert. She would have run if she thought she could have gotten away.

"What?" asked Carli. "What are you talking about?"

"I knew you'd keep looking."

"Grant, I am not from a cult. I'm your sister. Tessie."

"It's just like you, to pretend to help these people just to get to me," he said.

"Grant, what are you talking about? You're the one who asked me to help with Outreach. I'm not with a cult. It's me. Tessie. Your sister."

Grant stood a moment. He continued to stare, now with anger in his eyes. "Look, if you want me, just take me back. But leave my friends on the streets alone."

"Grant, I am not from a cult."

"If your name is Tessie, why have you been calling yourself Carli?" he asked.

"It's a long story." Grant continued to stare. "Look," said Carli. "I am not from a cult. I don't want to take you anywhere," she said.

Grant said, "I don't want to see you with any of them again."

"I don't want to hurt anyone. I want to help," she said. "And I'm glad you asked me to help with Sarah and Vera. I won't abandon them." She turned slightly so as to look directly into his eyes. They stared back, with the feel of bullets about to hit their target. She said, "I can prove it. Listen ...," she said. Carli sang their childhood song. Then she said, "We all used to play on the street – the Delaney twins, the Humphrys, the Santiagos ... And ... 'Cranky Flower' was our secret password."

Grant looked stunned. He said nothing more. Just turned and left. Carli watched him weave his way through a crowd of people on the sidewalk. He walked quickly and disappeared down a stairwell to the subways. Carli phoned Mercy and Dr. Greenberg with an update. Then she slid shut the door to her apartment and poured herself a drink to settle her nerves.

The next day, Carli swung down past Wilson's park. She was disappointed to find his bench empty. Carli continued along to look for Vera. The Third Avenue standpipe at Thirty-Seventh Street stood alone. Carli took both absences as signals for her to return to her studio. There, with Lila and Terrance alongside, Carli set painting aside to begin a sketch of her two little street dogs. She could practically draw them from memory. In a few short months, Lila and Terrance had become the constants in her life. They had uncertain pasts, but their current challenges were minor and few, like deciding when to chase a ball around her studio floor, and when to sleep. It was a good life they had. When Carli finished, she started shopping from the comfort of her window seat. Flippin' Dog had exactly the going-away gifts she was looking for. She felt good about her purchase of new collars with their names embroidered on them. Yes, she would miss the two of them. She would also be forever grateful that they had brought Henry back to her, even if he didn't know her.

Three days later, as Carli exited Four Bridges, she ran smack into Grant, with his arms wide open. She nearly screamed. He dropped his arms, but Carli continued to shy away. Was the old Grant back, or was this a ploy to grab her? Were his accusations of cult-ties buried behind them? She wasn't sure she wanted to know. Except she had to know. Why didn't he know her? Why wouldn't he admit he was Henry? And why did he threaten her?

"Come, visit Cedric with me," he said.

"I thought you had him covered," said Carli, continuing to keep her distance. "I'm fine sticking to Vera and Sarah."

"No," said Grant. "Cedric needs you."

"What do you mean?" Carli looked at Grant for several moments, wondering if he would bring up the cult and change back to the frightening expression of his last interaction with her. Grant continued to look like his old self. Carli slowly started walking.

"Wrong way," said Grant. She froze.

"What do you mean?" She could only hope Mercy would hear her from inside if she yelled loud enough.

"He moved," said Grant.

"Moved? Oh, no," she said. "The hospital?"

"No, and he wants you to visit." Grant was smiling. "At the shelter." Grant's turquoise ring caught a flash of sunlight as Grant placed his hands on her arms. "He's in." Looking directly into her eyes he added, "Don't know if it's for good, but it's a start."

Carli studied Grant's face. She wanted him to remove his hands. "How?" she finally asked.

"He was ready."

"That's it?" she asked.

"Yup, that's it. He's at a transitional place," said Grant. "He'll be applying for something more permanent, and, hopefully down the line, a job as well. Deena, the social worker up there, thinks he'll be ok for it, but they have to continue to check his TB first, for his sake and the sake of others. They'll evaluate him for a bunch of other things too. It'll take him longer than he thinks. Doesn't know how out of touch he's become."

"He needs socializing, you mean," said Carli.

"They all do," said Grant. "Just has to take it day by day."

Together, they walked to Cedric's new home. It was comforting knowing exactly where to find him. Carli and Grant paused while a funeral cortege with black limousines blocked their route. Carli took another long look at Grant, out of the corner of her eye. So far, so good.

"He had another run-in with the cops," said Grant. "Better with them than with the stinking can snatcher. At least they're trying to help. I didn't bother to tell you about it. It couldn't have hurt that he had been inside with people who cared about him. At the hospital, that is."

They climbed the steps to the shelter and Grant said, "Wait here. You have to pass some bunks to get to the lounge area. Might be someone sleeping." Carli watched Grant disappear into the building. Two men exited as Carli waited. A third wandered inside.

"Hey, Kid. Heard you don't like my calendar," said Cedric. Carli loosely clutched Cedric's forearms and shot an unwelcome glare at Grant. The information was meant to be privileged.

"New pants, Kid?" she asked.

"They gave them to me." His eyebrows lifted. "Actually gave them to me." Cedric glanced between Carli and Grant. He looked like he had won the lottery. "I won't be taking no free lunch or anything, but the pants are good. This lady, Deena, said I might get some park job. That sounds okay."

"Indeed," she said.

"She says I might have to share a kitchen," said Cedric. "That's not going to happen, but don't tell her that." Cedric winked. His secret was safe.

"I promised Cedric I'd keep checking on him," said Grant. "I hate like hell to lose my friends." Carli would have felt better about Grant's statement had he not used similar words discussing Carli's potential plot to poison his friends, but Cedric smiled, revealing his familiar toothless chasm, and Carli couldn't help but feel a sense of gratitude. "I'm keeping his cart for him too," said Grant.

Leaving the shelter, Grant said, "I told you once, the best thing you can do while they're on the street is keep on making contact, keep showing you care, and hope to somehow connect." Carli nodded. "Well, it doesn't stop just because he's in," said Grant. "Between you and me, I worry about them just as much when they're in somewhere. He's about to be tested. Not by a cold wind, cold stares, or TB, but it's just as hard, usually harder. Now he has to finally face the things that put him out in the first place and find a way to move forward. Hearing a few extra supportive words doesn't hurt."

Grant walked slowly. "There's always a chance he'll be back out, maybe even tomorrow. Sometimes it takes five or six tries before they stay for good. That's why I keep checking." Carli looked to see if she had heard him right, to which Grant nodded.

"Congratulations," he said. "Let's celebrate. What do you say to dinner at week's end?" The old Grant was back. But Henry was still missing. And somewhere between them slinked a threatening stranger.

TWENTY

GRANT ARRIVED at Carli's wearing a spring tweed jacket, Oxford shirt so well pressed it looked new, and brown Oxford tie shoes, which also looked new. "To Lucy," he said, handing Carli a single white rose. "And to Cedric," he added, leaning to kiss her on the forehead. Grant was intent on the evening's details and didn't notice Carli's eyes solidly affixed to his every move.

"The best place in town is the piers," he claimed. They caught a ride to the edge of Manhattan to dine within view of the Statue of Liberty and New York's rippling harbor.

"What's new?" he asked, once seated at an oversized table for two.

"Nothing. Some things change. A lot doesn't."

"Gets stagnant sometimes," said Grant, "but mosquitoes need stagnant water. Their season's coming up fast here," he added.

"What are you talking about?" she asked.

"Oh, nothing." The arrival of drinks interrupted their conversation. Grant proposed a toast. "To Cedric. God rest his soul. I mean, may he long find peace inside ... resting. And, to you." Grant rattled Carli's glass. "Knew the minute I saw you with that chowder that I wanted you with me." Carli stared, frozen by his gaze. "It's not that I wanted Lucy to die, but I did want to meet you again." Grant seemingly tried to backtrack. "You know what I mean, right?" Grant smiled and shrugged at the same time that he turned his palms upward, and added, "What? You reminded me of someone. It was that split second you turned from the chowder bin," he said. "I thought you were my ex-wife, but only for that second." Grant quickly changed the subject. "I want you to be the first to know. Next winter, I'm shooting for another atrium."

"Huh?"

"They're going to love it," he said.

Carli was stunned, once again, and unable to speak. He had jolted her with both thoughts, but it proved only the start of an awkward meal with extremely disjointed conversation. Grant continued to speak of atriums, street lives, and the piers. Through it all, he sipped scotch and occasionally pulled a breath mint from his tweed pocket to pop in his mouth. He crushed the mints forcibly, grinding them with his molars and nervously swallowing the pieces.

"Do you ever stay in bed all day? Just slip under the sheets, all clean, and stay all day and all night?" he asked.

"Haven't done that," she said. "Unless I was sick."

Grant let it drop.

"Short walk?" he asked. The park was nearly empty.

"Ah, look at her!" Grant's eyes surfed across the choppy waves to Lady Liberty, with her sparkling lights and verdigris shroud. He released a hefty sigh.

"She's beautiful," said Carli. She had never seen the statue from so close at night.

Grant handed her a pair of vintage binoculars. "Those scopes never work," he said, nodding at the viewers on the promenade. "Got these at the thrift shop. Probably from someone's estate. I'm sure whoever owned them had ten other pairs."

Masking tape patched the strap together. Carli focused on the statue, and Grant began reciting. "Give us your tired, your poor, your indigent, your downtrodden, your huddled masses … God knows we have a number of those here." His tone changed. "Just look around, Liberty. Look around."

Carli pulled the glasses from her face. He was taking liberties. With the inscription on the Statue of Liberty. What was going on?

Grant stared at her. "What's the matter? We have poor. We have indigent. We have downtrodden. In fact, I'd say we're doing a damned good job of collecting, wouldn't you?" Carli suddenly felt the weight of Lady Liberty's two hundred and twenty-five steel tons plunging through her chest. Canada, Sarah, and Wilson had all been tossed through rough waves, but why was Grant bringing it up now?

Peering through the binoculars again, she stated boldly, "We have them all right. It's up to us to help."

"Well, my dear, there's no second verse with instruction on that, but, hey, I think we can do it – give this Mother of Exiles a second verse."

Carli heard Grant fiddling with his jacket. The next moment, he was blocking her view. As she lowered the binoculars from her face, she stiffened and nearly dropped them to the ground. Grant balanced perilously on a grouping of three wooden posts. They jutted upward several feet from the depths of the water. Each post looked barely wide enough for a seagull to rest upon, yet Grant was on them, a good three feet from land. Grant's jacket lay in a heap near her feet. As he raised his arms to the sky, his shirt billowed out behind him like a sail catching wind. Waves chopped against the posts and sent water splashing over his shoes.

"Grant, what are you doing? Come back on land!"

Grant laughed. "I'm getting a better view."

"Grant, please ..."

"Give me your tired. Give me your poor. Give me ... oh Christ, just give 'em all to me. I'm ready. We have shelters. We have drop-ins. We have work programs. We have lunch lines." His voice broke into a cynical laugh. "We have two-for-one sales. We have discounts. Bargains. Don't hold back. We're ready for them." He slapped his arms down to his sides and addressed Carli directly. "We're ready, right?" Before she could answer, Grant started broadcasting again. "Yessiree. ... Oh, Carli, I love it when it's like this out here." His energy and mood had refocused.

"Please, Grant ..." Wind whipped against her face. "Come down ... or ... sit. Yes, sit."

"On a beautiful night like this? No way." He held his arms straight out, with his head nearly straight back. "Just look at those clouds. Like a herd of flying carpets. They're moving. Wish I could jump on one and go." A gust of wind caught Grant. He jerked his head down from the sky and waved his arms for balance.

"Henry! No!" Carli froze. She hadn't meant to say it.

Grant turned his head toward her. "Say what? Can't hear you."

Dear God, she thought.

"Grant, I'm going to call ... for help. We need help. If you don't come down, I'm leaving."

"Go ahead and yell, but you're safe with me."

"Anybody? Can anybody hear me?" Wind carried her words uptown. "Help! Is anybody here? We need help!" She waited in silence, then called again. "We need help! Is anyone around?"

A voice suddenly sounded. "Hey, man. You crazy? Get down from there." The stranger moved toward Carli. She nearly cried.

"Can't you see it's dangerous out there?" the man asked.

"Heyyy, want to join me?" asked Grant.

The man extended his hand across the watery gap, and Grant instinctively responded with an outstretched arm of his own. The two barely locked fingers before the stranger's handshake turned into a sharp tug. It brought Grant lurching forward and falling to the ground on top of the man.

"What'd you do that for?" asked Grant.

"Didn't your mother ever tell you not to climb on things like this?"

"I was fine," said Grant.

"You weren't thinking of jumping, were you?" asked the stranger. "Water's mighty rough around here tonight and gets deep mighty fast. Currents can run the water out in no time and take a body with them. Not a good place to get wet."

"I love this place," said Grant. "No worries, mate."

"Sure," said the stranger. "But you scared your lady, here, half to death." Turning to Carli, he said, "Best bet is to get him home."

Shaking his head, he added, "Haven't seen anyone do this for a while. Long while." Home, thought Carli. If the stranger only knew.

From the sidewalk in front of her building, Carli watched the cab with Grant slide away from the curb. It wouldn't matter to the driver that his next stop would be a storage facility. Too bad she couldn't tell him she knew. As soon as she stepped into her apartment, she dropped to her knees.

TWENTY-ONE

CARLI HALF-EXPECTED Grant to stand her up for having hauled him off the piers. Instead, she found him ready to tackle some of their Outreach visits together, as Carli had requested. Grant was definitely her brother. She needed to learn more, and figure out how to help. She was definitely in deep.

"Sleep okay the other night?" she asked, leaving St. Mary's.

"The city hardly sleeps a wink, and neither do I. Can't afford to. Vera needs a pillow, by the way. I saw her after I dropped you off, on my way back down to the piers."

Carli stopped walking. "You went back down?"

"Sure. I needed to see Canada. Had to tell him about a new Chinese restaurant that makes an excellent egg roll. The driver didn't care. He got a bigger fare. Took me to Vera, Canada, and then home. I tell you, that man was born to drive. Rishad Agoul. Good ol' Rishad. Bet he would've taken me to Harry and Sarah if I'd have asked."

"Rishad?" asked Carli.

"Pretty sure that was his name. I've got his picture at my place," said Grant.

"Picture?" she asked.

"Yeah, from his cab. Nice touch, don't you think?"

"Grant, you stole his ID."

"Nah. It was like a business card. I'm going to call him next time."

"Grant, I'm telling you, you took his ID. He needs it back." Carli stared, as she did many times over the next week. No one else seemed to notice. In fact, most everyone found Grant a welcomed spark of life roaring into their lives, even if he reeked of muddled conversation.

"Grant, your mints aren't working," she said finally.

Grant smiled. "That bad? I tried this new cordial last night, and the taste *really* stays with you. Won't happen again."

"No, Grant. It's not only the mints. It's all of you. What is wrong?" asked Carli.

"Wrong? Nothing," he said. "Everything's good. Will I see you tomorrow?"

"Yes." Clearly, a reasonable conversation was impossible. Nothing could have prepared her for this.

Though smelling less like alcohol or mints over the next days, Grant continued to race through visits. Carli finally pulled him to a halt with a tug on his shirt. The sound of fabric ripping in her hands stopped them both.

"What's going on? You aren't acting right," said Carli. "And I need answers."

"Not acting right? Who says what's right?" asked Grant. "Suppose we lived in some remote landscape ... or one of those tree house platforms in a tropical rain forest. What would be right, then? All these people living outside might be right because housing wouldn't have the same meaning. They'd be sleeping outside in the forest, and we'd be out there, and Madison and Sarah would be doing just fine out there. No one would bother them, not even us, because it would be okay and we'd all be acting right. As far as I'm concerned, all these other people dressed in their designer fabrics, cut into shapes known as suits, droning to cubicles or corner desks, are the ones who aren't acting right. Sitting at a desk isn't normal. If it were, all the other animals would be doing it, but they aren't. So, what's right? It's all relative, Carli."

"Your drinking is noticeable," said Carli. "You're all over the place." She tried to talk as gently as possible. "I think it might help for you to see someone, a professional."

"For what?" he asked.

"For how you're acting. I'll go with you if you like. I know a good doctor."

Grant stared. It was deadly. Finally, he said, "Tomorrow?"

Carli nodded.

"Tomorrow I'm booked," he said. "Have to see my agent. Booked solid."

Carli closed her eyes, only to feel his hands pressing on her shoulders. "I'm fine. Trust me," said Grant. "Every so often a person has to let go. Speaking of go, I have to check on Cedric."

Grant was nearly at the light, while Carli remained fixed to the sidewalk, both fuming and defeated. She steered her way to Sarah.

As soon as Carli said hello, Sarah pulled a wad of newspaper from one of her bags and began unravelling the limp paper packaging. Buffy's picture was framed. It had a piece of plastic to cover and cardboard for backing. Together, they gently held Buffy on display in a recycled frame with a faux wood decal finish.

"Beautiful," said Carli. Sarah tried to smile, but smiling didn't come easily to her. "Buffy will last longer like this. Nice."

Sarah nodded, then rewrapped Buffy's portrait and put the bird away. She glanced at Carli and then stepped slowly to the far end of the bench, seeming to leave her bags entrusted to Carli's care. Carli watched intently. Sarah slowly walked toward the man vending popcorn. Her legs were swollen like bloated zucchinis, the result of too much time with her legs in a vertical position. Sarah needed a bed to reduce the edema.

Sarah seemed to agonize over a possible purchase. No one stood in line in front of her, but she was unable to step to the counter. For the several minutes that Sarah stood, Carli turned her thoughts to Grant. His illness, or addiction, was out of wraps, just like Buffy. How close to being like Sarah was he? She recalled the clutter of his storage room as she glanced at Sarah's bags. It was no wonder he knew the system and understood their problems. Dear God, she thought.

Sarah hobbled to her fortress, having made the leap. Sarah tossed a few pieces of popcorn to the ground. In a flutter, the pigeons arrived. Sarah continued looking straight ahead when Carli said, "I have to leave," but her expression seemed to change ever so slightly to reveal a hint of disappointment.

———

Carli opened her apartment door, and Grant walked in. "Nice place," he said.

"I'm glad you made it," said Carli. She knew it was risky, and wished she hadn't felt the need to put Kristin and Mercy on notice that he was coming for a visit, but she was willing to give it a try. Dr. Greenberg had given her an idea, even though she hadn't precisely endorsed it. Thankfully, Grant looked clean-shaven and didn't smell of alcohol. "I was pretty sure you'd want to say goodbye to them before we took them to Thelma," she said, "and without all the commotion going on with Lucy's service." Just as Carli finished speaking, Lila and Terrance came skidding out of the bedroom. "Speaking of the devils," said Carli.

Grant squatted down. "Hey ... hey guys," he said. Lila and Terrance wagged and wiggled, happy to have a visitor. Grant patted each of them as they pranced. "They look great. Like real dogs. Yes, you do. Yes, you do. Real dogs. That's you," he said.

"They definitely remember you," she said.

"Of course, you do," said Grant, still talking with the dogs. "You guys are lucky little hounds, yes. Lucky little L and T. That's who you are."

"Come, let's sit. No need to squat," said Carli. "They'll follow. Might even jump onto your lap."

Carli led the way to the living room, with Grant and the dogs following. After several more minutes of watching Lila and Terrance, Carli drew Grant's attention to a table of family photos. "That was my old dog," she said. Grant looked at the photograph and nodded. Carli looked carefully at Grant. "He was amazing," she said. Grant continued to look at the photograph. He shifted his eyes to the other photographs sitting alongside the first. Carli had placed several images of young Henry and Tessie alongside her picture of Tura. Mom and Dad in a family portrait, a couple of shots of the neighborhood, and one of their home completed the collection. Grant seemed deep in thought. Carli watched in silence. Finally, Grant said, "Nice dog." It wasn't what she wanted to hear.

"You said you had a dog," said Carli. "What was he like?"

Grant slowly shook his head. He turned back to the photographs but said nothing.

Carli found herself rubbing her thumbs together to quell her nervous energy. Grant continued looking at the photographs.

"He was gentle," said Grant. "Sort of calm for a dog. Not like these little terrier types. Lila and Terrance, I mean. He'd follow me around, pretty much anywhere, and lie down and sleep or watch. I think he used to fetch a tennis ball, but don't really remember."

Carli remembered. She remembered a lot. Bonaventura fetched plenty of tennis balls and alternated between calm and fully-loaded dog. He used to chase a lot of things, squirrels included, but enjoyed a nice long nap too. Mostly, he looked to participate in whatever was going on. The front porch, where he slept in the photo, was his favorite spot from spring to fall. From several feet above street level, he could keep cool in the shade and oversee all the neighborhood action. Often, Carli's porch was the center of activity; a place for cards, checkers, and popsicles. During the winter, Tura shifted between the kitchen and living room floors, depending on where people were congregating. Tura was not particularly independent.

Grant gazed at the photographs another few moments. "I was trying to protect you," he said very slowly. "I know who you are."

Carli took in a short breath and tensed. She lifted her phone from her chair and prepared to hit speed dial.

"I wish I didn't have to do it," he said.

"Do ... what?" she asked, ready to jump.

"You know, leave you," said Grant.

"What do you mean?" she asked. "You need to leave now?"

"No, crazy ..." Grant gave an outburst of a laugh. He turned toward Carli and showed a slight smile. "I meant before. In college."

"Oh, my God," whispered Carli. "It *is* you."

"Yes, Tessie. It is."

Grant stared at Carli and slowly began to open his arms, inviting a hug. Carli wanted to run right into him but remained still. Tears streamed from her eyes and she couldn't move a foot forward. All she could do was stare. Henry was finally back.

"I can't believe I found you," she said. "Why did you say you didn't have a sister?" she asked. "And you didn't know me? Why did you say I was from the cult and poisoning people? Oh, my God. It's you, Henry. It really is you." Carli finally opened her arms and moved forward to embrace him with all the power she had within. "I missed you," she said. "And I worried enough to last hundreds of lifetimes. Oh, my God, did we ever worry. Where have you been?"

Grant seemed to be holding in tears, but Carli soon felt several soaking through the shirt covering her shoulder. "I missed you," he said. "I really did. Mom and Dad too. But I couldn't go back. And I couldn't tell you that."

"What do you mean?" she asked. "We looked for you. Day after day. Year after year. We needed you. What happened?"

"I couldn't lead the Nirvu to your doorstep," he said.

Carli stepped back a step, rattled to hear him speak of the cult by name again. "I don't understand."

"You're shaking," said Grant. "Are you okay?"

"I need to sit," said Carli. "This is a lot to take in. And you knew me ... but didn't say anything."

"I had to make sure."

"I can't believe it's you," said Carli. "I mean, I knew it was, when you talked about Tura in the park, but, like I said, I still don't know why you said you didn't know me."

"I didn't know you. Not until the Meadow. I was shocked. I don't understand your name change."

"That makes us even," she said. "Why are you Grant?"

"I told you, I had to protect you. From them. If they knew I was alive, that Henry was alive, they would have gone straight to Mom, Dad, and you ... with a plan – an ugly plan – to get me back, and then likely kill me," he said. "Might have killed you three as well."

"What? ... Why?"

"I learned pretty early on that things going down in that group were bad. And I mean bad."

"We got the message," said Carli. "The FBI was investigating them for human trafficking. The Bureau tracked us down."

"That's what I mean. If the Bureau could find you, they could too. It was a creepy group. Not what I signed up for. My friends were there one day and gone the next. I didn't know what happened to them. That explains it."

"They told us it was global," said Carli.

"Figures," said Grant. "They had a lot of different nationalities slipping in and out. Like I said, instinct told me I had to get myself out of there. Fast. I didn't know exactly why. It wasn't like I could ask to leave, and they'd just open the door," said Grant. "No, I had to escape. It was the only way. I left a note. Said I was going off to kill myself because I didn't feel worthy of the cult. I said no one would ever find my body. Snuck out in the night. It took a couple of weeks to get away. Hiding. Running. Hiding again. I thought they might not care. Might not come looking. I didn't fit in with them. Thought they might be happy to lose me. But they cared. I heard them, at least five times, out looking." Grant sat for a moment, as though reflecting on the chase. Carli couldn't believe he had hidden like a hunted animal. Grant looked up. "I saw them poison two who tried to leave. Gave them tea. Laced with poison. They watched them slowly die. And then they laughed." Grant quieted and closed his eyes. Finally, he said, "Henry had to die. And he couldn't ever go home. Couldn't ever lead them to you. Or Mom. Or Dad."

Carli tried to nod, but couldn't move. As though sensing the severity of the situation, Lila and Terrance placed their heads to the ground between their outstretched paws and stared, wide-eyed, but silent. Carli's apartment had never felt so still.

"I can't ever be Henry again," said Grant.

"I get it," said Carli. "I get it," she said more quietly. "But it sounded like the Feds got to them," she finally added.

"I'm not risking it," he said. "Not risking it."

Carli nodded ever so slightly. Henry was dead.

"And I'm never calling you Tessie again. If the wrong person hears it, we might both be dead."

It was a concession she could make. But his argument seemed riddled with holes.

"Why'd you change your name?" asked Grant.

Carli told Grant about TSW Inc. and her previous concerns about the Church Run.

All Grant said was, "You always were the Chicken Little of the neighborhood."

It was exactly what Carli needed to hear. It was also exactly what she expected to hear from Henry. She would have been happy to not say another word, but she ventured into another dark crag. "Speaking of neighborhood," she said. "Where do you live now? You get out to see everyone so easily that, for a while, I wondered if you were living downstairs here."

"That would be the day," said Grant. "No, this is definitely out of my price zone. I'm over on Lexington Ave., 184. A nice second-floor penthouse. Well, not really a penthouse, of course. But plenty good for me."

"Have you been there a while?" she asked.

"No. Still kind of moving in."

"Moving's a lot of work. Especially here, in the city."

"A lot of work anywhere," he said. "Unless you're running for your life and leave everything behind."

Carli continued to gaze at Grant. He, too, stared back. "I can't believe I finally found you," she said. Then, she lightly touched his arm. "How are you doing? You've had me worried."

"Worried?" he asked. "How so?"

"You know ... you were drinking during the day. That doesn't sound healthy."

"I'm fine," he said. "Not to worry. Seems you've done enough worrying about me, like you said. I'll be fine."

Carli studied his face. She knew she was looking at another "case." "I'm here to help. You know that, right?"

Grant nodded. A resigned smile rose, but he was struggling. "Mercy already talked with me. Gave me the name of a place. I'll be okay," he said.

"There's something else," said Carli. "I confided in Mercy. Someone else, too. I told them I had found you."

"What? No!" Grant sat upright, fully alert. "Tell them you were wrong. Tell them your brother is dead. And don't tell anyone else. I'm telling you; that fucking cult is still here somewhere."

"Okay," said Carli. "Okay. It will be all right. I'll tell them." She touched his arm again, and said, "I'll be safe. You will be too." As Carli's words sounded across her apartment, she couldn't help but question herself. She had always been able to trust him. What if they were still looking? For both of them. Being together *would* make it that much easier for them. But could she have sunk so low as to lose faith in a minister – Pastor Miller? In Mercy, whose every hour was spent helping others? And in Kristen? No, Kristen was a sister.

TWENTY-TWO

CARLI WENT to Lucy's service alone. Grant never called, never showed. Lucy had been in Elmsville for several months, but the ladies of the town wanted an outside tent gathering. It pushed the formal service into June. Carli missed most of the service, with fears and questions about Grant plaguing her thoughts. In fact, she was close to panic mode. Had he run, she wondered, now that he knew she was his sister? Now that he knew she had talked about him? Would she find him when she returned to the city? And how had she missed it all? First thing upon her return, she would confront him again, in front of Cooper's Storage, if need be. Now, more than ever, she prayed for strength.

Carli navigated the first ten minutes of her drive back to the city through a curtain of tears. Leaving Lila and Terrance made her life feel empty. Had it not been for the cheerful sight of early roses on the edge of the roadways, she might have cried longer. But she had other concerns as well. Every so often, she glanced at drivers in nearby cars to see if they were looking her way. Several times, she contemplated the cult as she checked her rearview mirror. Finally, she told herself to pull herself together. That didn't stop her from veering off the highway at a different exit than usual to head to Grant's apartment. She needed to know he was safe and still in town after his no-show.

Grant's building was a somewhat older building, with a few exterior cosmetic updates. She was surprised to see a doorman sitting behind a counter.

"I'm here to see Grant ... uh, Grant on the second floor." Carli suddenly realized she didn't know her brother's last name.

"On the second floor?" asked the man.

"Yes."

"Had a man named Grant there for a while. But he's gone now," said the man.

"Gone?" Carli's voice filled with fear.

"That's right."

"Did he just leave? This morning?" asked Carli.

"No, no. The owner rents it out as a week to week. I think Grant was here for a week. Maybe two. Sometime back. Now, it's someone else. Nice couple. Came in a little while ago, maybe a week or so. They're here 'til the end of the month, I think."

"He's not here anymore? Grant, I mean?" asked Carli.

"No ma'am."

Carli called Kristin on her way home and found her friend waiting outside her building when she arrived.

"How was it?" asked Kristin.

"You don't want to know. But I'm telling you everything, like always. We have a lot of catching up to do. Come on in. I'll tell you when we get in my apartment."

Carli and Kristin rode the elevator in silence. As soon as Carli opened her door, Carli's tears rolled down her cheeks. "I need a dog," she said. "Two dogs. You won't believe what's gone on here."

Kristin listened to news of Grant and of Lucy's memorial. Together, they searched for weekly apartment rentals and found the second-floor unit listed as a short-term rental, exactly as the doorman had said.

"Why do you think he told me that?"

"Why do you think?" asked Kristin.

"Right," said Carli, thinking of Grant's storage room. "Right. But he did actually rent it. For a week or two."

"So, what are you going to do?" asked Kristin.

Carli lifted her head out of her hands and said, "First, I'm going to cry with my friend and have a glass of wine. At least, I found him, and he's alive. But right now, I almost wish I weren't."

"How was it?" Grant asked, meeting Carli at St. Mary's.

"Final goodbyes are never easy," she said. Grant looked marginally better than the day he dumped his tray in front of the lunch crowd. "It's the right place for her," she continued. "And for Lila and Terrance."

Grant barely nodded.

"I met Lucy's doctor," she said. "He did what he could."

"With her diabetes, you mean?"

"Yes. Lucy did the rest."

"Like all of them."

"Nobody likes a faulty body," she started, giving Grant a fiery stare. She nearly reopened the doctor issue, but stopped.

"Why didn't you come with me?" she asked.

"Overslept," said Grant.

"Overslept? Have you been making visits?"

Grant gave a fairly lifeless shake of his head. "I gave myself a vacation. Call it a long weekend."

"Grant, you don't look so good. You really should see a doctor."

"No. Drop it. I'm fine." His voice was defensive.

"Grant, I mean it."

"I'll check them tonight."

Carli watched Grant leave the church, presumably to settle into bed, since it didn't look like he could do much else. Then she made another trip to Four Bridges.

"He needs help," said Carli.

"That place where I got you the appointment does well with things like this – drugs, disorders, or both," said Mercy. "You know it's a private place and keeps everything anonymous. Do you think he'll go?"

"He wouldn't consider it when I brought it up. He snapped at me and shut down."

"Most don't want to hear it," said Mercy. "No, they don't see it in themselves. Or just don't want to. They usually either go the denial route or the super-sensitive, don't-talk-to-me-about-it route. But Grant, he's seen so much of it ..."

"He didn't go to Lucy's service either. Didn't call. Nothing. But I just saw him at St. Mary's, and he said he gave himself a vacation. I'm worried it's related to his visit with me." said Carli.

"On account of his learning you're his sister, you mean?"

"Right." After Grant's cult admonition, Carli felt uneasy speaking about her relationship to Grant.

"Maybe. Maybe not. It's not totally surprising he skipped out," said Mercy. "He probably figures he did what he could. I doubt he felt any reason to dwell on something he couldn't change. Maybe he's already done his grieving. He hasn't been by here for a while, either." Mercy paused. "You've got my cell; in case you need me. Or just plain want me," she said. "Same difference. Day or night."

"When he does stop in here, remember he doesn't want you, or anyone, knowing I'm his sister," said Carli.

"I'll remember. When he stops in, or if he happens to return my calls, it sounds like the first thing I'll be doing is presenting him with the Avenue Partners option again," said Mercy. "In the meantime, you keep taking care of yourself. Yes, indeed. Number One is you." Mercy's face sparkled, with the lipstick du jour, a deep, earthy maroon, making a particularly vocal statement. It matched her dress, of course.

Carli took her sketchpad to the piers on an impulse. She looked at Lady Liberty, but she soon found herself sketching the piers instead.

Maybe she would add them to her show. The waves sounded like silly laughter, causing her to pause. She sat a long while, listening to the foolhardy water, suddenly flooded with memories of her youthful Henry. In turn, she considered the others. Who were they once? Before they were here. How had they all been lost? How had Henry been lost? She wanted to fill in the pieces. Carli looked forward to her afternoon visit with Dr. Greenberg. She had much to discuss.

———————

After she visited Dr. Greenberg, Carli knew, more clearly than ever, that Grant needed to make an appointment. Such an odd thought for two kids from her middle-class family. Two days later, she raised the subject again.

"If I go to the doctor, will you call off the dogs?" asked Grant.

"Yes."

"Fine then." As far as Grant was concerned, no help was needed, but he agreed to let Carli make the appointment. Then, Grant skipped out on his appointment and vanished the entire week after. When Carli finally reached him, he seemed to sense he should give it a try. Carli helped schedule another appointment.

When appointment day arrived, Carli made sure to walk Grant to Avenue Partners. Approaching the building, he suddenly put his hand on Carli's shoulder and said, "Hey, I feel fine. Let's go to the park instead."

Without a word, she pressed the call buzzer and escorted him inside. Damned if he wasn't right; going to the park sounded more fun. Carli left Grant and spent the next hours trying to think of anything else but him. She had told the doctor everything she knew. She had described the piers, alcohol, and bouts of withdrawal and mania. All Carli could do now was wait and pray, a hostage to circumstance. Then it dawned on her. Again. The antidote. She ran to Avenue Partners, hoping to arrive in time.

She caught up with Grant seemingly seconds after he emerged onto the sidewalk. As expected, he seemed distracted by internal thought. No doubt he had come face to face with some difficult notions. It took a long, quiet minute before he was able to push himself out of his closed steel shell.

"She gave me this booklet to fill out," he said.

"I got one too. When I went in," said Carli. "Background information. It helps."

"Maybe she could just use yours. Don't want to spend my life answering questions."

"Do what you can." She offered to help, knowing simple paperwork might seem insurmountable if Grant were clinically depressed.

"I have to get blood tests too," he said. "This all seems pretty worthless."

"She wouldn't order them without reason," said Carli. "An easy answer would be nice, rather than a bunch of tests and appointments. But it will take time. She's already been a big help to me."

"That's just it. I don't have time," he repeated. "And I don't think it'll do diddlysquat."

Grant was acting just like Cedric. No matter. He needed help, and needed someone he trusted to support him and gently nudge him along.

"I'm walking you home," she said softly, knowing Grant's answer before she said it.

"No need," he said.

"I have to." She could tell he hurt. "I can't walk away this time. I can't turn my back on my brother. I have to help."

"No. I really don't want that."

"I know you don't, but I know better. I know about Cooper's Storage. Let me walk you home. There's no reason to hide from me. I want to help."

Grant stared her down, showing no specific emotion, but Carli knew plenty had raced through him. All he said was, "I'm going," and he darted through cars to the other side of the street. Carli stood watching, and believing she might never see her brother again.

She hailed a taxi after Grant disappeared, and headed to the storage unit, not to talk, but to make certain he made it home. There was no telling what she had just done or what it might cause him to do. It was so damned hard being patient. A good block from Cooper's, she slammed shut the car door and slid into the alcove of a quiet building across the street. For almost an hour, she squatted in the shadows, her legs aching from their contorted pressure. Finally, she watched Grant arrive home by foot, with a familiar brown bag tucked comfortably under his arm. He scanned the neighborhood before crossing the threshold. She would wait ten minutes and leave.

When Carli straightened slowly, she was unaware Grant had slid back outside.

"Hey!" he yelled. "Wait!" He held a bushel of clothes in his arms, clearly headed for the laundromat. "What are you doing here?" he asked.

"I'm leaving," she said. Grant stared her down. "Just wanted to know you were okay."

Surprisingly, he said, "Don't go," his anger gone. "It's been a long day, and I don't like surprises."

"That makes two of us, and I've had a few of them lately."

"You tried to help. I get it. Thanks." Carli smelled the alcohol, of course. "Come on in," he said.

Grant was silent as he led her inside.

"Why are you living here?" she asked.

"What I want to know is how you knew." Carli didn't want to admit she had followed him and spied, but Grant took the news well.

"The house doesn't make the man," he said. "It's common sense and simple economics. I could pay many more hundreds of dollars a month for a single room, shared bath, peculiar neighbors, and be strapped for the rest of my life. Or, I could grind it out on the subway, smelling everybody's end-of-the-day grime and inseam odors, only to live at the end of the line with a roommate who does God knows what. I'm not the roommate type, and it would make it harder to keep track of them. Disability? No. Housing run by corrupt landlords doesn't work for me either." He took a deep breath. "And neither did living on the streets." His words fell on her like a lead anchor, and she must have shown it.

"Yes, I was on the streets." He spoke slowly, and dispassionately, like the steady roll of a clothes dryer's drum. "A year and a half on the streets. How do you think I know them so well? Not individually, but the street sleepers and The Sweepers, in general. I know what they feel, what they see, hear, and go through." He stared at Carli and nodded slowly.

"One day, I got myself in. A couple of months before Mercy showed up. She knows, but no one else inside, not anymore. Outside, yes. I'm their example. Look at Rocky. He followed me in."

Carli swallowed. Confidential *had* been Mercy's middle name. She hesitated, and then asked, "Where did you sleep?" Grant stared, as though assessing her ability to handle the facts. She asked again, "Where?"

"With Madison. Midtown Synagogue. It was safer then. Less crowded too." Carli closed her eyes a few seconds. Then, gazing at the metal storage room wall, she reached a hand in his direction. It caught him on the shoulder.

"Yeah," he said, sighing deeply enough to raise and lower her hand, "there's a lot you don't know. Nobody knows."

It was like Lucy's dogs; she was compelled to follow.

"Why did you go in?"

"Hah!" Grant's voice echoed back to life. "That's the easy part of the story."

Carli waited.

"I ended up in a crack house. Didn't mean to. I was looking for a new place to stay and hadn't hooked into this place yet. Madison told me there was a place somewhere around there, with a roof, no tenants, etcetera. As soon as I walked in, I knew I was in the wrong place. There was a whole group of them, a whole bunch of knives, a couple of guns, and a shot went off. Somehow, I was running faster than I knew I ever could, and they missed me. After that, I figured I'd been given another life, and I'd better use it. Funny how little things can change a man's perspective." A grin rose on his face.

Carli felt her knees weaken. "You sold drugs, with Canada?" she asked. "That why you two are so close?"

"Actually, I played chess for a living, and sold a few pints of blood."

"Blood? Chess?" she asked.

His grin vanished. "Sure. In the park. Near the piers. I could take money off of everyone, especially with a few beers in me." His voice spiked with excitement. "It was like I saw the entire game in front of me as soon as the other guy made his first move."

"A gambler," said Carli.

"I was good. Still am."

"You gambled with me too."

"Had a feeling." He suddenly jumped topics. "Carli, I don't have many options. I found one that works, at least for now. My ten-by-fourteen's only two hundred and fifty bucks, with heat, water, electricity, and privacy included. Sometimes I pay the guard extra to keep a lid on it, call it a bonus. His name's Neuman, by the way. If I have to move, there are a couple of others to choose from." He paused for a moment, then said, "That's why I don't want doctors, tests, change. I have what I can handle, and it's all I can handle. I know that. I've got stuff going on. I know. Ever since that fuckin' cult. I know."

"How can you work with them, and not with yourself?"

"How? Just can. I choose to. I'm not your average guy. Surely you see that."

"Grant, the house doesn't make the person, but it's the person I'm worried about. I don't want you to stay like this. There has to be a better solution. Sometimes you're all over the place, sometimes you are fighting to get out of bed. It would have been nice to get an easy answer today; neatly wrapped, no rough edges, and no question marks. But it doesn't work that way. It takes time. You, of all people, know this. Give this a chance. Please."

Grant looked at her for a long while, but she knew he wasn't looking at her at all. Knew he was looking inside himself.

"Carli, let me tell you about testing. Let me tell you about giving it a chance." He was suddenly on fire. "I went to the doctor for you. No other reason but to get you off my goddamned back. Neither you nor the doctor knows the half of it."

Carli braced herself.

"You want to know about hospitals? About rehab centers? You want to know about me? Dear God, woman! Here it is. I'm only going over it once, so listen carefully." His sudden anger was threatening. She checked the distance to the bin's door.

"I've been inside every hospital you can name, either with so-called clients or by myself. But that's getting ahead." His voice calmed. "I was married. Once upon a time, I was a lawyer. I told you about my job, but I don't think you believed me." Grant retrieved a business card and newspaper clipping to share as proof that he had both passed the bar and been an up-and-coming person in the field. Carli wasn't surprised he had managed to legally change his name, finish college, and study law online and in person. Wasn't surprised at all. He was always so damned gifted.

"Now I'll tell you about me, what I didn't tell the doctor. Way back, we used to work hard and play hard. Drank and snorted, just about every last one of us. I was good at what I did, like I said, and loved the game, loved the ride. We all did. We were big, and I mean big. The whole scene was a giant high. After about ten years of it, they put me in detox, my friends did. Thought I should dry out. So, I did, and they thought it worked, but I'm really good at staying functional. They welcomed me home, I did the usual shit and then got bored. The fun was gone. So, I told my wife I was given a bonus vacation, which she believed, of course. Sometime in there, I met a shrink. We talked and he prescribed. I was officially depressed, but the stuff he gave me landed me in a psych ward. Had a bizarre reaction. Don't know how long I was there, and don't care. Sometime around then, I got some other stuff to take and went back to work. Going to AA, I got beat into believing all drugs were bad, so I stopped taking it. Going to AA was part of the deal for staying on the job. Anyway, they said work was slipping. Without billable hours, I was booted. Lousy bastards just shut me out, even though I know many of them must still be on plenty of stuff. Look at Madison's clientele, for chrissake. Anyway, I was out. Out of work, love, marriage, out of my mind, but no one else could see what was wrong. I guess I rebelled and tried to start a new life by myself, without the rules. It was one hell of a mental crisis and midlife crisis, and I hadn't hit midlife. The thing of it is, it wasn't altogether awful. Think my wife was glad to see me go. Maybe the kids too. Two boys."

Carli couldn't believe it. She was an aunt. And she had never met her nephews, let alone her brother's wife. Dear God.

"Basically, I drifted," said Grant. "Lived with a friend for a while, but then I decided to see the big apple pie from a different vantage point. Something about the Statue of Liberty that I had to see. Anyway, I wanted to see how long I could live without a paycheck, see how nice people were. It was just another game and a change from all the people who weren't so nice. Call it another gamble. And I was up for it. First night, tried a shelter. Second, third, same thing, all okay. By the fourth night, I thought I had the system down. Figured I'd hang out as long as I wanted, freeloading by day, sheltering it by night. Only that's the night I watched some guy get his coat slit open, and part of his body with it. So, it was good riddance to the shelter and hello sidewalks. Hard to believe it looked better, 'cause, God, was I scared. Slept by day, and stayed up all night, like a bunch of them. After a while, I figured I ought to do something steady for food money. Tried a bunch of things – courier, sidewalk tie sales, though not all legal. Tried driving a car but had a couple of close calls with wrecks. My favorite was selling peanuts at the stadium."

Grant shifted position, looking more animated.

"Yessiree. Peanuts in the park. Got to see all the games. Got a whole lot of baseballs in here somewhere." Grant glanced around his bin. "Found beer when I had to, and boy did I sell." He lifted his arm in the air and waved it holding an invisible bag of peanuts. "I'm nuts! I'm nuts!" his voice boomed. "Get your nuts here."

"You didn't."

"Absolutely. In the face of competition, you have to make a name for yourself. After a while, I got tired of being out there at certain hours. Basically, lost another job. I had a great idea to scalp a whole bunch of tickets but was nabbed, and they took the tickets without paying. Lousy bums probably sold them themselves. Before you know it, I was out, completely, with Canada and chess. You know the rest."

The bin was so silent she heard the air moving in her ears.

"Look, I drink sometimes," he said.

Carli closed her eyes for a moment, as a tear welled. "Did you tell the doctor?"

"I told you, I went for you. As for me, I know I have crap. I ask myself what is wrong with me. I ask that all the time. But I've found a way to beat it. I get by. Forget I even went today. Hell," he said with a laugh, "compared with where I've been, I'm on top of the world."

He reached for her arm. "We can't choose our bodies or our minds. We can only control the extraneous crap like job, zip code, etcetera."

Carli continued to beat back tears. For as much as he had told her, she knew there was likely more he had left out. It didn't matter. What mattered was building a future. For Grant, whoever he was now, she had all the time in the world, and she wasn't going to let him down.

Carli looked over his room, pulling details of items she had only scarcely grasped during her prior flash visit. Sneakers still lined a wall, but the jumble of pizza boxes now crowded the opposite corner. Clothes lay everywhere. How had he selected ones for the laundromat?

"Nice bike," she said, looking at his vintage, thick-tired bicycle.

"Royal? She's quite a roadster." Grant nodded and smiled, as though reminiscing.

"Royal? You named her?"

"Doesn't everybody? Name their bike, that is? I mean, just look at those fenders. Royal blue if I ever saw it. The bike I used for deliveries was stolen long ago, but ol' Royal's been good to me. I'll have to take you out on her sometime."

"One seat and two people? No thanks."

"You've never ridden double before? Wobbled around on those handlebars? Once you get going, you cruise. I mean, really cruise with the weight of two."

"Never have. Thank God," said Carli. "If the Delaney twins taught me one thing in life, it was don't ever ride double."

"Hah! I remember them," said Grant. "Always fighting over who rode and who pedaled. I thought you and I tried it a couple of times."

"I never had the courage," said Carli. "Followed you into a lot of things, but somehow stayed clear of that one."

"Midnight's always the best time to ride," said Grant. "Midnight to about two or three in the morning."

"What? Over my dead body."

"I'll call you sometime. And, don't worry, I'll go slow for starters."

Carli stared at his smile for a long time before asking, "What's with the sneakers?"

"Do a lot of walking. Like you don't know that. Sometimes it's easier to just buy in bulk. In case they get wet or something. I guess I could ditch a few. What do you think?"

"Looks like you could open an outlet store, but I doubt you'll outgrow them."

Grant quieted and looked at Carli a few moments. "You haven't said anything about Mom and Dad."

Carli nodded slightly. "No ... I haven't." She lifted her eyes to his. "Moved," she said. "You know ... how we all used to joke about the neighborhood moving a few blocks over as one after the other moved into the cemetery?"

Grant nodded. He was silent for a few moments. "When?"

"Dad went first. About twenty years ago. Mom, just a few years ago. She would have loved seeing you. Both of them would have. I bet they're looking down on us right now," she said.

Grant reached his hand over to touch Carli's arm. "It's okay. We're all good."

Carli bit her lip and nodded.

"Hey, remember how we used to play Mother-May-I and hide-and-seek in the cemetery?" he asked.

"Memories I'll never forget," she said. "Leaning against those headstones to take cover, and being scared out of my wits that some dead person would spring up and grab me."

"Hah! Me too," said Grant.

"You're kidding." Carli stared. "You always seemed fearless."

"Outside," he said. "Only on the outside."

"Well, holy crap. If that place scared you, it's no wonder I thought I was going to die every time I went in there," said Carli. After a moment of reflection, she said, "We were pretty horrid, the lot of us."

"What do you mean?"

"The way we stomped on Mrs. Ryan's grave? I mean, every time we played in the cemetery, we had fifteen kids jumping on the ground, like we were doing some kind of dance ritual."

"Oh, right. Groundskeeper must have wondered why it was always trampled to smithereens in that one spot," said Grant, laughing as he spoke. "But she was a grump, wasn't she? Didn't like anyone. Never fit in on the street. I remember the grownups talking about her. When she was alive."

"Something must have pushed her to act the way she did," said Carli. "Something must have hurt her pretty bad. Or scared her. Pretty strange in our neighborhood."

"A definite outlier," said Grant. He looked toward the metal ceiling and smirked. "Your dream came true, Mrs. Ryan. We all grew up, and you can finally rest in peace. Sorry for all of the disturbances."

Half an hour later, content with Grant's safety, Carli headed home. Grant headed out with her. "About time I did my laundry and scouted around for a few of the guys," he said.

TWENTY-THREE

CARLI WANTED to run into her studio and close the door shut to the world outside. Time was ticking, and the paint wasn't flowing fast enough to meet her show's timeframe. She looked at her unfinished sketch of Lila and Terrance and recalled them clicking across the wooden floor as she painted, occasionally checking in with gentle nudges to her leg. She hoped they were out for a walk or rolling on a nice green lawn. She smiled. She had done the right thing. It was with this frame of mind that Carli started painting.

Hours later, Carli settled into the corner of her window seat to phone Pastor Miller.

"Thanks again for helping with Lucy," she said. "It was nice to see her home and surrounded by people she knew."

"It certainly brought relief," said Pastor Miller. "Closure is always good. And it was nice to hear of all the good times, as well."

"Yes," said Carli, "it was."

"Thelma, by the way, is mighty happy with your gift of the dogs," he said. "I spoke with her earlier. She's struggling to keep up, but I imagine they'll all adjust."

"I was just thinking of them," said Carli. "I was imagining them taking charge of those expansive lawns. Scampering their hearts out."

"Lovely thoughts, indeed," he said.

"Speaking of closure," said Carli. "I have some news. It's confidential."

"Oh?"

"I found my brother. Henry."

"Oh, my word, Carli. You must be thrilled."

"Yes and no. It's not so simple."

"What do you mean?" he asked.

"He's Grant. As I suspected." Carli let the news sink in.

"Did you say, 'Grant'?"

"Yes. Grant is my brother, but no one can ever call him Henry again. And I will never be Tessie to him." Carli had dismissed the crazy notion that Pastor Miller might be part of the cult, and gave the details of Grant's escape and his continuing attempt to protect her. Then she said, "As far as I can tell, Henry really is gone. Grant is not the person I knew." She neglected to say her brother was living in a self-storage unit.

———

Carli's next impromptu visit to Wilson yielded a single golden nugget. Wilson had studied chemistry. But that was all he shared. He didn't say where he studied, worked, or learned scents. He simply couldn't remember. After sitting quietly for another fifteen minutes, Wilson slurred out a single word. He framed it as a question: "Princeton?" Then he shrugged. Carli watched him settle into another foggy slumber. Finally, she thought. Then she went looking for Vera.

She rounded the corner of Vera's favorite block and stopped. Vera was in her usual spot, standing alongside the standpipe. Another woman stood nearby, and they seemed to be conversing. Maybe she was another Outreach worker, or maybe Vera had a friend, an actual friend. Something Carli knew for certain was she wasn't part of the cult. She also knew the stranger was not part of The Sweep. Carli couldn't quite make out Vera's expressions. Didn't know if she was enjoying the visit. As Carli continued watching, a blue city bus rolled alongside the curb. Several passengers stepped off. Right after, the woman near Vera slowly climbed the four steep steps into the bus, using arm strength and the handrail to ascend. Vera didn't so much as wave. Just settled against the standpipe.

"Vera. Vera Dear-a," said Carli.

A smiling Vera turned to watch her walk the final steps. "And what color socks are you wearing today?" Vera asked.

"You tell me," said Carli. "I don't remember." Together, they inspected Carli's maroon socks, which sort of matched the rest of her attire.

Vera said, "I gave my green ones a break today." She lifted her pant leg to reveal a blue sock on one foot and a yellow sock covering the other. Carli hadn't worn socks this mismatched since Halloween, decades ago.

"What's this?" asked Carli.

"I don't know. Just what I had," said Vera.

"You know ...," said Carli, "well, maybe I'll just ask you something, instead of telling you something."

"What do you mean?"

"If you mix your yellow sock and blue sock together, what do you get?" asked Carli.

"A pair of socks, I guess."

Carli smiled. "Okay, let's not say socks. What happens if you mix the colors yellow and blue together?"

Vera stared into the air, then slowly started nodding. A smile began to show. "Uh-huh ... yes, ma'am. I see exactly what you're saying." Then she flashed her eyes straight at Carli and said, "You know what they call that?"

Carli shrugged and shook her head.

"Karma!" Vera's eyes sparkled. Actually sparkled. Carli had never seen Vera so positively animated.

"Let's hear it for karma," said Carli, raising her fist into the air.

"Karma," said Vera, raising her fist. As soon as she did it, Carli saw Vera's smile vanish, and Carli immediately felt awful for having prompted the outburst.

"Vera, oh Vera. That looked painful."

"I'm all right. ... I'm all right," she said.

"I'm so sorry I caused you to do that."

"Ain't no one's fault but my own. I ought to know I can't go doing those things anymore."

A few months ago, Carli might have felt pity. Today, she reached an arm toward Vera, stopped just short of touching, and felt sheer determination. "Vera, I want to help, and I am pretty certain a doctor could make a few of these joints of yours feel less pain. Maybe even get you dancing someday. Four Bridges can help. I know I've said this before."

"That you have," said Vera. "Plenty of times."

"Just think of all the fist pumps we could do together," said Carli.

It got another smile out of Vera.

"Tell me when you're ready. I'll go with you," said Carli. Vera nodded and Carli asked, "Want a coffee? I'm getting one."

Vera smacked her lips. "Why not."

Carli's eyes met Vera's. "Two coffees coming right up." She couldn't believe it.

When Carli returned, she placed Vera's cup on the standpipe and handed Vera the sugar and creamers. "Did I see you talking with someone before I got here today?" she asked.

Vera said, "Yeah. I don't know who. See her here a bunch. Catches the M103 pretty regular."

"She must live or work around here. If you're seeing her this much," said Carli.

"Work," said Vera. "Said she was heading home."

"I wonder if she knows about the Minnix House," said Carli.

"Better not, or I won't talk with her again."

"She could work there, you know. Someone works there. Cleans the rooms. Does the cooking. Works the front desk," said Carli. "You think anyone else who used to live there when you did is around anywhere?" asked Carli.

"Doubt it. Ain't no more Minnix House like it used to be. Every-one's got moved out. Me included," said Vera. "Of course, there were those who were older. They're likely dead and gone. Why you asking me this stuff, anyway?"

"No reason. Just curious," said Carli.

"Well, don't you let that curiosity of yours get you in trouble. Like that curiosity that killed the cat," said Vera. "You heard of that one?" she asked.

"Yes. Of course. Listen," said Carli, "it was nice talking. You take care of yourself, okay?"

"Yes, ma'am. That I will. Always do."

———————

Twice the following week, Carli met Grant at his storage-room home, for peace of mind. And to lay out options. It was a struggle. She continued to encourage him ever-so-gently to visit Dr. Greenberg. What she wanted to do was hurl him head over heels into her office. Grant wasn't interested. One day, as they heard rain falling across the roof, they cleaned his bin together. In all respects, his room mirrored Grant: passable on the outside, and a mess within. Unread newspapers concealed more grease-splotched pizza boxes. Several contained entire pizzas, garnished with dead roaches and the skeletal remains of a mouse. Together, Carli and Grant bundled and tossed papers and boxes, along with a rainbow sprinkling of drugs – prescription, over-the-counter, and illicit. He claimed they kept him normal, just like, she learned, his many cups of coffee, which, oddly, calmed his body.

Carli wondered how he appeared as cleanly dressed as he did when they sorted clothes into one pile dirty, one pile clean, and one pile unsalvageable. The clean pile didn't measure up. On several occasions, what looked to Carli to be garbage items were quickly retrieved by Grant. From his "thinking chair" – a bright red beanbag chair now centered in the room – he gave his approval or disapproval of items she deemed suspect.

"That? No way," he said, as she confidently tossed a hole-riddled tee shirt into the trash bag. "Walked around with that one for over six months. One day, when it was snowing like a bitch, and I didn't have the system down, it was the first and only thing I could find to tie around my head. I thought my ears would fall off, it was so cold. For some reason, I had to go outside. Needed something. That skimpy tee shirt felt so warm, just getting the wind off my head. Yessiree, that tee shirt is a lifesaver and a keeper." Grant smiled. "I considered using it for a brush rag – for paints – but couldn't, not even in the shape it's in. It would be like defacing it. No, that shirt is being retired, hung over the big arena. When Sarah says she wants to keep her bags, she means it."

Behind a pile of books, Carli found a slew of well-worn sketchpads, along with oil paintings coated with dust. "I thought you were an attorney. Look at these. Now I know what you meant by a 'brush rag.' Thought you were talking about something for painting a bedroom or something."

"For the record, I was an attorney, but I get inspired from time to time. It's really just a hobby," he said.

It was clearly more. Several were finished and looked a lot like portraits of people she knew—Madison, Sarah, and Cedric included. Others looked like wild masses of colors, and still others, ponderings of the deepest depths of one's soul.

"Nice," she said, looking at Cedric's image. "You had formal training."

"Sure, in grade school," he said. "The teachers weren't impressed. You remember them, right? Didn't like different, and mine were definitely different. No... I was trained by the masters in the museums."

Carli wanted to forget the museum. Grant did not.

"I think about them, with their brushes and canvases," he said. "Wonder if they sat or stood, if they threw a bunch of stuff on there, spur of the moment, or planned it all out. I wonder what the faucet looked like where Mr. Monet, or should I say, 'Monsieur,' got his water, and how different it was from Cezanne's spigot. I wonder who sold Renoir his oil paints; if they worked at night or middle of the day. Wonder how they sounded when they spoke out loud, or to themselves."

"Ever sell any?" she asked.

"When I needed money. A couple."

"Now that these are back out, maybe you'll finish them," said Carli.

Grant smiled but said nothing.

With one week left in June, Grant started another bout with the bottle. He hid it reasonably well from strangers, but Carli was no stranger.

"Just enough to keep me down," he said, responding to her probe.

"Self-medication. Let's get you home."

Inside his room, Grant sprawled on the mattress and said drowsily, "See why I chose you for Outreach? Won't let me get away with anything. I still want to know why you said, 'Yes.' I mean, I know you *needed* to do Outreach, but I don't know why. Were you still looking for me?" asked Grant.

Carli hesitated. "I had my reasons. I saw everyone at the Church Run and Lucy's church, and something pushed me. I had always hoped to find you, but I gave up believing it was possible. I knew how it felt to lose you. I didn't want others to lose their loved ones. Helping two women seemed reasonable," she said. "And it was time. For me to give back. After decades of work for myself and my company."

Grant looked intrigued and waited for more. Carli took a long look at Grant and said, "Please, let's give Dr. Greenberg another try."

Grant took in a deep breath, and slowly shook his head. "You think she could help you?"

"That's just it, Grant. She *is* helping me. And I'm worried about you. Your slip is showing."

"Say what?"

"What's under is sticking out. Gretchen commented, and I wouldn't put it past Wilson to offer you his bottle. How can you nudge them to get inside, when you are practically still out? They're not going to trust you anymore. Things like not showing up for a week at a time will make a difference."

"Hah!"

"We can't let them down. I can't let you down," said Carli.

"We aren't letting anyone down," he said. "At least, I don't think we are. You come with me tomorrow and take a good look. You'll see. We're helping. We're doing lots of good for them. And, if you think it matters, I'll visit them twice as much as usual this week."

They set off together the next morning to make their visits. Cedric was a courtesy call of sorts. As he and Grant talked, the trends of thought were brief, cursory. Grant looked agitated. Cedric, wrapped well into his own dealings, seemed not to notice. Grant had been right. They left with the score Grant – one, Carli – zero.

Canada was next. Surely, he knew as much about Grant as any of them. Grant was accepted, blemishes and all. It was another point for Grant. To Sister Anna and the kitchen crew, including Gretchen, Grant was always welcome. Any irregularities had long ago been accepted as quirks of his personality or sporadic deviations from the real Grant. The true test came when they caught up with Vera. Grant's impulsive habits and words seemed to lighten the day's load. Grant had been right. No matter how he came to them, they trusted him. What made him so good was he *knew* them, and he was always there for them. It was both reassuring and distressing.

"We have another stop," said Carli.

"Who?" asked Grant.

"Rocky."

"What do you mean? He doesn't start his shift for hours," said Grant.

"I made an appointment. He's waiting."

In a side room at Four Bridges, they found Rocky and Mercy sitting on the same side of a fold-up table.

"Hey, man," said Rocky.

"Heyyy," said Grant. "What're you doing here? Everything okay?"

"I need to talk to you," said Rocky.

"Anytime. What's up?"

"It's not about me this time." Rocky looked directly at Grant and brought his hand to his chin, as though to think a moment. When he lowered his hand to the table, Rocky said, "Hear you might be having a bit of a tough time with something."

Grant clenched his teeth slightly, enough for Carli to see the muscles of his face tighten. Grant looked from Rocky to Carli and, finally, to Mercy, before saying, "What do you mean?"

"You know, all those years, you held me up 'til I figured out how to take better care of myself. ... I want to thank you for those years. I needed you," said Rocky. "Could never have done it alone. I know I already thanked you before. But now what I'm wondering is, is this my time to help and *really* thank you for everything you've done for me?"

"What are you getting at?" asked Grant.

"Look, man, I'm just wondering if maybe you could use someone to lean on, or talk to."

"I'm not getting what you're saying," said Grant.

"Okay ... right ... Here it is. Straight up. Just like it should be." Rocky's tone remained gentle, but it had grown more firm. He waited a moment, as though mentally composing his words. Then he said, "Grant, I understand, as well as anyone, what it is like to need help and deny that need. We both know what I was like and all the gyrations I went through to ignore these lifelines that people were tossing out to me. That includes you, of course. To me ... and others here ... it looks like you might just benefit from grabbing onto one of those lines. I see you sometimes in not-so-great shape. Not like you usually are. And I'm 100 percent positive you see it too. In yourself. No way you couldn't. And you know, as well as any, what's out there for you. Fortunately, or unfortunately, I bet you also know what's out there if you don't grab ahold of one of these pretty damned soon."

Rocky took in a deep breath to let his words settle in. "Look at me now. And think of where I could have ended up. Would have ended up. Grant, seems like sometimes you're drinking on the job. You're racing around the city with no time to stop. Or you're out of commission for who knows what reason. Come on, man, don't you think it's time to see it in yourself? Aren't those the words you said to me a bunch of times? See it in myself? And think of everything I could do once I did see it? Yeah, those are your words all right. So, I'm here talking as a friend. Someone who really needed you. And someone who still needs you. Still. Today. And someone who's been in some mighty uncomfortable shoes. I'm here to say, you need to let yourself get some guidance. Don't just think about seeing a doctor, or whoever you need to see."

Rocky looked straight into Grant's eyes. "Go and see them. Take that first step. That really difficult first step. Once you do, every step just follows. Well, maybe with a few detours, but it follows, man. It's only one step. And it's a step in a new direction. That, in itself, makes it scary. But think of all the people you've helped to take that first step. Last count, I think I heard you say you'd gotten over thirty of us moving in better directions just in the last few years. And I know, absolutely, for certain, no doubt whatsoever, that you've got a whole lot more people to help out here. Just look at everyone in that room behind you. And you're so good at it. Grant, man, I'm here for you, but you know who's got to take that next first step. Also know, if anyone can do it ... and if I did it ... you can do it"

Grant looked around the room, avoiding eye contact, and began to nod. Then he looked directly at Rocky, turned his gaze to Mercy, and landed, finally, on Carli, all the while continuing to nod. Quietly and slowly, Grant said, "Thanks for your concern." He returned his eyes to Rocky. "I'll think about it. Pretty sure I'm okay, but nice knowing you care."

Mercy straightened up, pulling all eyes upon her. "Grant," she said. "I'm in a tough position here. You know what I'm getting at?"

Grant knew.

"I'll give you some time. But I can't give it forever. More importantly, I want to see you doing what you do best because you're in your best condition. I don't want to lose you to something that can most likely be helped."

Grant continued to nod his head, slowly and gently.

"And, Grant," said Mercy, "you know I'm always available for you, twenty-four seven. My operator is standing by. And think about it ... Carli, here, came to me and is getting some help. Rocky ... well, you know he's living proof of what good changes can take place when you let others help. And I know you had a lot of hardship going on, long before you got here. If nothing else, you might feel better just talking to Dr. Greenberg, or someone like her, about all of that. Get rid of some of those scars. Those lingering things can surely tear a body apart if they don't get healed. See it all the time. All different situations. You know I do."

Grant shifted in his chair. For the most part, Carli kept her eyes glued to Mercy. She knew the two other pairs of eyes would feel threatening enough for Grant. For many more moments, the room remained silent, except for the occasional sound sauntering in through the space under the closed door to the drop-in center. Finally, Grant said, "I'll think about it. I need some time. I don't think I'm as bad as you're all making me out to be, but thanks for your concern. Thanks, Rocky. I appreciate it."

Carli looked over and felt awful for having arranged the meeting. She had never seen him so thoroughly wounded. Rocky stood. "Anytime, man. Anytime. Got to get me some dinner somewhere before I check in for work."

TWENTY-FOUR

"COME ON IN. Come see the babies." Thelma held open her front door, and Lila and Terrance ran to Carli's feet.

"Lila! Terrance! Look at you!" said Carli. "But first, a hug for you, my friend." Carli reached toward Thelma.

"So glad you made the drive," said Thelma. "I was hoping to see you again, and sooner rather than later."

"I have news to share. And I want to show you my paintings. It's a whole other side of me I want you to finally see," said Carli.

"First, follow me. You know where the kitchen is. We can get a little something to give us energy. Lila and Terrance will be asking for something as well."

Carli felt like a feather floating effortlessly on an invisible current of air, soft and warm. Seeing Thelma smiling, instead of fighting to retrieve a friend or planning a memorial service, and seeing Lila and Terrance enjoying the privileges of having won over another heart, were all she needed for a fabulous day.

"So, what's this news you wish to share?" asked Thelma.

"It's about my brother," said Carli. "I found him."

"You what? Oh, Carli, this is wonderful. How? And where?"

"The tricky part is I found him, but he doesn't want others to know. I only tell you because I don't want you to spend the rest of Time worrying about me, on account of having lost him. As far as everyone is concerned, my brother is presumed dead, or still missing."

"Oh," said Thelma.

"The fact is, he's very different than he once was. He's convinced the cult he joined in college will come for him, or for me, if they know he's alive."

"So, he is alive?" asked Thelma.

"Yes. He changed his name. And that's about all I can say. This makes it sound more mysterious than it is."

"Are you in any danger?"

"As far as I can tell, not at all," said Carli. She refused to acknowledge her own, lingering fear.

"It seems to me, if they wanted to find you, they could have long ago. It's not very difficult to look people up these days. If I can do it, I figure anyone can," said Thelma.

"I agree," said Carli. "There's something else."

"I hope it's as good as this first bit of news, which, by the way, I will consider to have never heard," said Thelma.

"I knew you would understand," said Carli. "It's part of our special bond."

"Indeed. And thank you for taking me into your confidence. You're right to think I would have worried about you forever," said Thelma.

"The other news is this. I've been living a bit of a double life. You know me as Carli Morris. A lot of people know me by that name now. The truth is, I lived most of my life as Tessie Whitmore. I built my business on that name. My reputation too. A college friend was named Carli, although her last name wasn't Morris. The fact is, I chose to call myself 'Carli' out of fear. I am ashamed to say it arose out of fear of people like Lucy, when she was on the street. I see, now, how ignorant and wrong that was. A bad reflection of who I was. But this has been a good lesson for me. I am fine owning up to it," she said.

"Well, I understand. It is sad, of course, but not difficult to understand at all," said Thelma. "We are often threatened by things we do not understand. And, unfortunately, sometimes there is a threat of danger from people who suffer with mental health challenges. Seems to me, your visiting a number of them is ample reason to feel good about yourself, not beat yourself up over a name change. On top of that, name changes aren't all that unusual," said Thelma. "A friend of mine writes novels. Doesn't want a single person to know her real identity. Those musicians with their stage names – more examples of name changes, though I guess for them it's a branding thing. But when you think of it ... why would you label a girdle as female shapewear? Another name change, right?" Thelma was sweet. A dear, sweet friend, who truly did understand.

"I'm sorry you lost her," said Carli. "I wish she could have walked back into your life, as my brother did."

"Oh, dear Carli, we do not control these things. I am simply grateful she now rests in town, alongside her William. Every day, I picture them smiling at one another, probably even holding hands."

After a refill of their coffee cups, Carli retrieved two paintings from her car. A smile erupted across Thelma's face as she looked at the finished waterscapes. It justified the many hours Carli had struggled to regain her artistic expression and skills. Carli looked at Thelma, as the woman continued to view the paintings. She hoped to have a fraction of her grace and wisdom as she moved forward in years.

"When did you say the show is?" asked Thelma. "We surely must get a contingent down to see it."

"It is supposed to be in five months—November—but I don't know if I'll be ready. So much else is taking up my time. I'm worried I'll have wet paint dripping from the exhibit," said Carli.

"Let it drip!" said Thelma. "With paintings like these, a little excess liquid will look plenty authentic. Who knows, might even be written up in the newspapers as an innovative trend. Maybe dog portraits will have fur flying off of them."

Thelma had done it again. All Carli said was, "You are a gift!"

It was a hot afternoon, nearing July, when Carli and Grant sat in Gloria's and he said, in a calm, unemotional voice, "I'm trying it."

Carli checked the menu. "Trying what?"

"The tests ... Dr. Greenberg." He pulled the fifteen-page evaluation booklet out of his pocket and slapped the crumpled pages on the table.

Carli latched onto his eyes. He had made it sound as though he were doing it on a lark. Grant's resigned look told her he was all in. At least, for the moment.

While Grant faced Dr. Greenberg, Carli took on her own visits and made extra stops with Cedric and Wilson. All the while, she hoped Grant was actually placing his trust in the doctor's hands.

Cedric emerged from the shelter with an ear-to-ear smile, after another resident stepped past the bunks to give a knock on his door. Carli hated having to meet outside. She wanted to finally see Cedric seated on a legitimate sofa or chair. She was, however, more than happy to accept a set of stone steps in lieu of a bag full of cans.

"You look good, Cedric," she said. "Real good, Kid."

"Back at you, Kid. But you always looked good." Cedric's wry smile forced a smile of its own onto Carli's face.

"How're things?" she asked.

"Pretty good. I'd say I am acing my tests, and Deena – you know, the lady here – is helping me with a bunch of things. I think I might get a kitchen of my own, after all. It's not like I don't know how to cook. I do. But I don't feel like seeing if some roommate knows how to cook."

"I'm a lousy cook," said Carli. "I usually burn things. Eggs, hamburgers, bread ... doesn't matter."

"Not me," said Cedric. "I keep an eye on it. That's the trick. Can't let it go off on its own."

"I should try that," said Carli. "Honestly, anything could help." She looked at Cedric and realized her bad cooking didn't matter a bit. "Who gave you the haircut?" she asked.

"Grant took me out."

"He's been by?"

"We did a BOGO down in the Alphabet City neighborhood when

we visited a Parks Department person. This new place was trying to drum up business. Real nice place. Lots of seats. Clean. Nice barber, too. Grant and I even split the cost. He refused to let me pay. And, of course, I refused to let him do it."

"Like I said before, Kid, you're looking good," said Carli. "I'm glad Grant's keeping in touch. You know he'd miss you if he didn't."

"Yeah, yeah, yeah. No need to get all mushy on me."

"So, I'll be back soon. It's always good to see you, Cedric. Always good," said Carli.

"Okay, Kid. Like I said before, back at you."

Carli watched Cedric return to his building, practically skipping up the stairway and through the front door. Hallelujah. It had really happened. Carli looked to the sky and smiled.

Vera was not at her standpipe. Carli waited half an hour at the deli, but Vera didn't appear. Carli moved on, in search of Wilson. Two blocks from the pocket park, she reached in her bag and pulled out another of her older perfume bottles. After a spritz on each wrist, she walked the final blocks. She couldn't tell if Wilson was awake or asleep until she was well within the park. Wilson lifted his head, as she had seen him do before. Knew she was coming.

"Who's there?" he asked.

"Carli's here," she said. "How are you today, Wilson?"

Wilson stretched his arms over his head, then rubbed his eyes. "Is it afternoon?" he asked.

"About 1 p.m.," she said. "I had a free moment and I wanted to see you."

Wilson looked straight across the table. He closed his eyes another moment, opened them briefly, and then closed them again. He looked like he might fall asleep sitting upright. Maybe she should come another time. "I can leave you be, unless you want to walk with me to Four Bridges."

"Too nice to be inside," said Wilson. "Just give me a minute here. I'm ... I'm getting there." Wilson opened his eyes again and took in a deep breath. He could easily have been on his sixth shot at the bar.

"What's that you got on?" he asked.

"Aha. You tell me. You know it?"

"Yeah ... maybe. Got some vanilla or something in it. Or maybe it's ... no, definitely vanilla. And citrus."

"Here," she said. Take a look." Carli pulled a frosted glass bottle from her bag and slid it onto the table. Man-weeks of branding, marketing, and advertising had undoubtedly gone into the product and its packaging. It was sensuously shaped and topped by a pewter-colored cap with an intricate design. The odd partnership of bottle and bench would likely turn the advertising team over in their graves, or put them there. Wilson lowered his head to assess it. The fog didn't seem to be lifting very fast, except suddenly Wilson said, "I've got it. Yes. Seen this one. Must have been ten years ago. Came out for Christmas sales. One of the big ones."

"Vicissitudes. From 2009," said Carli. "How do you know this?"

"I told you. I was a chemist or something. Did all this stuff with fragrances and perfumes and stuff."

"When?" she asked.

"I don't know," said Wilson. "Must have been a long time ago, right? I mean, I've been here a long time, right?"

"I'm not sure," she said. "What exactly did you do?"

"What do you mean?" he asked. "I don't know. I just did all kinds of stuff. You know, chemistry stuff. With perfumes. I don't know what I did. I think I just did it. Know what I mean?"

"Well, sort of, but not really," said Carli. "Maybe you can tell me more about it another day."

"Sure," said Wilson. "Not much to tell. I just did it, I think ... I don't know." Wilson was smiling. Carli didn't know if Wilson even realized he was doing it. She was about to ask what he was thinking, when he said, "Lily of the valley lady." Carli did a double take of Wilson. Then she looked to the sidewalk. She couldn't believe it.

"Wilson, you're amazing. And here's what I'm going to do," she said. "Next time, I'm bringing a couple of bottles. Of perfume, that is. I want to hear what you have to say about them. Maybe you'll have a lot to say, or maybe nothing at all. Doesn't matter. I'm just curious."

"My opinion?" asked Wilson. "You want to know my opinion? Sure. I can tell you. What do you want to know?"

"I want to know if you're doing okay," she said.

"Yeah. I'm okay. Already told you that. Didn't I?"

Carli collected her perfume and swung her legs over the picnic bench, ready to leave. "Just wanted to make sure. Glad to hear it," she said. "Remember about Four Bridges if you need anything. Mercy's in there the rest of the day."

Wilson lifted a hand slightly off the table. It fell down quickly and made a noticeable thud upon landing. Carli wondered how his body stood up to the pounding of alcohol. His condition was worrisome. She also wondered how long ago he concocted perfumes. Now all he was mixing were different brands of wine. Oddly, it made sense he chose wine for his habit. There were, after all, infinite varieties, and each carried a unique fragrance. A perfect opus major for a *chimiste des parfums* she thought, dredging up her high school French lessons and giving Wilson a proper-sounding profession, likely worthy of his past.

TWENTY-FIVE

CARLI CAUGHT up with Harry sliding out of St. Mary's. She walked with him into the shadows of the highway. "I heard you used to be with your daughter," she said.

Harry shrugged. "Yeah, I guess." He walked another two minutes before adding, "We kind of had a blowup. Didn't like the way I acted around the little one; Jessica's her name." He grunted. "Must be near five by now. Who knows, maybe older." Stopping momentarily to reposition his bags, he said, "Probably as cute as can be. Guess I deserved it." It was clear, from his posture, he missed them.

"Where are they now?" she asked.

"Probably where they always were. Don't care a damn about me. Probably think I'm dead. Figure I'll never see them again, and it won't bother them at all. Doesn't matter."

"People change."

"Look, let's drop it," said Harry.

"Sure," she said. Despite what Grant had told her, and how many times he had dismissed it, the past *did* matter. It had to. Sooner or later, Carli would bring up Harry's family again.

She left Harry, before reaching his barrel, to head Uptown. Sarah sat with bags stacked up on a bench, as usual, but something was noticeably absent.

"Where's your cart?" asked Carli.

"Gone."

"Why?"

"Stole."

"Someone stole your cart?" asked Carli.

Sarah nodded once, casting her eyes to the ground as she did.

Seven bags and a woman left intact, but the cart – rusted and squeaky – was stolen.

"How did you get these here?" asked Carli, motioning to the pile of bags.

Sarah waved her arms to show she had carried them. Then she looked away, wary of prolonged eye contact.

Carli considered the process. It must have been difficult, physically and emotionally. "Who?" she finally asked.

Sarah folded her arms and shut like a clam. Carli repeated the question. Twice. Her pigeon woman finally answered.

"Same one. Hit Len … ny."

Carli froze. Sarah had seen it – Lenny's attack. Of course. She slept in or near the park every night. How could she not have seen it?

"Lenny?"

Sarah nodded.

"Who?"

Sarah stared, puzzled. "I told … him."

"Told who?" asked Carli.

"Told … Grant."

"Who?" Carli asked again. "Who did it?"

"Har … ry. Told … Grant."

Carli stiffened and felt the blood of her pulse throbbing in her neck. It was Harry. Grant knew all along, but hadn't said a word. Had out-and-out lied. Face to face with a police officer. With two, in fact. Or, perhaps, he didn't know at the time. If only she could remember that first day more clearly.

Sarah's scant words explained a lot, like the reason Grant was after

Harry; he had his number and wanted Harry to know it. Carli sighed. Harry, the man who looked like her elderly uncle, the man who was missing his granddaughter, and the man she had just seen, was a part-time thug. Carli looked at Sarah without her cart and boiled. Harry and Grant had some explaining to do. But not just yet. After months of Grant's knowing, a few more days wouldn't make a bean's worth of difference. What she didn't know was enough about Harry and how to confront him.

"I'll look for a new one," she said.

Sarah shrugged as though it didn't matter, but Carli knew it mattered a lot. Seven bulging bags were seven bulging bags, and Sarah was no bodybuilder.

Leaving Sarah, Carli couldn't help wondering if it was Harry who had paid a visit to Cedric's place. Time was when she believed they looked out for one another, but, obviously, there were bad eggs.

At half past six o'clock the next morning, Carli arrived at Sarah's to watch her come to grips with her new predicament, and help lug the plastic to the park. It is what Grant would have done, or so she thought. Now she wasn't sure, since Grant had dined with a criminal and turned his back on the crime.

Carli spotted Sarah huffing toward the park, lugging two bags alongside her, while keeping watch over her shoulder for the five left behind across a busy street. In fact, Sarah stopped smack on the street's centerline, with cars passing and honking both ways. She peeked at the left-behinds and readjusted her grip on the two she hauled. Then, she shuffled through streaming traffic, placed the bags on the curb, and started back for the rest.

Carli dashed to Sarah's side, offering to help in silence. She picked up two bags and nodded. Together, they stepped off the curb like mother cats transporting kittens. When the operation was complete, and Sarah was settled on her bench, Carli said, "I'll be by later to help."

She headed to the shadows of the elevated highway to seek out Harry and Grudge. The two were already up and out, but Sarah's cart was boosted against a trestle, looking like part of the bridge. She wanted to take it, but doing so could endanger Sarah. If Harry happened to go looking for it again, Carli wanted him to know she had taken it, not Sarah.

Carli walked away empty-handed. Taking Harry's "new" cart would be robbing him, too, and not only of his new cart, but of his trust. There were other ways to keep them both, but it didn't mean she wouldn't ask him about it very soon. After all, hadn't Grant tapped Harry on the back about Lenny?

With the logistics of street life being new to her, Carli didn't know if Sarah might have a way of finding a new cart on her own. But when she returned, as she had promised, she saw Sarah's bags jumbled on the bench, with no cart by their side. Together, they schlepped the bags out of the park. Many people stared. None gave a hand. According to Grant, Sarah didn't go far – across the street and up and down a few blocks was about it. Without a cart, she likely wouldn't be leaving her neighborhood or going to Lucy's church. The next morning, following another bag delivery to the park, Carli set off to find Sarah a new set of wheels.

It took some searching, but Carli finally found what she needed tucked in the corner of a dusty top shelf at First Avenue Hardware. She steered her acquisition onto the sidewalk, wondering how long it would take for it to mellow to the rusty patina of street life.

Carli was certain Sarah would scorn a gift, so she helped move bags one more time, and waited until after dark to make an under-cover delivery. Surrounded by night, Carli slid the cart under a shrub near Sarah's favorite bench. With any luck, Sarah would lay claim to it before anyone else. Carli fled fast, shuddering at the thought of Sarah being out by herself near the empty park, at this very moment, and night after night.

The next morning, as soon as Carli spotted Sarah, she smiled. Sarah was already chatting with the pigeons, with her new cart sparkling in the morning sun. For all Carli knew, Sarah saw her leave the cart and claimed it in the middle of the night. The new cart was a bit wider than Sarah's first, and the woman had tied two bags to the sides using strands of mismatched twine. The bags in the middle anchored their weight, and Sarah could now push her pram with bags no longer piled so high as to block her view. She could walk with two hands on the handle, instead of using a hand to balance the top bag. Going over curbs would be easier. In some respects, the theft was a blessing, but Carli hardly felt like thanking Harry. Yes, it was time to find Harry for a talk.

Carli slid into a seat directly across the table as soon as Harry and his tray sat at Lucy's soup kitchen.

"I heard you got a new cart," Carli said, reaching for salt for her lunchmeat.

Harry glanced up.

"Where'd you get it?" she asked.

"Found it."

"Near Sarah?"

"Just found it." After taking a bite he added, "But I sold it."

"Sold it?"

Harry continued eating. "Needed it, but then didn't, so I sold it."

Someone else was now walking around with Sarah's cart.

"Why didn't you give it back to Sarah? And why did you take it in the first place?"

"I had my reasons."

"But she needed it," said Carli. For all the good she had hoped on Harry over the past months, Carli momentarily despised him.

After lunch, Carli returned to the park. As she sketched, Sarah approached with shiny new cart wheels making crinkling sounds as they rolled over the gravel path. Carli looked up to see Sarah reaching her hand straight toward her to offer a plastic bag. Instinctively, Carli reached to accept it but immediately regretted doing so. Nothing jingled like a bag full of coins.

"Cart," Sarah said slowly.

Carli tried returning the bag, but Sarah turned, and her cart turned as well, ready for another crinkly stroll.

"Sarah, wait ..."

"Sister! What's up?"

The moment Carli heard Kristin's voice on her phone, she smiled. "Hey. Good to hear your voice," said Carli. "I'm doing a bit of research."

"Paintings? That kind of research?"

"No. Perfumes. Trying to find Wilson, last name unknown, occupation chemist ... possibly ... but also unknown for certain. I mean, how many Wilsons could there be in the perfume world?"

"Wilson ... the man in the park?" asked Kristin.

"Yes, that Wilson. He claims he used to be a chemist. In the perfume industry. I don't know if it's true, but he has an incredible nose for fragrances. I don't know how he does it. A lot of him is in a fog, but, somehow, his nose picks up these scents. And knows them. Like, identifies them. You should see it. It's amazing."

"Sounds like a gift."

"Well, with any luck, it will be a gift that tells me a bit more about him, and helps get him out of that damned park," said Carli. "I'm hoping something, or someone, will let me make a stronger connection."

"I thought you were only visiting two women," said Kristin.

"That was the idea, but how can I not help a man with a childlike smile, who wouldn't harm a flea, and who is grateful to receive two new coat buttons? A man who somehow knows perfumes ... and who seriously needs to turn in his bottle before he dies with his head on a park bench."

"Good points."

"I mean, he's not just a drunk in the park. He's Wilson," said Carli. She paused, realizing the full meaning of her words.

"So, give me the deets. I'll help you search. Two keyboards are better than one."

"You're always a team player," said Carli.

"You got my back. I got yours."

"So, here's the thing ... what I likely need are old annual reports, company publications, or maybe an industry directory. I'm guessing from five years ago to fifteen years ago. I'm just getting started. I considered calling our friends who did *Workables* and *Living Easy*, to see if they can give a few leads to *Fragrance Industry* or *Fragrance Creators* materials."

"Good idea," said Kristin. "Let me do that for you."

"I have no idea if Wilson was a higher-up, production chemist, or master blender of some sort. If I had to guess, I would definitely go with the latter. All he said was 'chemist.'"

"Any reason to think he'd make that up?" asked Kristin.

"Could have. But he said he studied chemistry. He also said 'Princeton,' but I didn't get anywhere with that. Maybe I just didn't have the right range of years."

"Maybe, but honestly, this all seems like we're being total creepers. What are you going to do if you find out something?"

"I'm trying to come up with anything that will connect. I have no intention of telling anyone who isn't trying to help," said Carli.

"It still feels like creeping. On the other hand, people look for all types of information about all types of people. I guess this is no different."

"Who knows?"

"Hey, the other reason I called is I want to know about your vacation. Are you still taking it?" asked Kristin.

"It sounds so weird when you say it like that. Sounds like we're talking about taking time off from work. You know, like when you have to schedule in your time off from the office," said Carli.

"Those were the days, right? At least for one of us. The other one, here, is still living it."

"Yes, I am going," said Carli. "Well, I hope so. I'm worried about leaving Grant. He said he saw Dr. Greenberg. Hey, I didn't tell you about that, did I?"

"No. You're holding back on me. Fantastic."

"I guess I believe him," said Carli. "As long as there is no major emergency, it's Wyoming here I come. Can't wait. Two weeks of total brain crunch with my artistic side."

"You need to get away," said Kristin. "Not only for your painting, but for you."

"Agreed. I definitely need to get out there for my show though. The whole premise is to have contrasting landscapes from oceans to mountains. To show the different power of it all. I considered adding in desert works but decided to make that a separate study. I'd likely drop dead in the desert heat right now, anyway."

"Oh, God. Forgot about that," said Kristin. "Head to the mountains, Sister."

"I will, but right now I'm heading to sleep. Long day. Thanks a billion for the call."

TWENTY-SIX

DR. GREENBERG'S evaluation returned a simple translation: bipolar disorder, or manic depression. Grant was a man of many internal faces, whose bouts with alcohol served as last-ditch efforts at home-made fixes meant to level his head. His unexplained absences were proof positive of depressive waves far too massive to swim through by will alone. It was no wonder he left rehab, apparently several times. It was a matter of biochemistry, not will and not steps. The diagnosis left Carli feeling helpless once again, and wondering if she could have any impact. It was up to Grant to make the right decisions.

Doctor Greenberg prescribed mood stabilizers and psychotherapy to sort through baggage and heal emotional wounds. Grant was one of the luckier ones, having thus far been spared delusions and other debilitating psychoses known to difficult cases. He could never be cured, but he could be helped. That was the news before Independence Day weekend.

Carli watched Grant struggle with his diagnosis in textbook style. There had been comfort in denial and ignorance, even when it gave free run to an uncomfortable being. While relieved to have a known condition, he was angry. He felt betrayed by a malfunctioning brain and emotionally wounded at having a named mental illness, even if he had likely known of it all along. Grant fell into the quiet and safety of his room, where he digested the meaning of his diagnosis and became spiteful of the world, which included Carli.

The drugs would kick in over a couple of weeks, and demanded careful monitoring, as too much could be as bad as none. In fact, too much could be lethal. Carli gave him time before making her way to Cooper's storage. In the meantime, she painted on pins and needles, waiting it out, and swatting away the many "what-ifs."

"Do you feel like working?" she asked, when she finally visited.

"Outreach? Sure." He smirked bitterly. "Was working all along, and I'm supposed to be getting better."

Carli nodded.

"On second thought," he said, "don't really feel like going today."

Carli didn't feel like going out either, but she went. It was Vera who crossed her path first, after picking Carli out from a mass of pedestrians and calling her by name first. Carli called back. "Vera Dear-a, what's new? How are you doing?"

"I can't complain. Nothing good comes from complaining. Say, where's that Grant? I need to ask him something."

"He stayed home today," said Carli.

"Have you seen them ticketing for boxes again? I thought I saw that dumbbell new cop," said Vera.

"As far as I know, The Sweep's been quiet," said Carli. "Did the cop bother you?"

"I thought I saw someone else getting bothered. That's all. No one did nothing to me."

"Tell me, how're your joints doing?" asked Carli. "It looks like you're walking a bit worse on your left side. What's going on?"

"Some days it's better than others. Sometimes, I think it's all that sleeping on the ground that does it to you. Puts a lot of pressure on the hip, you know. Then I think I could be in a nice, comfy bed and still have this happen 'cause I sees a lot of older folks its happening to and they all got beds, at least so I thinks. I don't complain."

"I can get you mobile medical if you want it," said Carli. "Told you about this before."

"And I told you I wasn't interested," said Vera. "Like a hundred times."

Carli sighed and stared at the women's feet. "You don't deserve this, Vera, and I know you tested out the atrium. Doesn't that tell you something? Listen to yourself. I'd like to help if you want to do something about it. It's okay to change your mind." Carli paused a moment for Vera to consider her words. Then she took another risk. She knew Vera could always walk away, but something told Carli she wouldn't. "I just wonder," said Carli, "wouldn't your husband want you to take care of that hip of yours? And your feet?"

Vera looked directly into Carli's eyes, seemingly stunned. Then she slowly lowered her gaze to the ground. The next moment, Carli was certain she saw Vera's eyes flicker in the direction of the old Minnix House, before quickly returning to their downward gaze.

"Vera Dear-a, we're due for some nasty thunderstorms this week. Please, stay safe," said Carli.

Vera knew. She *knew*. But she couldn't do it. Not yet. She said, "I'd best be getting home," and began walking.

"Wait," said Carli. "There's something else."

Vera halted her step and raised her eyes. Her head maintained its downward tilt. "I am going away for a bit," said Carli. "Not right away, but I want to give you this heads-up. I don't want you thinking I'm leaving you if you don't see me."

Vera nodded.

"Maybe I'll bring you back another gift," said Carli. It brought a smile to Vera's face.

"Thanks," said Vera. "You know, for giving me the heads-up."

Not finding Cedric at Penn Station during the past months gave a peculiar thrill every time Carli walked past or came up from one of the subway trains. Some days, Carli went out of her way to visit his spot, just to stare at the empty space. It was a welcome reminder, so she went again on her way to Wilson's.

What she saw, nearing the glass tower, made her slow her step. A figure was stretched on the ground near Cedric's old resting place. It wasn't Cedric. Thank God. The man didn't flinch when Carli stepped near. Maybe he was the punk can stealer, or maybe someone else – someone new.

The man, out cold, was a good catch for the cops if, as Vera said, they were out. If he was moving in, he was poorly furnished, with not a bag on him. She hoped he had a different story, like a long night out and a missed train ride home. She would tell Mercy and check back the next day. With any luck, transit cops, or street cops, would remind him there were better places to sleep. It could be the best "worst lesson" he might ever get. Right now, Carli had another important stop.

Before Carli was a block from Wilson's park, she realized she was smiling nearly ear to ear. Surely other pedestrians noticed, but no matter. She couldn't wait to hear what Wilson would say about the four bottles of perfume tucked inside her bag. Maybe he would recognize them. Surely, he would identify some of the separate elements of their scented blends, just as he had done with the others. Carli couldn't wait to share her new game with him. She hoped he would be as excited about it as she was, and hoped the fog of his wine had not yet settled around his bench. Carli hastened her step.

When the park came into sight, a wave of disappointment washed over. The picnic bench sat empty, save for a few weeds clinging to one of its legs. Nobody stood near the back wall. A couple of brown sparrows flitted past, picking up seeds from the ground, but Wilson's park was otherwise empty. Carli leaned against the outer fence and felt her mouth turn downward.

As Carli cut through library park, she saw the screamer, the woman Grant had loosely pointed out on her very first day of Outreach. Carli still didn't know her name. Carli watched her, standing, mumbling, and very much self-contained. For some reason, Carli decided to approach. A few feet away, she said, "Hi."

The woman gave one angry, fast, penetrating look at Carli and sounded the alarm. With Carli as her target, she screamed loud and fast and rattled words off her tongue like lottery balls bouncing in their glass container. The car alarm woman continued to honk and flash and Carli turned and walked swiftly away. The woman's voice followed Carli down the block but, thankfully, the woman did not. The contact had gone nothing like Carli had planned. She couldn't wait to get home and raise a paintbrush to her canvas.

Carli stared at her unfinished waterscape and saw her life swirling around on the watery surface, like powerless flotsam being lifted over swells, pummeled under breakers, and churned up by waters receding from the shore, only to have it repeated. She lowered herself to sit cross-legged on the wooden floor, with her head leaned all the way down into her hands on her lap. Grant was a mess. She couldn't save Vera or Wilson. And Lila and Terrance were no longer dancing their happy toenails across the room.

In a few moments, she resettled with her back flat on the ground and eyes looking to the ceiling. She had crossed tough roads before. Countless times at work. Occasionally she had felt overwhelmed by the demands and details and had felt lost, but it had always worked out. In the end, she had her internal compass to guide her. Carli knew her patience and faith were part of that compass and were both being tested. Surprisingly, she also realized it was okay. As she continued to stare at the ceiling, Carli no longer felt she was failing, but merely being impatient, and, perhaps, still untrusting. Yes, patience and faith would see her through. Isn't that what she saw daily on the streets? Men and women, with nothing but faith?

Despite her renewed willingness to be patient, it felt like an eternity before Grant was ready to rejoin Outreach. In the meantime, Carli painted and kept track of Vera, Sarah, and the others becoming increasingly familiar. The man at Cedric's place never returned, but another new one popped up at Gloria's – same time every day, his clothes barely changed. The worst news was Wilson did not look well.

Jaundice was a threatening sign that his kidneys and liver were in decline.

Carli frequently visited Cooper's to assure Grant of her support. One day, finally, he was ready to go out.

"You're looking better," she said, as Grant paced quietly alongside her.

"I feel worse, like I just got the brains and body of a turtle. All I want to do is sleep."

He wasn't angry, simply cynical.

"You're doing better, trust me. It takes a while."

The street people were seemingly blind to his evolution. He remained adept at masking, of course. If *she* hadn't known how he felt, how could anyone he visited know?

"Maybe you need a change of dose. Doctor Greenberg will know when you check in." In truth, steadying his chemistry could be as much an art as a science, and every patient could be a study by trial and error.

By the following week, the shadows of depression had lifted further, and Grant's manic upheaval had softened, making him more the person Carli had known in between extremes. No longer feeling fettered, even *he* applauded the doctor's drugs. Carli and Grant celebrated with Chinese takeout. Canada had told Carli where to go for Grant's favorite. The weight of the world was finally off her shoulders.

They sat in his storage room and ate in the company of sports talk radio.

"Ever listen to anything other than sports?" she asked.

"You mean music? Nahhh. This keeps me in touch with the lunch crowd."

Carli rolled her eyes. "If you go to lunch, you hear everything anyway."

"I like to hear the arguments and opinions. It's the blood and guts of America. I mean, people actually stop what they're doing to call in on this stuff because it means so much to them."

"Must be the lawyer in you."

"Bad subject." He leaned forward to fiddle with the radio, moving past portions of pounding music, news, a scratch of static, before suddenly stopping to say, "Wait … shh. Hear that? Sounds like …"

Carli became still, thinking the bin had company.

Grant tweaked the radio again. To many, the latest news story would mean nothing. To Grant, it was a special bulletin, which stopped his talk mid-sentence. A water main near the highway – Aquaman Harry's highway – was broken. Streets were flooding. A gas explosion might have caused it. Grant and Carli exchanged panicked glances, nervously awaiting details.

"No one hurt," the man's voice reported. "Crews working to remove several from the scene."

Carli sensed they were someone they knew.

"Harry." Grant jumped up. "And Grudge."

"The closest hospitals are Bellevue and NYU," she said.

"Harry and Grudge won't go unless they have to. I'm sure they'll be moved for the night if it's them. Housed somewhere – men's shelter most likely. Harry and Grudge won't like it."

"Are you sure you're all right?" she asked.

"I'm going."

On their car ride toward the river, Carli dialed the hospitals. No admittance yet.

"That leaves us two to find," said Grant, as he shifted forward in his seat.

Police barricades circled the broken main and several blocks around it. Fire trucks idled. Gas company trucks flashed yellow warning lights. Power and gas were off, and foot-deep water flooded streets and sidewalks alike, swishing against steps of several buildings and racing toward drains and the river. Harry's reputation had suffered a blow with Sarah's cart, but all Carli envisioned, as they eased up to the police line, was a helpless old man trying desperately to maintain his balance, while wading through a relentless torrent of water. Despite what he had told her, Carli knew he would do his best to survive for the sake of his granddaughter. She also knew he could easily go down if he caught a swell the wrong way.

"Where are they?" Grant didn't waste a second.

A police officer turned abruptly. "We're waiting for special units. An old man over there won't come out. Says he won't leave a grudge, or something like that. Think he's a bit wacko; shouted and started to kick, so we've called for backup." The officer seemed concerned.

Grant sloshed past.

"Hey! You can't go in there."

Grant kept wading until the woman caught Grant by the arm.

"Harry! Grudge!"

All was still while Grant waited for a response. "Harry! It's Grant. And Carli. I need you out! Now!"

The street suddenly seemed as quiet as a cemetery. "Harry!" he yelled again.

A soft noise eked its way across the murky water. "Grant?"

"Harry!"

The officer loosened her grasp, and Grant sloshed freely forward. On Grant's order, two first responders followed.

"Is Grudge with you?" called Grant.

"He's hurt."

Grant tried moving faster, sending a rippling current reeling around him.

"Grudge is a man, the name of a man," Carli informed the police officer by her side. "He's an amputee and needs a wheelchair. He's probably stuck, and Harry wouldn't leave him."

Within minutes, Grant emerged from the shadows, with Harry clasping his side and Grudge riding half piggyback, half sidesaddle on Grant's hunched over back. One first responder carried several bundles, and the other followed with Grudge's wheelchair hoisted over his shoulders, well above the waterline. Harry and Grudge's warming barrel remained behind.

"What happened?" Grant asked.

"I wasn't here," said Harry. "Came back and found him in six inches of water. It was running by fast. Tried to get him up but smacked his head."

Grant looked at the gash, with the help of emergency lighting. Grudge was going to the hospital.

"You saved his life," said Grant.

"Ah, for chrissake, I had to. No way I'd leave another Vet behind. Never. It was hell, pure hell back then, and we got them all out. Had to get Grudge. Now get outta here and take care of him. I gotta get some rest."

"Where are you going?" asked Grant.

"Don't know. Might try a safe haven for the night."

"Good idea. They'll get you some dry clothes. Say, let me have those. They're wet and heavy. You trust me, right?"

Harry nodded and handed over his belongings. Grant promised to have them washed, dried, and returned by morning. It was better, Grant said, than leaving them soaked and muddy by his bunk, and far better than having to clean them himself or have someone toss them in the garbage.

"First bed he's had in quite some time. Hope it feels good," said Grant. "So good that he goes in more often. I know how he thinks. This could be the only chance for change."

Carli's thoughts had drifted. "Why didn't you tell me about him?"

"What do you mean?"

"I mean, one day I'm walking Harry to his highway, hearing his story, and thinking he's had it tougher than he deserves. Later that day, I hear from Sarah he's the one who put Lenny in the hospital."

Grant stopped abruptly and stared into the distance.

"Sarah said she told you. What gives?" asked Carli.

Grant chuckled. "Carli, the street can make you do things you wouldn't otherwise do."

"I don't understand," she said. "How could you do that to Sarah? Ignore her and steal her trust?"

"I didn't ignore her, believe me. I gave you to her … and she lied to you."

"Huh?"

"I saw it all," said Grant. "Harry didn't do it. It was your good friend Sarah who gave Lenny the brick gift."

Carli studied Grant carefully. Sarah barely crept out of her skin long enough to say five words, let alone clobber someone on the head.

"My guess is Sarah was trying to preserve her spot, preventing the new kid from moving her out. She knows Harry goes over there from time to time, so she framed him. In fact, he might have been there; I'm still not sure. I saw someone in the distance but couldn't make him out. But I saw her, and I know she did it."

"If you saw it, why didn't you stop it?"

"Was over before I could do anything."

"Why didn't you help Lenny?"

"I did. I left the scene and called for help. Actually, it arrived faster than usual. Better to leave an anonymous tip than to be dragged in."

"You didn't report her?"

"She belongs somewhere, but not in a cell. The way I see it is this: if she happened to see I was there, she knows I won't turn her in if she ever happens to get in a jam. That can always be useful knowledge. You just keep working on her. I know you can do it."

"So, that's why you kept asking Harry about it?"

Grant nodded. "Seeing if he was the one I saw, and seeing if he planned on saying something to anyone. Don't think he cared one way or another, if it was him who was there."

"He must know. Why else would he steal her cart?"

"Stole her cart? Must have been looking for a wheel for Grudge's wheelchair."

"He what?"

"Was looking for a wheel for Grudge. Harry took the cart from Sarah, or bought it from her or traded her for it, for all I know, because it had wheels. He was trying to get one for the front of the wheelchair. Where was that old shopping cart, anyway? Didn't see it out there."

"Sold it. Said it wasn't right."

"Hmm. The wheel must have been the wrong size. Either that, or it was too rusted to remove." Grant resumed walking.

Carli followed a couple of steps and stopped. "Jesus, Grant, I feel like an idiot. Here I was looking at Harry like a criminal. How the hell do you know all of this, and I don't know any of it?"

"You were working on Sarah. Only saw her side. But it was good timing, you coming onto Outreach when you did. I was getting nowhere with Sarah."

"Why didn't you tell me?"

"You would have seen her differently."

He was right, but it stung.

Hoisting Harry's belongings onto an empty washing machine, Grant threw dark colors in one machine, light in another, and laid out papers, plastic bags, and assorted trinkets to dry on the row of empty washers. It was eerily reminiscent of Bert's sidewalk store that Grant had introduced Carli to on her first days of Outreach. Ever since, she had seen Bert every time she passed by Thirty-Fourth Street. The difference was Harry's trinkets – can opener, wet matches, and lighter fluid – were more substantial than Bert's expired mailer coupons and outdated catalogs. Grant put Harry's duffels and backpack into separate machines and started them washing, gentle cycle. Carli placed her hands on his arms. "Thank God, you're here. Welcome back."

Together, they dried and folded even the most ragged items and stuffed them back into Harry's packs. Next morning, they provided "home" delivery to a safe haven shelter closest to his trestle.

"Better than the pricey dry cleaners," said Grant, presenting Harry his goods. "By the way, how'd you sleep?"

"Bad. How's Grudge?"

"Should be out today."

"Where's he going?"

"My guess? Here for starters."

Harry raised his eyebrows. "You can give him my spot. And don't go looking for nothing else for me. I'm not going in."

"We'll see," said Grant. "We'll see."

Aquaman's home took two days to fix with nonstop, around-the-clock, overtime workers. It had been a big one; Harry and Grudge were lucky to be alive. After tearing up a full block of pavement, the neighborhood was as good as new. Harry disappeared during the repair but moved right back in, clean clothes in tow, once things were back to normal. Grudge made the move back as well.

"I'm sure he was riding the lines," said Grant, from inside his own room. Carli thought of Harry volunteering to find a spare part for his friend's wheelchair and then huddled in a subway car, with lights flickering as it passed through station after station. It killed her. After all, he had saved Grudge's life. She looked closely at Grant, from head to toe, wondering how close he had been, or might still be, to sleeping on a train. Every day still presented a delicate situation, forcing her to continue walking the silent tightrope hovering between support and hands completely off. What's more, she now knew each one could be a full-time job, with no guarantee of success. Grant had long been her sounding board. She was on her own now.

TWENTY-SEVEN

AS AUGUST ENDED, Grant looked steadied in body and mind. Dr. Greenberg's drugs and discussions were finally working. For the first time in a long while, Carli felt safe leaving him. He promised to pay special attention to Vera while Carli took time away. Carli believed him and freely packed for her two-week painting expedition to the western United States, many needed miles from the frazzled streets of Manhattan.

From the picture window of her cabin at Triple R Dude Ranch, Carli looked across grasslands to the purple craggy mountains of the Tetons. They were awe-inspiring; nearly ten times taller than Manhattan's tallest skyscrapers. Broader and sturdier as well. Unlike Manhattan's tallest buildings, known to sway several feet in high winds, the only things swaying in the mountains were the stately stands of evergreens and birds in their branches. The mountains stood firm. Had done so for millions of years, rather than a mere century or two. As they sat, framed by her window, the mountains of the west put Outreach in perspective. Carli thought about Lucy, Grant, and all the others now woven into her life. She thought of all that had to get done ... when they were ready. Compared to the million-years-time frame of mountains, Outreach time flitted past in nanoseconds. But it was just as Grant said, time passed, nothing more. That's what Carli learned, looking out her window at Triple R.

The next day, Carli brought her sketchpad up a moderately ascending trail and sat upon a rock bench of sorts – really only a convenient assemblage of rocks chipped from the mountain behind her. She looked down on a valley and across to another range. For the past months, she had worked hard to capture the allure of oceans, in some of their many robes. They had a multiplicity of personalities—choppy or calm, angry and furious, or soothing. As she sketched the range in front of her, she thought how strange that its peaks had likely risen from oceans. Then she wondered why oceans were always vast, but never majestic, and mountains were always majestic. Was it because they didn't tower overhead? It was like two very different siblings, one staid and true, the other as variable as the moon and winds that manipulated its currents and stirred up its waves.

In truth, the western landscape was also vast. There was enormity in it; from the mountains to acres of forest and prairie land, to rivers that stretched for miles, and waterfalls that cascaded thousands of feet. Carli would have to make this sense of scale jump from her paintings when she worked from the day's rough sketches.

She moved from a study of size and scale to a study of form. Whereas water and waves curled, mountains angulated; the Tetons in particular. It would be millions of years before water and wind softened their sharp edges. Carli couldn't wait to highlight their juxtaposition of shape and form.

Color was next, also offering the yin to the ocean's yang. The oceans lacked purple. Lacked the reds needed to bend them in that direction. The mountains, however, showed a bounty of purple-twinged gray rock faces and forested evergreens tempered by their lavender-gray shadows. The one element that ocean and land shared was a vast and changeable sky, with its many nuances of light. Yes, Carli knew light and lighting would be key, as usual.

As she continued to look across the grassland, Carli could picture the exhibit. No, she could feel it! The mountain color palette would hang on two of the gallery's adjoining walls. The waterscape palette, on the two others. Working together, they would enclose the rectangular room with a flood of strong, deep, rich, and complex colors. Together, they would create a continuum of brazen earthy surroundings. Against the gallery's white walls, they would be truly shocking, perhaps even overwhelming. Wasn't that what they deserved? Like Carli's waterscapes, the western visions would be big. Several would be six-feet by nine-feet each; massive, honest statements of her subjects. If you are going to brand, she thought, brand big. Carli set down her sketch pad. She couldn't believe she was creating so freely again. It felt like a dream. If only time weren't getting so short.

One night mid-expedition, Carli lay in bed, surrounded by the chirping sound of crickets in the mountain grasses. As kids, she and Grant had camped out in their backyard, entrenched in a nearly deafening cacophony of a similar late-summer choir. It wasn't easy being tough with Grant, she thought. She had always looked up to him and had often deferred to him. It would be so much easier to let him get away with it – the fibs, odd tales, and continued assurances that everything was fine – but it couldn't possibly end well. Softly encouraging him, ever so gently, without pushing so hard as to send him into a shell or an angry snap, was so damned difficult. But just as he was having to fine-tune his medications, she was having to fine-tune her relationship with her brother. Not stepping up to the plate would simply make her a codependent of sorts. Could a person really be a "sort of codependent," she wondered? No, of course not. She faced herself—literally rose from bed and looked at her reflection in the two-foot square mirror in the cabin's master bathroom—and said, "You can either be a codependent or a true sister and friend, tough decisions and all." She closed her eyes, folded her arms across her chest, as though to protect herself with a hug, and said, "Dear God, please help me to see what is right and do what is right so Grant will be safe. Please protect him, as you have all the years, and keep him well. And please know how grateful I am for having Rocky, Mercy, and Dr. Greenberg here to step in and help." She flipped the light switch and returned to bed for a night's rest.

———

A week later, Carli filled her carry-on bag with her sketches, artist pencils, and notes. She added to it the gift for Grant. Finally, she slipped in a couple of sandwiches to tide her over during her airport time and flight back to New York City. With a last look around the cabin, she threw her carry-on over her shoulder and argued with her roller bag the entire bumpy trip over the gravel leading to her car. She had finally found a worse evil for luggage than Manhattan's sidewalks. As usual, for as good as it was to get away, she was ready to return home.

———

Carli arrived at her apartment to find Grant waiting outside on the sidewalk, a bouquet of raging red tulips in his hand.

"For me?" she asked.

"Give me your bags. We have work to do," he said.

"What's wrong?" she asked.

"Wilson. In the hospital. His system's close to collapse. It doesn't look good. Thought you should know. Lucky me, bringing the bad news. Welcome home."

Carli quickly digested his words.

"His kidneys are at about 50 percent functionality, and his liver is practically shot. They have him on something to help with his detox. It's a lousy game of wait and see."

"When did this happen?" she asked.

"Couple of days ago. The nurses look fearful, what with him jaundiced and vomiting. Wouldn't be surprised if they tried to scrub him down sometime soon, or next time."

"Scrub him down? Next time? What do you mean?" she asked.

"Oh, I don't know. Let's just go."

As they rode through traffic, Carli took a long look at Grant. "Good to see you. How are you?"

"Terrific," he said. "Except for this. I missed you."

Wilson slept under a pile of blankets. His color still had a jaundiced sheen to it, and his breathing was shallow. Carli thought of Wilson grabbing the fragrance of pear or lily of the valley out of thin air, and she desperately wished he were well enough to smell them now. Grant pulled Carli aside, so as not to wake him. "He's going to be here a while. At least, we can hope for that. The alternative is six feet under," said Grant. "Mercy and the doctors have a place lined up for him if they can keep his body functioning enough to stay alive. It has the best support system around. Counseling, groups, and medical liaisons to keep him tied to his doctors."

Carli wanted to share perfume in the park with him, not watch him die. She gazed at Wilson and then closed her eyes and prayed. Moments later, a young female nurse peeked into the room, circled the bed, checked the monitors, and left. Carli watched Grant's eyes follow her around and then stop when they came back around to Carli. He smiled a sly smile.

"I used to love the old uniforms," he confessed. "Those white stockings reminded me of a swan's long white neck, and those pointed hats they used to wear reminded me of wings and a tail."

Carli wondered why he had chosen now to share this information. Grant shrugged off her stare like a cow casually swishing a fly with its tail.

"How long until we know if any of this working?" she asked, leaving the hospital.

"More than a minute. Less than a year," said Grant, with little emotion but an odd certainty.

"What?"

"Don't know. It's out of our hands," he said.

They walked quietly. She wondered if she had strength enough to continue. If Wilson's body gave out, she would face another loss, surely a setback for her painting. The worst of it, though, was it would be far more painful than she ever could have imagined; she had grown fond of Wilson, even if he peed in public. Carli wanted desperately to save him from his alcohol-coated life.

"Where to first? Wilson?" Carli asked the next day.

Grant looked up for a moment. "No. The piers. Let's catch some sunshine."

"Grant, he looked like he was on the verge of dying. He might already be dead."

"It's a nice day for that, too. Let's go."

Grant began walking. Carli caught up and stopped him with a hand against his chest.

"We're checking Wilson, right?"

"Sure, why not."

"Wait," she stopped him again. "Are you all right?"

"Sure." He stared blankly and resumed walking.

Wilson's outer appearance was unchanged, but his doctor hailed certain test numbers as evidence of slight internal improvements. Wilson strained his eyes when Carli and Grant approached his bed. Then, he gave the weakest of smiles. To Carli, it felt like a first magnificent sunburst after a horrible deluge.

Wilson's lack of strength made the visit brief. Less than fifty words were exchanged between them. Carli held in tears while Grant, for some reason, inquired about the nurse.

Once outside, Carli pried again. "Grant, how were your tests?"

"Fine," he answered.

"What were your numbers?"

"Don't know," he said.

"What do you mean?"

"I couldn't do them. Was busy with Wilson. It's pretty ugly, but he'll die soon enough."

"Grant, you promised."

"Yes, promised to take care of them. We're doing it, right?"

"I think your dose needs a change."

Carli phoned Doctor Greenberg.

"Without seeing him, or knowing the levels," said the doctor, "it's unclear. My guess is he's gone off."

"Off?"

"Yes. Off his medication."

"Why would he do that?" Carli slowly asked.

"Because he thought he could get away with it. Or just wanted to. He must have been feeling better. Not uncommon at all, if this is what happened. Tell him to come see me."

Carli shut her eyes. "Oh, dear God," she barely whispered. It was Lucy's denial all over again, but worse.

"Am I seeing you this week?" asked the doctor.

"Yes. Definitely."

Carli phoned Kristin next. All she said was, "Help."

"What's wrong?" asked Kristin.

"Everything."

"Uh oh."

"Grant's off his medication. At least, it seems like it. Wilson, the perfume man, is in the hospital, and in horrible shape. I haven't been out to see Vera or Sarah yet. That makes more than two weeks without a visit."

"Sister, that sucks."

"On top of it all, I doubt my paintings will get any attention. Why does life always do this?" asked Carli.

"Don't know. It just does. But I have faith in you. You'll get through it."

"I was so excited to tell you about my trip. It was awesome. I was truly doing it."

"Details, Sister. Hand them over. I could use a good distraction. I have a couple of tough projects going on right now, myself," said Kristin.

"Sorry, I didn't even ask. We'll get to you, but first, Wyoming was spectacular. Through my cabin window I saw mountains. All around, it was so big and open and unlike here. No gutter water after a rain. Fresh air all the time. Crickets and mountains. Bison crossing grass-lands, and tiny ants crawling on mega-mountains."

"Better than roaches on the kitchen counter? No way," said Kristin.

"Oh, yes. Wayyy better."

"Lucky you. Did you get the material you need for the rest of your work?"

"Absolutely, and then some. You would have loved all the colors. You're such a color guru. Can tell the slightest variations in every-thing. You always got the blends on those materials perfect."

"Color is my inner soul," said Kristin, "which is why I am having such a lousy time with one of my projects. The client doesn't get it. The colors they like are fighting with the message. I'm at wit's end. I hate having controlling clients that are totally clueless."

"It's the worst. Sorry for you," said Carli.

"And Grant?" asked Kristin.

"Picture yourself in a canoe on a river. You're looking upstream at a dam that's making odd noises. It's like you know before it happens that the dam is about to split open and crumble apart, and you are going to be in an 'oh shit' moment that you can't control. You will only be lucky to escape, but you can't do a thing about it, except ride it out. And you'll likely go under on the way. That's Grant."

"Oh."

"And Wilson is bad off, like I said. It's a game of wait and pray," said Carli. "Even if they can get him detoxed, there's no guarantee his liver or kidneys can function enough to sustain him. It's going to be a long process. Or a very short one."

"Sorry, Sister. This is definitely the good news report, huh?"

"I so wanted to let him sniff my perfume samples. I couldn't wait to see his eyes light up, even if nothing much else could," said Carli. "I really thought it would be a great way to reach him. Looks like his wine beat me to it."

"Sorry to do this to you, Sister, but that client I just told you about is on the line here. Got to go."

"Hugs," said Carli.

"Back at you."

TWENTY-EIGHT

THE LAST THING Carli expected to hear was the buzzer to her apartment ringing in the middle of the night. She ignored the first buzz, thinking it might be a prank, or the night doorman mistakenly hitting the wrong button. He was new to the job since she had gone out west. The buzzer sounded again, and several more times after. Maybe someone needed help.

"Yes?" she barked into the call box.

"There's a man with a bike here to see you," said the doorman.

"Can you put him on the line?" asked Carli. "He probably doesn't have a phone."

Carli heard some muffled conversation and then heard Grant loud and clear. "Carli? Did I wake you?"

"Grant, what are you doing here? Are you okay?"

"I've got my bike. I'm a man of my word. Let's ride!"

Grant had arrived on Royal and sat with elbows resting patiently on the handlebars and with his chin in his hands. He beamed as Carli stepped outside.

"You've never been on the front of one of these before?" he asked.

Carli shook her head. "You know as well as any that I haven't."

"Not to worry. You'll be comfy in no time. Nothing to do but relax and leave the driving to me."

"No, Grant. Let's go. Inside. We're not riding right now."

"Of course, we are. Get on."

"No, Grant. It's dangerous." Carli reached for Royal and said, "Get off." Grant dug his feet into the sidewalk, and clutched the brakes with both hands. Carli tried jostling him a bit. For every bit that Carli jostled Royal, Grant jostled back. In fact, he finally pulled Royal so hard he ripped the handlebars from Carli's hands. Then he said, "Nice try ... Forget it."

Carli fought with words another few minutes, but to no avail. As much as she wanted to return to bed, she knew she had to keep an eye on him. He was clearly losing control to impending mania. If she let him ride off alone, she would worry about him all night.

After a short discussion on how to ride, she cautiously backed herself onto the handlebars. Grant lifted one arm into the air, shouted, "And they're off!" and started pedaling.

A few uncomfortable tilts taught powerful lessons on when and how to lean. Carli learned to keep a wide straddle so shoes stayed clear of spokes, and learned it was best to not block the driver's view. Mostly, she heard the Delaney twins bickering loud and clear as they went weaving down Fifth Avenue.

Grant pedaled block after block. The ride was generally smooth, and Carli began to feel oddly comfortable. Before she knew it, they were all the way downtown, approaching Wall Street. She never took much notice of Manhattan's hills, but, on more than one occasion, Grant had stood slightly to give the extra push needed to make the grade. She felt his breath on her neck.

When they slowed to a stop in the park at the island's southern tip, Carli slid from the handlebars, grateful to have her feet touch the ground. The water surrounding Manhattan looked beautiful lapping the concrete edges of the city. Nearly as soon as they arrived, Grant was ready to leave. They rode northward again, block after block toward Central Park, and then turned south once more. He didn't stop at her apartment. Instead, he said, "Missed something. We're going back down." Goosebumps inflated on Carli's arms, even in the August evening air. She feared they were headed for the piers. Around two in the morning, Royal slowed to a stop at the entrance to the Staten Island Ferry. Grant parked his bike quickly and loudly.

"Look at it," he said as they crossed the water by ferry. "The moon, I mean. It's full tonight. Pregnant."

Carli looked at the moon and then at Grant.

"Wanted to see the moon from the water," he said. "And the moon on the water. It's like shimmering silver!"

"Grant," she started, knowing he needed help, and certain he had ditched his meds.

"Shh," he said. "We're alone. With the waves and the sea. Listen." He was right. Not a single other person was with them in the passenger space on the ferry.

The ride across the water to Staten Island was followed immediately by a return trip to Manhattan. Grant pushed harder on the pedals as they road uptown. He talked as they rode, leaving huffs of breath to catch the wind in between his words.

"We have to keep going, Carli. It's too beautiful to stop. We might get to Heaven this way. I think we have to ride all night."

Grant's energy was overwhelming. His words raced in tandem with his pedaling legs and spinning body. If he could have made his dear Royal fly, he would have. As it was, he came uncomfortably close.

When he finally returned her home, Carli convinced him to stay, knowing she was staring face-to-face with the manic side of bipolar. The couch would be fine for his sleeping purposes, and she didn't want him out alone. The doctor was right. It was as though someone had flipped a loud, clanking light switch in storage, and had catapulted Grant into a radiant blare of white-lighted thought. He was heading back up. Only God knew how high or for how long.

Grant was interested to see the photos again. The ones of their family, including one of Henry and Bonaventura. Grant stared at that one for a long time. Then he straightened up and stared at Carli, seemingly deep in thought.

"What's wrong?" she asked.

Grant looked at the collection of photographs, then slowly said, "I don't know."

"You remember Tura, don't you?" she asked.

"The dog? Of course," he said.

"What about the people?" she asked.

"I know them," he said. "Yes. And I know you. It was good, wasn't it?"

"Very good," she said. She wished she could have it back.

By the time Carli awakened late morning, Grant and Royal were gone. Miraculously, she found him dining at St Mary's, as his note had directed. He had already visited Wilson, Canada, and most everyone else. She knew he hadn't slept and wondered what he had said to any of the street clan. He had a telltale odor of liquor. After lunch, and into the evening, they walked, as though desperately trying to walk off his jumbled thoughts.

Doctor Greenberg's message had been plenty clear: send him up to see her or tell him to phone. Carli looked at Grant, wishing she could. Repeated requests were met with denial. Her heart wept. It was his decision to make.

For five tense days, Grant was a mass of energy, changing thoughts and direction, jumping curbs, leaping over benches, bumping people in parks, expounding the merits of many things – love and parakeets and goldfish—to anyone who would listen, including crowds at Times Square, families strolling in the park, and tourists standing by the piers. Oh, how he gravitated to the piers. Carli spent several sleepless nights in storage. By the start of the next week, he made marginal sense to anyone but himself, if he even did that. He continued to yearn for the piers. She continued to chaperon.

After two more long nights traveling and talking, Grant was ready to return to his storage room and stay awhile, or so she thought. Carli studied him carefully after he flopped upon his mattress. Somehow, she believed him. She returned to her own bed for four short hours of sleep and hoping for a chance to paint and make her visits in the morning. She had as good as neglected everyone all week, except Wilson, who was slowly improving. She made a point of walking

Grant over to visit every day. Carli wondered how the rest were faring, especially Sarah and Vera.

As Carli prepared to walk at her pace, for the first time in days, Grant phoned, with a chilling request.

"Help! I need you. Fast."

Carli found the door to his room open. Grant sat comfortably in his thinking chair. A partially eaten cake sat in the middle of his mattress. The cake in his hand was chocolate frosted, the one on his mattress was topped with vanilla. Another dozen cake boxes, at least, were neatly-arranged in four stacks beside him.

"Grant, what is this?"

"Happy birthday to me. Happy birthday to me. Happy birthday to me. Happy birthday to me." He swung his fork through the air like a baton.

"It's your birthday?" she asked. Apparently, Grant was born in August. Henry, she knew, was not.

"Was. Yesterday," he said proudly. "Got a cake for each of my old college frat brothers. Delivered, even. Should have seen the delivery person! I need help getting these addressed and to the post office. Got one for you too. Vanilla or chocolate?"

Carli stiffened, hardly feeling relieved the emergency was about cakes. Mania had not receded after all. Dear God, help him.

Carli assisted with the wrapping and labeling of the goods. In the end, the cakes looked to be going out for delivery by special courier, but an extra tip slipped to Neuman at Cooper's, while Grant showered, assured Carli the cakes wouldn't get far, which was just fine. After, she walked with him, as slowly as she could, trying to keep him quiet – a difficult task.

A loud booming sound outside her doorway sent Carli bolting from bed and wondering if Grant and Royal had returned. Her next-door neighbor was moving out. With any luck, Grant was still in his room, but her call to him went unanswered.

The storage room door was locked. Grant was out. The guard – Neuman – confirmed it. "Left early this morning," he said.

She should have stayed after addressing the cakes. Oh, Grant, please ..., she thought.

Her gut told her he was at the piers. When she checked, he was nowhere in sight. She trolled the city by car, and then acquiesced to the game called "wait and see."

Gloria's was dead, except for the new man Carli had seen before her expedition. Her instincts were right. He was definitely moving in somewhere in the neighborhood. She looked at him and sent a partially committed smile. Maybe he would remember her, and the smile would mean something when it came time to try to get him in. Grant had always reached out to the new ones, so she wasn't sure.

Wilson opened his eyes as soon as Carli entered his hospital room. He was sitting upright in bed, propped up by pillows and surrounded on both sides by more of the steadying white supports.

"Good to see you awake," she said. Carli approached softly and spoke with a calm coating on her voice. It's what Wilson needed. "I've been visiting," she said. "Grant too. Well, was ... We didn't want to wake you."

"Ahh, you could have." Wilson's voice was raspier than usual and softer, as well. "I've got plenty of time to sleep."

Carli noticed he was shaking a bit, a sure sign his brain and body were not used to their lower-proof state. His color looked better, although she wasn't trained in the nuances of jaundice. "The doctor reports are good," she said.

Wilson's only response was a flicker of his eyes, from his bed to her face and back.

"I have something," she said.

Carli hesitated before reaching into her bag. The doctors had given her the go-ahead to share the scents if Wilson was willing. She watched his reaction when she placed four small bottles on a bed tray. Wilson was weak, and his grin barely slid up from one corner of his mouth, but she saw it. "Curious?" she asked quietly.

Wilson gave a feeble nod, barely raising his chin. It was enough.

Carli quietly twisted off a simple silver-colored cap from an aqua blue glass vial. She held the bottle in one hand, several feet from Wilson's face, and slowly waved her free hand over the opening to send its invisible floral scent floating toward Wilson's face. Wilson closed his eyes. She thought he might have fallen asleep, but many seconds later he looked back at her.

"It's *Oceans* by Antoine," she said, not wanting Wilson to waste energy speaking.

Wilson smiled, both with his eyes and with another slight upturn of his left lip.

"Some other day, you can tell me more about it," she said. "I'll bring these others back next time too." Carli gave the bottle a quick tilt downward, with one finger covering its open neck. It was just enough to collect a single oily drop on a finger. She dabbed part of the drop on the sheet on the left side of Wilson's bed. Then she walked around the foot of the bed and back up the right side, continuing to slide her finger across the bedcovers. It would be just enough, she thought. Wilson's gaze told her she was right. Carli took ahold of Wilson's hand, as gently as possible, and said, "Rest well."

From Wilson's bedside, Carli traveled to Vera's place. Luck was on Carli's side.

"Vera Dear-a," she called.

Vera swung around, a smile lighting her face. It was such a gift to see. "I thought you got lost somewhere," said Vera. "Either that or got some kind of amnesia and didn't remember where to find me."

"I told you I was going away," said Carli. "I wanted to see you days ago, but something else came up."

"Well, you missed a good one," said Vera.

"Good what?"

"Couple nights ago. Fireworks. Just like Fourth of July, but shorter. Over at that tennis stadium," said Vera.

"You saw them from here?"

"Of course. Just like last year. Well, not from right here exactly, but you didn't think I crossed the river to see 'em all the way in the other borough, did you?"

"Lucky you," said Carli. "You always liked a good show."

"Yes, indeed." Vera nodded and smiled.

"So, are you doing okay?" asked Carli.

"I guess so. I don't like to complain," said Vera.

"Guess so? What's wrong?" asked Carli.

"We had a bunch of storms while you was gone. Thunder booming. Lightning like the fireworks. And rain. Whooeee! Did we ever have rain. Like cats and dogs. Water was flowing on some of those streets like rivers. Day and night."

"Did you go in anywhere? You know, to get out of it all?"

Vera cocked her head slightly to the side and shrugged. It was the answer Carli expected. "My place has a good enough overhang," said Vera, "but the water coming off some of the awnings nearby was splashing up. Didn't have any place for it to go. I put some plastic over me though. It did okay."

"Vera, please, remember what I said last time I was here?"

"What part of what you said? Sometimes you say a lot of different things. I'm not complaining, mind you. Just saying," said Vera.

"The part about ... you know, your husband. The part when I asked if he would want you out here," said Carli.

"I remember. Sure, I do. I've been thinking about it," she said.

"I have something for you," said Carli. "It's not socks."

Vera looked at Carli with her brow raised. Carli reached into her bag for a single photograph that she had laminated not once but twice before she went to Wyoming. The second she placed it in Vera's hand, Vera brought it to her chest, where she embraced it with one hand over the other. "Oh, Lordy be," she said. "My home." Vera looked ready to keep the simple gift close to her heart all night, at least, but moments later pulled it away from her chest to gaze at it and, no doubt, consider a flood of good memories.

It had taken Carli hours of digging to find an old real estate brochure of Vera and her husband's Minnix House early post-opening.

She hadn't minded. The Historical Society had moved right up Carli's list of fascinating city attractions, alongside the main branch of the library. Its collections presented intimate stories of architecture and people, which together helped make the city. Were the heart and soul of it in fact. Carli made the find, then made the copies and laminated them. Maybe if Vera could bring it with her, with memories of her husband, she would one day be willing to leave the standpipe and sleeping alcove. Time would tell. It was worth a shot.

Canada was nowhere to be seen. Carli figured he was working Wall Street since a check of his usual Midtown spots found him nowhere. She did another check of Grant's room. The lock was still in place.

Carli found Sarah on her bench, with no lure and no popcorn. Carli sat near, and Sarah looked up. They sat silently for five minutes, maybe more. Sarah was off duty. Carli was perfectly fine with this.

When Carli returned to Cooper's the next morning, she found the outer lock missing. Grant was back. She stood outside for a moment to listen. Then she whispered, "Grant?" No answer came, so she placed her ear on the door's metal finish. "Grant?" she whispered again. "Are you awake?"

Grant's was the only door with a lock inside as well as out. He had installed it himself, of course.

"Open up. I want to see you," she said. Something told her he was listening. "I have sandwiches," she said. By God, they were the same words from the Church Run.

The door stayed shut, but she heard him shuffling. After several soft knocks and no response, she slid herself to the floor to wait, thankful he was home. "I brought food," she said. Five minutes passed, and she launched another plea through the door. Then another. Finally, she heard the shaking of the lock.

He was unshaven, unchanged, hardly dressed for the street. How quickly the transformation occurred. With the roller coaster changing course, the dog-eared Grant was back. She wanted to wrap her arms around him and protect him from everything. Instead, she barely grazed his shirt sleeve with one finger. Truly, he was fragile.

Pizza boxes and telltale signs of Chinese food littered the room. New shoeboxes climbed the wall. Royal lay parked mid-room. Grant bit into the deli sandwich and dropped it onto its wrapper. It wasn't what he wanted. Most likely, nothing was. Carli eased down upon the floor. He spoke a few words. They were lifeless waves of sound, flat and empty, gone almost before they flowed from his mouth. She knew the answer, but asked anyway, "How do you feel?"

Grant didn't answer. Didn't seem able.

Carli spoke to fill the void. "Wilson was awake but awfully weak. At least he's still going in the right direction. I brought some perfume. He loved it," she said. Grant didn't respond "Vera was nearly flooded out when I was away, but she rigged up some plastic for protection," said Carli. "She's doing okay. Sarah was quiet. And Canada was nowhere to be found."

Grant's expression remained unchanged.

"I heard the umpires might strike," said Carli. "That would put a quick end to the season." She looked at Grant's face. After a long silence, she said softly, "I know you don't want to hear this, but you need to see Doctor Greenberg. Please, let me help you."

Grant's eyes moved up a trifle with one of his next breaths, then slid down as he exhaled. He heard, but couldn't do it. Didn't want to go out, eat, walk, or even turn on the light. So, they sat quietly together in the dark. He was withdrawn deep inside himself, once again, and no amount of convincing would move him until, or unless, he somehow managed the energy. With a blanket around her shoulders, Carli prepared to sit and keep watch. Tomorrow, she thought. Please, tomorrow.

When Carli awakened, still sitting upright, Grant was asleep and looked to be staying put. She gathered her bag, left a note on the floor, and rested her hand lightly on his shoulder. Before slipping through the open door, she slid the inside padlock into her bag. The bin would be safe, locked or not. No one ever came to the sixth floor; Grant had practically purchased penthouse privacy from

Neuman. She wouldn't be long, and she refused to be shut out again.

Grant's bin was temperature controlled, nothing like the city's brutal August heat, which slowed everything. Call it wishful thinking, but Carli carried in her bag the four perfume bottles. How she wanted to remove their tops and send their fragrances wafting through Wilson's room in a fireworks of perfume. Before she entered his room, she braced herself for what she might find. Wilson was asleep. With sheets and blankets tossed loosely off his chest, she gained a more complete view of his condition. His skin-and-bones body looked mighty ill. Carli took a quick peek into his single closet, curious if anything was inside. As soon as she swung open the door, she reached forward. She couldn't help herself. She touched his favorite winter coat, hanging properly on a hanger, and nearly cried. Thank God they had let him keep it. This really was a topline place, she thought.

Carli paid another visit to Vera. She saw her standing at her usual spot, but before Carli could catch her, Vera hopped on a bus. It was one way to find cheap air conditioning. Carli was happy to let her ride.

At Lucy's church, most dined lightly. Many took in extra water and juice, although some still downed hot coffee with plenty of sugar. A few fanned themselves with napkins. Others simply sat still. Conversation at the op-ed table was loud, owing to the standup fan humming wildly in the room's corner. The talk of the day was the heat, of course. It was the fifth pronounced heat wave of the year; three days in the hundreds so far, and untold more expected. The weather headliner was coupled with news of faulty air conditioners, baseball stats, and a media queen marriage. Lanna was the only cool one in the bunch. She had a job, salaried and insured. No amount of hot air could bring her down. At last, another success.

Though curious to learn what Sarah did to beat the heat, Carli trusted fully in the woman's ingenuity and ability to stay cool. It was Grant who needed her. She was on her way to Cooper's when Canada caught her exiting St. Mary's. "How're you doing in the heat, big guy?"

"Fine, fair lady. You?" Canada always called her "lady" now.

"Awful. Can't stand it," she said.

"A body gets used to it. Just like the cold," he said. "Library's a good spot. Or some of the subways, but you have to get one of the Wall Street routes. They have the best equipment."

Canada never wore shorts, not even as August had sauntered in and was sweltering its way past. A few of the others did. He likely knew something they didn't. "Come, talk with me a minute," she said. Carli beckoned him over, but Canada insisted they walk to a set of steps near a corporate fountain. With the blessing of a light breeze, the fountain's cool mist brushed against them, as he knew it would.

"I know you and Grant go back quite a ways," she said.

"That we do," he said.

Carli wanted to say, "Actually, Grant and I go back a long way too." Instead, she said, "He's struggling with something."

"Grant? Moods or booze, most likely. Am I right?"

Carli turned to face Canada directly. "You've seen this before?"

"Oh, yeah. Seen just about everything with him. He could say the same about me. Is he up or down?"

"Just started going down. I know there's medication that can help. But he isn't taking it."

"Not surprised," said Canada."

"Will you keep an eye out for him?" she asked.

"Sure. I doubt I can do anything about it, but I'll keep a watch out and see if he needs anything."

It was exactly what Carli needed to hear.

Grant was awake when Carli returned. He asked about Wilson, before turning to the subject of death and an edgy talk of knives. Grant began explaining details of carving and sharpening, serrated edges and smooth. She didn't like the tone of it. A small steak knife lay exposed on his mattress. She picked it up with a dirty plate and headed to the bathroom on the pretense of cleaning. Water flowed swiftly from the faucet and gurgled down the drain. Was he bluffing or, God forbid, preparing? She hated how well he played poker. When she returned, she said, "We need to see the doctor."

Grant looked up, with no change in his expression.

"You mean so much to them," she said. She relayed news of Vera and the bus, lunch at Lucy's, the new job for Lanna, and the particulars of Marvin and Leo. Then she said, "Canada asked about you." It was news of Madison that interested Grant most.

"He wants to see you, but you ought to see Dr. Greenberg first."

Grant's stare remained vacant. It didn't surprise her to hear him say, "Tomorrow."

TWENTY-NINE

FROM A DISTANCE, Carli spotted Sarah holding a bottle of water against the side of her face. Carli chuckled. She *knew* Sarah would have a few street tricks to combat the ills of the weather. Sarah sat very still, ignoring the pigeons. Carli guessed it was another measure to conserve energy. Carli stepped near, and Sarah slowly lowered the bottle from her face. A pulse of adrenaline surged through Carli's body. Staring back was a gaping wound on the side of Sarah's mouth. It had untidy edges of flapping flesh, and it was bloodied, red, and raw. The rest of Sarah's left cheek, from eye to chin, was a black-and-blue mess.

"Oh, my God, Sarah! What happened?"

"Rat." Sarah squawked out. "Looked ... for ... you." Dried blood on Sarah's clothes said it must have been a gusher.

"You need a doctor. Now."

Sarah nodded. "Go ... in."

Carli studied Sarah carefully. It sounded more permanent than seeing a doctor. Carli had passed her over in the park, trying to help Grant. All along, Sarah had needed her. Had wanted her. After all the pigeon talk, feedings, paintings, over-the-shoulder investigations, all it took was being there. The foundation had been set. Carli gently touched her arm and silently thanked God the woman was persistent.

"Okay," said Carli. Sarah tried to nod. Carli pulled out her phone.

"Where?" asked Sarah.

"Police," said Carli. "To ride to a hospital."

"No." Carli looked up. The look on Sarah's face was frozen scared. "Wait," she said.

"The police will help," said Carli.

"Wait," said Sarah.

A voice on the phone asked for details. Carli held it at bay as she questioned Sarah, "Why?"

"Mon ... ey," said Sarah.

"You don't have to pay," said Carli. The phone voice probed. Carli asked for more time. It no longer mattered. In the frenzy of the past days, she had pulled "a Grant" – the phone was dead.

"Keep," said Sarah. "For me." It didn't sound like Sarah was concerned about payment. "Lots." Sarah stared intently.

Carli thought a moment. Even if it was only a dollar, she knew it was important. Then again, it could be more. Much more. It had happened before. "Sarah, let's see a doctor, and find you a place. I'll hold your money for you. How much is it?"

Sarah studied her face carefully, as though looking for something specific. Carli didn't know what. Her voice was as harsh as ever. "Seven ... ty? Eight ... y?" She shrugged and began unloading her plastic bags until reaching one, in particular, at the bottom of her cart. After prying it from the cart's metal womb, she pulled out several piles of folded newspaper and then the brown, fake-leather satchel, with a roll of toilet paper tied to its strap. All that remained in the plastic bag was Buffy's framed portrait. Swinging the toilet paper roll aside, Sarah slid the bag over to Carli, unopened. Sarah looked straight ahead for a moment, before turning her eyes toward Carli, and giving a slight nod.

"Sarah, just tell me how much ... ," she began.

Carli's words were cut short by darts of panic shooting from Sarah's partly closed eyes. Carli unlatched the buckle and pried the bag open. It was as though she had found Lucy's pictures again. Crumpled bills—tens, twenties, fifties, and hundreds—jammed the satchel, covering bundles of neatly-stacked bills.

"Okay," said Carli. "Lots." She looked straight at Sarah and said, "I'll take care of it. Anything else?" Sarah shook her head.

With all bags, save the satchel, piled on the cart, Sarah and Carli bused the baggage out of the park. Even with the new shopping cart, it was a bulky load. As Carli carried the satchel, she felt eyes of many upon them. Blood, after all, was blood.

A call box brought a police officer from the Outreach squad straight to Sarah's side within minutes. He understood an ambulance would scare the woman away. So, he gently shielded Sarah's head, and held her weight with one of his arms, as she jostled her way onto the black vinyl interior of his car. Her bags fit nicely beside her. The cart settled into the trunk. Sarah was going in. Carli had the officer phone Mercy with the report.

Were it not for the money and cart full of bags, Sarah likely would have gotten help on her own. Certainly, she knew where to go, though fear might have kept her out. The money explained a lot, like why she never went in before, why she never took a shower, or put her bags in storage. A doctor's recommendation would surely get Sarah moved to one of the more private shelters. Carli was certain Sarah would actually go in this time. She was ready.

Carli demanded kid-glove treatment. Didn't want to see her woman back on the sidewalks and refused to leave her. The park would be fine with one less person. Carli stood by Sarah's side until a social worker completed the papers, and the doctor made his review; the suturing process wasn't pretty.

At last, they brought Sarah to a bed. Her swollen legs and battered body finally had a mattress, and her head a clean pillow. Carli took the satchel and one extra bag Sarah relinquished to her care. First thing in the morning, Carli would return to visit. Buffy's mama was finally in! For five minutes, Carli sat on the doorstep to Sarah's building and cried.

Grant was no spring flower when Carli returned. In fact, he idled like a car burning oil, and his black haze pushed Sarah's news far afield. Grant had pulled out *his* ace. A handgun rested on the floor, bedside, barely visible under the sheet spewed off the side of his mattress. The black-barreled revolver screamed at Carli in silent sirens.

"Grant," she said softly. "What are you doing?"

She managed one step forward. She wanted to run but didn't dare leave. Grant remained fixed to his bed. Did he intend to kill her too? She inched closer. Grant made no move toward the gun. He was painfully silent.

"Where did you get that?" she asked.

"This?" Grant managed to point a finger at the unwanted intruder. It was as though he was pointing it straight at her. "Just had it," he said. "Used to wear it."

"Why ... is it out?"

"Rats." He paused and stared her down. "Heard 'em. Ugly sons of bitches." His voice sounded ugly and slow; so slow, there was a pause between nearly every word. "It's the problem ... with everyone storing food here," he said.

"There are better ways to get rid of rats," she said.

"You took my lock." His monotone felt threatening. She might have preferred anger. She wondered if the steel intruder had bullets enough for both of them.

"Yes," she confessed. "I wanted ..."

"Leave," he demanded.

Carli focused on his face. Leaving was what she wanted to do. Others were far better trained at this than she. Yet, she was afraid to go. Afraid of the possibilities. "Grant," she started. He glanced up, and she looked straight into his eyes for several long seconds. Then she said, "Henry ... please ..."

Grant peered at her for many moments, silent and still. "What did you say?"

"I didn't mean to say it," she said. She moved a step closer. "I didn't mean to say it."

Grant moved his hand slightly.

"Please, Grant, let's see a doctor. Now."

Barely raising his eyes, he said, "Leave. Now." His finger seemed poised.

"Grant, you can't ..." She wondered if he would point it at his temple or down his throat. She saw a violence-filled struggle for the weapon to stop his intentions cold. She saw gunshots to her back and to his front. All of this she saw in a mere flicker of a second. In the end, she acquiesced to his request. He seemed far too sedate to do anything, let alone end his life.

Three steps back took her out of the bin. Two more removed him from sight. She heard no sound, no leap toward the gun. Grant was silent. The gun was silent. Carli ran quietly, fearing what she might hear. God, she silently prayed, don't let him do it.

Carli grabbed Neuman's phone. It was a call she had hoped to avoid. It was a long seven minutes before first responders arrived – six of them from many sectors. Thankfully, the gun was never raised. Carli grabbed it from his bed and hid it in her bag before others saw it. Grant had made no move to claim it. For all she knew, it wasn't even loaded, but the last thing Grant needed was to be charged for an illegal weapon in New York City. Grant went peacefully. Something inside him must have known. Perhaps he had wanted her to walk in, as she had, to be his gun's safety lock, and answer his pitiful cry for help, the cry he couldn't put into words. Oh, surrounding blackness.

Far from feeling like she had saved him, Carli felt she had abandoned him when she handed him over to a system of strangers. It was the worst thing she had ever had to do. She described the inciting incident, his appointments with Dr. Greenberg and diagnosis, and his recent refusal of prescribed medication. Against his former wishes, she told them she was his sister. It was now up to him.

Carli walked the streets in a haze of guilt and loss, wanting Henry back, but knowing how ill he truly was. How could he see it in everybody else, and ignore it in himself? That was the illness. Dear God, she thought, let him see it.

He was placed on suicide watch. Though he hadn't made a direct threat, Carli's account of the gun, news of the knife, and Grant's overall intent and demeanor were evidence enough for his examiner. His supervision was constant, his means few, and the care good.

During the next days, drugs flowed back into his body. He responded well. Perhaps it would only be a matter of time before he would be his renewed self, but it could be a rocky road, and he would have to be willing to travel it. For now, he at least seemed safe.

Carli shared the news with Mercy.

"It's mighty hard to do what you did," said Mercy. "It was the right call. The only call. You'll see."

"I hope you're right."

Street visits were bittersweet in their semi-empty state. Sarah had spent several sleepless nights inside. As much as she wanted in, she didn't. At least she wasn't sharing space with a rat, and she seemed comforted by Carli's visits. Grant was heading in a better direction. Wilson's park looked like it was waiting, just waiting, for another to come along. Carli found Canada resting lazily on a bench in a park near the library. He was just the person she wanted to see.

"I had a problem with Grant," she said. "I wanted you to know."

Canada listened intently as the news percolated. Both agreed a person could hide things. Canada seemed to have less to hide than many others, perhaps because most of Canada's baggage had already surfaced and was carried in the open. Carli knew Grant wanted Canada off the streets, not only for Canada's sake but for the sake of others. It was Grant's belief that Canada could even join the Outreach team, and maybe even partner up with Grant. At least that's what Grant had said. Carli didn't know what to believe of Grant's words. Clearly, no one had been poisoned. Yes, three had died over the past year, but not as Grant envisioned. His poisoning theory was just a bad memory associated with his gruesome departure from the cult. Nevertheless, Carli tested the waters and quickly learned that Grant had, indeed, talked with Canada about doing Outreach. Several times, as a matter of fact.

"Grant's right," he began. "I know a lot of them. Wilson ... well, he was going to be out until some emergency raced him in. That's just what happened. Who knows if it is too late for his body. Harry's hurting as bad as any. I figure he looks after Grudge to direct his loss and feel more useful. That Spaceman Irving has issues. Most everyone stays clear, but I don't think he'd hurt an ant. The Screamer's a weird bird, and nobody knows her name, but she's still a person somewhere in there. We just have to find her again. There are a whole lot of others you might not know too well since you're visiting a couple of ladies, but I know them."

"What about you? What keeps you out? Grant's so certain you could go in, and, what's more, reach others."

Canada tried to smile, a clear cover. "I'm not sure I can start over," he said.

"Why not?"

"Just the way it is," he said. "Afraid, I guess."

"People change. Getting inside would give you a better place to think about it. And think about a different way to help others. On the street and down on Wall Street."

Carli left him to consider it and found herself strolling past Sarah's bench in the park. On this spectacular summer's day, the park, bustling with people, felt oddly empty. Sarah had been a part of Carli's park for as long as she had done Outreach, and even before she had known Sarah by name. It was empty, too, without Grant. She didn't bother going to Lucy's church. There was no one she wanted to see. She skipped out on Vera, put off Harry for another day, but phoned for an update on Wilson, and learned he was holding steady.

THIRTY

"CARLI ... OR SHOULD I SAY TESS ..." Grant looked deeply into her eyes. "I want out." He continued to stare deeply for many seconds more. "I don't want to be here any longer, even if I have some liver problems, as they say."

Carli held him close. It had been almost a week, with daily visits, sometimes for hours, that Carli had carried the guilt of sending him to the hospital. Finally, she heard the words she had hoped for. She continued to hold him close in her arms, overwhelmed by the power of love.

The next day, he asked about the others. Finally, she could share the news of Sarah.

"No way!" Grant's voice boomed.

"She asked me to keep something." Carli paused. "Her money. Don't know if she's staying put, so I didn't check it with anyone."

Grant was interested. "Some of that probably came from me. Dropped a share of twenties to her over the year."

"Really?"

"A benefit of living where I do. Usually have extra to pass around."

"She conned you." Carli spilled the details. "It was nearly eighty thousand dollars. All kinds of bills."

Grant buried his face in his hands. Muffled laughter grew into a hearty laugh, as infectious as ever. He, of all people, appreciated a good con.

Sarah Melissa Stewart, Carli thought to herself, thank you for bringing him back.

"Technically," said Grant, "you ought to tell the shelter so they can figure her assistance and benefits right. Non-technically, I suggest you keep ahold of it for a while longer to be sure she's staying, like you said." Carli agreed.

"Speaking of living where you do," said Carli, "what was with the apartment on Lexington Ave.? The one you told me you lived in when you first visited my apartment?"

"You went?" he asked. "Hah! I should have known. Just something I do, rent one of those short-term vacation rentals every so often. Different places across Manhattan. To keep Nirvu off my trail. Don't want them to know where I really live."

Grant's words of the cult sent shivers through her body. She said, "Grant, I think we're safe. Both of us."

Grant shook his head ever so slightly. Maybe it wasn't time yet for him to be released after all. "I see," was all she said.

"By the way," he added, "Canada stopped by. Thanks for telling him."

———

Discharged from the hospital, Grant dismissed any suggestion of moving out of his storage room and sharing space in Carli's apartment, even on the most temporary basis. He did visit a few times, once to officially meet Kristin.

"You remember her, right? This is a long-time friend," said Carli. "Just about everything I've done over the past few decades, I have done at least once with Kristin."

"That's right, Sister," said Kristin.

Carli noticed a strange look on Grant's face. "It's a nickname. She's not really my sister."

Grant laughed and then looked at Carli for a long moment. "Don't you think I would know that?" he asked. He continued to grin and look Carli straight in the eyes. "You know what else I know?"

"Haven't a clue," said Carli.

"If you two are as close as you say you are, Kristin, here, likely knows exactly who I am, maybe even knows more about me than I know about myself."

Carli and Kristin were silent.

"Just as I thought," he said. Grant gently tapped Carli on the arm, as he had done through childhood. "It's okay. I get it." Then he looked at Kristin and said, "I'm sorry you got to know her all these years and I didn't. She's a good one."

Henry was back.

In another few days, Carli and Grant met at St. Mary's. It was like starting over. It felt terrific. The energy he carried was better than ever. Carli guessed most of the street clan would never know how lucky they were to have Grant visiting. She certainly would.

Walking into his storage room afterward, Carli saw he had cleaned. Much had been tossed, and even more had been sorted. Paintings lined one wall, clothes another. She saw so many from Outreach skillfully captured on canvas. She didn't recall seeing as many paintings during her other visits. The shoes he kept were organized in pairs; his shirts and pants were folded and stacked.

"Where did it go?" she asked.

"New Hope Thrift. Where else?"

"Should have known. It looks great. Say, Thelma would like us to visit. She'd like to meet this man called Grant. Knows he helped her friend Lucy."

"Give me a week," he said. "Maybe Tuesday."

It was barely midnight when Grant phoned several nights later. He sounded desperate.

"Man, I just had a nasty crash. Stomach hurts like a bull's inside, but Royal looks salvageable."

"I'll be right over," she said.

"No need. Just want you to know. I might be late getting out tomorrow."

"What were you doing riding in the rain?" she asked.

"You call this rain?" he asked. "Hah! It's a deluge! But I couldn't sleep. Thought a ride would help wind me down."

"Are you sure you're all right? I can take you to Emergency."

"No. I'm fine. I didn't call to worry you. Get some rest. I'll see you in the morning."

Carli clicked off her phone and tried to fall asleep. Half an hour later, she grabbed her car keys. He was right; it was a deluge. She couldn't imagine controlling a bicycle through the intermittent river-ways winding from buildings to sidewalks and streets to drains. Her car's wipers couldn't keep up with all that was falling. It made for very slow driving, even with relatively few cars. Most of the taxis, she suspected, were carrying show-goers home post-performance, at least those who had been lucky enough to beat others to a cab.

Carli found his storage bin unlocked and with its light on. Grant lay spread across his mattress. His room was even tidier than the days before. He had even hung his wall tapestry from the ceiling. It hid the tangle of ugly wires, but he had cut a hole in it for the lights. It looked like a canopy bed. The room looked oddly cozy and, at the same time, spacious. She stepped past Royal in the hall, with part of its front fender badly bent.

"Knock knock," she whispered. "It's Carli. I came anyway."

Grant didn't move.

Carli stepped closer to sit on his mattress edge. She noticed his clothes were soaked through. His hair, too, was wet with rainwater. Wet sneakers covered his feet, and a slight puddle lay on the ground beneath his left shoe hanging over the edge.

"Grant," she said. "It's Carli. Wake up. You should change into dry clothes."

Grant didn't move. She touched him lightly on the shoulder and said his name one more time. As she did, she stiffened. From her hand to her chest and her head to her feet she felt the awful, undeniable grip of panic. Everything hit at once – the small plastic bag of white pills on the bed, one half of a pill near his turned head, his bloodless, pale face, and his way-too-still body. Her hand didn't rise and fall with his breaths. It didn't move at all.

"Grant!" she screamed.

Carli dialed 9 -1-1. Then she began chest compressions with all her might.

"Please, Grant. Wake up!" She tried shaking him alive. "Grant ... Grant ... Henry, no!" She continued CPR. No pulse and no breath responded back. As soon as emergency teams arrived, they began the resuscitation and naloxone routines. Come on, Grant. Come back. Please, come back. She said it over and over to herself, as she helplessly watched the others.

Grant's heart suddenly came to life. "Oh, Dear God," she whispered. "Thank you. Yes, thank you, Lord." She watched the team assess him. Grant's face gained a blush of color. Ten seconds later, his heartbeat stopped, and it all ended again. For good. He had been given only ten more seconds of life.

Carli stared at her brother, feeling as though she might faint. Then she made a rash decision. Yes, it was the right thing to do. She dialed Wilson's hospital. The conversation was brief, with a disappointing result: without a directive from Grant, he couldn't give Wilson his badly-needed organs. Besides, she was told, Wilson's body wasn't yet strong enough for major surgery. Carli sat on his mattress edge again, lowered her head to his back, and wrapped her arms around him, wondering what had gone wrong.

"Just when I had you back," she said. "Dear God, please tell me what happened. And why you had to have him."

In automated fashion, Carli went through the practicalities of moving Grant for an autopsy and addressing other arrangements. It was almost sunrise, but the sky was still dark when she knocked on a cardboard box near the Midtown Synagogue.

"Canada?" she called. "Mad? It's Carli. Are you here?"

"Who's there?" asked a voice from the box near her feet.

"Carli, from Outreach. I need Madison. It's an emergency."

"Emergency? He's down at the end. Closest to the bank," said the voice.

"Carli?" It was Madison's voice.

"Come out," she said. "Please. I have to see you."

With the streets still dark, and the group's having chosen a sleeping spot away from the night lights of stores, Canada's familiar gray hoodie was almost upon her before she saw him.

"Sorry to wake you," she said. "It's about Grant."

"Where is he?" Canada asked.

"It's bad news," she said. "It's ... well, he's gone. It happened a few hours ago."

Carli thought she saw Canada stumble backward a step before he asked, "What happened?"

By now, the other boxes were rustling.

"I don't know," she said. "I don't know. Grant called and said he crashed his bike. He said he couldn't sleep. I went to check him, and he was still soaking wet and sprawled across his mattress with a bag of pills. One pill was broken in half on his mattress. I'm thinking he took the other half. I need to know something. Did you give Grant any pills lately?"

"Pills?"

"Yes, white pills ... here, look. I need to know what this is." Carli took a pair of pills from her pocket and said, "Close your eyes a minute." She switched on the spotlight of her phone and focused it on her hand.

"Let me see one of those." Canada held a pill between his fingers and lowered it into the light. Carli saw him squinting to get a better look. "I've seen these before," he said. "They're bad news."

"Are those the ones?" asked one of the other men.

"Think so," said Canada. He passed the pill over to the others for a second opinion.

"That's the one. Has the red fist. See it?" said one of the others.

"Saw it," said Canada. "I'm gonna kill him."

"What are you talking about?" asked Carli.

"I don't ever, and I mean ever, deal any of these," said Canada. "These are to help you sleep. A bunch of them got on the market. Often around college campuses. Those kids take one kind of pill to keep them up and get their work done. Then they take one of these to get to sleep. From time to time, someone adds in some fent, and it becomes a killer. Might only take half a pill to do it. In fact, be careful how you hold it."

"Fent?" asked Carli.

"Fentanyl. Tens of thousands dead from it a year," said one of the others.

"Oh my God," Carli whispered. "He said he was trying to sleep."

"It creeps into other types of pills too. Like, party pills. You sure it wasn't the crash?" asked Canada.

"We're checking," she said.

"Well, my guess is we'll know in a couple of days, autopsy or not. If this is what we think it is, we'll hear about a rash of overdoses. I could kill the guy who's doing this."

"Oh, my God. I had no idea," said Carli. "I thought maybe you gave it to him. Why didn't he get something from the pharmacy?"

"I don't sell this stuff." He looked straight at Carli's eyes. "I can't believe it." He opened his arms wide to share a hug. Carli felt his chest gently contract and lurch as he released some of his pain.

The last thing Carli recalled was collapsing on Grant's mattress. It smelled like his shampoo, and the sheets were still wet from the rain. This time he was truly gone, the boy who had held her captive when he playfully tugged her pigtails, and the man who teased her and captured her with his laugh. Late afternoon, after nearly a full day's sleep, Carli crawled into his thinking chair. She touched the sides as though she were touching Grant. She looked at his paintings. They were the only things she had left of him that revealed his soul. There was no good answer. Never would be. On the heels of sadness, she hated everything, including herself. Why didn't she come over right after his call? He would have been alive. She could have saved him.

Sister Anna, Mercy, Gretchen, and the others held a simple, private prayer of thanks in the lunchroom of St. Mary's. Carli left it to Sister Anna to deliver the news to those who could handle it. Mercy was in her own state of shock and grief. For the first time ever, Carli saw Mercy wear black.

One afternoon, Carli found Canada leaning against the wall of the synagogue, taking a day off from work. "You okay?" she asked.

"Nothing you or I can do about it," said Canada. "I'm sorry it happened to you. Hard to lose someone."

"You lost him too," she said.

"Not like you did."

It took a moment for Canada's words to sink in. When they did, Carli directed her eyes straight toward Canada's.

"He told me," said Canada. "One of the days I visited him at the hospital." Carli slowly nodded. "He was happier than anything to have you in his life. All he ever wanted to do was protect you. Never hurt you." It was what Grant did all his life. It was her brother's way.

"Did Grant ever tell you why he got off the streets?" she asked. Canada shook his head. Carli told Canada about the dirty drug den. "It's like you were meant to help them. You already got Grant in by sending him into that rattrap and making him think."

Canada smiled painfully. "Could be." Then, seized by something unseen, he raised his eyes skyward and shook his head. "You knew you'd get me. One way or another, you knew, didn't you? Well, rest in peace, bro. Rest in peace."

Carli and Canada locked eyes. Then, as though by some hidden signal, both knew it was time to move on.

"I'll go see Mercy," said Canada. After taking a step, he added,

"Grant's right. I know them all. We used to talk, Grant and me." He turned quickly, but not fast enough to conceal a wet drop sliding from his eye. A hand raised to his face confirmed it. Carli wished more than ever Grant could be with her, flesh and soul, to witness it. Finally reaching Canada, the boisterous stalwart, felt empty without him.

Carli entered and left St. Ignatius several times, searching for answers. Then she fit herself back into Grant's room, content to keep everything out of her life for as long as she could. She joked cynically, calling his storage room "Grant's Tomb," but the real tomb, she knew, had been his body.

Late one evening, feeling oddly immune to danger or, perhaps, simply unable to feel much of anything, Carli stood at the ferry terminal. The boat for Staten Island was docked, and the water was calm. She moved to the piers. They stood strong against the gently lapping water. "You bastards," she barely whispered. "You got him. You finally got him."

She walked along the empty streets near City Hall, convinced the powers that be were solving nothing at all, for weren't they all still out? Sleeping church after sleeping church seemed to jump in her path. She scorned them all, but Carli knew her anger was simply a part of her grief. Unfortunately, she had felt it before. Just north of Grand Central Terminal, she saw two light-colored vans surrounded by a cluster of people. The Church Run. No doubt, Canada had met it at one stop or another along its route, along with others she knew. She didn't stop. Couldn't bear to. Wanted nothing to do with them. What she needed, more than anything, she couldn't have.

Kristin was a good sounding board, as always. She even took a couple of afternoons off from work to sit with Carli on the window seat, either in silence or conversation.

"It's ironic," said Kristin one afternoon. "All this time, Grant claimed others were poisoned by the cult, and he ended up on the wrong end of something totally different ... but exactly the same."

"Maybe. Or maybe Grant was right. Maybe the cult was poisoning people ... and they finally got him."

Kristin gently took ahold of Carli's arm. "I hate to say it, but I wondered that myself. It couldn't be, could it?"

Carli lifted her eyes to Kristin's. "Time will tell," said Carli. "I'm banking on Canada being right."

"What do you mean?"

"If others start making the news, we'll know it was some lousy dealer. And if others are anything like Grant, they'll drop like flies ... very soon."

"In the meantime," said Kristin, "you can't make up for losing him by going out at all hours of the night by yourself. I mean, retracing all of his steps, and doing these night visits you've been doing, isn't safe. And," said Kristin slowly, "it won't bring him back."

"Canada comes with me sometimes," said Carli. "And I don't think we really look for anyone. Mostly we just walk the streets. Sometimes all we do is sit on a bench in the dark and listen to our hearts. At times, mine sounds like a kite soaring because I think of how loving he was. And how much I loved him. Other times, my heart feels like it's gurgling down a drain, and it can't get through, so water is backing up, and it's making this awful sucking sound. That's how it feels sometimes."

Carli felt warm tears roll from her eyes. "I finally had him again."

"I am so sorry, Sister. I really am."

Carli sat alone through the cremation, clutching his turquoise ring; his police cap was with him. When the nighttime Run from First Church came creeping into the City two weeks later, Carli sought it out. Pastor Miller was welcoming, as always. She had already phoned him about Grant. He opened his arms to her, and she to him, knowing Pastor Miller had relied on Grant to help the same ones he was helping.

"It was a bad pill," she said. "A couple of others made unexpected trips to the hospital on account of them. One other died."

Carli visited Vera, Sarah, and Wilson as best she could. Visits felt empty. A few times, Canada walked with her, chaperoning and nudging the street clan. He even slept a few nights in a shelter, and, as promised, he had talked with Mercy. Yes, he was seriously considering a change. Carli was too. It was time to find Tessie again, and undertake a new mission, one that only Tessie Whitmore could tackle.

THIRTY-ONE

CARLI PRACTICALLY DANCED into Elena Rossi's Galleria, eager to present her idea. The prospect of seeing Tessie Whitmore's waterscapes and landscapes was already creating a buzz, but Carli knew she had more important works to share. Through all her days with Outreach, she had come to learn she had to connect the two worlds; the ones in the atriums with the ones outside. Of all the people who could help the people on the streets, by helping the ones reaching out, it was the patrons with their passion, compassion, resources, and clout. Carli had to reach them. And she, herself, as Tessie Whitmore, had just the right kind of clout to do it. So did Elena Rossi.

Carli quickly made her proposal: a show of street people. Not an exhibit of their art. That had been done plenty of times. Rather, an exhibit of them—portraits of people. Of Sarah and Vera, Harry and Grudge, Cedric and Wilson, and so, so many others. Individuals, who lived outside in the city. The patrons' city. Tessie's city. What's more, Carli knew there had been a different beginning and, with any luck, could be a different end to their stories. It was time to show not only portraits, but the essential links between street lives, former lives, and future lives back inside. Elena applauded, in her typically-quiet-mannered but influential way. To add impact, the exhibit would travel the city. Rocky's building would host the opening month, with Elena's Galleria and Tessie Whitmore underwriting the exhibit's move through many of the city's protective glass walls. Patron parties at the Galleria and other exhibit locations, along with invited speakers, would up the ante. The exhibit, showcasing the need for Outreach, and the need for others to reach out, had Elena Rossi's immediate support.

For the next weeks, oil fumes swelled in Carli's nostrils as she brought the people she knew from the street to life in full color across paint-laden canvas. Thelma gladly lent photos from which Carli portrayed young Lucy Birdwell. Vera said, "Why not? Count me in. I'd like to show some folks a thing or two." Then there was Sarah. When Carli met Sarah at the shelter, the woman said very little, which was no surprise, but Carli could tell she was glad to see her and relieved to be safe back inside. Sarah had been a dam ready to burst. When it finally broke free, it had all gushed out. Only it gushed out red. Red for the violence, for the beatings, for the misunderstandings. Her fiancé had been abused as a child. In turn, so was she … by him. It must have been hard coming from the one she most loved. Yet, she felt prolonged and stinging guilt that he had died in the crash, and she had not. Pigeons might well have become her only safe havens – if one left, another glided easily into place, and flapping wings couldn't hurt her.

On the first of the month, Carli handed Neuman cash for the next month's rental of the room at Cooper's. Something inside her wasn't ready to close the account. She found comfort in being as close to Grant as she could be in its dark and tinny innards.

Neuman had taken Grant's death hard. It didn't bother him that Carli took ownership of Grant's room. Carli's attempts to save Grant proved ample evidence that what was Grant's was now hers. Halfway to the elevator, Neuman's voice tripped her up. "Hey, you want his second unit too?" Carli came to an abrupt stop.

"Second unit?"

Neuman rode with Carli to the sixth floor. On the opposite end of Cooper's, far around the outer wall from Grant's living room, was

Grant's second rental. Neuman had thrown it in for half price. Had it been closer to his living quarters, Carli would have smelled the paint. Would have seen his other paintings before now. Together, she and Neuman lifted open the metal door to reveal a studio floor splattered with dried pigments, a corner of artist brushes, turpentine, tubes of oil paints, and canvas in every stage of completion. It suddenly made sense; explained the occasional paint on the cuffs of his sleeves and across his pants. Neuman left her to contemplate another mystery of her brother.

Later that same day, Carli approached mailbox 2647 at the city's Main Post Office, wondering what additional information she was about to uncover. The key to the box had been hanging in Grant's room, alongside the box reserved for his door locks. With the key engaged in the door to 2647, Carli reached inside and retrieved a single item – a post card. It directed her to collect the excess mail before it was destroyed. When Carli reached the mail counter, she was given a stack of letters bundled together and curled over by a pair of sturdy rubber bands. It must have been months since Grant had stopped in.

Seated under Grant's canopy at Cooper's, she stared at unpaid credit card bills, no doubt the result of manic spending. How did he even get the cards? If anyone could do it, he could. She came across a letter with a simple return address: New Jersey. It was postmarked nearly nine months prior, and looked as though it might have already been opened. Maybe Grant thought it was from the cult and never bothered to retrieve mail after it arrived. Carli tensed as she pulled out the letter. Inside was a name and address. Nothing more. Goosebumps rose on her arms; Carli now had access to one of Grant's sons, and a new way to keep Henry in her heart. Maybe Grant knew exactly who sent it, and had left it in the box for safekeeping, or, at least, for the cult not to find in his bin.

Carli gazed around the tin walls until her sight fell into the corner of Grant's room. Cedric stared back; a perfect portrait of a man with his cans. Grant had even captured the gap in his front teeth and all the personality that went with it. Carli felt herself brighten inside and out. Yes, she was adding it to the exhibit!

Over the course of the next month, Carli mounted several of Grant's pieces and was privy to a surprise find: sketches of herself done in soft 5B graphite. A letter tucked between his renderings didn't surprise her at all – an offer of admission to a Chicago art school. He hadn't gone, of course. To Grant, the act of applying was probably another manic fling, a passing squall that he abandoned when he envisioned the framework of a new and better dream or fell apathetically ill to the barbell weight of depression. Most likely, he never bothered to reply. The postmark was a few years prior.

An occasional tear streamed down her cheeks and soaked into Carli's smocks as she worked. They were for Cedric and Sarah, Canada and Wilson, Vera and so many others. Of course, they were for Grant, as well. She cried at the irony of working like a maniac to meet the show's deadline; cried with love, with grief, and for Grant's missing the fruition of this worthy dream. Carli gained strength from her commitment, both to herself and to everyone on the streets and their broken families at home.

She stumbled through rounds, knowing she couldn't abandon them. That had already been done to them at least once before, in one way or another, by loved ones, the system, or their own bodies. And now they had no Grant. She knew she was no replacement. No one was. With all his special qualities, troubles included, he sparkled brighter than anyone through the lunchroom, through the night, and through the protection of each and every corrugated cardboard home.

Canada helped Carli share the news of Grant's passing with Cedric and Wilson. It was a big blow. Cedric accepted the news in stunned silence. It hurt to see him this way. Grant had worked so hard to help him. She, of all people, knew what it meant to have Grant bound into his life and then lose him. It would be up to Carli and Canada to check on Cedric. As Grant had said, you had to keep hoping for the best and forever lend support when they faced their biggest barriers. Wilson had simply cried when they sprang upon him the permanence of

Grant's absence. After the news sank in, he buried his head in his hands. He asked Carli to bring his coat from the closet. With the material surrounding him, Wilson clutched one of Grant's coat buttons and quietly sobbed.

"It'll be all right," said Canada. "We'll get through this together. I'm pretty sure he's still with us." He'd said the same to Cedric.

Sometimes when Canada walked with her, Carli wondered if Grant had ever spoken with him about taking care of her or taking care of the street clan. She sure wished Grant could speak with him now, but she realized she was actually learning patience. Wasn't that what Grant had always recommended?

On one of the first cold days of autumn, Carli sat with Canada on the same stone steps where she had watched him greeting his people below when she and Grant had searched for Cedric. After a few quiet moments, Canada lowered his head and spoke softly. "You know," he said, "losing Grant hit me hard. Real hard. It's not the same out here."

Carli nodded, unable to speak.

"I keep thinking," he continued, "about what happens if one of my guys down there turns out to be another Grant." Canada nodded at the building where he usually set up his backpack office. "What if I'm pushing someone out onto the street, when maybe I could be helping them go in ... and maybe helping another Grant find himself again." He stopped to look straight at Carli. She managed a half-smile. "Maybe I could do it."

Carli took a deep breath in and slowly exhaled.

"Yes, you could do it. In fact, I'm pretty sure you've already started."

Grant was clearly still with them all.

A week before Thanksgiving, it was time to make it all count. Every loss. Every gain. Every fit and start. Inside Rocky's atrium, Vera watched Carli and Kristin pull the protective wraps off Carli's paintings and seemed mighty thankful to have been invited to help supervise, as Carli had described it. When Vera said she had pushed the limits of her arthritis, and she turned to leave, Carli said, "Wait, I have something." Vera turned around. "You never saw the second painting I did of you," said Carli. She removed the wrap from the last painting and slowly turned it for Vera to see.

Vera pulled her hand to her face. "Oh, my ... Oh, my. Oh ... my. Look at this." Vera's mouth remained open as she panned across the painting.

Carli said, "I have something else." She pulled a postcard-sized print from her bag. It was laminated, an exact print of the painting. When she handed it to Vera, she saw Vera's outstretched hands begin to tremble. Together they looked at the print of Vera and her husband standing along a sidewalk, with the Minnix House – Vera's house – standing clearly in the background. "I wanted you to always be with your Minnix House and ... you know, your best friend."

"Darling, darling, darling," said Vera. "Thank you. I wondered why you wanted to see that old photo of us two. This means ... well, it means the world to me."

"It can go anywhere in the world with you," said Carli. "Or, maybe, just anywhere in the city. You'll always have him with you."

Vera continued to rest her eyes on the print. "Uh-huh, you sure know. You sure know," said Vera.

As Vera pushed through the revolving glass door, Carli knew that she had finally reached her Vera Dear-a.

"A bit lower on the left," was all Carli needed to say. Philip, the building manager at First Century Properties, was happy to oblige, having hoisted the last of Grant and Carli's paintings onto the lobby walls. It was a clean sweep, and a good one. She wished Grant were here to see it.

"Are you all right?" asked Rocky.

"Yes." She nodded. "Are you?"

Rocky nodded and said, "It's a nice thing you're doing for all of them."

Carli walked the floor. It was unsettling seeing Vera through the atrium's glass window, wrapped in a new, full-length trench coat, standing close to the wall half a block away, and seeing Vera in an oil wrap, striking a similar pose in her first work of Vera, right beside Carli in the atrium. It shook her, knowing Harry and Grudge would be shacked up outside again tonight, when part of them was inside, practically shaking hands with every office worker who crossed the marble floor.

Oh, Grant. She whispered his name silently, speaking with her inner voice—the voice a person can't control but always hears inside their own head. Thankfully, Carli's inner voice was kind and worked in synch with the rest of herself and the world around her. It wasn't menacing. It wasn't controlling. Others, she knew, weren't so lucky.

On the walls, Carli viewed the best work of her lifetime. There were four portraits for Lucy, renderings created from Thelma's collection of photos: in childhood, swinging under a tree; in love, dancing with her beau – William – her gown trailing, with softness and a lover's drape to it. She was also reflective as a widow, resting sullen eyes on her husband's portrait; and vulnerable, curled up and sleeping with her dear Lila and Terrance, gray hair covered by a teal-green winter hat. Finally, Lila and Terrance, well-groomed, with matching teal collars and ribbons, sat next to a bench at the Elmsville church. Carli closed her eyes and swallowed hard, remembering all it had taken to bring Lucy home and to give Lila and Terrance to Thelma.

After a moment, her eyes moved on. Wilson looked stately at his Princeton, New Jersey, prep school, and far less prestigious in a second portrait, clinging to a bottle wrapped in a brown paper bag, the same color and texture as his hair. Thank God he was still alive. "Conflict" depicted a troubled young adult – Lenny - meeting with a counselor. It was juxtaposed with "Conflict Too (2)" which showed him as a child, sitting in the shadows of his mother and an aunt, dreaming of his lost father. He, too, was going back home. Mercy and his aunt had finally reached him again, and he was willing. "Trusted Vets" showed Harry and Grudge in uniform, right next to "Common Bond" depicting their new two-person regiment. "Hope" was named not for a person, but a circumstance: Lanna in her new job. "Freedom" was a simple portrait —a bicycle with royal blue fenders, leaning against a light post, with no chain and lock around it. Under it, the sign read, *"Just as a child learns to ride a bike by toppling, sometimes falling, and getting back on, these men and women must learn and be helped to ride again. And they can."*

Next in line was "Simply Sapphires" with Sarah wearing her sapphire heels in a corporate office. Carli had found the photo mixed in with the money. The last time Carli visited Sarah, her woman in blue had spoken a full sentence. Several in fact. They did not come easily, but they came. Just in time for the show, Carli had fleshed out her sketches of Central Park and the Plaza. A number of sleepers rested on the benches. All of these were joined by "Triumph," and Rocky exalting the world in his work uniform. Carli, of course, knew it had taken many triumphs along the way – the triumph of going to a clinic, of admitting the need for help, of pushing away abusive substances, of simply facing every new day … and facing himself.

Suddenly, Carli felt resentful. Grant had just gotten it all together. He could have been here, standing next to her. Carli was back to putting on the biggest show of her lifetime, even bigger than the collection of art around her. She understood, now, how Grant had masked it all. He was a Master, indeed.

Carli viewed Grant's work last, as she posted a sign next to his paintings.

"These works were done by a man named Grant White. He was gifted in many ways. He was homeless for part of his life and then chose to help the home-less by gently encouraging them, in his own remarkable way, to move off the streets and into shelter. Before that, he was Phi Beta Kappa and a New York attorney. He was also my brother. I knew him as Henry."

Carli stared a long while at "Henry and Tessie," a painting of them standing arm in arm as children. Bonaventura—beautiful Tura—sat in front, looking up at them in his dog-happy way. She then looked at the many other photos and paintings of her brother from their childhood and read the next sign.

"Often, one has no choice but to follow what life gives you. As an adult, Grant was given bipolar disorder and he chose not to treat it. Later in life, not long after he was admitted to one of the country's top art schools for advanced work, he died of an accidental overdose. May those who see this exhibit reach out, as Grant did, to the many who are given difficult life challenges. No one says, 'When I grow up, I want to live in a box on a sidewalk.'"

Carli stared at his work for many more moments. She smiled at the sight of Grant's paintings of Madison and Cedric. She imagined him painting and saw clearly his arm and hand traversing the canvas. She had added to the exhibit Canada's portrait of denial. Surprisingly, Canada had recognized denial's sad picture and had owned up to it when he saw it in his painted reflection.

Carli sat among the plants in the atrium for nearly an hour, watching many rushing by, in their usual way, with their usual quiet clamor. A few were inexplicably drawn in, taking time to look and ponder, perhaps even willing to take the next bus or train home. Would it mean anything in the end? The leaves of the plants brushed together as she slid down the granite wall and glided gently into a circle of critics.

"I've seen this woman," said one observer.

"Yes," said Carli. "Usually halfway down the block. Her name's Vera. Some street people don't want to be approached, but Vera would like it if you said hello."

The young man nodded and walked outside. Carli watched him walk that half block and saw him turn and look back as though seeking reassurance. Then, even from a half-block away, Carli was certain she saw Vera's face turn a smidgeon brighter. He must have called her by name.

ACKNOWLEDGMENTS

My gratitude overflows for several outstanding editors who helped make *Clean Sweep* the novel it is. Thank you to Stephen Parolini for thoughtful and astute comments on early drafts, helpful nudges, critical suggestions, and an affirmative, educational, and kind pen. Not only did you help bring greater depth to the characters and a more complete story out of rudimentary drafts, but you pushed me to become a better storyteller and writer. Thank you to Mary-Theresa Hussey for copyediting that went above and beyond as though undertaken by a detective who noticed, questioned and investigated all, and pointed out invaluable options for strengthening this story. Thank you to Louise Stahl for proofreading with the utmost of care, professionalism, good humor, and a welcome touch of humanity. I feel most fortunate to have worked with each of you, my creative and talented editors. Also, thank you to Kathleen Lynch/Black Kat Design for presenting a wonderful array of cover options, and developing a professional, appealing, and appropriate final design to bring readers together with this story.

In addition, I extend gratitude to many former teachers for lessons taught at Kathleen Laycock Country Day School and Greens Farms

Academy in Greens Farms, Connecticut; and at The Taft School in Watertown, Connecticut. To each of you, I am indebted.

My love of family is second to none. To the family that has gotten me through my debut novel and much, much more, you are my strength, and I thank each of you with never-ending love: my husband Chick, for offering unwavering support and for standing beside me through life's many travels, both rough and smooth, and for encouraging me to pursue my dreams, varied as they have been; my daughters, Bonnie Lee and Emily Lee, for cheering me on and showing me what awesome can look like; Emily Lee, for reading drafts and commenting wisely, and Bonnie Lee, for staunchly holding out for the published hardcover; my brother, George Barata, for a lifetime of steadfast big-brotherly support, as well as an hysterically keen understanding of human nature and motivation, plot—both real and fictionalized—and life's many stories; and the memory of my mother, Ellen Morrison Barata, and father, Joseph G. Barata, both writers, and readers forever, who gently shaped the person I have become through their own exemplary actions, and humble appreciation of life.

ABOUT THE AUTHOR

E. B. Lee was raised in Weston, Connecticut, where she enjoyed the best of a then-rural town and easy train access to the high-energy world of New York City. She brings together elements of both worlds in her debut work of literary fiction, *Clean Sweep*, a heartfelt story of human connection, tough choices, and compassion. Ms. Lee and her husband have two grown daughters, one middle-aged dog, and have loved a variety of family pets along the way. Ms. Lee now writes in North Carolina and Connecticut.

Sign up for E. B. Lee's author newsletter for a fun look at the writing life, thought-provoking musings, and news of future releases. www. eblee.me

Also, check for posts in Quinnifer's Book Club, a blog about dogs and books and the magic of both. www.littlebrowndogpress.com

DISCUSSION QUESTIONS

1. Chapter 1 of *Clean Sweep* opens with our protagonist, Carli Morris, helping to deliver sandwiches to homeless men and women living on the sidewalks of Manhattan. If you were in Carli's shoes during this overnight mission, how might you have felt when Lucy was found? What might you have done?

2. By the end of chapter 3, we learn more of Carli's past. Do you think Carli would have reacted differently to Lucy, and to Lila and Terrance, if she had not lost Henry? At this point in the novel, what most drives Carli's actions: guilt for not having saved Henry, a lingering sense of sadness and loss, a genuinely strong desire to help others, a combination of these, or something else?

3. We first learn in chapter 4 that Outreach is about connecting with people who are living on the sidewalks, in the parks, in other outdoor spaces, or on public transportation. It is about encouraging street homeless to recognize the benefits of accepting help and voluntarily moving into some sort of housing. Moving inside is now prioritized by a number of programs as a critical first step in enabling help for other problems. Imagine spending 48 hours on the streets. How much time

might you have to spend traveling to secure meals, water for thirst or for taking medication, bathrooms, showers, dry clothes if it rains or snows, heat, or air conditioning? Where would you stay without shelter? How safe would you feel? How would you feel if people glared at you, spat on you, or talked negatively to you?

4. In Chapter 7, Carli watches a stranger – a homeless woman in blue – for over twenty minutes as the woman inspects her belongings. What does this tell you about Carli and her inability to turn her back? Have you ever noticed or watched someone who is homeless and living on the street or in a park? For how long?

5. In Chapter 8 we meet Mercy. I will let you in on a secret. Mercy was not always Mercy. She was initially named Theresa. An editor pointed out Tessie (Carli's real name) might likely be a nickname for Theresa. Two characters with the same name would not do. So, Theresa became Mercy. But Mercy almost became Izzy, short for Isabella. Why? The meaning of "mercy"—being associated with compassion or forgiveness *based on one's power to punish or harm*—was not the sentiment I wanted attached to this character. Also, the name Izzy seemed well-suited to this character's strong personality and flamboyant exterior. In the end, however, I set Izzy aside because I like the way "Mercy" sounds. It is soft-sounding, easy to read, and easy for other characters to say in dialogue. It rolls well off the tongue of my internal reading voice. "Izzy" has a harder sound. I feared this would negatively impact the voice of the novel and lend a different feel to the reading experience.

Choosing names for characters is not always easy. Consider the names of the characters in *Clean Sweep*. Are they memorable? Distinct? Do they need to be? Is a name better if it is not memorable? Are the *Clean Sweep* character names likable or not? Does any particular name impact the way you see that character?

6. Before reading *Clean Sweep*, what might you have thought of a homeless person you saw on the sidewalk, a bench, or sleeping in their car or in a subway car? If you came across someone like Wilson —who you first meet in chapter 9—how might you have viewed him if you did not know him or know his story, as Carli comes to know it? Might you have labeled him as a "bum," drunk, lost soul, victim of bad circumstance? How would his appearance – a man in need of a shower and with clothes coated with food and a bottle held in his hand – influence your thoughts? Might you have felt at all threatened? Indignant? Sad? Concerned? Indifferent? Compassionate? Something else?

7. Chapter 10 introduces the City Sweeps, which move street homeless off sidewalks, ostensibly for the benefit of a neighborhood and for those who are homeless. In *Clean Sweep*, we see that individual characters living on the streets sometimes prefer to stay put. Is it "right" to move street homeless off the streets? Is it right to allow individuals to live on the streets? Consider the visual results of a Sweep. How different does a city block look with or without desolate beings in sight? Might a homeless person's presence impact your perception of your surroundings? Could it make you feel a different sense of safety or different sense of cleanliness in your surroundings? Would you feel threatened or turned off? Would it not be noticeable? Or, might it seem normal, and either unchangeable or in no need of being changed?

8. In chapters 13 and 15, Carli confronts denial, not only in herself, but in those on the street as well. Denial slides into *Clean Sweep* in several other chapters. Denial can be a strong personal defense mechanism. It comes part and parcel with a number of mental health challenges and addictions. Denial can be a double-edged sword, providing temporary respite, but also prohibiting steps to longer-term solutions. What characters in *Clean Sweep* employ denial, knowingly or not, to help with their situations, and how does each of them manifest their

denial? How difficult do you think it is to break through the walls of denial? Does the break have to come from within?

9. Compassion and human connection are vital elements of *Clean Sweep*. Both are seen as strengths and saving forces, but, as we see in Carli's story, compassion and connection can have associated vulnerabilities. Can a person have true compassion or human connection without opening one's heart and allowing oneself to be vulnerable?

10. While writing *Clean Sweep*, one of my biggest challenges was revealing behavior and conversation indicative of Grant's mental health prior to letting readers in on his condition, as later diagnosed. In fact, I started dropping hints about Grant beginning in chapter 4. When did you first notice conversation or action on his part that raised a red flag for you? How did you react? Did you shrug and ignore it? Did you believe I had simply written something in a strange manner? Did you feel he needed help?

Fiction often requires readers to suspend disbelief, but was Grant's action of moving street homeless into an atrium an act you found difficult to accept? Were you enthusiastically pulled along by his excitement and magnetism? Or did you have doubts? It seems Carli struggled with both excitement and doubt. How did you react when, in chapter 15, Grant exclaimed, "Cruise wear is out"? Did you find his statement funny, due to its oddity? Did you think, perhaps, Grant is getting a bit wacky? Did it come to mind that he might be struggling with a chemical imbalance and mental health issue? Chemical imbalances known to cause mental illness can go unnoticed for periods of time, even by family members and others closest to individuals with these imbalances. In retrospect, these signs often seem more obvious. If you were Carli, at what point would you have said, "Hey, something is off"? What does her taking action to help say about her character?

11. For each person who experiences chemical imbalance and/or addiction, there are usually several more people – family members or

friends – who share the associated struggle of seeing unusual actions, thoughts, and pain in someone they love, and in being unable to singly create desired changes. Grant's condition allows us to see this very personal impact on Carli. Would *Clean Sweep* have resonated with you in the same way if we had not been privy to Carli's despair and heartbreak resulting from this personal connection? As a society, we have come a long way in reducing the stigma associated with mental health issues and addictions. Have we come far enough? Do we do enough to make help available to those in need?

12. A novel is a series of scenes. Together, they create a progression of actions, both external and internal to characters. Some scenes are more conversation-oriented, others are more action- or event-oriented, and still others are more setting-rich, reaching readers through descriptions of "place." Aside from the overarching messages of *Clean Sweep*, do any particular scenes stick in your mind more than others? If so, why are they memorable? Does it have to do with any of the following specifically: Setting? Conversation? Action? Language? A particular phrase? A specific thought? An emotional impact the scene has on a character or on you? Another reason?

13. Art is an important thread running through *Clean Sweep*. It is part of what defines Carli's life, and it becomes a defining element of Carli's contribution to those she most wants to save. Did you find the art scenes: interesting in and of themselves? Or as a forewarning of sorts? As symbols of Carli's state of being? Or something altogether different? What do you feel about the role of art in *Clean Sweep*?

14. How do you feel about Grant's death? Was it necessary? Did you want a different outcome? How does it add to the story or tie into Carli's life-affirmative transformation? How does it draw you into the story told by *Clean Sweep*, or turn you away, hoping to change the outcome?

15. The subtitle for *Clean Sweep* is, "A Novel." It is simple, straight forward, and standard protocol for literary fiction. When all was said and done, I followed protocol, but I seriously considered taking a risk, and adding more specific information to the subtitle. I wanted potential readers to know more about the essence of this story when they read the cover. Some of the alternate subtitles I considered were, "A Novel of Hope," "A Novel of Newfound Hope," "A Novel of Human Connection and Hope," "A Novel of Conviction," "A Novel of Faith and Conviction," "A Novel of Compassion," "A Novel of Devastation and Hope," "A Novel of Trust," and, "A Novel of Faith." Should I have taken the risk? What would you have thought of a more descriptive subtitle? Would you have chosen any of the above or something else altogether? Please, let me know your thoughts. I am curious!

16. Who are your two favorite characters? Or, with which two characters did you feel the strongest connection? Why?

17. Is *Clean Sweep* a story about Carli, or men and women living on city sidewalks, or, perhaps, is it about a larger societal issue of mental health issues, poverty, and homelessness? What do you think?

18. What would you change about this novel? Or any of the characters?

19. The final chapter of *Clean Sweep* gives details of Grant and Carli's art exhibit, in which characters we have met on the streets are depicted before, during, and after their street life. We considered earlier the role of art in Carli's life and in the novel. Let's now consider a different aspect of art: how much does art merely reflect the world, and our impressions of the world, and how much can it influence change in the world? Do you believe an art exhibit such as Carli's could prompt any types of change in a real-life situation? What impact would this exhibit have on you?

20. Are you happy with, or satisfied by, Carli's final transformation and her drive to help through her art? Does it seem appropriate?

21. As Carli notes in her art exhibit in *Clean Sweep*, "No one says, 'When I grow up, I want to live in a box on a city sidewalk.'" Will you remember this if you happen to see someone who is street homeless? Will you remember they once had a very different past? Did reading *Clean Sweep* change your views of someone you might see on the streets, even though the exhibit and the characters in this story are fictionalized?

A NOTE. AND ONE MORE QUESTION.

Several readers of early drafts of *Clean Sweep* were Manhattan residents, and gave this feedback: "I expected to find Wilson and Cedric and the other street homeless characters of *Clean Sweep* on the streets when I walked out of my apartment. I also expected, and wanted, to see Carli's art exhibit." How real did the characters and situations of *Clean Sweep* become to you?

Share your thoughts on *Clean Sweep*. Please, send an email my way. Eblee.author@gmail.com

REVIEWS ARE ALWAYS APPRECIATED!

REVIEWS HELP OTHERS decide if *Clean Sweep* might be a book they would like to read. I would like to have as many interested readers enjoy *Clean Sweep* as possible.

IF YOU HAVE A MINUTE, would you kindly consider leaving a review of *Clean Sweep* on my Amazon Author's page, your Goodreads page, or social media posts, where other readers might find it and learn your thoughts? A few lines or phrases will do just fine if you are pressed for time.

I am happy you found *Clean Sweep*. I hope you enjoyed it.

Best,

E. B. Lee